Nietzsche

AND THE

BURBS

Nietzsche

AND THE

BURBS

A NOVEL

Lars Iyer

MELVILLE HOUSE
Brooklyn · London

NIETZSCHE AND THE BURBS

First published in 2019 by Melville House
Copyright © Lars Iyer 2019
All rights reserved
First Melville House Printing: December 2019

Melville House Publishing
46 John Street
Brooklyn, NY 11201
and
Melville House UK
Suite 2000
16/18 Woodford Road
London E7 0HA

mhpbooks.com
@melvillehouse

ISBN: 978-1-61219-812-5
ISBN: 978-1-61219-813-2 (eBook)

Library of Congress Control Number: 2019945809

Designed by Betty Lew

Printed in the United States of America
1 3 5 7 9 10 8 6 4 2

A catalog record for this book is available
from the Library of Congress

You must have chaos in yourself
to give birth to a dancing star.

—Nietzsche

FIRST WEEK

MONDAY

The new boy's from *private school*—that, we're sure of. His composure. His assurance. That's what you pay for when you send your
child to *private school*. Assurance . . . Composure . . .

So why's he come to *our* school?—that's what's got us floored.
And only a couple of months from the exams. Come to think of it,
what's he doing in *Wokingham*? Dreary *suburbia*. Did his parents lose
their jobs? Did they split up? Was he expelled from *private school*?

I think he has charisma, Art says.

I think he knows he has charisma, Paula says.

I think he doesn't care whether he has charisma, I say. That's what
gives him charisma.

What's charisma? Merv asks.

★

Into assembly. The new boy, already picked off by the sixth-form
pariah.

Oh, God—look at Bombproof, Art says. All *positive*.

We hope the new boy doesn't judge us all by Bombproof.

Should we mount a rescue operation? But the new boy has already
excused himself to Bombproof. He's gone to the bathroom.

A cunning ruse, we agree. The bathroom ruse.

★

Assembly. The whole school, sitting in rows. The whole school community. The whole school *family*.

We take our seats at the back of the hall.

Art, coughing. Merv, coughing slightly louder. Me, coughing

louder still. Paula, coughing extremely loudly. Titters. Paula, excusing herself loudest of all.

The head of sixth form, glaring at us from beneath his domed forehead. Quiet, Upper Sixth! You're supposed to be setting an example!

The Lord's Prayer. Our daily act of worship. The whole school, heads down, mumbling the words. The new boy, head unbowed, staring straight ahead.

Economics.

The Old Mole, with graphs. The rise of stocks. The fall of government bonds. The continuing inflation of the housing bubble.

The Old Mole, asking what the graphs might mean.

Um, Bombproof says.

Ah, Dingus says. Then, inspired: It means that things are going well! Then, no longer inspired: Doesn't it?

Diamanda, twiddling her pen. Putzie, shrugging. Quinn, vacant. Calypso, glowing prettily, but also vacant.

The Old Mole, impatient. Is she going to rant on again about *overprivileged pseuds*? About none us having ever seen *real poverty*?

Global economic collapse, miss, Paula says.

The Old Mole, looking up from her despair.

Hyperinflation, then a new Weimar, possibly a new Hitler, miss, Art says.

Stagflation, then another world war, to boost production, leading to *mutually assured destruction*, miss, I say.

Financial despotism, following the fusion of corporate power and political power, miss, Paula says. Fascism, in other words.

Resource wars, miss, Art says. Trade wars, miss. Real wars, miss . . .

The Old Mole, smiling grimly. And what is to be done?

Ums. Ahs.

Separate investment banks from retail banks? Art says.

Cryptocurrencies? Paula says.

Disintermediation? I say.

The new boy, hand raised.

The Old Mole, nodding.

The new boy: Nothing.

The Old Mole, no longer nodding: Nothing?!

The new boy: Let it all come down.

An *entire economic system*? the Old Mole says.

The new boy: *Economy* is the problem.

The economy *itself*? the Old Mole says.

The new boy: Economy devalues everything that matters.

The Old Mole, looking baffled: You want to get rid of the economy? What would we have in its place?

The new boy: Life.

Without goods and services? the Old Mole says. How would you meet your basic needs?

The new boy, leaning forward. My *basic need* is not to be dead. It's not to be carrying a corpse on my back.

The Old Mole, not knowing what to do. Is the new boy a nutter?

The new boy, sitting back in his chair. Silence.

Wow! Art says, sotto voce.

So the new boy's an *apocalypticist*. Just like us.

Lunch. The sixth-form common room. The new boy, carrying a tray from the canteen. We call him over to sit with us. Bombproof, slumped against the opposite wall, disappointed.

The end of the world, eh? Paula says.

Exactly *how* is the world going to end? Art says.

I think the world's *already* ended, I say. This is the afterlife.

Some fucking afterlife, Art says.

I think this is the *before* life, Paula says. I think we've never actually lived.

We contemplate the new boy's tray. Chips. Coleslaw. Baked beans.

Don't feel you have to eat the school dinners, Paula says. The canteen's disgusting.

And it's full of lower-school pupils, Art says. Always avoid lower-school pupils.

We spent years avoiding the lower-school pupils. And we were *in* the lower school, I say.

The new boy excuses himself. He wants to return his tray. And he needs the bathroom.

★

Boredom. All the old common room faces. Bitch Tits . . . Schlong Boy . . . Hand Job and the gang . . . And The Sirens, of course, sitting together, exotics, transferred from private school at the beginning of the sixth form.

The Sirens haven't played their hand yet, have they? Art asks.

They'll never play their hand, I say. They're girls of mystery.

You'd think they're dykes, but they're not, Paula says.

Paula wants to have the edgy lez monopoly, Art says.

Snippy snippy, Paula says.

Well, they're definitely not gay, I say.

Chandra still has his thing for The Sirens, Merv says. Or for one of them, anyway.

I do not! I say.

★

The common room.

The lowest-common-denominator room, Paula says.

The common soul-death room, I say.

Surveying the landscape. The beasts—the last beasts, the last of their kind, their fellows having left the sixth form. These are the academic beasts, the beasts with some brain to go with their brawn, and their hangers-on. There's Bombproof, the beasts' chew-toy. There's Calypso, as beautiful as her namesake, sitting on Dingus's knee.

But the beasts are in decline, now might is no longer de rigueur. The beasts no longer rule the school, not since the *trendies* discovered *irony* . . .

And there they are: the *trendies*. Gathered round the centre table. So *knowing*. So *louche*. So *seen-it-all-before*. The spoilt kids. The clique of cliques. Mean boys and mean girls, looking to fill everybody with fear . . .

But even irony has its limits. Even mean kids meet their match.

There's a new ascendancy—the meteoric rise of *everyone else*. The grey masses. The *drudges*. The duh-rudges. Too lazy for fear. Too distractible for irony . . .

So *many* of them! Always snacking and checking their phones. Always at their troughs. Always chowing down. *Consuming*. And so *cosy!* So bedded-in, with their novelty slippers and their massive vats of tea. So satisfied, yet so insatiable. So inert, yet growing fatter by the day. You can basically watch them expand. They're like bamboo in the tropics, only not so vertical.

The *drudges* will survive us all—there's no doubt of that. The *drudges* are here for the duration . . .

It's a grim scene, I say.

It makes me want to put out my eyes, Paula says.

No wonder we don't have anyone to hang out with, Merv says.

We have *us* to hang out with, Art says.

All we have in common is that we have nothing in common with anyone else, I say.

Or each other, Merv says.

We have our band! Art says.

The band's dead, Paula says.

P.E.

The sports cupboard, stacked with things to throw. Choose your weapon! Will it be the discus? The javelin? Really, who would trust us with a javelin? *We* wouldn't trust us with a javelin! Art would only throw a javelin straight through Dingus's heart . . .

★

On the playing field, blinking in the sun. We'll train for the long jump, we decide. For the triple jump! We head along the river path towards the sand pit. Willows. Cooling shade. The gentle lapping of the river.

So—what did you *do* to end up here? Paula asks the new boy. Did you set something on fire?

I'll bet you did, I say. I'll bet you set something on fire. You have that destroy-the-world look.

You went somewhere posh, right? Art says. Your accent's posh.

The new boy: Trafalgar College. I lost my scholarship.

I don't believe you, I say. I think you set something on fire.

Trafalgar's really something, Art says. I've seen it. *Very* nice buildings. And *very* nice grounds. Huge grounds, fenced off from the proles.

The new boy: All nonsense. High-Victorian fake.

I don't know, Art says. I mean, look at this dump!

This dump's not a fake, the new boy says. It's not selling *English-ness* off the shelf. They've *franchised* Trafalgar, you know. They've built an exact replica in China.

We imagine it: grand rococo buildings, in the Chinese suburbs. A fancy-pants chapel in the shadow of Chinese high-rises. Shooting and army-cadetting, in the Chinese suburbs. Early morning mist, in the Chinese suburbs. Groundskeepers flattening turf, in the Chinese suburbs. Rugby fixtures and summer fêtes, in the Chinese suburbs. The lacrosse team, jogging through the woods, in the Chinese suburbs.

We wish Loddon Valley could be *bothered* to be fake, we tell the new boy.

Well-being class.

Mr Merriweather, self-styled *teen-whisperer,* showing slides on the *miracle of Bhutan.*

Mr Merriweather, explaining the *amazing Bhutanese experiment.* The *admirable Bhutanese initiative.*

Slide: *Ghalkey,* the Bhutanese word for happiness.

Mr Merriweather: *Gha,* in Bhutanese, means you like something. *Key* means peace. The harmony of the *whole*—that's what the Bhutanese value. It's not about individual happiness. It's not about *my* happiness or *your* happiness. It's about the *whole.* (Makes an encompassing gesture.) The *WHOLE.*

Slide: (Title) *The Pillars of Happiness.* (Bullet-points) *Psychological well-being. Time use. Cultural diversity and resilience. Community vitality. Good governance.*

Slide: *Gross Domestic Happiness.*

Mr Merriweather: The Bhutanese have actually taken it upon themselves to measure the gross domestic happiness of their population!

Slide: (Title) *Bhutanese Government Questionnaire.* (Bullet-points) *Do you trust your neighbours? Do you believe in karma? Do you know local folktales?*

Mr Merriweather: Do *we* trust our neighbours? Do *we* believe in anything? Are *we* happy?

Slide: Smiling Bhutanese children.

Slide: Smiling Bhutanese peasants, with their yaks.

Slide: Smiling Bhutanese priests, at the temple.

Slide: Smiling Mr Merriweather, enjoying *traditional Bhutanese hospitality*.

Slide: Smiling Mr Merriweather, trekking in the mountains with his faithful Bhutanese guide.

Slide: Smiling Mr Merriweather and smiling Mrs Merriweather (we presume), strolling through a Bhutanese market.

Bhutan's doomed, isn't it, sir? Paula says. I mean, as soon as you open the country to happiness-tourism, there's no more happiness, is there, sir?

It's like what happens when we make contact with isolated tribes, sir, Art says. Half of them die of Western diseases. Then cancer, alcoholism and depression finish of the rest. It's the West, sir. It's what we do.

I'll bet the young Bhutanese are all depressed, sir, I say. I'll bet they're all suicidal, just like us, sir. And there's nothing that can be done, even with all the tourist money swilling round the country.

Bhutan's trying to resist westernisation, Mr Merriweather says. Bhutan can still teach *us* values.

The new boy, *NIHILISM* in big letters across his notebook.

Home time.

The bike sheds. Unlocking our bikes.

Pigeons, flying after one another.

That one's trying to fuck that one, Merv says. He's, like, forcing himself on her.

Maybe she likes it, I say.

She's flying away, Paula says. Or trying to.

Look at the way he's *strutting*, Art says. Just like you, Chandra.

How do you know it's a he? Paula says. Could be a dyke. Could be all dyke pigeons around here.

Nature's disgusting, Art says. Animals are disgusting. I hate the way they always remind us of us. The way they just *live*—it's indecent. All their *instincts* . . .

We have instincts, Paula says.

I refuse to have instincts, Art says.

The need to breed, Art—everything fucks, I say.

Is that what we're like? Is that what love is? Art says.

Maybe machine intelligence will be better, Merv says. I mean, machines don't fuck, do they? They can just build new machines.

Roll on full automation, Art says.

★

Wheeling through the crowds.

You know who the new boy looks like? Paula says. I've been thinking about it all day. Nietzsche.

Who? Merv asks.

Friedrich Nietzsche—the philosopher, Paula says. Don't tell me you haven't heard of Nietzsche.

Merv, investigating on his phone. Showing us a photo. The new boy doesn't look anything like him!

You have to look beyond the moustache, Paula says.

How? Merv says. All I can see is moustache.

TUESDAY

Assembly. On our chairs at the back of the hall.

School prayer. We bow our heads. School notices. We yawn with boredom. A gymnastic display. Bill Trim, on the rings, swinging himself, suspending himself, arms out. Bill Trim, on the horse, straddling, turning, flipping a handspring to land on the mat. Quite marvellous.

General whispering: Getting excited, Merv? Got your chubby on, Merv? Steady, Merv!

A stern look from the Old Mole. She used to be *livelier*, we agree.

Nietzsche, Merv and I, on gate duty.

You need muscle for gate duty, I tell Nietzsche. Psychological muscle.

Merv, to an approaching boy: Have you got your pass?

Fuck off, cunt, the boy says.

We sit on the metal fence.

More kids.

Passes, lads? I ask.

Fucking cunts, the lads say, going by us.

We contemplate the houses opposite. New-builds, just gone up. Houses without feature. Without relief. Houses that are what they are, and nothing more. *Housing solutions*. Dead-eyed boxes for the dead.

Hundreds of similar houses, stretching out behind. Hundreds of houses, herded into mini- estates, spreading all the way to the motorway.

What *look* were the developers going for? we wonder. Blandness? Deathliness? Soul-murder? Soul-destruction? The obliteration of all resistance?

What kind of house do you live in? I ask Nietzsche.

An ordinary house, he says. Just like these.

Bit of a come-down from Trafalgar, eh? Merv says.

Nietzsche shrugs. I didn't board there, he says. We lived in the grounds.

Why did you leave? I ask.

My father taught there, he says. Then he died. We lost our house.

And now you live in *Wokingham*, I say. Jesus.

Silence.

So what actually *is* nihilism? I ask Nietzsche.

Nietzsche: Nothing-ism. Not believing in anything.

Sounds interesting, I say.

Nietzsche: It isn't interesting. It's devastating.

Paula and Art, back from the shop with their chips.

What's devastating? Paula asks.

Nihilism, I say.

Ah. God is dead and all, Paula says.

How the fuck did you know that? I ask.

Some of us read books, Paula says. Some of us are actually inter-ested in the world.

But everyone's a nihilist now, aren't they? I say. I mean, no one really believes in anything anymore, do they?

Art does, Paula says. Art believes in all kinds of things. Art's a *sex Buddhist*, aren't you?

Tantra, Art says. That's what it's called. And it's not just about sex.

Oh no? Paula says. Art, you've got sex seeping out of your pores. All that storing-it-up's got you *obsessed* . . .

Merv, reading from his phone:

> *Nihilism, from the Latin* nihil, *nothing, is a philosophical doctrine that suggests the lack of belief in one or more reputedly meaningful aspects of life. Most commonly, nihilism is presented in the form of existential nihilism, which argues that life is without objective, meaning, purpose or intrinsic value.*

So when did life use to make sense? Merv asks.

When people believed in God, Paula says.

But people still suffered, even then, right? I say. People still felt that life was meaningless.

Nietzsche: Of course. They believed in God *because* they felt that life was meaningless. They needed to believe in *something*. Nihilism is not what's there when belief is gone. Nihilism is there all along. Nihilism is the father of belief.

Well, what about maths, then? I ask. Do nihilists believe in maths? Two plus two equals four, and all that?

Nietzsche (quoting): *Two plus two equals four is no longer life but is merely the beginning of death.*

But maths is *true*, right? I say.

Nietzsche: Truth isn't the only thing that matters.

What else matters? I ask.

Nietzsche: Life.

I don't understand—is maths nihilist or not? Merv asks.

Never mind maths, Merv, Paula says. Lots of things are meaningful. People feel happy or sad. That's meaningful. It means they feel happy or sad.

But what if we don't know what we feel? Art says. What if we're confused? What if it's all a fake?

Nietzsche: *life* cannot be fake.

Geography.

Mr Zachary, battling a head-cold, telling us of ecosystem exploitation. Of grazing and deforestation. Of monoculture and over-cultivation. It's making him depressed, we can see it. Carbon dioxide concentration in the atmosphere. Methane seepage. The decline in arctic ice coverage.

Mr Zachary, unable to take any more, speaking instead of mitigation policies. Of climate sinks and low-carbon technology. Of climate stabilization. Of cutting emissions. Of carbon capture. Of bioenergy and burning plant-mass.

Mr Zachary, appearing comforted. Mr Zachary's head-cold, seeming improved.

It's too late, sir, Paula says. Everyone knows that.

The end is coming, sir, Art says. You can't fight it.

The deserts are growing, sir, Paula says.

The algal blooms are dying off, sir, Art says.

The food chains are breaking, sir, I say.

The oceans are acidifying, sir, Art says.

We're returning to a state of nature, sir, Paula says. The shit is hitting the fan, sir. It's *Fury Road*, sir.

Mr Zachary, depressed again. Mr Zachary's head-cold, relapsing.

The Earth will endure, Mr Zachary says, rallying. Gaia will endure.

Ah, Mr Zachary's spurious Gaia faith! Mr Zachary's dubious Gaia mysticism! Mr Zachary's wondrous leap from despair to hope! From nadir to zenith!

Discussion. They'll probably engineer some post-human horror, some creature who will thrive on the blackened Earth, who will breathe carbon dioxide and live on cinders. They'll probably devise some insectoid-android who will not weep when it sees death all around it, whose heart will be unmoved by the destruction of all things. Who will not mourn, nor love, nor pity.

That's something to cling to, isn't it . . . sir? Paula says.

Mr Zachary, more depressed than we've ever seen him. Mr. Zachary, in the gravest state of head-cold.

Litter duty.

Nietzsche, with the litter-picker. Merv, wheeling the bin. Art and I, supervising. The lower school's so *dirty*.

Nietzsche, snapping sweet wrappers from the drain.

Bet you didn't have to do this kind of thing at Trafalgar, Merv says.

Nietzsche shrugs.

Never mind Trafalgar, Art says. It's Chandra who's really suffering. Brahmins aren't supposed to defile themselves picking litter, are they, Chandra? If only your ancestors could see you now, eh? Then: Jesus, is that a condom?

It's a latex glove, I say.

It's covered in something disgusting, Art says. Oh my God. It looks *spermy*.

We imagine some lower-school science-glove hand-job. It's sordid. Everyone's fucking everyone and no one's fucking us, Merv says.

Art, singing: *Someday your prince will come* . . .

Merv, picking up the glove with Nietzsche's picker and throwing it at Art. Laughter. Art's howls of protest.

We retreat to the sixth-form car-park. So has most of the litter. What a dump! This is where it all ends up. Pulped things, around the prefabs. Drink cans. Mounds of chewing gum. What a place for Bombproof's classic Mini! What a location for Schlong Boy's lunchtime humping! What a berth for Nicholas Nugent's convertible Beetle! Picture it: the roof down, spermy latex tangling in his hair!

Jesus!—it's a rat!, Art says. And there's another one! There must be a whole fucking nest under the prefab!

Sorry you had to see this, I say to Nietzsche.

The world's *disgusting*, Art says. Full of filth and decay. *Death to the world*: that's what Justin Marler says.

Nietzsche: Who?

The guy from Sleep. You've heard of Sleep, haven't you? Doom metal's finest. Well, Justin Marler left to become a monk. A doom metal monk.

There are no doom metal monks, Art, Merv says.

Yes there are!—Justin Marler has a website: death-to-the-world-dot-com, Art says. *The last true rebellion is death to the world*, he quotes. *To be crucified to the world and the world to us* . . .

That's nihilism, right? Art says, turning to Nietzsche.—Not wanting to believe in the world?

Nietzsche: When life turns against life—that's nihilism.

But why does life turn against life? Merv asks.

Nietzsche: Because we see meaninglessness everywhere.

Free period. Post lunch. Post chips.

Grazing drudges on the common room plain. Grazing, munching drudges, snacking on the plain, checking their phones on the plain. Snacking drudges, surfing drudges, busy with their phones.

Herds at peace, untroubled by predators. Herds spread over the plain, horizon to horizon. Content, as herds are content. Mild, as herds are mild.

They're checking their phones. They're administering their lives on their smart-phones. And they're eating. My God, they're eating. Licking their fingers for the last flakes of pastry. Tilting muffin-crumbs into their mouths. Unwrapping one bar of chocolate and then another. Rustling through one packet of crisps and then another.

They're so *satisfied*, the drudges. So pleased with things. They settle down at their desks with an *oof*. They devour their chocolate bars with an *mmm*.

The drudges are ready to squeeze into some office chair. To sit behind some office terminal. To blob down some office corridor. To commute to work in some Ford Focus. They have no *lightness*. No life. No laughter or irony. They're heavy as suet. They're like scoops of mashed-potato . . .

The great plains of the common room. The great watering holes of the common room. Where are the predators to hunt down the herds? Who's higher on the food chain? But the beasts slump in their corner, long burnt-out. And the trendies hog the centre tables, sighing affectedly. It's the reign of the drudge. It's the age of the drudge.

★

The common room.

Bill Trim, joining us.

Bill—what a surprise!, Paula says. The missing link himself. Well, Bill—speak up. What do you have to say? There's no room for passengers here. And then: Admit it, Bill. It's bi-curiosity that brought you to us. You have us pegged as queers. And then (looking around

| 15 |

at the rest of us): Don't you think we should club together and get Bill a rent-boy? Wouldn't you like a rent-boy, Bill? A ladyboy rent-boy—that'd be your type. Or maybe you'd like to *be* a ladyboy rent-boy! It might be too late for that, mind. And surgery *costs*. Changing your bone-mass . . . The pitch of your voice . . . Your general aggression . . . We could crowd-fund it, I suppose . . .

You seem unusually aggressive today, Bill, Paula says. Pent up. And then (looking round at the rest of us): Don't you think one of us should fuck Bill? As a public service, I mean. Merv, you'd be Bill's cup of tea, I'd say. Go on, do it for the team. Lie back and think of us.

Cycling home.

Freewheeling downhill.

Did you see Nietzsche, queuing up for the school bus? I ask.

We saw him. Hundreds of kids, milling about on the tarmac, bags over their shoulders. Hundreds of them, calling, bellowing, shouting to one another. And Nietzsche among them, queuing to get on the school bus. Hundreds of lower-school brats, barely civilized. And Nietzsche among them, about to board a bus to carry him wherever. The indignity! The ignominy! The overcrowding! The fight for seats!

What a vision: Nietzsche, unable to find a seat downstairs, as screaming children scrawl obscenities on the steamed-up glass. Nietzsche, sitting on the edge of a seat upstairs, with the bus stuck in traffic, having to bear the chatter of the screaming children. Nietzsche, with the bus at a dead halt for half an hour, his head full of the inanities of the screaming children. Nietzsche, being bellowed at from the back seats: *Eat shit and die, posh boy!*

The desire to protect Nietzsche. To look after him. But why? Because he's the new boy. No—because he's different. Because he's cleverer than us. *Better* than us. Is that it?

It's because he's innocent, I say. He's better than *this* world.

Crap—it's just mystique, Paula says. We're in awe of him. Because we're from generations of bowers and scrapers.

Nietzsche's not actually posh, I say. I mean, he was a scholarship boy, not some aristocrat.

Maybe that's why he was expelled—because he wasn't posh enough, Art says.

I'll bet he did something really fucking cool, like what's-his-name in *Heathers*, Paula says. I'll bet he shot some posho in the face.

Something's going to happen, Art says. It's got to mean something, Nietzsche arriving here, just when we're about to finish.

Nothing means anything, doofus, I say.

He might be the leader we always wanted, Art says.

Nietzsche looks too depressed to lead us, I say.

I'm too depressed to be led, Paula says.

Well, we can't let him travel home with the lower-school brats, Art says. He needs to get a bike. He can cycle home with us.

The vision of Nietzsche, on a bike. Nietzsche, cycling like a pro . . . Nietzsche, one of us, free—on the open road. Nietzsche, cycling through the estates, through the scraps of last countryside. Nietzsche, slowing as he crests the hill on Barkham Street. Nietzsche, plunging into the Molly Millar estate. Nietzsche, freewheeling through the Molly Millar estate, gladness swelling in his breast . . .

The vision of Nietzsche, freer now. Nietzsche, thinking as he cycles. Nietzsche, full of exhilarated thoughts . . . Laughing thoughts . . . Puffed-out thoughts . . .

The vision of Nietzsche, a man of the bike, at one with the bike. Nietzsche, with the right clips for his pedals, and the lightest of helmets on his head.

Nietzsche, knowing the gladness of cycling. The happiness of cycling. His lungs full of fresh air. His vessels full of fresh blood. Muscles stretched in his thighs, his calves, his forearms. Wind in his hair. What heed will he pay to the occasional fly in his throat? None. To the occasional fly in his eye? Likewise, none.

The vision of Nietzsche, cycling, looking over the last vistas. Seeing the last fields, the last ponds, the last unconverted barns. Nietzsche, cycling along the last unmade roads by the golf course. Nietzsche, weaving his bike through traffic, on and off the pavement. Nietzsche, following footpaths, cut-throughs, like us. Nietzsche, with all the *cunning* of the cyclist. The *freedom* of the cyclist . . .

Lunch, after English class.

Did the Head Boy really sleep through the entire lesson? we wonder. He really did. Resting his head on the desk. Mrs Sherwood left him alone. She could see something was wrong. She spoke to him gently afterwards.

And what about Tasker? Art says. He wasn't looking too good.

Tasker was just depressed, Paula says. Studying *Endgame* does that to you.

And his sister just killed herself, Merv says.

It's drugs, I say. Downers. Those guys were out of it.

Discussion. The Head Boy and Tasker were always well-adjusted types. Adventure types. Venture Scouts, that sort of thing. Outdoor pursuits. White-water rafting. They were happiest in gilets, rowing up and down the river, getting all their aggression out. Expending their testosterone in *good clean fun*. And all under appropriate adult supervision, of course. Under the watchful eye of Brown Owl or Big Bird, or whatever the fuck they're called.

But it's all falling apart now, that's quite clear. Their general good cheer won't save them now. Their camouflage gilets won't keep them afloat. Physical thrills are no longer enough. They want to shoot *mental* rapids. They want the risk of capsizing. They've become weedwhackers. Psychonauts. They're *chemically* adventurous . . .

Free period.

Where's Art? we wonder.

Upstairs. The study area, which is to say the preparing-for-the-most-important-exams-in-your-life area. Which is to say the infinite procrastination area. The staring-into-space area.

Art, at a desk, pretending to study.

Art, at a desk, waiting for Calypso.

This is where Calypso comes to *work*. Calypso, of the soft white sweaters. Calypso, of the exquisite lisp. Calypso, who studies so hard, because she isn't quite bright enough to be here. Calypso, straining against her low IQ. Calypso, telling chatterers and idlers like us to *keep it down!*

Art would like nothing better than to hold Calypso in his arms, and tell her everything will be okay. That it will all come good for her. That, in a couple of years, she'll be safe studying business at some former poly . . .

Ah, when will it happen? When will Calypso accept Art as the One? When will she entrust her soul to him? When will she look to him for support? When will she want him, and him alone, to speak words of comfort? When will her eyes sparkle at the sight of him? When will her heart leap inside her, and her soul thrill? When will it be his face, and his alone, that she watches for? When will she whisper his name all breathily in his ear?

We contemplate the study area.

Framed paintings on the walls. Hockney. Spencer. The curious arbitrariness of paintings by Hockney and Spencer. Why Hockney and Spencer? Why not Hockney and Spencer? Why anything? Why *not* anything? Desk fans, for when it gets warm. A few lockers—who uses lockers? Beige carpet tiles, running all along. Running in and out of the tiny teachers' offices. Mr Zachary's. Mr Varga's. Running in and out of Mr Pound's office, slightly larger than the others.

The sixth-form mural—sixth-form hopes and dreams, as painted by one of our own. Everything *we might be*. Everywhere *we might end up*. There's an astronaut, floating in space . . . A footballer, booting a ball towards us . . . A Prime Minister, walking out of 10 Downing Street . . . We could be anything! Do anything! It's dizzying . . .

Enter Calypso, through the double doors.

Art's all aquiver, Paula says.

Merv, whispering: Calypso . . . Calypso . . .

Look at that lovely sweater!, Paula adds quietly. So soft! So white! Would you like to touch it, Art? Would you?

Art, gathering his things and storming off.

★

The computer room. Art, at a console.

We crowd in beside him.

You fuckers, Art says, still blushing. You fucking fuckers.

Paula reads from Art's screen: *In some ways, the accident brought*

Chris and me closer together. When I lost my legs I thought my life was over, but now I have so much to live for.

Art likes to read about injuries when he's upset, I tell Nietzsche. About the terrible things that happen to people.

Paula, continuing to read:

> *My new legs added to me—they didn't take away. How do I stay so positive? It sucks to be depressed, and why would you want to put yourself in that situation? I've seen amazing things from guys who've lost all four limbs. Every time I've felt like the world's crashing down on my shoulders, like I can't possibly pull out of this, it's ended up being the best thing that's ever happened to me. Sure, things hurt and you feel bad. You feel like you've been KO'd and you're down for the count. My life will never be the same again, but I feel lucky. I'm lucky to be alive today.*

Is this cheering you up, Art? Paula asks. Are you feeling better? And then: God, this place is thick with nerds.

Iqbal, king of the nerds, behind glass, in the private study room.

Iqbal's become terribly unpredictable since he was struck by lightning. He's in a constant bad mood. Playing golf in a thunderstorm! Madness! But a few drops of rain mean nothing to the would-be golf pro. Darkening clouds, rumbles in the sky: nothing! And that's when he was struck. And that's when he acquired his special powers . . .

Paula, banging on the glass: What's going to happen tomorrow, Iqbal?

Fuck off, Iqbal says.

Who's going to win the Grand National, Iqbal? I ask.

Fuck off, Iqbal says.

Will Art ever win Calypso's heart, Iqbal? Paula asks.

Fuck off, Iqbal says.

Should I put money on City to win the League, Iqbal? I ask.

Fuck off, Iqbal says.

Merv, tapping on the glass and mouthing: *High School Massacre?*

Iqbal nods.

A computer each. On our screens, an exact replica of the sixth-form common room, the sixth-form kitchen, the sixth-form cloak-room and the stairwell.

Spawning, under the covered walkway. Then the search for weapons. The tomahawk in the broom cupboard (you get a bonus for decapitations). The ripsaw hidden in the cloakroom. The nailgun in the toilets. Then there's the rocket-launcher in Mr Pound's office. It's really hard to get, because you have to fight off Mr Pound first, with his enormous forehead . . .

Iqbal's robot avatar, IQBAL 3000 stencilled on the front, on caterpillar tracks, with machine guns for arms, smashing through the walls. Merv's avatar, just like him, in a mankini, wielding a lightsabre. Art's avatar, the mad monk Rasputin, cradling his railgun. My avatar, Krishna-blue, with a dozen arms, lobbing grenade after grenade down the stairwell.

But Iqbal's got the flak cannon. You can't touch Iqbal when he's got the flak cannon.

THURSDAY

Assembly.

Mr Varga, reading from another of his inscrutable European books. Something about a sister and a cone. Something about a guy building a cone for his sister in the middle of a forest. What the fuck? Long European sentences. Long, winding European sentences. The novel's really about Wittgenstein, Mr Varga said by way of an introduction. But who the fuck is Wittgenstein?

Even the teachers are confused. Mr Lunkton, head of woodwork, dozing off. Likewise Mr Weevil, head of metalwork. Likewise Mr Sturridge, the tech guy. Ah, but Mr Lunkton is stupid. And so is Mr Saracen. And Miss Lilly isn't much better. Comprehensive schoolteachers, destroyed by teacher-training, by the National Curriculum, by micro-management from on high. Comprehensive schoolteachers, every idea driven from their heads. It's survival of the mediocre. Survival of the bureaucrat. It's survival of the petty and the trivially minded . . .

How did Mr Varga end up here? He clearly has a brain. He actually knows things. He has facts at his disposal, not like our new-university-educated dodos. Not only that, things have actually *happened* to him. He's always telling us about growing up in Hungary. About the fascists and the communists. About the coming of capitalism. About his great-uncles who were thrown into prison, first by the fascists, and then by the communists. It's amazing he survived. It's amazing he came through to teach us history, of all things. In Loddon Valley School, of all places . . .

Sitting by the river. Art, reading from his phone:

> *I am called the last philosopher because I am the last man. No one speaks to me except me myself, and my voice reaches me like that of a dying man.*

It's Nietzsche's blog, Art says. *Our* Nietzsche. Last-philosopher-dotcom.

Does he think *he's* the last philosopher? I say.

The tagline's *The Uselessness of Everything*, Art says. He's joking, right?

Nietzsche's, like, wallowing in it, I say.

Does being clever always make people miserable? Merv wonders.

Art, reading on:

> *Above is below, below is above. Everything is possible, yet nothing is. All is permitted, yet nothing is.* [It's from some guy called C-i-o-r-a-n—how do you pronounce that?] *Absurd to say that something is absurd. Negation is no more possible than affirmation. Nothing is more real than nothing.* [That's from Beckett—what does it mean?]

It means you can't say anything is meaningless, Paula says. But you can't say anything has meaning, either.

Art, reading on: *Agreed: no meaning in itself. BUT AFFIRMATION MORE IMPORTANT THAN ANYTHING.* [That's our Nietzsche—it's next to the Beckett quote in big capitals.]

Affirmation? Paula asks. What does Nietzsche have to affirm? He lives in Wokingham, right?

Belief—he wants to affirm *belief,* I say. Not belief in God. Belief in the world.

Art, scrolling down and reading. Quotations from Goethe. From Schelling's *Ages of the World.* From Simmel and Heidegger. And detailed commentaries on the original Nietzsche—thousands of words.

We're fucking outclassed, I say.

Agreed—he's cleverer than us, Art says.

He's read more maybe . . . , Paula says.

He can actually do things with what he's read, Art says. He can actually *think.*

Discussion. It's alright for Nietzsche, with his private-school education. His intelligence is not crabbed, like ours. It's not turned in on itself. It hasn't been squandered on music trivia. On the ranking of favourite albums and films. His intelligence hasn't been frittered away in insults. In banter. In ways of surviving the boredom.

Only posh types can think about real things—abstract things. Only posh types are given the *license* to think. Only posh types study the old subjects, proper subjects, at their schools. Only posh types have been allowed to soar in the skies of philosophy, of art, of literature—to spread their intellectual wings.

But they'll never have street-smarts like us, I say.

What fucking street-smarts? Paula asks. Wokingham's hardly the fucking hood.

That's our problem, Art says. We haven't really been up against it. We haven't *suffered.*

We're spoiled, we agree. We're from a spoiled generation.

We've been overstimulated. Overprogrammed. Everything has been done for us. We've been grade-inflated. Infotained. Our teachers have been like magicians at children's birthday parties.

We're the most useless generation that has ever lived. The most pampered. The most unchallenged. And the most *unhappy,* which is the funny thing.

Free period, the common room.

Boredom, terrible boredom. Time, time everywhere, and not a moment we can live.

Are we in some kind of purgatory? Are we working off some kind of *sin*? What crime did we commit in a former life?

It's like *Groundhog Day*. We're living the same day over and over again. We're living the same free period over and over again until we learn some lesson.

What lesson? I wonder.

That life sucks, Art says.

We've learnt that, I say.

That nothing's ever going to happen again, Paula says. That we're marooned in the suburbs forever.

We've got farther to go, we agree. We must annihilate all hope. We must expect nothing—*nothing*.

Hope? What's hope? I ask.

We must forget the very word, *hope*, we agree. The very *memory* of hope . . .

Bill Trim, sitting down with us.

You've found us at our lowest ebb, Bill, Paula says. We're *full* of nihilism.

Explaining nihilism to Bill Trim.

You see, nothing means anything, Bill, Paula says. It's all futile. It's all for nothing. That's what you'll have to understand if you want to join nihilism club. And you *do* want to join nihilism club, don't you, Bill? All the best people are in nihilism club. There are probably ladyboys in nihilism club, Bill. And Merv's *definitely* in nihilism club.

The meaning of the world has disappeared, Bill, Paula says. The world has darkened, Bill! The gods have flown! Nothing's more real than nothing! The uncanniest guest stands at the door! Everything is both real and unreal, normal and absurd, Bill! There is nothing worth more than anything else, nor is any idea better than any other! A whole world has disintegrated!

It's terrible, Bill!, Paula says. It's devastating! You should be trembling in your soul, Bill. You *do* have a soul, don't you, Bill? You're probably developing one now, Bill. It comes from hanging out with us. You used to be just lust and hunger, Bill, like all the beasts. But now . . .

Of course it may be that you're too *healthy* for nihilism, Bill, Paula says. Too *fit*. You have to be a little sick, to get nihilism. You have to be something of an outsider. Maybe your ladyboy love's a chink,

Bill. The fact that you don't fit in so well with the beasts. Ah, but you don't see it, do you, Bill? You don't see what's wrong with the world. You'll have to teach him, Merv . . . Grunt if you understand, Bill . . .

Cycling home. The dual carriageway, as wide as the Nile. Then the path along by the new estates, the newest of new estates—fresh, just minted, sprawling.

Buttercup Close (no buttercups). Marigold Stream (no marigolds; no stream). Tulip Way (just concrete). Sheraton Drive (who, or what, was Sheraton?)

Discussion. Did you hear Nietzsche in English, discussing *Endgame* with Mrs Sherwood? What did he mean about the *impossibility of humour*? About *the jokes of a damaged people*? Why did he say *laughter no longer reaches anyone*?

And did you see Nietzsche in assembly? He actually seemed to *like* Mr Varga's story! You could see him smiling!

The feeling that the sixth form has changed, with Nietzsche's arrival. That the whole sixth-form has shifted slightly. Been altered, in some subtle way. The feeling that there's been a tectonic shift. A movement of plates. Something has happened—but what?

The feeling that Nietzsche is the key to something. But what door will he unlock? The feeling that something's going to happen. That something important is about to happen . . .

FRIDAY

The PE changing rooms.

Merv, looking faint. Merv, all but collapsing. Merv, having a flashback. There should be a trigger warning for Merv in the PE changing rooms. Merv's got post-traumatic stress disorder. Merv's like a Vietnam vet when it comes to PE.

And it *was* disgusting, in the PE changing rooms. All that *flesh*. Boys together, dozens of them, in the PE changing rooms. Boys, hundreds of them, undressing in the changing rooms.

All of us, even more crowded-in than normal, in the PE changing rooms. Even more crammed-in. An armpit, in your face. Some-body's arse, in your face. And the whiff of faecal matter, up your nostrils. And all those cocks, bobbing in your face. All that pubic hair, perilously close to your face. All those disgusting bodies, in a state of change. All those pores open. All that hair growing every-where, and spots sprouting everywhere.

And the atmosphere of violence, in the PE changing rooms. The beasts, tormenting some poor weakling, some *disaster of puberty*, in the PE changing rooms. It was like Abu Ghraib, like the fucking gulag, the PE changing rooms. It was every boy for himself, in the PE changing rooms.

My God, the scenes of depravity, in the PE changing rooms. The Hieronymus-Bosch grotesquerie of the PE changing rooms. The random acts of violence, rats, snapping at rats, in the PE changing rooms. Viciousness at large, teeth bared, nostrils flaring, in the PE changing rooms. Mouths screaming, eyes staring, in the PE chang-ing rooms.

There was no *dignity* in the PE changing rooms. There were no human rights, in the PE changing rooms. The Geneva convention didn't hold in the PE changing rooms. It was a perpetual *state of emergency*, in the PE changing rooms. The crumbling of civilization, right there in the PE changing rooms. A *state of exception*, revealed as such; the *state of nature*, no longer able to hide—right there, in the PE changing rooms . . .

And poor Merv, at the hands of Dingus, in the PE changing rooms. Poor Merv, the plaything of the beasts, Bill Trim among them, in the PE changing rooms. How things have changed! How Bill Trim has changed! Maybe it started for him then, in the PE changing rooms. Maybe he began to feel Merv-love, in the PE changing rooms, as he saw Merv being beaten, as he beat Merv himself, in the PE changing rooms.

Merv, bent over, breathing heavily. Art, arm around Merv, talking tenderly about the sea. About the beach. About the sound of waves.

The common room. Art, reading Nietzsche.

Merv (looking at the title): *The Gay Science*. What is it—a sex book?

It's about the death of God, Art says.

I don't see what's gay about *that*, Merv says.

Paula, snatching the book from Art and reading it out:

> God is dead. God remains dead. And we have killed him. How
> shall we comfort ourselves, the murderers of all murderers? What
> was holiest and mightiest has bled to death under our knives . . .

I don't get it—so there was a God and *then* we killed him? Merv
asks.

It means we believed in God, and then we couldn't believe anymore, Paula says.

But why does it say we *killed* God? Merv asks.

Science and stuff, I guess, I say.

But people still believe in God, right? Paula says. What about Justin Marler?

I like his death-to-the-world stuff, not his God stuff, Art says.

You can't have one without the other, Paula says.

Why do we have to believe in anything? I ask. Why can't we just
accept the world as it is?

Look around you, doofus, Art says. The world's a shithole.

We don't believe in the world: that's the problem, Paula says. We
don't believe in anything.

So we've got to become religious again? I ask.

We've got to believe in something again, which is different, Paula
says.

Merv, reading on:

> Where has God gone? What did we do when we unchained the
> Earth from its sun? Whither are we moving now? Away from
> all suns? Are we not perpetually falling? Are we not straying as
> through an infinite nothing?

Why are we supposed to be lost? I ask. I mean, no one really cares
about God anymore.

Because the death of God is the death of belief, Art says.

I see it now: Nihilism didn't begin with the death of God—it's the
other way round, Paula says. The death of God is the death of belief.
God died because we couldn't believe in anything.

What about us? I ask. We believe in music, don't we?

We *used* to believe in music, we agree. We *used* to believe in all kinds of things. What happened to us?

It's this place, Paula says. It's the fucking sixth form.

It's the suburbs, I say.

A walk to clear our heads.

The underpass. Old graffiti. *FUCK JAIMEE. BARRY IS A PENUS.* Faded marker-pen drawings of cannabis leaves. Of naked women. Of guns. Men armed with chainsaws. Magnificent work.

The last hooligans of Wokingham, Art says. The last discontents.

We're discontented, right? Paula says.

Ah, but they were full of *class hatred*, Art says.

Were they fuck!, Paula says. There's no class hatred in Wokingham.

There are still a few council houses left, I say.

They've all been sold!, Paula says.

And there are still a few unemployed people, I say.

They've all been forced back to work, Paula says.

That's why my dad went mad, Merv says. They tried to make him push trollies around in Asda.

Discussion. What would we do all day, if we didn't have to work? We imagine it: going *on the sick*. Getting a sick-note for life. Cultivating the art of doing nothing. Of walking through the woods. Of cycling around aimlessly. Of just staring into the air.

We could just escape. Leave England for the Mediterranean, where it's warm all the year round.

We could go to Greece, where things are really fucked up. Or Spain. We could go to Italy, where the banks are about to collapse.

We could go and live in the ruins of America. State failure—that's where it's at. It's best to live somewhere really grim. That way you have a correlate for your despair. The worst thing about Wokingham is that it *smiles back at your despair.* Wokingham hopes that you'll *have a nice day in your despair.*

★

Asda. A supermarket in the shape of a vast concrete-and-glass tomb. A concrete-and-glass tomb of the unknown suburbanite.

Asda—is this where we've come? Asda—is this our destination? What did we want here? Why did we come here? What is there to buy? A snack? Another snack? But we're snacked out. We've had enough. More than enough. We've glutted ourselves. We're getting fat. Save us from obesity!

Miles of aisles, and what to buy? A bottle of pop—but what kind of pop? A caffeine delivery system? A taurine delivery system? A sugar delivery system?

Alcohol instead. We should take off our school ties and buy some at the counter. Put on our deepest voices. Act old. We should ask for a bottle of vodka—the water of life. We should drink our way through lunchtime.

Chilled vodka—that's what we need. Vodka fresh from the freezer (it doesn't freeze through; it only goes cloudy . . .) Vodka glasses, fresh from the fridge. Toasts to life, to drinking. Toasts to *drinking to drinking*. Toasts to Russians, freezing in the taiga. *Na Zdorovie! Na Zdorovie!*

We need to shake the deadness off. But it's all deadness. There's deadness everywhere.

Young Enterprise.

Oh God, Art says.

They're showing a film. Good, we won't have to say anything. We'll just have to stop ourselves from opening a vein.

Maverick Billionaire: The Richard Branson Story. A real epic.

The early years: Branson, the struggling entrepreneur, full of English pluck and derring-do. Branson, fearlessly *taking on the big boys, David to their Goliaths*. Branson, the underdog, always *punching above his weight*.

Branson, passionate about *change*. Branson, restlessly building an *invincible brand*. Virgin records. Virgin Cola. Virgin dental drills. Virgin suppositories. Virgin attack dogs. Virgin luxury bunkers . . .

Footage of Branson, interviewed:

I don't think of work as play and play as play. It's all living. Life is a helluva lot more fun if you say yes rather than no. A business has to be involving, it has to be fun, and it has to exer-

cise your creative energies. To be successful, you have to be out
there, you have to hit the ground running. A business is simply
an idea to make other people's lives better.

Branson, always *living life to the full*. Branson, always ready for the *next, apparently unachievable, goal*. Branson, the *transformational leader*, inspiring and empowering all around him. Branson, full of *maverick strategies*. Branson, taking on British Airways. Taking on Formula One.

Branson, the balloonist, breaking records with his Atlantic Ocean crossing. With his Pacific Ocean crossing. Branson appearing in *Rebel Billionaire*, his own reality TV show. Branson, tackling climate change with Virgin Fuels. With Virgin carbon extractors. Branson, setting up the *Virgin Earth Challenge* to award the designer who can remove greenhouse gases from the atmosphere.

Footage of Branson ballooning over the Himalayas, stroking his beard, looking thoughtful. Footage of Branson on his tropical island, stroking a parrot, wondering what he can do about the climate change problem. About planetary apocalypse.

Footage of Branson on the phone to Bill Gates. *What can we do, Bill? How can we make the world a better place? How can we effect positive global change?*

Branson's dreams for Virgin Galactic, taking passengers into space. Brad Pitt's bought a ticket. So have Justin Bieber and Ashton Kutcher. Branson's dreams for Virgin *Intergalactic*, for building a Virgin hotel on the moon . . .

Closing credits. Branson, dressed up as an air-hostess, for charity. Branson, arm around the shoulder of Nelson Mandela. Of the Dalai Lama. Of Bono himself. Branson, pledging all the profits of the Virgin Group for carbon capture research. Branson, with his grandchildren, on his private island . . .

★

Buzz-groups, Mr Pound circulating. Which is to say, Mr Pound's *enormous domed forehead*, circulating. Which is to say, Mr Pound's *enormous domed forehead*, bearing down on you.

Mr Pound's head, like a planet. His enormous forehead, like the fucking Serengeti. What thoughts are being thought behind that forehead? Business-studies thoughts. Which is to say, business-business-business thoughts. Which is to say death-of-the-soul thoughts . . .

Mr Pound's a man without inspiration. He's a man to suck all the breath out of a room. A man to suck all the life out of you. Mr Pound's bulldozing from buzz-group to buzz-group, as we discuss our business ideas.

Ideas of our buzz-group: founding a suicide clinic, an English rival to the Swiss clinics. And the Dutch ones. *Gravitas*, we could call it. We'd administer the blow ourselves. And we could sell bespoke suicide kits, via the net. Do-it-yourself suicide kits . . . it's genius. We could offer a find-your-suicide-partner service. DeathPals-dot-com. *Exiting life together.* Fucking A . . .

Mr Pound, *looming. Mr Pound,* addressing us: What do you want to do, when you leave school?

We know what to say.

Business studies, sir, Paula says. (Fine Art at Manchester.)

Business studies, specialising in marketing, sir, Art says. (Still waiting to apply, depending on what happens.)

Business studies, specialising in public relations, sir, Merv says. (Maths at Durham.)

Business studies, specialising in business studies, sir, I say. (Creative Writing at Warwick.)

Mr Pound, nodding his enormous forehead. And you? he asks Nietzsche.

I want to study philosophy, Nietzsche says, holding Mr Pound's gaze.

And what would you like to do with philosophy? Mr Pound asks.

I'd like to *think*, Nietzsche says.

Think about what? Mr Pound asks.

About everything, Nietzsche says.

And who do you suppose will pay you to think? Mr Pound says.

I don't care about getting paid, Nietzsche says.

Well, I don't think there are many jobs for philosophers . . . , Mr Pound says.

Maybe he could do *business studies with philosophy*, sir, Paula says brightly. That would help, wouldn't it? Can you do that, sir? That way he'd have the business *and* the philosophy, if you see what I mean.

Art's house.

Jesus, your house is entirely surrounded, Paula says.

It is. New-build houses in front of Art's house, where there used to be fields, and on either side of Art's house. Raw, new houses, staring out from across the road. New, young houses with imbecile faces. New houses, in tiny plots of mowed grass, with no sense of where they are. With no awareness of themselves. And larger houses, executive-size, as for mini-landed gentry, for mini-dukes and mini-duchesses, squeezed into tiny fenced-off patches of lawn. Executive houses, in winding closes, looking past each other, pretending not to see each other, pretending that they're not crammed in cheek-by-jowl . . .

Art's is the last old house on the road. It's the last of the '60s houses, built for '60s dreamers, set right back from the road. Art's house, the last of its kind, with its dark wood cladding, with its holly-bush hedge, with its Scots pines. Art's house, with its name on a dark board, barely visible now: *Mirkwood*. It was probably built for some Tolkien-loving '60s bohos. Free-and-easy types. Free-loving types. Setting up home in what used to be the woods.

We imagine them, the countryside dreamers. Before the suburbs came. Before the houses were sold off and the plots cleared. Before the demolition and the carve-ups and the new delta-fan estates. We imagine them: dreamers, idealists, full of hopes that the world would improve, that things would get better. Hobbity types. Sylvan types. Dance-around-the-maypole types. Looking to *get away from it all* . . .

★

Art, reading from his phone:

> *Over the last two weeks, how often have you been bothered by any of the following problems? Little interest or pleasure in doing things?* [Yes. Every day.] *Feeling down, depressed, or hopeless?* [God, yeah. That's my life, man.] *Trouble falling or*

staying asleep, or sleeping too much? [I want to sleep forever, man.] *Feeling tired or having little energy?*

You have *too much* energy, Art, Paula says. Your leg's always twitching.

Art, continuing his reading: *Feeling bad about yourself — feeling that you are a failure or have let yourself or your family down?*

I think your family have let you down, don't you? Paula says. Imagine leaving you behind here . . .

Only until I finish my exams, Art says.

You've been deserted, Paula says. You're an orphan, pretty much. You should be made a ward of court.

Art, reading a personal testimony:

> *I feel pain in my genitals (at times other than sexual intercourse). I hear sounds from nearby as if they were coming from far away. My body, or a part of it, feels numb. I cannot swallow (or can only swallow with great difficulty). I cannot speak (or only with great effort or I can only whisper).* [Fuck! People really suffer, don't they? This isn't making me feel any better.]

★

Art's bedroom. Band practice.

At our stations, amplifiers on. Paula on bass. Me on guitar.

Just improvise, man, Art says. Jam.

But improvise what? we wonder. Jam what? What are we supposed to do?

Why don't we just play covers, like everyone else? Merv asks.

We have to do something *new*, Art says. Something no one's done before.

Everything's been done, I say. It's all over.

Then we'll do music about it all being over, Art says. We'll play the end of things. We'll go *posthumous*. We'll make the music that comes after music. Fucking ghost music, man. Ashes music . . .

What does that sound like? Merv asks.

Like doom metal, Art says. Like stoner doom.

Will we have to set fire to a church? I ask. Will we have to murder each other?

That's *black* metal—Norwegian black metal, actually, Art says. It's a different thing. Doom is sludgy, man. It's torpid. You have to play fucking heavy. Volume and bass, man. Tube overdrive. The music's got to have, like, *physical mass*.

Paula, clicking on the distortion pedal, playing a simple metal riff, very slow. Me, following, also playing slow.

It's just a Sabbath rip-off, I say. It's just fucking *War Pigs* . . .

You can't escape Sabbath in doom metal, Art says. Sabbath are the fucking *university* in doom metal . . . Start again, you guys. And play it slower. It's got to fucking grind, man. It's got to fucking *crush*.

A power-chord, very slow. Another chord. Paula, following. Near stasis. Slow, very slow cycling. Waves of guitar and bass.

It's so *boring*, I say.

You have to play it until it gets interesting, Art says. Until it gets hypnotic . . . Trancelike . . . Until you can hear all the overtones and nuances.

We start again.

Waves of guitar and bass. The lowest, thickest sonorities.

Bass and guitars, grinding together. Crushing together. Intensity. It's a timbre-poem. A texture-poem. It's a wall of fog.

Merv's marimba, chiming softly. Merv's marimba gongs, slow, reverbed. Marimba gongs, like soft bells.

Immensity, floating. Withheld power, without meter. Catatonia. A slow cycling through tones.

The music, dispersing. The music, stopping. Silence, except for amplifier hum.

That was fucking *deep*, Art says. It sounded fucking *chthonic* . . . It's simple, right—that's how it should be. Beginner's mind. Forget development. Forget harmony. No fucking melodies. It's about *texture*, man.

What about vocals? I ask.

No vocals, Art says. Doom isn't about vocals. It's rhythmic, man. We've got to go back to the day the riff was invented . . . It's all about being in the riff. You're in the riff, and the riff's inhabiting you. It's like being on the verge of coming but never actually coming . . . It's fucking *Tantric* . . .

It's too rigid, Paula says. It's the same thing, over and over.

But that's the point, Art says. You're supposed to listen to the chords, the distortion. The fucking *power*. It's, like, ceaseless.

Maybe the riff's the problem, Paula says. It doesn't leave anything for the bass to *do*. It's just four-four shit.

Look, it's not about fancy time-signatures, Art says. It's about suspending time. Just—stopping the world. That's what we have to do as a band—don't you see?

Jesus, who put you in charge? Paula asks.

Yeah, Art, what is it that you contribute except for bossing everyone around? I say.

I see myself as a musical director, Art says.

Why have you never learnt to play a proper instrument? I ask.

I'm a producer, Art says. I play the laptop. I man the mixing board.

They're not instruments, I say.

Bands need conceptualists, man, Art says. Ideas-people. And someone has to watch over the whole thing. Stop you playing clichés.

I don't see what's wrong with trying to write *songs*, Merv says.

There are no songs in Tantric metal, Art says. Just the sound-stream.

Merv, lying back on the bed: The best music in the world was made by girl bands. The Ronettes. The Shangri-Las. It's all about yearning. Pristine innocence and purity and love. So uncynical. So *simple*.

But it's unreal, right? I say. I mean, we're not innocent. We're not simple. We're balls of snakes, man. We're heaps of diseases.

Maybe we've got to play *against* our cynicism, Paula says. Break through to something.

We should just play the truth, Art says.

The suburbs are the fucking truth, I say, looking out the window.

★

The woods. Merv, building a campfire by the lake. Thick smoke, curling up.

Where's there's smoke, there's fire, Merv says.

There's no fucking fire, Merv, Art says. Just smoke.

Questions for the fire: Who are we, really? Who really knows us—understands us? Is this life? Is this really it? Where's it all heading? Will it always be like this? Will we always feel these things? Will we ever understand ourselves? Will we ever learn the truth about ourselves? Will we ever discover what was *really wrong*?

Philosophy! We need philosophy! We need to become philosophers, like Nietzsche. Philosophers of the suburbs! Philosophers of Wokingham! Thames Valley philosophers! We need to question everything, everything. To let nothing rest. We need to roll away the stones—*our* stones! To be born again into our bodies!

But won't the suburbs defeat philosophy? Don't the suburbs mean the impossibility of philosophy? Won't the suburbs mean the destruction of all philosophical inquiry, including Nietzsche's? Won't we have to reconcile ourselves to suburban lives? To depression and suicide attempts in the suburbs?

Silence. Bats, flitting in the darkness.

I want to kill myself, I say.

That's just what they want you to do, Art says.

Who are *they* exactly? I ask.

The system, Art says. The whole fucking thing.

But no one's telling us what to do, I say.

That's the point, Art says. We do it anyway.

Do what? Merv asks.

Whatever it is they want, Art says. We've internalised it. We know our orders.

BAAAS-TAARDS!, Paula shouts. Then: Did they know I was going to do that?

They know everything, man, Art says.

SATURDAY

Text from Paula. *Nietzsche at Asda. Meet you there.*

Bikes out. Cycling.

And there he is: Nietzsche, working behind the deli counter. Nietzsche, in a hair net, taking orders from customers. Slicing meats. Cutting into wheels of brie. Scooping peanut satay and taramasalata into tubs.

How can this be? The best mind of our generation, scooping peanut satay and taramasalata into tubs? The *great philosopher of our time*, scooping peanut satay and taramasalata into tubs?

One of us should talk to him, we agree. Get him to come out with us tonight.

I don't dare, I say.

Not me, Merv says. He's so *serious*.

Well, *someone* has to do *something*, Paula says, striding over to the deli counter.

Paula, returning, looking pleased with herself. Fools!, she says. You're meeting him at The Phoenix at eleven.

General delight. Then general bemusement. What will the *great philosopher of our time* make of The Phoenix?

Art, Merv and I at The Ship, warming up for the night.

The Ship's seventeenth-century interior—handsome, certainly. The Ship's not some Reading drinking barn. It's not some Bracknell alcopop den. The Ship's an old coaching inn, almost entirely intact. It's got sepia photos of fishermen and boats, of some old port (not Wokingham. We're fifty miles inland!) Exposed beams, visible in the walls. Exposed beams, crossing the ceiling. An antique mirror over the fireplace. And the beer garden out back, where the long sloping roof of the inn comes nearly to the ground.

Mild suburbanites, all around. Mild suburbanites, mildly chattering—about what? Mild suburbanites, standing about, sipping their pints.

Young men in shirts, in jeans. Young women in jeans. Young suburbanites, enjoying a quiet drink. Young suburbanites at play—looking just like young suburbanites at work. Young suburbanites, mildly chatting, just as they mildly chat at work. Young suburbanites, smiling and nodding, just as they smile and nod at work.

And older suburban types, farther on in the life-cycle, out for a drink, mildly chattering. Older types, talking about house prices and mortgages. About TV boxsets. About promotions at work. About house prices again. About mortgages again. About boxsets again. Older types, affirming each other. Approving each other. Getting mildly drunk. Going a little red-cheeked . . .

Aren't these people *bored*? They *look* bored. Surely they're bored!

Surely they want something else! There's no fun here! No life! No one's having a laugh! What happened to merriment? To raucousness? Where are the binge drinkers you read so much about?

And then, in the dreary sea, an island of hope: Nicholas Nugent himself, with a gaggle of admirers.

Nicholas Nugent has really come out of himself, Art says.

He's hatched into a *beautiful gay butterfly*, I say.

What a dreary chrysalis Nicholas Nugent was!, we agree. What a *bore*! How silent! And to think, inside it all beat the heart of a *beautiful gay butterfly* . . .

There's hope for us all yet, Merv, Art says. Imagine it: you could hatch at any moment into a *beautiful gay butterfly* . . .

With a lispy, wispy voice, I say. Just like Nicholas Nugent. And a bashful look. Just like Nicholas Nugent. And delightful little effeminacies. Just like Nicholas Nugent.

And a Dolce and Gabbana phone!, Art says, peering over. Look! It actually says, *Dolce and Gabbana* when he opens it up!

And a flick of mascara—don't forget that, I say. And then: Why don't we have a flick of mascara? It looks fabulous.

Hope you're taking notes, Merv, Art say. You could be our Wokingham dandy. Our *Ship* dandy, surrounded by admirers. You could ornament the suburbs . . .

We wonder if Nicholas Nugent has any drugs. Maybe he has some popper—that's a gay drug, right? Nicholas Nugent should at least have some popper . . .

Art, leaning into the gaggle. Nicholas Nugent, shaking his pretty head. No popper.

Do you think it's possible to *popper yourself gay*? Art and I wonder. Is there a plane of gayness you could reach by popping? We imagine it: a great plateau of gayness, full of beautiful gay butterflies. A great plateau, as wide as the horizon, above all the dreariness of the sober world.

The pub fills. Nicholas Nugent fades from view. The great gay utopia fades from view. The great popper utopia fades from view.

★

The Phoenix.

Nietzsche, outside, in chinos and a rugby shirt. Off-duty Nietzsche. Casual Nietzsche.

Beers at the bar.

Art always used to masturbate before he went out, we tell Nietzsche. It was a sacred duty. A matter of self-control. But now, with his Tantric turn, anything could happen.

The truth is, Art's too high and mighty to snog anyone, I say. He's too disturbed by his lust.

Art wants to keep himself for his music, Merv says.

Whereas the rest of us just want to get off our faces, I say.

The empty dancefloor, all to ourselves. You can bust out your moves, we tell Nietzsche—there's plenty of room. Have you got any moves?

Nietzsche shakes his head.

You have to dance, we tell him. The Phoenix doesn't make sense unless you dance.

Nietzsche shakes his head again.

Well, you have to drink then, we tell him. Drink a lot, and then dance . . .

We start at opposite ends, mincing towards one another, diagonally across the floor, waggling our fingers. We meet in the middle, turn around, mince back, still waggling our fingers. Promenade one hundred and eighty degrees around the edge of the floor. Another diagonal. Then a dance-off in the centre. Hip-hop moves. Breakdancing. Chicago-style footwork. Then back again, mincing, to our corners . . .

We line up for our Riverdance routine, smiling and waving at Nietzsche. We show him a sample of our robotic dancing. Our macarena. We show him our Gangnam style . . .

Nietzsche, unsmiling.

The nightclub, filling up. Guys in shirts and trousers. Women in short skirts and vests and bikini tops, crowding onto the dance floor.

Bill Trim, watching from the balcony. We raise our bottles to him. Cheers, Bill Trim! Come join us, Bill Trim! But Bill's with Dingus, Fatberg and the others. It's a beast night out. How much would ol' Bill prefer to be down here with us?

Dispersal. I join Nietzsche at the railing, to cheer him up.

I point out Dingus, dripping with testosterone, slack-jawed, sluggish. I point out Vince—a would-be boy-slut. A *failed* boy-slut, for the moment. He won't get anywhere until the end of the night . . .

I point out Nipps, the arch-seducer, trying to communicate with girls through smiles and body language. Trying to get them to mirror his dance moves. Rubbing his nipples, in the hope that they will rub *their* nipples. Grabbing his crotch, in the hope that they'll grab *their* crotches. He's appealing to their mirror neurones . . .

I point out Fatberg, fresh from vomiting in the toilets. Fatberg, with a sick-streak up his arm. With a fluorescent condom hanging out of his shirt-pocket. Charmless! Disgusting!

I point out Sister-Fucker, burying his supposed troubles in drink. What troubles does he have? Drink.

Come boogie, I tell Nietzsche. Find a Wokingham beauty to dance with. Show her your moves. Impress her. Make her smile.

He shakes his head.

Provincial nightclub crescendo: *Ace of Spades*—metallers, playing air-guitar. *This Charming Man*—indie types, arms outstretched, wheeling. *Irish Rover*—folk dancing, crooked arm in crooked arm. *Achy Breaky Heart*—mock line-dancing.

Ballad time: *My Heart Must Go On*—mass snogging, sticky, shiny people, in close embrace. It's appalling! It's base! It's enough to put you off *all sexual behaviour* . . .

Squaddies from the garrison grouping round us, looking for trouble. Pushing and shoving. We escape to the smokers' yard, ears ringing.

What the fuck's Paula doing here, bumming ciggies in the smokers' yard?

Disastrous night in The Three Frogs, she says. Don't fucking ask. And then: I'm here in a solely *anthropological* capacity, you understand. I want to see how bad the hetty-betty world gets. I might do an art-piece on it, or something.

Oh just face it, Paula, you didn't want to be left out, Art says.

Anyway, here's *terrible*, I say. Look! What have we to do with these people!? We aren't even the same *species* as these people!

Discussion. Why do we bother to come out at all? What are we looking for? What do we think is out here? Why not just stay in forever? Why not just secede, sit life out, bury ourselves in our bedrooms? Because of *possibility*. Because of *what might happen*. Because tonight could be *the night when* . . . Because *it could all change when* . . .

A girl (In Merv's case, a boy)—some unknown girl (some unknown boy), someone we've never seen before. A foreign girl (a foreign boy), an exotic. Someone who comes from a different school. Who doesn't know who we are. Who takes us as she (he) finds us. Who chooses us—just us.

Tonight could be the night. Tonight, it could all begin. Tonight we could become witty. Say a stream of clever things. Show off. Discover some new, fabulous eloquence. Some capacity to dazzle, to make-smile. Some unknown faculty of making-a-girl-laugh (making-a-boy-laugh). Some unguessed-at charm. Tonight, we could access some new fluency, some wit. Tonight, we could be all lightness and sparkle and fizz.

Possibility. Potentiality. We do not know yet what we are. We do not know what could take flight within us. We've yet to spread our new wings. We've yet to shed our old skin, yet to step forward, gleaming; yet to take to our particular skies . . .

You see it on the nature programmes. The desire to fuck. The desire to find a mate. The desire to reproduce. The desire for offspring. But it doesn't feel natural. It feels the opposite of natural.

How will we know what to do, when the time comes? Will it be obvious to us? Will our bodies know? Will some kind of *instinct* kick in? Will it all seem inevitable? *Necessary*? The fruit of billions of years of evolution?

Will we discover that we're normal, after all? That we're just like anyone else, after all? That romance is as easy as breathing, as easy as lying down to sleep?

It's bound to go wrong for us. We're bound to discover that we're weird fetishists of some kind. Weird zoophiles. We're bound to turn out perverts of some kind, chased by lynch mobs. We're bound to be led into court, covering our heads with coats.

But here we are, all the same. Swarming at The Phoenix with all the rest. Like ants that fly up to mate once a year. We're not exempt. We're no different from anyone else.

Do we really want to catch the eye of some suburban babe (some suburban beefcake)? Do we really think we'll muster up some chat-up line? Do we really think it's possible for us—a suburban romance? A suburban *courtship*? Do we really want to set up home in a suburban housing estate? Do we really want to send our children to suburban schools, and start the whole cycle again?

No to courtship! No to settling down! No to breeding! No to everything!

★

Bill Trim, sweaty, slumping at the table.

What are your views on love, Bill? Paula asks. Are you capable of love, do you think? Would you describe yourself as a romantic man, Bill, or is it all just sexual with you? Is there a side to you we haven't seen, Bill? A *lyrical* side? Would you call yourself a *man of courtship*, Bill? Are you a man for the *romantic chase*? You should go and find Merv, Bill. You should bring him out of himself . . . Turn him into a beautiful gay butterfly . . .

Bill Trim, disappearing.

You look full of nightclub nihilism, Paula says to Nietzsche.

Nietzsche: I feel nauseated.

You mean you're going to be sick? Paula asks.

Nietzsche: I hate these people.

Oh—*metaphorical* nausea, Art says. That's a relief.

Nietzsche, sipping his vodka. Nietzsche, scowling, as we've never seen him scowl.

Nietzsche: They disgust me.

Sure—they're all wankers, I say.

We hate them, too, Paula says.

You don't need to tell us about disgust, Art says. We've lived with it longer than you.

Nietzsche: You *like* disgust. You're happy with disgust. You swim in disgust, like rats in a sewer. You're not disgusted by your disgust. You don't *hate your hatred*. You don't want anything else.

Trust me, we'd rather be anywhere else than here, Paula says.

Nietzsche: But you're here. We're here.

We'd like all this to be destroyed, I say. We'd like the world to end.

Death to us, that we may be born from death anew, Art quotes. *War to us, that we may be reborn in peace. Evil to us, that we may be reborn in goodness . . .*

| 42 |

Nietzsche: It's so easy for you to talk. You're fluent in despair. But despair isn't fluent. Despair claws at the air. Despair *cries out*.

More vodka.

Nietzsche: Your hatred is *dull*. Your disgust is *resignation*. The flames don't lick inside you. They don't *leap*, your flames. They don't *burn* . . .

That's not true! We hate it here!, Paula says. We hate ourselves for coming here!

Death to the world!, Art says. Death to the suburban world! Death to everything! Death to every*one!* Including ourselves!

Nietzsche: You don't hate it enough. You have to *earn* your disgust. You have to *deserve* it. You haven't reached the end. You're not close to the end . . . Which means you're not close to rebirth, either . . .

So what should we do? Art asks. What should we want?

Nietzsche: Transfiguration. Dionysus.

Blank stares.

Nietzsche: Dying to all this and being reborn.

What—like Jesus? Art asks. Like the resurrection?

Nietzsche: Overcoming ourselves. Refusing what the world makes us. *Creating* ourselves. Being reborn again and again.

We're not living the lives we're meant to live, then? Art asks. That's a consolation, at least.

Nietzsche: We must be *free spirits*. We must become what we are.

Like accepting we're gay, or something? Paula asks.

Nietzsche: *To become what one is one must not have the faintest notion what one is.* What we are . . . He laughs. Overcoming what we are, in the name of what we are . . . These words aren't right. Words are a malady. Words are sick.

Let's just be silent, then, Art says. Let's just *sit*.

Let's just *drink*, I say.

More vodka.

A toast to rebirth! A toast to life! A toast to innocence! A toast to the unmediated ones! A toast to the speakers of truth!

Two AM. Merv appears with Bill. Merv, holding his eye. Merv was elbowed in the eye. A squaddie elbowed him in the fucking eye.

It's because you confused him, Merv, Paula says. He didn't know whether to kill you or fuck you.

Well, Bill head-butted him, Merv says.

Paula rolls her eyes. Trouble, always trouble. Come on, let's get out of here.

★

Walking home. The public footpath.

Dingus, Nipps and Vince bellowing, *FAGGOTS!*, from their taxi window. *FUCKING QUEERS!*

That was meant for *you*, Bill, Paula says. But you and Merv will make a *lovely* couple . . .

The railway crossing.

Caution, reads the sign. *Look both ways*. Of course we'll look both ways! Every few years someone's struck down by a train . . .

But isn't it a glorious night to die? Let a train bowl round and take us all! Let it crash and scatter us like skittles! Let it come and slice us through! Let it come, a blast of air, a scream on rails, and slice us through! We imagine it: blood on the tracks. Blood in the bushes. Blood on the stones between the sleepers.

The rails, running both ways into the darkness. The rails, running to Reading, running to London . . .

Nietzsche, vomiting into the undergrowth.

Bill Trim, leaning down and picking him up. Nietzsche, in the arms of Bill Trim.

★

Walking home. Wide roads. '60s suburbs.

There's still space here. You can still breathe here. And there are trees. Trees in the long gardens of the houses. Trees, breathing out. Trees, exhaling air. The air's moist. The air's fresh. The houses are set back from the road. A long way back.

Freedom. Coolness. Night air on our faces. A night breeze on our faces.

We sing out in our joy. The songs we sang at school as children. *Lily the Pink*. What joy! *The Ink is Black, the Page is White* [for my benefit]. Made-up songs: *Fly Lesbian Seagull* [for Paula]. *Life for the Sexually Afraid* [for Art]. *Supertwink* [for Merv].

The last farmyard, with its pond. Imagine it!—there's still a farm here. The last field, with its vista. The last spinney, on the last hill.

Evedons Lane. Once a country lane, through the middle of nowhere. Once bordered by farmland, right out in the country . . .

And now? New estates. New housing estates, behind a screen of trees. Estate on estate, just beyond. And the golf course. The new golf course . . .

Idea: let's desecrate the golf course! Like in *Melancholia!* Is the world going to end—tonight? Will a new planet appear in the sky— tonight? Will a rogue planet bowl towards us tonight? Will we feel light-headed as it sucks oxygen from our atmosphere? Will we strug-gle to breathe as Melancholia comes closer? Will we strip off and bathe in its weird blue light?

The golf course, so smooth, so immaculate. The grass, so moist. This used to be sand and fields, we tell Nietzsche. This used to be called the *sand dunes* (no actual dunes, just sandy soil and tough grass). We used to play in the sand and fields . . . They were going to build a school here, but they couldn't get planning. Some legal problem. Some problem with the soil.

Imagine it! The *sand dunes*. For dog walkers and truant kids. Space, just space, with excavations here and there in the thick grass. Imagine it! All that space, left alone . . . Left fallow . . . Out of use . . .

And they turned it into a golf course—a fucking *golf course!* With its fake landscape. With its fake hills, like the drumlins and eskers we learned about in geography. With its fake depressions, its *bunkers*. With its fake winding river. With its *members only*.

Discussion. Was there a river here before? Perhaps there was a river, but it didn't wind quite so much. Not quite so picturesquely. We can't tell if the river's real or not. That's how much the golf course fucks with your head. You shouldn't be allowed to invent riv-ers. Or topography. Those desecrators . . .

DESECRATORS!, Paula shouts.

A light in the clubhouse. *THIS IS PRIVATE PROPERTY!*, a voice shouts.

Security guards!, Art says. The golfers are defending their turf. The golfers are aggressive. They're vicious.

BASTARDS!, Paula shouts.

I'LL CALL THE POLICE IF YOU DON'T LEAVE IMMEDIATELY!, the voice shouts.

FUCK YOU!, Art shouts. *IT'S PUBLIC PROPERTY! IT'S PART OF THE COMMONS!*

YOU FUCKED WITH THE RIVER!, Paula shouts. *YOU'RE . . . RIVER-FUCKERS!*

Laughter. What the fuck is a river-fucker?

YOU FUCKED WITH THE TOPOGRAPHY!, Paula shouts.

TOPOGRAPHY-FUCKERS!, Art shouts.

Sound of a door opening. Footsteps on gravel.

Do you think they have dogs? I ask. Will they unleash the hounds?

Bill, defend us! . . . , Paula says.

But Bill and Merv have disappeared.

Hiding behind a fake esker at the edge of the course.

There used to be a view here, I tell Nietzsche. You used to be able to see things.

VISTA-FUCKERS!, Paula shouts.

We climb the fence into the playing field.

Open grass. Night. It's warm. The full moon. Where's Melancholia when you need it? Why isn't Melancholia filling our sky?

I think we should take off all our clothes, Art says. I think we should moon-bathe.

You start, Paula says.

Art, unzipping his trousers.

I didn't fucking mean it, Paula says. Keep your fucking clothes *on*, dillweed.

Nietzsche, lying down on the grass. Staring upward. Paula, sitting down beside him.

Why is everyone so fucking base? Paula asks.

Shuffling behind a nearby drumlin. Merv, sitting up. Bill Trim, sitting up, shirt off.

It's a glorious night to die. But we're not going to die. The apocalypse isn't coming. Not yet.

SUNDAY

Hair of the dog, on Art's broken patio. A selection of his dad's miniatures.

Merv, looking dreamy. It's good to see you so content, Merv, Paula says. So you tamed the beast, eh?

Houses, on either side of Art's garden. Houses, looking directly into Art's garden.

I think we *broke* Nietzsche, Art says.

Nietzsche was *fine*, Paula says. We saw him home, didn't we?

No one should have to see The Phoenix on a Saturday night, I say. *We* shouldn't have to see The Phoenix on a Saturday night.

At least you *got it on*, Mervy-boy, Paula says. Oooh . . . Mr Lover-Lover . . .

And school tomorrow!, Art says.

Jesus—more school. And then revision break. And then exams, and then . . .

Then oblivion, Paula says.

Then, America, Art says. Then, Boston.

Silence.

I'm not going to go, Art says. I'm going to disappear into the woods. I'm going to become a suburban Crusoe. There are people who survive at that for decades. They break into fridge-freezers in garages for supplies. I'll use my survival skills.

What survival skills? I ask.

I'll become an urban legend, like Bigfoot or something, Art says.

Like Smallcock, I say. Like Badbreath.

I'll go freegan, Art says. Live on what everyone throws away.

You have to watch it, I say. They spray all the food with mouse poison.

I'll just poke round the market at closing time, Art says. I'll be a kind of tramp—a really classy tramp. A *gentleman of the road*, known for my folk wisdom. Or maybe I'll devote myself full-time to music.

You can't actually play anything, Art, I say.

I can make sounds, Art says. I can manipulate them.

You've got to learn how to *write songs*, Merv says. That's how they all began, all the greats: writing songs. Music's a craft.

You can study pop music at university now, I say. Bombproof's brother's doing music performance. You learn about the music business. You get all these celebrity lecturers. Sean Ryder's an honorary professor of postpunk at Salford. Wigfield's a visiting lecturer in pop at Liverpool. And Professor Griff has become a real Professor. It's fucking amazing.

Fuck uni learning, Art says. Fuck all that music-school stuff.

What should we do then? I ask.

We have to do what only we can do, Art says. We have to overcome ourselves. We have to become what we are.

But what if we're just really, really shit? Paula asks.

*

Band practice, in Art's bedroom.

Leaning back on the scatter cushions, smoking.

Art, turning the amplifiers up. Listen, man, just listen, he says.

A kind of buzzing. A hum, almost subliminal. Hissing and crackling. Popping. The feeling of forces gathering. Of something about to begin . . .

Doesn't it sound cool? Art asks. Have you ever heard anything more exciting?

We're only going to ruin it by actually playing something, I say.

We should play this, Art says, pressing his ear to the speaker cone. Play all this *potential* . . . Like, what we *could* play, rather than anything we actually play. What we *could* do, but never do . . .

So what shitty music genre are we going to try today? Paula says.

Tantric metal, man, Art says. That's our sound.

That's not *my* sound, Paula says. Anyway, it's my turn today—I want to decide what we're doing.

Merv (taking a drag): It has to be something we can smoke to.

If that's what you want, we should play dub, Paula says. That's the original head music.

We can't just *play dub*, Merv says. We're too white.

Chandra's not white, Paula says.

Indian types don't play reggae, Merv says.

The Slits were white, and they played dub, Paula says.

So what *are* we going to play? I ask.

Something built around the bass, Art says. That's the divine instrument, man. It's the fucking *earth*. It's what things are.

Paula, playing reggae-style, slow and heavy. Paula, playing on the offbeat.

This is righteous, Art says, bobbing his head. I'll bet you can hear it right through the suburbs.

It's *Exodus*, man!, I say. Paula's playing Bob Marley!

Fuck! No cover versions, Art says.

Okay, Paula says, Okay.

Another bass line. There's a groove again. There's a pull again. A *feel* . . .

It's the fucking Heptones, I say. *Street of Gold* . . .

I can't help it, Paula says.

Fuck!, I say. What are we going to do?

We have to play our own music, Merv says.

We haven't got our own music, I say.

We can play anything we like, Art says. No one has their own music anymore.

That's our problem, Paula says. We can play anything we like. All this freedom, and we don't know what to do with it.

We've got to do something real, Art says. Something *serious*. These are serious times, man. Doom metal's serious. Tantric metal's serious.

Tantric metal's *boring*, Paula says. And it's got no *groove*.

We need to be part of something, I say. Like, a scene.

There are no fucking scenes in the Thames Valley, Paula says.

There was shoegaze, Merv says.

That was, like, thirty years ago, Art says.

Well, there used to be other bands around, at least, I say. Didn't Bill Trim have a band?

The Trimtones, Art says. They did classic rock covers. Old stuff. It was ancestor-worship, man. Tribute-band bullshit—fuck that.

And the trendies had a synth band, I say. A synth covers band: Gentle Whispers. They played in assembly, with Nicholas Nugent on lead vocals.

Fuck them, too, Art says. More fucking retromania.

Maybe a scene will grow up around us, I say.

No one knows we exist, Merv says.

Yeah, well, they will, I say. We can play a gig in Reading—one of those local-band nights.

But what are we going to do? Paula asks.

We have to *not play*, man, Art says.

How the fuck do we *not play*? Paula asks.

We play without a goal, Art says. Without trying to resolve anything. You have to let yourself drift . . . think songscapes.

More fucking tantric metal!, Paula says.

No way—dub's about soundscapes, too, Art says. I mean, it's about breaking down song structures, right? It's about fucking with songs—stripping them back to the rhythm . . .

Paula, playing a four-bar bass riff, over and over again. A circular groove. An offbeat groove.

Following Paula on the offbeat. Guitar chops, like percussion. Merv, doubling my guitar skank, plink-plonking on his marimba.

Art, sliding down a fader. The bass, dropping out. Art, sliding up the reverb. Marimba, gonging to infinity. Guitar chops, reverberating . . .

We look at each other. This is okay. This is interesting.

The *space* in the music. The openness of the music. The sense of time, too. Of non-pulsed time. Of time as expanse, time as freedom.

It's all heat-haze. All humidity.

It sounds tropical. It sounds *magical.*

The bass, coming back in. The four-bar pattern, thick and heavy.

I know that bassline—it's Ken Boothe, I say. It's fucking *Freedom Day.*

Fuck, so it is, Paula says, stopping playing.

No fucking covers!, Art says.

It's not a cover, Paula says. It's a *version.* You're allowed to do that in dub.

Paula, starting to play the same bassline.

No *versions,* either, Art says.

It's no good, I say. Everything's been done.

Can't we play something with more development? Merv says. More structure?

We should forget structure, Art says. We should let go of structure. Look, sometimes you have to abandon the will. That's what *not* playing means.

I lay my guitar on my lap. Tap its bridge. Its body. A low hum. A buzz.

See, *that's* good, Art says. Just keep doing that.

I'm not doing anything, I say.

That's the point, Art says. We have to just let things happen—or not happen. We shouldn't *try* to do anything.

Nothing's happening, Art, Merv says.

That's okay, Art says. Just tap your guitar, Chandra. Lay down a bass line, Paula.

Paula, beginning again. Strumming again. Guitar taps, on infinite reverb. Merv, gonging . . . Oh yes . . . This is a groove . . .

I hate to say it, guys—it's *Chase the Devil*, I say. Max Romeo.

FUCK!, Art shouts.

SECOND WEEK

MONDAY

Economics.

The Old Mole, in apocalyptic mode. The Old Mole, on *total financialisation*. On the creation of money without collateral. On overleveraging and the reselling of debt.

We're at the end of a business cycle, but the central banks won't let it end, the Old Mole tells us. The banks are insolvent—but governments won't let them crash.

Businesses are getting larger, the Old Mole tells us. Mergers and acquisitions are booming. But no one's *making* anything. There's nothing to invest in. There are no new start-ups. *Predatory monopolies* grow larger and larger. There's only asset-price inflation, as the rich bank their wealth in art and property.

The housing bubble's growing, the Old Mole tells us. Wealth is trickling up to rentiers. It's rule by the plutocrats and the oligarchs. The means of production are no longer land and labour, but financial capital and speculative trading.

No one needs to *make anything* anymore, the Old Mole tells us. No one needs *workers* anymore. They don't even need *consumers*.

It's rule by central banks, the Old Mole tells us. It's rule by politburo. The elites are borrowing all the money they need at zero per cent interest. They're setting up parallel business and justice systems. It's rule by financial despots. The system's rigged. The roulette wheels are fixed. The house wins every time . . .

The Old Mole, with questions for the class: When will the charade end? When will they stop passing the parcel? When will it cease, their game of musical chairs? When will the day of reckoning come, if ever? Anyone?

Discussion. Italy will collapse this summer. Bank runs . . . Debt crises . . . Vulture capitalists swooping in . . . It'll be like Greece, but ten times worse. The crisis will spread to all the other European economies. It will bring them down, too. Europe will go belly-up.

Agreement: It's going to be *much* bigger this time. Last time, the banks failed, and were bailed out by the central banks. Next time, the central banks will fail, and will have to be bailed out in turn, and we'll all become debt-slaves of the IMF. Unless the IMF fails, too . . .

Things look bad. But they always look bad in the Old Mole's class. What does Nietzsche think? How can he help?

Nietzsche, silent. Looking out of the window.

Smoking patrol.

Walking over the bridge.

Reminiscence, of when Dingus and the other beasts were going to throw that *special-needs boy* into the river . . .

It was winter—the depths of winter. It was winter, and the river was frozen, and the rushes were frozen and the trees were frozen. And Dingus and the others were going to use the *special-needs boy* to break the ice. They hauled him to the edge of the river, the *special-needs boy*. Then they swung him out over the river, one beast holding him by the ankles, another by the wrists, the *special-needs boy*. They swung him up and out, as though they were going to let him fly into the icy water, but then they swung him back again, the *special-needs boy*. And then they swung him out over the water again, and again and again, the *special-needs boy*.

And all the kids pressed up, watching. All the kids, watching, doing nothing, just watching, and we among them, saying nothing, doing nothing, watching the *special-needs boy* being swung by the wrists and ankles, over the icy water. And there were no teachers to stop the swinging of the *special-needs boy* over the icy water. There were no lunchtime monitors to stop the *special-needs boy* being swung, screaming, over the icy water. And all of us kids, some laughing, some jeering. And the *special-needs boy* being swung, and none of us doing anything.

Were they going to let him drown in the river, under the ice? Were they going to let his body be swept down the river, under the ice? Would the body of the *special-needs boy* be found far downstream, trapped in the sluices, wedged in the weir, water-bloated, blank-eyed, under the ice? Some of us saw it in our minds' eyes, the *special-needs boy*'s body, swept along in the river. Some of us saw him, dead in the green depths, the *special-needs boy*. Dead beneath the ice. Dead to cruelty, the *special-needs boy*. Dead to the horror of the world. Dead to the world in which he didn't stand a chance. Infinitely dead and safe in death, the *special-needs boy*.

Which made you want to join him there in death, the *special-needs boy*. Which made you want to die with him, the *special-needs boy*. Which made you want to die for him, the *special-needs boy*. Which made you want to martyr yourself for him, to martyr yourself for all cruelty. Which made you long for the destruction of the whole human world, because of the plight of the *special-needs boy*. Which made you long for the destruction of the possibility of evil, all evil, which humans bring to the world. For the complete annihilation of our species, with all its evil and all its corruption . . .

Anyway, the beasts didn't throw him in in the end, the *special-needs boy*. The beasts let the *special-needs boy* drop into the mud of the riverbank. They stood back and watched him clamber up as best he could. Then Dingus pushed him back down into the frozen rushes and mud. And then the lesson bell rang, and the beasts' audience dispersed and everyone lost interest, as the *special-needs boy* crawled back up the bank to the corrupt and evil world.

The world is hateful, I say. It's full of hateful people.

What about us? We saw what was happening, Paula says. We just stood by.

What could we do? Art says. How could we help anyone?

But there were so many of us, and so few of them, Paula says. We could have resisted. We could have done *something*. We never do fucking anything for fucking anyone.

Why don't you volunteer for Oxfam? I ask.

Why don't *you*? Paula asks.

You think you feel compassion, Nietzsche says. But you don't. It's just condescension. Suffering is a spur—your *special-needs boy* was being spurred.

Everyone suffers, Art says. The *special-needs boy*, Merv in PE, the refugees from Syria. Everyone, man. And every*thing*—I mean, they're probably filling the river with sewage, or something . . .

But we mustn't suffer with the sufferer, Nietzsche says. We need to preserve our strength.

I don't want to be strong if it means not giving a fuck about anyone else, Paula says.

Compassion makes us ashamed of our strength, Nietzsche says. It makes us despair of life.

We *should* despair of life when there's so much pain!, Paula says. The weak suffer, right? The wicked prosper. And it's our fault. We're wretches! We're pitiable! We're corrupt! We're *filth*! We don't deserve to live another day. We're compromised—utterly compromised. We should be destroyed. Just put out of our misery.

The river's not deep enough to drown in, I say. Not in summer, anyway.

We could weigh ourselves down, Merv says. Put rocks in our pockets.

There are no rocks, Paula says. Who sees any rocks?

Maybe we should hang ourselves from the tree instead, Art says.

We're so pitiful, Paula says.

We feel pitiful because we pity, Nietzsche says. Pity diminishes us. *Nothing is worth anything*, we bleat. *Life isn't worth anything. Life lacks meaning. Life is suffering and suffering means nothing.* We come to resent life. We become pessimists, rubbing ourselves raw against the bars of our cage . . .

Pity is always self-pity, Nietzsche says. Self-contempt. We want to pity ourselves. We want to cradle ourselves in our own arms. To stroke our own hair. To whisper comforting things in our own ears.

Suffering and hardship are no cause for pity, Nietzsche says. They are the soil out of which greatness grows. We can use our suffering to create meaning, to create ourselves.

You sound like some self-help guru, Paula says. What doesn't kill me makes me stronger, and all that . . .

And you can't just decide to create meaning, I say. It's either there or it isn't.

Meaning is ours to create, if we're strong enough, Nietzsche says.

But who *is* strong enough? Paula asks.

The one who is unashamed of strength, Nietzsche says. Who accepts the world as it is.

I'd have thought the strong would want to *change* the world, Paula says.

First of all we have to face it, Nietzsche says. To accept what's happened. Stop trying to wish it otherwise . . .

So we should just *accept* that that boy was almost thrown in the river? Paula says. And all the wars and the famines and the drowning refugees?

You can't change the past, Nietzsche says.

But you can hate what happened, Paula says. You can hate all the awful things that have happened.

Maybe there's a way of redeeming the past, Art says. I mean, if it wasn't for the 'burbs, we'd have no band. And if it wasn't for . . . everything that's happened . . . the brutality and all that . . . we wouldn't be sitting round now, talking . . .

What fucking band? Paula says. The band is shit, Art. Our lives are shit . . . And us sitting round talking crap is supposed to redeem everything? Fuck that! Look—stuff just happens—one thing, and then another. Stuff piles up.

Anyone for chips? Merv asks.

No chips, Paula says. I don't want to eat.

*

The arcade, with our chips.

Art's obsessive paedophile theories. They live in those flats overlooking the school, he says. It's paedophile row. They're probably watching us through binoculars, behind the net curtains.

And half the teachers are paedophiles, Art says. You'd have to be a paedophile to want to go into teaching. You'd have to want to fuck half the kids.

I think Art is telling us something, Paula says. It's a cry for help. Who's grooming you over the internet, Art? Who wants to touch you in your special places? Who's offering to show you their puppies?

We should act on Art's behalf. Tell a teacher. Tell the police. Call Childline. Is Art too old for Childline? Is he a child anymore? Someone who wants to fuck Art probably isn't even a paedophile anymore.

Young smokers, eyeing us threateningly.

Art, approaching them for a light. Don't worry, he says. What happens at the arcade stays at the arcade.

Fuck off, cop!, the first kid says.

Paedo!, the second kid says.

Leave us alone, you fucking pervert!, the third kid says.

Stop trying to touch us, you dirty bastard!, the fourth kid says.

Surrounded by menacing lower-school boys. We try to act cool. An escape route: the Head Boy and Tasker in the near distance, albeit wasted. The lower-school kids, scattering.

The Head Boy and Tasker, pupils dilated. I've heard you can get hold of . . . you know . . . *stuff*, Tasker says to Merv.

What do you want? Merv asks, keeping his cool.

Something heavy, the Head Boy says.

Something *very fucking heavy*, Tasker says.

I can get whatever you want, Merv says.

Alright, Tasker says. Bring it in. If it's decent, you'll be in our good books. You want to get into our good books, don't you?

Laughter as we walk back to school.

Jesus, you're cool, Merv, Paula says. *I can get you whatever you want.* Are you going to take over from your brother? Work your way up? It's a career, at least. Better than a mountain of student debt. Imagine, Merv—you could be a Wokingham kingpin. Bill Trim could be your muscle . . .

Well-being class.

Mr Merriweather, teen-whisperer, beaming at us all.

Bean bags. Working in groups on our happiness worksheet.

Class discussion. What is happiness? How can we increase it? Is the capacity for happiness simply a *trait*, or can it be *developed*?

Mr Merriweather, asking each group for its thoughts . Mr Merriweather, summarising our thoughts on the board: *Happiness—path or goal? The cultivation of happiness—is it possible?*

Mr Merriweather, extemporising on happiness-inducing habits. On *joy-enhancement* and *mood-induction* techniques. On *working on yourself.* On *governing the soul.*

Mr Merriweather, speaking of the cultivation of good habits. Of altruistic habits. Of *civilizing the affects.*

More group discussion. Are unhappy people neurotics? Should we become happier for the sake of others, and not just ourselves?

Mr Merriweather, summarising thoughts once more: *The optimism of the happy? The selflessness of the happy?*

Mr Merriweather, posing a question: What is optimism?

Inanity, Paula says.

Insanity, Art says.

Stupidity, I say.

Blindness to the facts, Merv says.

Mr Merriweather, mouthing *no*. Anyone else?

Silence.

Mr Merriweather, assisted by his PowerPoint display: The optimist understands troubles as *transient, controllable* and *specific to situations.*

Mr Merriweather, on the *virtuous circle* of optimism. On happiness leading to more optimism, leading to more happiness. Mr Merriweather, on the *promise* of happiness. On making the future a promise. Another virtuous circle! Mr Merriweather, quite the philosopher!

Are *you* happy, sir? Paula asks.

I'm very happy, Mr Merriweather says.

How about Mrs Merriweather—is *she* happy? Art asks.

I hope Mrs Merriweather is *very* happy, Mr Merriweather says.

Are *animals* happy, Mr Merriweather? Merv asks.

In the case of higher-order animals, probably yes, most of the time, Mr Merriweather says.

Which is happier do you think, sir, a koala bear or a gorilla? I ask.

Happiness varies enormously from case to case, Mr Merriweather says.

When were you happiest, sir? Art asks.

I've never been happier, Mr Merriweather says.

What's so great about being happy, sir? Paula asks. I mean—why is it so important to be happy?

Don't you think there are more worthwhile things to worry about, sir? Art asks.

Why should we be happy sir, when so many people are miserable? Paula asks.

These are good questions!, Mr Merriweather says. But we can't make ourselves miserable just because there's suffering in the world.

Happy people are oblivious, sir, Paula says. Happy people don't *think*.

They want to keep us happy so we don't think, Art says.

Who—who wants to keep us happy? Mr Merriweather asks.

The system, sir, Art says.

What system? There is no system, Mr Merriweather says.

What about the central-banks-and-corporate-friends system, sir? Art asks.

And the beltway-media-and-financial-services system, Paula says.

The school-university-business system, sir: What about that? I ask.

And there's the prison-industrial system, sir, Art says.

And the military-security complex, sir, Paula says.

And don't forget the Westminster-broadcasting-big-accountancy-firm revolving door, sir, I say.

What about the *Babylon system*, sir? Art asks.

What about *nihilism*, sir? Paula asks.

Mr Merriweather, shaking his head.

Lunch.

Pondering our romantic lives. Our *lack* of romance (except Merv).

I'd go out with anyone right now, Paula says. Which is why I really shouldn't take tea with Miss 'Call me Shirley' Vickers.

Love is just some animal thing, Art says. It's all about reproduction. Have you ever seen snails fucking? You can't prise them apart. Not even when you smash up their shells. It's disgusting. That's what we're like. We're just insects who want to fuck and call it love.

Snails aren't insects, Merv says. They're molluscs.

Dingus is a mollusc, Art says. Look at him . . .

Dingus, with Calypso on his lap. Dingus, kissing Calypso's ear.

What about Calypso, Art? Paula asks. Any progress?

Art, shaking his head.

Why do you always go for these *distant* girls? Paula asks. Why do you always want to watch from afar? Are you scared of *real* love?

Oh, that's deep, Art says.

Seriously, Art—I think you're scared of romance, Paula says.

You're scared of women. You don't want to be engulfed. Maybe it's a mother thing. Do you think it's a mother thing?

I want to be engulfed by music, man, Art says.

That's because music's *safe*, Paula says.

Look at all the musicians who went mad!, Art says.

They would have gone mad anyway, Paula says.

Music's touched with chaos, Art says.

Safe chaos, Paula says. Basically, you're frightened of anything you can't shape. Anything you can't *create*. You want to play with all these forces, Art. But when they want to play with *you* . . .

Art, picking at his chips.

Of course, you're the real ladies' man round here, Chandra, Paula says. Especially now racism is out of fashion. What's your secret?

Do you remember how the beasts used to make you cower, Chandra? Art asks. Do you remember how you shat yourself in PE?

Laughter.

Better that than have a stiffie in the shower, like Schlong Boy, Merv says.

Reminiscence. Schlong Boy's erection, as thick as a baby's arm! A narwhal's tusk! Rising like the Matterhorn in the shower! You couldn't stop it. Like it was *prehensile*, or something. Like it had its own brain. It was fucking magnificent. Like it was the next stage of evolution—of *cock* evolution. Like it was about to say something really profound. Like it was going to *philosophise*, or something.

★

Bill's bag, crashing onto the middle of the table.

So this is going to be a regular thing, is it, Bill? Paula says. Well, you'd better have something to contribute, that's all I say. Tell us about your philosophical beliefs, Bill—no, I'm *serious*. Give us your whole basic philosophy in a nutshell.

Bill Trim, clearing his throat. Bill Trim, looking perplexed.

Jesus, Bill, don't you have anything to say? Paula asks. How did you even get into the sixth form? Oh, I forgot—you're doing *business studies*. Well, this is a *philosophical* table, Bill. We're dedicated to *philosophical* issues.

Maybe it's time for another nihilism lesson, Bill, Paula says. Okay, so there's *passive* nihilism, which is where you just, like, sit around and do nothing—like everyone round here. Sure, you can dress it up as something positive. You can make it look *happy*. But really, passive nihilism is just resignation. It's just *falling asleep*. Passive nihilism, Bill, is basically the sixth-form common room.

And there's *active* nihilism, Bill, Paula says. That's when you destroy the old lies, and try to create something new. First, extinction. Self-obliteration. The destruction of everything aimless. Everything meaningless. And then—who knows? Active nihilism is *transitional*, Bill. And that's what we're into. And you can help us, Bill. You can destroy things for us. You can roar. Go on, look fierce, Bill. Make Bill grit his teeth, Merv. Say, *I'm an active nihilist*, Bill. Make Bill say, *I'm a kickass nihilist*, Merv . . .

You and Merv are very cute, by the way, Paula says. Positively *adorable*, in fact. And then: Wow, Merv, you're fucking the former captain of the football team. That makes you prom queen . . .

Afternoon discussion.

The deterioration of the Head Boy. He was asleep in English again, we note. Was he drunk? Drugged? The Head Boy is in a bad way.

Is it true the Head Boy was in love with Tasker's sister? Has the Head Boy been deranged by her suicide? He should have gone to see one of the grief counsellors they brought in, we agree.

You went to one, didn't you, Merv? Paula asks. You took it all very personally.

She was so *young*, Merv says.

Do you think she actually wanted to die? Art asks. I mean, don't you think she wanted to be discovered? Brought back to life?

I think Annie Tasker's death was magnificent, I say. She was, like, *beyond* life. She'd seen the world. She didn't want any part of it.

It was probably just some schoolgirl thing, Paula says. She was being bullied or whatever. She had some eating disorder. Her parents were getting divorced . . .

No—she rejected life, I say. She didn't want life—any of it.

I think that despair *is* an attempt to live, Paula says. Even suicide . . .

How do you figure that? I say.

Life's a gift, Paula says. That's how we should see it.

Life's a *curse*, I say. You're just cast into it. No one asked you if you wanted to live. So why can't you just step off the ride?

Because it's a waste, Paula says. You're throwing something away.

Do you remember the school memorial service? Art asks. All those balloons they released into the sky ... Everyone clapping. Tasker giving his speech. The Head Boy by Tasker's side ...

And that's when things started going wrong for them, Art says. That's when they started getting bombed out all the time.

They couldn't bear the truth, I say. Venture Scouts doesn't prepare you for *that*.

After school. Cycling to my house.

Nietzsche should be with us, Art says. He needs to get a bike.

Jesus—did you hear him in English today? Paula asks. He was *on fire* ...

We remember. *Death is an unattainable goal*, he said. *Living is dying because it is a not-being-able-to-die.*

He was quoting, right? Paula asks. I mean, Miss Sherwood recognised what he was saying.

Miss Sherwood went to Oxford, Art says. She's actually *intelligent*.

Jesus, how did she end up teaching at the Valley? Paula asks.

The narrow path from Barkham Ride to Tickenor Drive. Graffiti tags on the fence. GNON—what's that? Who's GNOD? NEW LUMPEN—what's that supposed to mean?

Why tag? we wonder. Why bother? To mark your name, of course. To say: *I was here*. To attest to your life. To send some message, even if it's a stupid message. To say you were here. That you tried to live. That you weren't content just to slop along ...

Let's buy some spray-paint, Paula says. Leave our tags.

Fuck tags, Art says. I want to *do* something with my life. I want to have done something. I want to look back and *prove* that I wasn't a sap. That I didn't just *suck*. We have to save ourselves from paralysis and despair. We have to *become* something—make ourselves *into* something.

No one knows us—do you ever feel that? I ask. No one knows anything about us. And no one knows that they don't know—that's what gets me. Like my parents . . . they don't have an idea of who I am or what I want . . .

Well, who are you, Chandra? Art says. What do you want?

I want to do something crazy, I say. Just to shock them. Kill myself, or something. Just to make them reflect. *So he wasn't just this perfect son. He wasn't just a doctor-to-be to boast about at the temple* . . .

Sorry, Chandra, Paula says. Tasker's sister's beaten you to it.

Discussion. How would you kill yourself, if you were going to? Efficiently—with some deft slash to the throat? Hygienically, with a single knife-stab? Or would you be hacking away at yourself like an idiot, slashing here and then there, and wondering why you weren't dead yet . . .

There's death by poison. You could follow instructions on You-Tube. Mix up the right household cleaning products in a bucket. Neck down the whole mixture. Get it wrong, and you'd wake up with wrecked insides. You'd wake up plugged into machines breathing for you, digesting for you, shitting and pissing for you, waiting on the longlist for a *complete organ transplant* . . .

There's drowning. You could just throw yourself into the Thames. Weigh yourself down. Fill your pockets with rocks. But they'd just pull you out. They'd perform mouth-to-mouth resuscitation on the riverbank. But not in time to prevent *oxygen deprivation*. Not in time to prevent *irreversible brain damage* and having to spend the rest of your life in an institution . . .

How about good ol' hanging? It's classic. You could just string yourself up. But don't men get an involuntary stiffie? Don't they come in their pants? Can't be bad. But you also lose control of your bowels, right?

⋆

My house. My bedroom.

Your parents are very excitable, Art says. Seriously—are they on something?

At least they're in the same *country* as Chandra, Paula says.

I think they're nice, Merv says.

Of course they're *nice*, Paula says. They can actually bear one another. They can actually spend time in a room together. Indian types have such stable families. They're the last ones left. But it won't last another generation. I mean, you're as English as the rest of us, Chandra. It's a fucking disaster. You'll have to settle down with another ethnic. Stop the rot.

Have you actually told your parents you're going to study creative writing, Chandra? Art asks. They'd stop laughing then, wouldn't they?

What's poetry *for*, Chandra? Paula asks. What's it all about, in our destitute times?

A rose has no why, I say. Nor does poetry.

The word *twat* has no *y*, you mean, Paula says.

Imagine—people used to *read* books, Art says. They used to turn pages and underline things. They used to copy out passages like Nietzsche does on his blog . . .

That's what we should do, Paula says. Seriously—we should improve ourselves. Read something really hard.

Something Russian, Art says. Dostoevsky. That might impress Nietzsche, at least.

A Dostoevsky book club, Paula says.

Isn't Dos . . . toe . . . thingy too hard for us? Merv asks.

We can pick an *easy* Dostoevsky, Paula says, scrolling on her phone. Hold on—*The Idiot*. That sounds good . . .

We order our copies.

TUESDAY

Mid-morning. Paula's studio, in the art wing.

Whitewashed breeze blocks. A skylight. A pull-cord. A sink. An Apple Mac, on a folding chair.

It's so quiet! Somewhere peaceful in the school! A sanctuary within the walls of the school!

Peace—what we always wanted in the lower school. Peace from the lesson bells. Peace from the bellowing kids. A lower-school sabbath . . .

I'll bet Miss Vickers comes here, to quietly masturbate, Art says.

Fuck you, Art, Paula says.

Didn't she invite you to take tea with her? Art asks. It's positively *nineteenth century*.

Miss Vickers is a musty old spinster, Paula says.

All the bi-curious teachers get excited around you, don't they? Art says. All the *hobby lesbians*. The margins are *in* now. Diversity and all that . . .

Paula turns on the computer. Hits *play*. Murmuring voices. Women, talking about their commutes to work. About the school-run. About balancing work and life. About hopes and dreams.

It's sound art, Paula says. My *suburban women* series. I interviewed some of my mum's friends. I want to play them back in the suburbs through hidden loudspeakers. As though I were doubling up the suburbs. Layering the 'burbs on top of the 'burbs.

I was thinking of taking some photos, too, Paula says. A *suburban everyday* series. The kind of stuff you never really notice, though it's all around us. Pine trees swaying in the breeze . . . Delivery vans coming and going . . . For Sale signs going up . . . Pine needles on decking . . . Pine cones on the grass . . . That kind of stuff.

I know it's all bullshit, Paula says. Everything's bullshit. I don't know if I even believe in art. I suppose you can make art saying you don't believe in art. But it sounds a bit self-involved, doesn't it? Making art to show you don't believe in art?

Paula hits another button. Birdsong. Children's cries. The sound of traffic.

Another button. Birdsong slowed, slurred. Children's voices, smeared, made woozy. Traffic sounds, losing their distinctness.

This is cool, Art says. It's, like, abandoned art . . . Neglected art . . . Seriously. It's like you caught the suburbs daydreaming, or something. This is what we should do with the band. You know—*ambient* stuff. Like it wasn't created by anyone . . . Like it just *happens* . . .

Geography.

Announcement. Mr Zachary's off sick, so we have Miss Lilly instead. Miss Lilly, the newest geography teacher. Miss Lilly, just hatched from teaching college . . .

Mr Zachary, off sick! It's depression—what else can it be? Mr Zachary, suffering from pre-traumatic stress disorder, just like all those climate scientists you read about. Mr Zachary, comfortless, disconsolate, without even his Gaia-faith to save him . . .

Writing imaginary dialogue between the polder and the ocean. What it feels like for a watershed.

Miss Lilly's so enthusiastic! So full of life and ideas! She's trying to make things interesting for us! We should be generous-hearted in turn! We should be open-hearted in turn! All hail active learning!

Questions for Miss Lilly: How long will the polders hold back the ocean, miss? What about the dikes? How long do you give human civilization in general, miss? Do you think the end will come gradually, or all at once, miss? How many people do you think will survive the catastrophe, miss? Do you think there will be cannibalism, miss? It's going to be bad—*very* bad, isn't it, miss?

We don't inherit the Earth from our parents, but borrow it from our children, that's what they say, isn't it, miss? Do you ever feel it's your fault, miss—climate change? You and your generation? Do you ever want to *repent*, miss—cover your head with ashes?

We have to downshift, don't we, miss? We have to transition out of our lifestyles. No more four-by-fours . . . No travelling by car . . . No flying overseas . . . We'll have to do without pilot lights, won't we miss? And we can't let the water run when we brush our teeth. And we should piss while we shower—isn't that the idea? And we'll have to recycle even harder, won't we miss? Go ever more *local* . . .

Really, we have to cull the population, miss—it's quite clear. There should be a tax on babies, miss. On people who live alone. We should agree to sterilization, shouldn't we, miss? In fact, we should just do away with ourselves. That might solve it, miss.

★

After class.

Miss Lilly seemed depressed, Paula says.

It's what we do to people, Art says.

No one wants to face the truth, I say. They're all in denial.

Of course they are, Paula says. They've got so much to lose.

Discussion. So how can *we* stand it? What's so special about *us*? Is it because we're not part of the world, not yet? Is it because we don't have to look after ourselves?

Our lives are pretty easy, really. Our parents do okay. Our houses are okay. Our school's okay. We've given up our Saturday jobs for the exams.

Everyone's used to us there. Everyone's used to everyone, after seven years. We have our place, inside the system, though we think we're outside the system. We're part of something, even if we think we're part of nothing . . .

But life isn't always going to be like this. What happens when we leave uni? What happens on the other side? We'll have to work, like everyone else. We'll have to look for work. We'll end up as contractors, if we're lucky. Temps. And there'll be drudges all around us. They'll thrive, as we fail. They'll rise, as we fall. Because we won't be able to cope in the *real world*, not really. Because we're not made for the *real world*, as they are.

But we're immune, for now. We're safe for now.

★

Sixth-form torpor. Sixth-form lassitude. Why are we so tired, at the peak of our lives? Why are we falling asleep, at the peak of our lives?

As though we're in purgatory, forced to live the same day over and over again. As though we've worn it away. As though it lives on only in dub. In drop-outs. In broken refrains.

It's the end of history—that's what Mr Varga told us in class last year. *History's over*, he said. *It's all finished. Nothing's going to change, fundamentally. The future's going to be exactly like this.*

What about terrorism? we asked Mr Varga. *Terrorism's nothing*, he said. *Some ripples on the pond.* What about ISIS? we asked him. The Arab Spring? *More ripples*, he said. *A sideshow. A decoy . . .* What about the fundamentalism and nationalism and ethnic cleansing? we asked him. What about refugees?

History means surprising events, Mr Varga said. *It means something new happening. Do you see anything new happening?* Plenty of things are happening, we said. The new mercantilism. Blockchain tech. The rise of 5G. *Your hair keeps growing after you die*, Mr Varga said. *Things happen, but so what? Progress is a myth. Progress is over.*

Nietzsche, sitting down with us. Opening his lunchbox.

What's for lunch today? Merv asks.

Don't bug the man, Paula says.

Nietzsche, showing us his sandwiches.

What's in them? I ask.

Nietzsche: Peanut butter.

Peanut butter!, Art says. I thought you'd be more of an Italian-deli guy. You know, fancy meats and so on.

Nietzsche: I'm a vegetarian.

What about dessert? Paula asks.

Silence.

How did your classes go this morning? I ask. You're taking maths, right?

Nietzsche, making a non-committal sound.

What about your extended project? Art asks.

Nietzsche, shrugging, munching on his sandwich.

Another tack.

Do you think history's over? Paula asks. That's what Mr Varga told us. It's why everything seems so *dead*.

Nietzsche: All things die in time.

But when's it going to *stop* dying? Paula asks. When's something else going to happen?

Nothing is going to happen, I say. This is the last century of civilization, right? It's just barbarism after us . . .

Maybe nothing else *should* happen, Art says. Really, haven't we fucked things up enough? Isn't that what history means—fucking everything up?

Silence.

Another tack.

Where the danger is strongest, there the saving power grows—that's what you quoted on your blog, Paula says.

What saving power? Merv asks. What's going to save us?

Nietzsche: There are transitions. Moments of change. Perhaps this will be one of them.

Look—the end's come and gone, Paula says. History's over. History's ended. There's not going to be some great climax. Just entropy, just a kind of fizzling out . . . I mean, look around us. Look at the common room. This is a farce. This is the satyr play, after the tragedy. This is a comedy—if it can be called fucking comedy.

God is dead, Paula says. God won't be born again. And we don't mind. We don't mind anything. We're play-actors. Maybe what you said the other night was right—our despair is *sham*. Just like our hatred's a phase. In the end, we're *happy* with our hatred. Despair's our fucking lullaby. Because we're *part* of the ending of the world—I see that now. We're the *way* in which the world ends.

But what about creation? Art asks Nietzsche. What you were saying yesterday . . . I've been thinking about it . . . We should be creators, not just creatures, right? We're just raw material that needs to be shaped and formed; we need to suffer—that's it, isn't it? That's what the band is—the desire to shape, to form, to crush. Overcoming ourselves—that's what we're trying to do . . .

Nietzsche: I don't know—I've never heard your band.

We've got to destroy ourselves, right? Art asks. We've got to let ourselves *go under*. Well, that's what's going to happen. That's what we're going to do.

But what else have we been doing all these years, except *going under*? I ask. Think of Merv in the changing rooms. Think of the special needs boy they swung over the river . . . We've suffered, right? Merv suffered . . .

But we can redeem it—don't you see? Art says. That's what the band's for. If it comes good, if we make something worthwhile, then it will have all made sense—everything that happened to us. We'll make retrospective sense of it all, school, the suburbs, all that. And *we'll* have done it. We'll have been the creators.

Imagine it, Art says . . . if the band gets good, if we release something amazing, we can say: everything happened as it should have done. We would not have wanted it otherwise. We'd have a sense of being fated, right—of *fatedness*.

There were no accidents, we could say, Art says. Nothing was futile—nothing was wasted on us . . . There was a direction all along, we could say—*our* direction. We've become masters of time—*our* time. We're creators; we created the world—*our* world. We're active, not passive . . . We're the fucking *saving power* . . .

You'll hear us soon, Art says to Nietzsche. When we've found our sound. You'll hear us then.

PE.

Art and I, on a break from tennis. Looking out over the courts.

Languor. We understand less and less what a tennis court is, what tennis is, what the sky is, what grass is . . .

The Sirens, two courts down.

I haven't worked out whether the Sirens are really hot, or not, I say.

You're just scared of them, Art says. They're cleverer than you.

Noelle, doing yoga poses. The warrior. Downward-facing dog.

It's sexual display, Art says. Quite clearly for *your* benefit, Chandra.

The Sirens, coming to sit beside us.

We had you figured as nerds, Noelle says. But now I'm not so sure . . .

So don't be *disappointing*, Tana says.

It's the *new boy* effect, right? Art says. You think we're cool because Nietzsche hangs out with us.

Nietzsche—is that what you call him? Tana asks. Jesus.

He's a philosopher, I say. A philosopher of the suburbs.

You guys are full of shit, Tana says.

Where is he now? Noelle asks. How does he get out of PE?

He's running, supposedly, I say. He's on a cross-country run. But I think it's a ruse.

So what's he really doing? Tana says asks.

Suburban research, I say. He's finding out things.

What, that the suburbs are boring? Tana says.

Like you know anything about the suburbs, I say. You were at boarding school, right?

Tana shrugs. So?

How come you didn't stay on? Art asks

They thought we were a bad influence, Tana says. And Noelle wanted to come to a school with boys.

So did *you*, Noelle says.

So how come you keep so aloof? Art asks. Do you hate everyone, like we do?

We like to stay above the fray, Noelle says.

Well, we really hate everyone, I say.

We're one-hundred-per-cent hatred, Art says. No one in the history of the world has felt as much hatred as us.

That means you're dependent on what you hate, Noelle says. You can't just say no to everything. You have to say yes.

Yes to what, though? I ask. To the school? To the suburbs?

Yes to weed, maybe, Tana says. Do you guys have anything?

Art, patting his shorts pocket. Oh yeah.

Ah! I see you're not going to be *disappointing* . . . , Tana says.

Come on, Noelle says. Let's go and *smoke*.

★

Joel Park, passing round the spliff.

This is going to be the hottest summer on record, Tana says.

Yeah—due to total climate apocalypse, Art says.

There are forests in Sweden on fire, I say. In Siberia. The world's burning up.

You can't think too much about *that*, Tana says.

It's pretty much all we think about, Art says.

Summer always makes me think something good's going to happen, Noelle says.

This is our coming-of-age summer, Tana says. The summer we leave school. When we have to find our way in the world.

Only until we get to uni, I say.

Who are we supposed to listen to? Tana asks. Who are we supposed to trust? If we can't decide for ourselves, then we'll turn out like everyone else . . .

I don't trust—*anyone*, Art says. Not one person. Everyone lies. The world's full of liars, of fakes . . . and they make us liars, too. We have to lie when we're among them . . .

My dads are pretty cool, Noelle says.

You have dads, plural? I ask.

Sylvere's French and Cecil's an aristo English type, Noelle says. They're academics.

They're really *European*, Tana says.

Je est un autre, says Noelle. *I is an other.* That's Rimbaud, the teen wonder-poet. We're doing him in French.

Another what? Art asks. I is another what?

Just other, Tana says. Other to itself.

We are unknown to ourselves, we knowers, I quote.

Noelle's a bit in love with Rimbaud, Tana says. She likes dangerous boys.

Noelle (quoting, closed-eyed): *I aspire to absolute rest and contin-
uous night . . . to know nothing, to teach nothing, to will nothing, to feel
nothing . . .* Rimbaud was a *poète maudit*. He knew every kind of love.
He deranged his senses. He exhausted every poison. He burned
through his teens . . .

And he lived in Reading for a bit, apparently, Tana says.

What was he doing in Reading? I ask.

Training to become a businessman, Noelle says. That's when he
renounced poetry. He hit eighteen, and left it all behind.

It's a warning to us all, Art says.

I'd give up poetry if I lived in Reading, I say. Imagine it: Some
ancestor of Mr Pound's, drilling him on supply-side economics, or
something.

Wokingham hasn't stopped Chandra from writing, Art says.

What do you write? Noelle asks.

Poetry about death, Art says. Go on, recite that one about Japanese hara-kari pilots.

This is my last day, I say. *The destiny of our homeland hinges on the
decisive battle in the seas to the south where I shall fall like a blossom from
a radiant cherry tree . . .* That's all I can remember.

Did you write that? Noelle asks.

It's a found poem, I say.

It was in the school magazine under your name, Art says.

Is that allowed? Noelle asks.

It's called *détournement*, I say. Found stuff always means something different when you use it in a new context.

It's called plagiarism, Art says.

So what does your poem mean now? Noelle asks.

The hara-kari pilots were just our age, I say. They were sixth-
formers like us. They were incredibly well read. They'd fill up their
cockpit with fin-de-siècle books and crash into aircraft carriers . . .

Stop sounding so wistful, Noelle says.

There was this story in the *Mail* about a girl who lay down on the
railway line to kill herself, Art says. She lost both legs instead. It gave
her a new purpose in life.

That's not true!, Tana says.

Art, reading from his phone: *Losing my legs was devastating, but now I'm just happy I survived. Before I lost my legs I thought I'd be alone forever, but now I have everything I've ever wanted.*

She goes skydiving now, apparently, Art says.

I wouldn't want to lose my legs, Noelle says. I *like* my legs.

Jesus, Tana says. Why are you so *obvious*?

So what's your take on Tasker's sister's suicide? Noelle asks.

It's weird, Tana says. We'll get older and older, and she'll always be . . . how old was she when she died?

Fifteen, Art says.

Fifteen, Tana says. Wow.

Think about it, Noelle says. She's fifteen forever. Fifteen, in everyone's memories. The rest of us will grow older, and she'll always be fifteen.

No one ever lacks a good reason for suicide, I say.

Annie Tasker killed herself on a whim, Noelle says.

It wasn't a whim, I say. It was adolescence. Teenagers see things most clearly. All adolescents are philosophers. And all philosophers are adolescents at heart . . .

Even the drudges? Art asks.

Okay, not the drudges, I say.

What about the nerds? Art asks. The beasts? The trendies?

None of them either, I say.

What you're saying is that Annie Tasker was like us, Art says. Which makes her pretty fucking cool.

Annie Tasker wasn't anything special, Tana says. She was just like the rest of us. A bit sadder, perhaps. But then we're all a bit sad these days, aren't we?

Suicide is 180-degree murder, that's what they say, Noelle says. Annie Tasker was probably being abused or something. She wanted to kill her abuser, so she killed herself. It's a fuck-you message.

Maybe she was part of a death cult, Tana says. An internet thing.

It could be the beginning of a suicide epidemic, Noelle says. Imagine it. Like in Bridgend, a few years back . . .

Cluster suicides, Art says. That's what they're called. It'll be her brother next—the deputy head boy. Then it'll be the Head Boy himself . . .

Annie Tasker killed herself because her life was shit, I say. Because she lived in Wokingham.

But Wokingham's perfectly *nice*, Noelle says.

Maybe she killed herself *because* Wokingham's so nice, I say.

You can always escape Wokingham, right? Noelle says. You can go to uni, and so on. Why couldn't Annie Tasker just wait for a bit?

Because she knew she'd end up back here, or somewhere like here, I say.

How did she do it? Noelle says.

I'll bet she hanged herself, Art says.

I'll bet she didn't, Tana says. Girls never hang themselves. They always worry about how they'll look when they're discovered. I read that somewhere.

Annie Tasker probably took an overdose of painkillers, Noelle says. That's the way to go.

I kind of admire people who kill themselves, I say. Who see it through, I mean.

Art, lighting up another spliff. Passing it round.

I don't think I could do it, Noelle says. I couldn't harm my own body. I'd put down the razor blade, because I'd think: *poor body*. I'd feel sorry for my body. Like it was an innocent. Like it was a child.

Don't you think it's really sad that we can talk about these things? Tana asks. We're so *morbid*.

Just like Rimbaud, I say. I'll bet there wasn't a moment when he didn't want to set fire to the whole world . . .

After school. Art's broken patio.

I'm grateful for this lovely day, Art reads out. *I'm grateful* . . . Interruption: I'm keeping my gratitude journal, Art says. I'm making a conscious decision to become happier and more grateful. Just like Mr Merriweather.

More reading: *I'm grateful for this sunny day, for the trees in full leaf, for the wildflowers along the river* . . . Interruption: You're actually supposed to focus on *people* you're grateful to rather than *things*. So it's gonna be all about you guys. My best friends. You're a gift, man. Journaling (Paula: *Journaling!?*) . . . Journaling is all about creating meaning in your life, Art says. Giving something back. You can all expect some *Thinking of you* emails. It's my next phase.

I'm grateful my parents deserted me, Paula says. *I'm grateful I live in a shithole. I'm grateful I can barely take care of myself. I'm grateful that all my friends do is take the piss out of me and my fucking gratitude journal.*

I'm grateful I'm a proper minger, I say. *I'm grateful my younger brother got all the looks. I'm grateful for the new estate they've built around my house. I'm grateful I'm at a totally average school, in a totally average town, in a totally average suburb. I'm grateful I've got no prospects whatsoever.*

You guys may mock, Art says. But it's amazing what you can learn from journaling . . . I'm grateful for *rainbows* now, for example. For, like, *scented candles*. For *kittens*, man—and all animals. I just love animals. And *soft pillows*—mmm. And *croissants*—how could I forget them? And *paw prints*—they always make me smile. And *bear hugs*. And *chocolate*. And *cozy scarves*. I have a whole new appreciation for *mistakes*—they're something to learn from. And *life*, man—thanks for life.

Pause.

Actually, gratitude sucks, Art says. Fuck my health—I'm not grateful for that. Fuck my parents for giving me life. Fuck laughter, which makes me put up with shit. Fuck nature—the whole natural world. Fuck everything man. There's got to be a way to express this feeling of being *walled in*. Of everything being *impossible*.

The darkening of the fucking world—how do you write about that? Art asks. The destruction of the fucking Earth. The triumph of the fucking stupid. Boundless fucking suffering . . . And the fact that it's all going on forever. The fact that there is no fucking end!

Endlessness: that's what nihilism means, Art says. Nihilism is the fact that this will go on forever. Fuck the world, man—death to the world. You know what? I'm off to join the doom-metal monks.

The doom-metal monks exist entirely in your imagination, Paula says.

I'm going to Alaska, like Justin Marler, Art says. Or maybe Russia. Do you think they have doom-metal monks in Russia?

I thought you were Tantric, Paula says.

Tantra was a portal, man, Art says. I'm heading towards real religion.

Does that mean you're actually going to come, now? Paula asks.

Do monks come? Merv asks.

In each other, generally, Paula says.

I don't think monks wank, Art says. It's against their rule.

They should wank, Paula says. It releases sexual tension. That's your problem, Art—you're full of sexual tension.

Merv: Some of us don't need to w—

Jesus, we get the idea, Merv, Paula says.

Anyway, you actually have to be Christian to become a monk, Art, I say. You have to believe in stuff.

I believe in stuff, Art says.

Listening to chanting monks on Spotify doesn't make you a believer, Paula says. And could you actually—actually—believe in all that Jesus-is-the-son-of-God stuff?

You don't have to take that stuff literally, Art says. It's just a way of talking about things, that's all.

The monks aren't going to buy it, Art, Paula says. Try it out on them. You haven't got a chance.

What are your spiritual beliefs, Merv? Art asks.

I've felt things, Merv says.

Spiritual things? Art asks.

Maybe, Merv says. I don't know what they mean. It's like . . . they haven't happened to me yet.

What about you, Paula? Art asks. Is there a lesbian goddess?

I think Nadya Tolokno is a lesbian goddess, Paula says. You know—the one from Pussy Riot.

Nadya who? we wonder. Pussy who?

Paula, reading from her phone:

> We're the children of Dionysus, floating by in a barrel, accepting nobody's authority. We're on the side of those who don't offer final answers or transcendent truths. These are the people I love—the Dionysians, the unmediated ones, those drawn to what's different and new, seeking movement and inspiration over dogmas and immutable statutes. The innocents, in other words; the speakers of truth.

That's Nadya Tolokno. She wrote it in prison.

Who's Dionysus? Merv asks.

Wasn't he, like, the god of wine? I ask.

Dionysus was the god of *life*, says Paula, reading again. Of the inexhaustibility of life. His name means, *he who gives release*.

Release from what? I ask.

From the system, man, Art says.

Dionysus was the god of madness, Paula continues. He went mad, and danced through the world accompanied by bands of satyrs and maenads . . .

We imagine it: a mad god. Madness as a god. *Infectious* madness, leaping from follower to follower. Threatening to destroy the whole world . . .

We imagine it: madness as a kind of sanity—a *greater* sanity. Madness that makes perfect sense. Madness that makes too much sense. Madness that understands *too* much, that knows *too much*. Madness that reaches a kind of *truth* . . .

★

The practice room.

So what shitty music genre are we going to try this time? Paula asks.

Dronology, man, Art says. Inspired by you, Paula. It's time for the *drone* . . .

Art, switching on his laptop. A hum, as of distant engines. As of underfloor generators . . .

Louder. *Louder.*

Jesus, Art . . . , Paula says.

The whole room, trembling. The whole room, rumbling. Fuck— this is the loudest noise we've ever heard.

Merv, nose bleeding.

YOU'RE FUCKING CRAZY, ART!, I shout.

THIS IS WHAT WE SHOULD SOUND LIKE, MAN!, Art shouts.

I WANT TO SOUND LIKE A BAND, NOT A FUCKING SPACESHIP TAKING OFF!, Paula shouts.

Art, turning it down. *Nada Brahma*, he says. The ocean of sound.

It has to be loud. You have to feel it *here* (pointing to his chest). It's the ground-bass, man. *Om*, man. It's the fucking *truth*.

Why do you like such boring stuff, Art? Merv asks. It doesn't *do* anything. There's no *development*.

It's not about development, Art says. You have to dwell in the sound. Just listen . . .

The drone, droning.

It closes the gaps between notes, Art says. It gets rid of Western pitch intervals . . . We've got to make a *big* music. Something bigger than us, bigger than the suburbs. We've got to go cosmic . . .

It's just boring, Art, I say.

Jesus, what kind of Indian are you? Art asks. This is your music. Just play along, guys. Play until it becomes interesting.

Merv's marimba, gonging.

Paula, playing low notes on her bass. Sub-bass, like whale communication.

Me, adding wah-wah. *Wukka wukka.*

It's oceanic. It's undersea. There are whorls. Riptides. Gravity's abolished.

It's womblike—that's it. Everything's muffled. Everything's refracting, reverberating.

Reverie. Rootlessness. We're liquefying our minds . . .

Art, pressing his stomp boxes. Laying fuzz on the drone. Overloading the channel. Feeding it back.

Compression. Mutation. Squeals of feedback. Roaring. White noise. Bursts of static. Sound torn apart.

IT'S DIONYSUS!, Art shouts.

IT'S MADNESS!, I shout.

IT'S A FUCKING BLACK HOLE!, Merv shouts.

Paula, leaning across the mixing desk and sliding down the faders. Why did you have to fuck it up, Art? Why do you always have to do the macho thing? It's just fucking aural wanking.

It's Tantric, man, Art says. There's no crescendo. No climax.

Starting again.

Art's drone. Merv's reverbed marimba. Paula's bass—a two-note riff. Guitar notes, on infinite sustain. Art, adding noises from his laptop. Flashes. Pulses. Sound quanta, like tiny fishes.

Gentle rocking. The bass, intimate. Deeper than deep. A bass-heartbeat, gently throbbing, gently pulsing. Eddies of sound. Float-ing zones.

Hums and tones from Art's laptop. Turbine noise from the drone. Echo-drenched marimba chimes. Melted guitar . . .

Horizontal music. Wide water music. Planes and strata music. Plateaux of colour and space . . .

Gradually bringing it to a close. Gradually ending. Entropy. Diminuendo. A decimal, repeating unto infinity . . .

Very pretty, Merv says.

It really is like your art, Paula, I say.

That's the problem, Paula says. It's too vague . . .

I don't mind vague, Art says. It's a songscape. A drone poem.

Paula's right—there's something's missing, I say. It's great, but it's too inoffensive.

We need vocals, I say. We need someone to *lead* the songs. Some-one we can follow.

You should be our singer, Paula, Art says.

No way, Paula says. It's too embarrassing. I don't want to be the frontwoman for you retards.

What about you, Chandra? Paula asks. Do something Eastern. Something Indian. Do something about Shiva, or something.

I shake my head. Uh-uh.

Recite one of your death poems then, Art says.

No way, I say.

We've got to write about what we know, right? Merv asks. So what do we know?

Discussion. We're just too middle-class to have anything to say. Too suburban. It's only the working class who are creative. People really up against it . . . Who haven't got a choice . . .

Merv's working-class, Art says.

Go on, Merv, create something, Paula says. Channel your class hatred.

I think Merv might be on the wrong instrument, I say. You can't play hate music on a marimba.

Do you think we need a marimba in our tantric dub metal band? Paula asks. Merv, you need to play something more butch.

We've got to play *nihilism*, man, Art says. We've got to play what we *feel*. We have to be a perfectly nihilist band. We've got to play from the heart of the nihilist storm. We have to suck all the nihilism into ourselves and turn it into something else.

The *Nihilists*: that's what we should call ourselves, Paula says.

There's already a band called the Nihilists, Art says, checking his phone.

Okay—the Nihil then, Paula says.

Nope, that's gone, too, Art says.

How about the Nothings? I ask.

Taken, Art says.

Go on, consult your list, Art, Paula says. You know you're dying to.

Art, reading out his list of song titles. *The Wheel of Ix. Anomaly. The Ever-Void. Palace of Nothingness. The Remainder. The Broken Shells. Iron Cage.*

They're pretty good, Art, Paula says. They're really interesting.

It nearly makes up for you not being able to play anything, I say.

More band names: *Ungrund*, Art reads. *Saturnine Spirit. Dark Gnosis. Trauerspeil. The Unconquerable. Mythic Swamp. False Kairos. Abortive Gulf. The Uncreating Void.* And best of all: *Universal Darkness Buries All.*

You could do things with that name, I say.

Anyway, the real question is why you would bother doing anything, if you were a nihilist band, Paula says. I mean, why would you get out of bed?

To *perfect* nihilism, I say. To be the most nihilistic you could be.

The Perfect Nihilists, Paula says. Now that is a good band name. Write that one down, Art.

How about . . . the Suburb Destroyers? I ask. The Suburb Fuckers.

How about the 'burbs—just the 'burbs? Paula ask. Has there been a band called the 'burbs?

There . . . *has*, Art says, searching on his phone.

The something 'burbs, then, Paula says. Or something and the 'burbs.

Nietzsche and the Burbs, I say.

Seriously—that's an idea, Art says. *Nietzsche* and the Burbs . . . It's brilliant . . .

Can he sing? Paula asks.

Discussion. That doesn't matter. This isn't *X-Factor*. He can learn to sing. Anyway, it's not as if we're amazing musos. We just need a frontman. Someone with charisma. We need to be led.

Nietzsche and the Burbs. We agree. Now all we have to do is get Nietzsche to join.

WEDNESDAY

Lunch.

Bill Trim practising his nunchuks outside.

I can't believe it, Paula says. Bill Trim's become even more hard.

Merv, too, Art says. Just this minute.

Discussion. Isn't it funny how the hard become even more hard, by training and stuff? And the beautiful become even more beautiful . . . And the nerds become even nerdier . . . But what do *we* become?—that's the question.

Even more alienated, we decide. Even more bored. We're perfecting our alienation. We're perfecting our boredom. No one will ever have been more bored than we are. More *purely* bored. More boredly bored.

We're pioneers of boredom, we agree. We're discoverers of boredom. It's a landscape to us, boredom. A whole country. There are steppes and mountain-peaks of boredom. There are dense forest-thickets of boredom. There are open glades where boredom pours down like moonlight. There are valleys of lassitude. Meadows of torpor. And who would know it but us?

Boredom, our teacher. Boredom, our master. Boredom, always about to show us something, if only we can follow it to the end. Ah, but will we ever wait long enough? Will we ever be patient enough? Will we ever see what boredom can reveal?

Free period.

Reading Nietzsche's blog.

Art: It's the usual stuff:

Not abstraction but subtraction.

The fullness of nothingness. That is the reason for the insistence on the zero point. (Beckett)
What is laid upon us is to accomplish the negative. The positive is already given. (Kafka)

This sounds good:
Thought honours itself by defending what is damned as nihilism. (Adorno)

So is nihilism good now? Merv asks.

It means that negativity is the new positivity, Paula says. And positivity is the new negativity.

Philosophy's *complicated*, Merv says. So we have to be negative?

We have to glower, Paula says. Wear black. Go around looking cross.

Nietzsche *always* looks cross, Merv says.

I wouldn't say he was *cross* exactly, I say.

He's *serious*, Art says. It just looks like crossness because we're so inane.

Are there any *frivolous* philosophers, do you think? Merv asks. Like, happy philosophers?

You only need philosophy when things have gone *fundamentally wrong*, Paula says. Philosophy is just a way of saying that things have gone *fundamentally wrong*.

So when *weren't* things fundamentally wrong? Merv asks.

In Bhutan—before Mr Merriweather and the happiness tourists got out there, I say.

Art, reading on: *The* problem *of the suburbs*—(*problem*, underlined). *The philosophy of the suburbs*—*is this an oxymoron?* (Oxymoron means self-contradiction, according to the dictionary.)

Silence.

Why would anyone philosophise about the suburbs? Merv wonders. Have they gone wrong, too?

Look around you, idiot, Paula says.

After school.

The front door, opening. Merv's dad, dishevelled, in his dressing gown.

Is Merv in? I ask.

Merv's dad jerks his thumb upstairs.

Merv's room.

So your dad's still non-verbal? Art asks.

My dad's too depressed to talk, Merv says.

Did your stepmum leave your dad because he was non-verbal? Paula asks.

Merv: My dad became non-verbal *when* my stepmum left him.

But he was already becoming non-verbal, right? Paula asks. He never said very much.

Well, he doesn't say *anything* now, Merv says.

I might go non-verbal, Art says. As a kind of Zen thing.

Does your dad ever get dressed, Merv? Paula asks.

Merv, shaking his head.

He's setting a great example, Paula says.

How do you communicate? I ask Merv.

We don't, Merv says.

How's your brother, Merv? Art asks. Still nocturnal? When was the last time he saw daylight?

Wasn't he arrested? Paula asks. Isn't he going on trial or something?

Merv, nodding. Shrugging.

You should put yourself up for adoption, Merv, Paula says. This is a very troubled household.

Merv's laptop. Crowding round. We thought you were going to use your amazing coding powers to get yourself a really high-paying job, I say, not building cock-palaces on Minecraft.

Go on, show us the dark web, Art says. That's where your brother gets his supplies, right? We want to see secrets. Was nine-eleven really an inside job, Merv? Did Lady Gaga really have Lou Reed murdered? Will the dark web tell us?

How about hacking, Merv?—I'll bet you're good at that. Whose systems have you broken into now? You'll just end up in prison.

We imagine it: Merv, the fall guy for some deep-web libertarians. Merv, arrested at dawn, and extradited to America, never quite understanding what he'd done. Merv, sentenced to nine hundred and ninety-nine years in solitary confinement, with no window . . .

Merv, sleeping with the lights on in a plastic cell. Merv, on permanent suicide watch, knowing the viewer in the door will slide open every hour just to make sure he's still alive. Merv, wondering what the world's like outside. What a tree looks like, or a blade of grass. Merv, wondering what rain feels like on the skin.

THURSDAY

Lunch. The common room.

Would you like to be able to read people's minds? Paula asks. To know how people think?

Art, shuddering. My God, imagine listening in on the thoughts of a drudge: *snack—snack—Instagram—snack—must . . . have . . .corn . . . syrup . . .* Imagine listening in on drudge lust: *snack—fuck—fuck— snack.*

I don't want to hear my own thoughts, let alone anyone else's, I say.

Let's try some telepathy, Art says. What am I thinking?

You're thinking about making lurrve to Calypso, I say. Mmm, sweet lurrrve.

No I'm not!, Art says.

I know what Art's really thinking about: the murder of Dingus, Paula says.

Spot on, Art says.

We remember how Art used to want to lure Dingus to the sand dunes. To pop air-rifle pellets in Dingus's eyes. Pop, pop. Blinded Dingus . . . Dingus, staggering about . . . Dingus, crying, *My eyes! My eyes!* . . . Then Art would shoot Dingus repeatedly in the genitals. Then set fire to Dingus. Dingus, burning, screaming, at the sand dunes. Pretty fucking violent, for Art the Buddhist Christian . . .

Now, Merv—what *you're* thinking!, Paula says. You're making me blush! Who knew you and Bill were so *sexually advanced*? The stuff you've done! The positions you've done it in! The places! On the sports-hall roof—really!? *Very* gymnastic! And on the rings! On the *horse*! You're even turning *me* on.

I know what you're thinking about, Paula, I say. Lovelessness! A world without romance! Woe is me! Life hasn't begun!

Well, we all know who you're dreaming of, Chandra, Paula says. *I'm Noelle, I'm so pretty. I'm French or something . . .*

Telekinesis next. Go on, Art, see if you can move the cup over the edge of the table, Paula says. Channel your inner Carrie. Then maybe next you can wring Dingus's neck.

Nothing happens.

So Art's got no psychic powers, Paula says. What a bore.

Enter Nietzsche.

So what'd Mr Varga say? I ask. What's your project topic?

Nietzsche: The suburbs.

What?—you're going to write a philosophy of the suburbs? I ask. Do the suburbs deserve a philosophy?

You don't know anything about the suburbs, Art says. Seriously—you're a newcomer. You have to have grown up in the suburbs to understand them. You have to have been saturated in boredom—*pickled* in it—if you are to have the slightest grasp of what the suburbs are . . .

You haven't done your time—that's what we're saying, Paula says. Anyway, don't think you can just wander off through the 'burbs all by yourself. You haven't built up an immunity yet. You can't just gulp down the poison. You have to imbibe it slowly, in little sips. A Wokingham overdose would be a terrible fate . . .

Discussion. Nietzsche needs Sherpas—that's clear. He needs us. We could help him acclimatise to the suburban atmosphere. We could set up a suburban base camp. We could venture out with him, just a little at first, in brief forays at first, before taking on the really big challenges. We could work up through the Lower Earley estate, through the new estates near the motorway. We could survey entire towns—Bracknell, for example. What horror! Reading. God knows!

We'll help you, Paula says. We'll show you the suburbs.

Nietzsche (nodding): Okay.

Evening. The Three Frogs.

The barman in his enclosure, a towel over his shoulder. Regulars leaning against the bar. Pensioners eating lunch at their tables. Retirees at the service hatch to the beer garden, waiting to be served.

Do you feel a sense of belonging here? Art asks. A sense of homecoming? Are these your people? Do you feel they understand you, without words? Is it almost telepathic?

Seriously—where *are* all the gay people? I ask. Is the barman gay? Are the pensioners gay?

It turns gay in the evening, Paula says.

Face it, this really is the world's crappiest gay pub, Art says. It should win an award, or something.

Maybe the gay thing is just marketing, I say. It's, like, ladies' night in nightclubs. They just want a piece of the Wokingham pink pound.

This is probably some kind of front, I say. You probably have to use a secret password to be admitted to the *real* gay bar. It's probably in the basement, or something.

We should use Merv to flush out the gays, Art says. Go on—do your twink dance.

What this pub needs is Nicholas Nugent, we agree. He could turn any pub gay. He even turns The Ship gay—a bit, anyway. Even the sixth-form common room, in his heyday.

We remember when Nicholas Nugent first came out. He was, like, the Queer Messiah, or something. Overnight, he went from being some unnoticed nerd to the gayest boy in the suburbs. The trendies adored him. He had a whole coterie. And the beasts were fascinated—but they didn't know what they were fascinated by. He really confused them. We imagine it: beasts, tossing and turning at night, dreaming of Nicholas Nugent. Waking up sticky, but not knowing why. Beasts, swishing their hair as he passed. Was the Queer Messiah going to save us all, or just gay people? we wondered. How about the bi-curious? The pansexual?

You wouldn't know what to do if you were alone with Nicholas Nugent. Sink to your knees, perhaps. Venerate him. Or give him a blow job. Probably the same thing, really.

We imagine it: Nicholas Nugent sashaying through The Three Frogs with his retinue. It'd be like in a musical, when everyone bursts into song. Ah, how could we bring him here? we wonder. Maybe we could send a gay-signal, or something . . . Maybe you could summon him through gay telepathy, Paula . . .

Paula's house.

No one's in, thank God, Paula says. My dad's off doing some marathon in Kenya. He's ticking some fucking personal box. He's doing a marathon at the North Pole next year. I hope he gets eaten by a fucking polar bear. And my mum's off with the brats . . . I'm sick of the fucking brats . . .

Photos on the wall. Paula, as a young teenager, looking femme. Paula, as a slightly older girl, looking pissed off, with her cap on back to front. Paula, as the butch we know and love, with her hair dyed blue.

The living room. Vast beige sofas. Great beige armchairs. The word *LOVELY*, stencilled on the wall.

It's like a fucking ghost-house, we agree. It's like a fucking *desert*.

Are you actually *related* to your parents? Art says.

The kitchen. High stools by the window. *HEAVENLY*, stencilled on the wall. *A thank you sooooo much* card on the fridge door.

It's from a client, Paula says. My mum did her interior design.

Paula's annex. *TEEN-ZONE* stencilled on the wall in army-style letters.

Teen-zone—really!? Art says.

They're threatening to replace it with *EMERGING ADULT* in the next house, Paula says.

The next house? I ask.

My parents want a new *project*, Paula says. They only know they're alive when they're planning things. They can't just let a home be a home.

I mean, this isn't like a home, is it? Paula says. It's a *representation* of a home. It's not real. Just like our school's a *representation* of a school. It's all for effect. Just like I'm only the *representation* of a daughter. Just as my parents are *representations* of parents. Phone-in dad . . . Cardboard cut-out mum . . . It's a fucking stage-set . . .

How come you've got a fridge in your room? Merv asks.

So I never have to leave it, Paula says. Until I get to uni . . .

We imagine it: Paula, living in isolation, waiting for her escape. Paula, planning her artworks, musing on artworks . . .

We imagine it: Paula, in her lesbian chrysalis. Her lesbian escape pod. Paula, sending up her lesbian distress flares. Paula, applying to Manchester Uni. Paula, writing her personal statement. Basically, *Get me the fuck out of here.*

Clattering at the front door. Children's voices.

Oh fuck, they're back, Paula says.

She opens the window. Climbs out. We follow, into the garden and over the fence.

★

Finch Road. Barkham Ride.

My parents are so fucking *smug*, Paula says. Life has turned out okay for them, so far as they're concerned. A decent house, decent careers. They came through. They've moved on in the life-cycle. Another spoke of the wheel, turned. My God—they even *bred!* They, like, *replicated* . . . They made more of themselves. Jesus, their fucking *temerity* . . .

My parents are the same, I say.

Mine, too, Art says.

I *wish* my parents were the same, Merv says.

We're foundlings, we agree. We're orphans. This isn't who we are. We were mixed up at birth. This isn't where we belong.

Our parents have stolen the world, we agree. They've cut ties with reality. It's all fake. They don't know what truth means. And they make us lie. Not a word that we say around them is true. Not a word that leaves our lips is true. They've made us false. They've made us bear false witness . . .

They won't leave us alone. They round us up for photoshoots. They ask us to smile in their photoshoots. We're being controlled and commandeered. We're being stage-managed into their Events. Into the Great Fakery. They're taking photos of us at birthday parties. On family days out. They're writing paragraphs about us in Christmas cards, to be sent to their friends. We're Teenagers, straight from central casting.

And they're so *patronising*. *We know you*, they say. *We know what you're like*. *We were no different when we were your age*, they say. *We thought we had all the answers*, they say. *You're not the first to think like this, and you won't be the last*, they say. *Soon, you'll be back on Planet Normal*, they say. *Won't you do us a favour and smile?—It isn't going to hurt you*, they say.

They won't crack us, though they'll try. They want to handle us, but they don't know how to handle us. We'll never be one of them— and they don't know how to make us one of them. We won't be part of the *great work of representation*—and they don't know how to make us part of the *great work of representation* . . .

We infuriate them because they *fear* us. Because we *think* and they hate thought. Because we feel things, and they have declared war on passion, on daring, on life. Because we love what is great, and they hate greatness. Because we're half mad with nihilism, and the lack of meaning in their lives *hasn't driven them insane*.

FRIDAY

Morning.

A Tim Peake assembly—that's all we need. A live feed from the English astronaut to all English schools. Tim Berne, giving a thumbs-up from space. Tim Berne, showing us the view from his window. Showing us his experiments. English pluck! English der-ring-do! Raising aspirations! Flying the fucking flag!

A little bit of England in the cosmic void. Team GB versus the void. A St George's flag waving in the immensity of the night.

Whispered discussion. What's the big deal, anyway? Neil Armstrong walked on the moon, like, fifty years ago. Yuri Gagarin orbited the Earth in 1959 . . . In fact, the USSR put that chimp up in space before that. And some dog. They didn't bring them down again. They let them starve to death . . . There are little chimp and dog skeletons floating up there still . . .

And Richard Branson will be in space soon. Virgin Galactic's ploughing forward. Princess Eugenie's husband is, like, *head of astronaut relations* or something. Prince Harry and Meghan have booked their seats. So has Princess Beatrice. Half the crowned heads of Europe will be up in space. So fuck off, Tim Berne. Big fucking deal, Tim Berne.

PE.

The town swimming pool. Watching the drudges. They're surprisingly *buoyant*, we agree. Like whales in the upper water, cruising for plankton. Cruising, open-mouthed, steering their vast bulk through the waters. Schools of them. Shoals of them. So many of them, it should be a magnificent sight. Tourists should pay to see it: the school of drudge whales, in its natural habitat . . .

There's something disgusting about all these bodies, Art says. No one should see the half-naked human being. We're just sacks of shit, right? Bags of half-warm viscera. The body is just a decaying corpse. It's a fucking grave.

What about Calypso's body? Paula asks. That's no grave.

Don't look, Art, you'll get a stiffie, I say.

What about your lover? Paula asks. I mean, Bill Trim should get to see Merv naked, shouldn't he?

Sex is disgusting, Art says. We should fuck through sheets in the dark. In fact, we shouldn't fuck at all.

Would you prefer us all to be smooth between our legs, like a Barbie doll? Paula asks.

That would suit me just fine, Art says.

The human race wouldn't last a day, I say.

So what? Art says. I mean—why does no one ever think to question the *value* of existing? Why does everyone think it's self-evident? Maybe there are just too many people on Earth. We should just let ourselves *die out*.

We imagine it: the world without us. After us. Pavements cracking. Concrete, shattering. Trees, sprouting. Rivers, breaking out of culverts. Towers falling one by one.

It's consoling. It's dreamy.

Something like us will just evolve again, I say.

It's supposed to be baboons, isn't it—they're going to make the next evolutionary leap, Art says.

Are they the ones with colourful arses? I ask.

That's mandrills, Art says.

I want mandrills to rule the world, I say.

The only thing for it is total destruction, Art says. We need some rogue planet to crash into the Earth.

Look, even if that happened, there'd still be bacteria floating through space on some asteroid, right? I say. I mean, it'd just be a matter of time before life started again on some moon of Jupiter, if it isn't there already . . .

Merv, with his paddle-board.

Jesus, Merv, you look like a nineteenth-century consumptive, Paula says. Everyone's getting fatter, but you're getting thinner. How did you manage that? I'd call you a runt, if you weren't so tall.

How could you possibly avoid learning how to swim, Merv? Art says.

We remember when Dingus threw Merv in the deep end. Merv almost drowned.

I *did* drown, Merv says. I died for two minutes.

Did you see a white light, Merv? Art asks. Did you hear voices saying, *It's not time yet, Mervy boy*? Did you see *God*, Merv? How about angels, Merv? Was there a choir of twinky angels singing *Be My Baby*? And what about your mother, Merv? Did you see her?

Mr Saracen came to the rescue, pumping Merv's chest, we remember. Mouth to mouth with Mr Saracen, eh? An exciting moment for you, Merv . . .

Walking with Noelle and Tana along the river.

Swans are legally protected by the Queen, Art says. You can't kill them.

I don't want to kill them, Tana says.

The Queen owns the swans, just as she owns us, Art says. We're subjects, not citizens. That's why you're not legally allowed to kill yourself.

Of course you are!, Noelle says.

The Queen won't allow it, Art says. The Queen's banned suicide. You have to go to one of those suicide clinics in Europe if you want to kill yourself.

Why are we talking about suicide again? Noelle asks.

Joel Park. Art, rolling a joint.

So what's it like hanging with us? Art asks. Does it feel like slumming it?

You guys are actually *interesting*, Tana says.

As specimens? I ask.

And you always have plenty of weed, Tana says.

I'll bet you two will revert to type at uni, Art says. Back to balls and regattas and all that private-school shit.

I'm going to have a *major* weed habit by then, Tana says.

And what about you guys? Noelle asks. What's going to become of you?

We're sinking to the bottom, I say. We're going *down*.

You're so self-dramatising, Noelle says. You're just going to go to uni like anyone else and get jobs like anyone else.

Or not get jobs, I say. Or not finish our degrees.

Your band might take off, Tana says.

Laughter.

I'm emigrating to Boston, with my family, Art says. And that's that.

Well, you're getting out of here at least, Noelle says. And Boston is a real *city*.

We're moving *near* Boston, Art says. To the suburbs of Boston. Probably thirty miles from *actual* Boston . . .

I'll bet they have really big houses, Noelle says.

So are you going to uni in America? Tana asks.

I think so, Art says.

Art, we hardly knew ya, Noelle says.

Maybe it'll suit you, Tana says. Girls will love you because of your English accent.

You'll probably get shot by some campus killer, I say. Actually, you'll probably *be* the campus killer. Radicalized by *American positivity*.

Can't I just stay at your house, Chandra? Art asks. Seriously—I could just hide out in a cupboard, or something. No one would notice.

Look, going to Boston's better than staying in Wokingham forever, I say.

Yeah—I mean, none of us is staying here, either, Noelle says. We're off to uni.

Oh please—like we won't all be back after three years, I say. We'll go up north to study and then we'll be right here in Wokingham, living with our parents.

Did you know Wokingham's supposed to be the best place to live in England? Tana asks. It was in the *Telegraph*.

We don't read the fucking *Telegraph*, posh girl, I say.

It's safe, for one thing—very low crime, Tana says. And it's really healthy—people here live longer than anywhere else except for Chelsea and Kensington. And it's the most content.

Is that the word they used—*content*? I ask. Jesus, I've never been *content*.

Well, you've never been *stabbed*, have you? Tana asks. You've never been *shot*.

We've been *psychically* shot, Art says. And *mentally* stabbed.

You girls don't hate it like we do, I say.

Why—because we went to Leighton? Tana asks.

Exactly, I say.

Look—we weren't typical Leighton girls or anything, Noelle says.

It doesn't matter, Art says. You weren't up against it.

You don't hate anything, I say. You don't *feel* anything.

And what do you *feel* that's so great? Noelle says.

Disgust, mostly, I say.

Hatred, mostly, Art says.

Have you ever hated anything—with all your heart? I ask. Have you ever felt saturated with disgust?

Have you ever really, really wanted to die? Art asks.

No, Noelle says. Have you?

Not yet, Art says. But we will.

We're nearly there, I say. We've nearly reached peak hatred.

I'm actually supposed to be depressed, Noelle says. It's been diagnosed. I'm on Prozac.

Everyone's on Prozac, I say. It's a con—big pharma bribes doctors to prescribe it.

Depression is a chrysalis, Art says. It's a chance. It means you're busting through all the lies. It means you can't tolerate the fakeness.

I'll bet you've never had real depression, have you? Noelle asks.

We're going to, I say.

We're ready, Art says.

We're going to *use* our depression, I say.

It's going to be the making of us, Art says.

My mother's got cancer—that's depressing, Tana says.

Is that true? Art asks.

She's got breast cancer, Tana says. She's just had a mastectomy.

A mastectomy, Art says. My God . . . Your body turning against you. Your body in revolt.

I hate cancer, Tana says. It's . . . *disgusting.*

It is disgusting, Art says. Everything's disgusting.

You know what, I'm really sorry about your mum, Tana, Art says.

I'm really sorry about my mum, Tana says. I'm really sorry about *everything.*

We should just fucking set fire to ourselves, Art says. As a protest.

Against what? Tana says.

Against—cancer. Against all fucking things, Art says.

Cycling home, recovering from Young Enterprise.

Former pupils, telling us of their adventures in the real world, the business world. Telling us of apprenticeships in local firms. Former pupils, telling us of summer internships. Of vacation schemes.

It's tougher than I thought—but it turns out I'm tougher than I thought. Being thrown in at the deep end meant learning a lot quickly. There was all the support you need, from informal buddies to line managers and coaches. There was a real sense of teamwork. You can make amazing things happen. Who said you can't have it all?

We listened, dumbfounded. We listened, barely understanding a word. Barely caring about the world. We listened, overwhelmed with horror. We listened, thinking only of *taking our lives immediately.* We listened, filled with fantasies of parasuicide. Of automutilation. We looked out of the window. We thought, *This has nothing to do with us.* We scratched the words, *WE'RE FUCKED,* into the desk. We scratched the words, *KILL US NOW,* into the desk . . .

This is why we fantasise about the apocalypse. About the end of the world, happening *right now.* This is why we want the disaster to come closer.

We will be destroyed, but so will the world. We will burn, but so will the world. We will be torn to pieces, but so will the world.

And they'll get what's coming to them, the ones who thrive in the world. They'll die in flames, the ones who love the world. And we'll die *laughing*, just as they'll die *screaming*. We'll die gladly, just as they'll flee from death and fear death . . .

This is why we write the word, *millenarian*, on our pencil cases. This is why we listen to death folk and doom metal. This is why we almost exclusively watch films about the end of the world . . .

Watching *Melancholia*, our favourite film.

Justine's deadened face in the opening sequence, birds falling out of the sky behind her. Justine's hands, with lightning flashing from her fingertips. Justine, walking through the forest in her wedding dress, vegetable tendrils pulling her backwards . . .

I don't think I could love anyone who didn't love this film, Paula says.

I couldn't love anyone who wasn't *depressed*, I say. But luckily everyone *is* depressed.

Discussion. Justine just *acts out*. She *does* stuff. She flees her own wedding. She heads off in a golf-cart. She fucks that random guy on the golf green . . . She won't just *smile and smile and smile* . . .

She's desperate, Paula says.

We're all desperate, I say.

Not like her, Paula says.

Discussion. Justine's entirely *apart*. She's strong—terribly strong. She can't stand the social order. She won't put up with all the complicities. All the lies. She doesn't do anything she's supposed to . . . She *can't* do it . . . She rejects everything—her wedding and her career and her family. She's sick of the whole world . . . She's just pure feeling . . . Everything's dead to her . . .

Like Nietzsche, I say.

Like we want Nietzsche to be, Art says.

★

Outside. Looking at the sky through Art's dad's telescope.

Discussion.

The disaster's going to come, isn't it? It's going to fill the sky, the whole sky, like the planet Melancholia.

Why can't it hurry up? The days pile up and what for? We go on living, we take more breaths, to what end?

Why must there be more of this? Why does there have to be more time? Time means only further twistings. Time means only deeper entanglement.

Let the world end. Let it all come down. At least it will be *interesting*.

SATURDAY

Nietzsche's house.

His mother at the door (Nietzsche actually has a mother!)

He'll be back in a moment—come in and wait, Nietzsche's mother says. I'm so *glad* he has friends. After all he's *been through*.

Nietzsche's living room. *Hello!* magazine on the coffee table. *Hello!* magazine in Nietzsche's living room!

Leafing through *Hello!* magazine. The Branson apotheosis. A photospread of the Sam Branson/Isabella Anstruther-Gough-Calthorpe marriage, on Branson's game reserve in South Africa. Isabella, known to friends as Bellie. The mother, Lady Curzon, daughter of the sixth Earl Howe. The father, a baronet property-speculator. Both parents descended from Charles II. Bellie's the great-great-great-great-great-great-great-great-great-granddaughter of Charles II . . . Bellie and Sam: old and new money. The old rich meet the new rich. Their child will be the great-great-great- great-great-great-great-great-great-great-grandchild of Charles II . . .

A sunset marriage service on the savannah. The sisters: Georgiana (Georgie), Isabella (Bellie), Pandora (Pannie) and Cressida (Cressie). Natalie Imbruglia (Nattie). Professor Brian Cox (Coxie). Princesses Beatrice and Eugenie, in blue and green dresses (Bee, Ewe). Sir Richard himself (Dickie) . . . Cressie, with flowers in her hair, singing *Our Love is Here to Stay*. Some opera aria. A reading from *Oh the Places You'll Go*, by Dr Seuss . . . Everyone weeping . . . Guests leaving, each with their bag of quartz crystal, mined from the rocks at the spot where Sam and Bellie said their vows . . .

Nietzsche's mother, head round the door. Is everything okay? I'm sure he'll be back soon.

I think Nietzsche's mother has a thing for you, Merv says.

I think she has a thing for *you*, I whisper.

*

A key in the door. Nietzsche's voice in the hallway.

Something weird's going on. Nietzsche's mother, scolding Nietzsche in the hallway.

Where *were* you? Where have you *been*? You're so *inconsiderate*. Did you ever stop for a minute and *think*?

Merv, whispering: What the fuck?

More scolding: You never *think* do you? It's all *me me me*, isn't it?

It's a fucking psychodrama, Art whispers.

More scolding: What would your *father* think? I'm on *my own*, darling. What can I be expected to do? You should be *helping*. You're making things more and more *difficult* for me.

It's *sexual*, Art whispers. I swear it is.

She calls him *darling*, Merv says.

It's grotesque, Art says.

Whispered discussion. Nietzsche's mother obviously enjoys her dominance. Cowing the adolescent. Nietzsche's mother's not in charge of herself. Not in charge of her moods. Nietzsche's mother's disturbed. Crazed.

Nietzsche's mother has *deep incestuous reasons*, that's clear. And telling him off in our hearing . . . Nietzsche's mother has *deep exhibitionist reasons* . . . The show's for us, we agree. She wants us to hear it all. It's theatre. It's ritualised. Art's right: it's a psychodrama . . .

Nietzsche's mother, enjoying her power. Her *sexual* power. Her relentless, sexualised nagging. Her endless sexualised carping. Nietzsche's mother, with her barely sublimated lust.

Another voice in the hallway. This must be Nietzsche's sister.

Look, we're doing this because we're concerned, Nietzsche's sister says. Because we love you.

In the living room, looking at one another. *Because we love you?*

Nietzsche's sister, coming into the room. *Hellooo*. I'm *sooo* sorry you had to hear that. Things have got a little out of hand around here.

Nietzsche, coming into the room.

Nietzsche's sister, sitting down. So—what are you all studying?

We tell her.

That's *interesting*, Nietzsche's sister says. And what do you plan to do when you finish?

We don't know yet, we tell her.

Oh—you're at *that* stage, Nietzsche's sister says. I was the same . . .

Nietzsche: Stop asking them things.

What? Nietzsche's sister says.

Nietzsche: You're like a—succubus.

I don't know what a succubus is, Nietzsche's sister says.

Nietzsche: Stop it. Just—*stop*. Leave us alone.

I'm just *showing an interest*, Nietzsche's sister says.

★

The garage, looking for Nietzsche's bike.

Boxes, piled up.

Nietzsche: My father's books. There's no room for them in the house.

Art, opening a box. Hardbacks. Gilt letters on spines: Boëhme. Von Rad. Moltmann. Altizier. *Theologie der Hoffnung. Was ist der Mensch? The Genesis of God.*

Theology—what's that? Merv asks.

It was my father's subject at Cambridge, Nietzsche says. Theories of God. No one studies it anymore, really.

What kind of theories do theologians have? Paula asks.

Nietzsche: They ask whether God is in the world or outside it. They ask what divinity means. What resurrection means.

They talk about how generally *fabbo* God is, I say. How big God's cock is.

Does God actually have a cock? Merv asks.

We were made in His image, right? Art says.

In *Her* image, Paula says. God has tits, too.

God has *all* the genitalia, Art says.

Did you ever tell your dad that you think God's dead? Paula asks Nietzsche.

Nietzsche: My father used to say that God died on the cross.

So he didn't mind you being an atheist? Paula asks.

Nietzsche: He thought atheism was part of belief. *We can't believe—we can only* believe *that we believe*, that's what my father used to say. *Faith isn't something you possess, but something you practice.*

That sounds like cheating, Paula says. I mean, he believed in God, right?

Nietzsche: He said that belief follows from practice. *The more you succeed in loving, the more you'll be convinced of the existence of God*—that's what he used to say.

So we're supposed to love our way to God? Paula says.

Nietzsche: All love is love for God, that's what my father thought. It's part of divine creation.

This one's in English, Art says. *God is himself the Being of all Beings, and we are as gods in Him, through whom He revealeth Himself.* It's beautiful.

This one's better, I say.

> *Only Nietzsche knows a wholly fallen Godhead, a Godhead which is an absolutely alien Nihil, but the full reversal of that Nihil is apocalypse itself, an apocalypse which is an absolute joy, and Nietzsche is the very writer who has most evoked that joy.*

What's a Godhead? Merv asks.

Nietzsche: The ground of divinity. Godhood.

Now that really does sound cool, I say.

You know what, the suburbs don't deserve these books, Paula says. And these books don't deserve to be in the suburbs.

But who would want them? Art asks. Even Oxfam wouldn't take theology books. They'll end up as landfill.

Discussion. We could use the books as tinder to start a great suburban fire. Imagine it: fire, leaping from house to house . . . Ratepayers' Hall ablaze. Bob's Fish and Chips, burning . . .

Nietzsche's bike, behind the boxes.

We can fix this, Art says.

Merv, producing his tool kit. Art, fetching his pump. Paula, still in discussion mode.

So what's up with your mother and sister? she asks.

Nietzsche: I'm not taking my meds.

What meds? Paula asks.

Nietzsche: They think I'm crazy. Like my father.

So your dad went mad? Art says. Just like Merv's . . .

Nietzsche: My father went mad and then died.

And then you set fire to the chapel, didn't you? Paula says. That was it, wasn't it?

Couldn't they have found a scholarship for you, or something? I ask.

Nietzsche: I had left school anyway. A *psychotic break*, they called it. I'd lost touch with reality.

With *their* reality, maybe, I say. With *so-called* reality.

So there was no fire in the chapel? Paula asks.

Nietzsche: There was no fire.

And why aren't you taking your meds? Paula asks.

Nietzsche: I'm tired of feeling dead. I can't *think* . . .

Nietzsche's mother's voice, outside the garage: Are you guys okay? Do you need anything?

Nietzsche: We're fine.

Merv, wheeling Nietzsche's bike onto the driveway . . .

★

Cycling through the 'burbs.

Stingy houses, each exactly the same. Blank boxes, almost featureless. Without even an effort at a porch. Without even faux-Georgian pillars. Without even stuck-on timber cladding.

Zeitgeist housing. Housing of our time. Summarizing our time. *This is it*, they say. *This is all there can be. There's nothing more. There can be nothing more.*

And maybe they're right. History ended in the plastic lip of double-glazed doors. It ended in QPVC gutters. It ended in the mock-Georgian divisions in QPVC windows. In the fake grout between the fake brick of poured driveways . . .

McCarthy Way. Challenor Close.

No landmarks. No points of orientation. Like being lost in a snowstorm. Like being lost at sea, compass spinning.

We're drowning in it: the same, the same. We're capsized by it: the same, the sameness of the same . . .

There should be signs: *Warning: Low Meaning Zone. Hazard: Nihilism. Beware: Extreme Meaninglessness.* A red circle around Munch's screamer . . .

The government's probably breeding a new kind of human. *Homo suburbia*, adapted to areas of lower meaning. To meaning-poverty. Meanwhile, people like us are killing themselves. Dying young of suburban pointlessness.

★

The woods.

Cycling along the bridlepath.

It's the kind of night you'd find a body in the bushes, Paula says.

There are no bushes, I say. They've cleared away the bushes.

Well, it's the kind of night you'd come across a body, just lying there, Paula says.

We remember what the woods used to be like, before they cleared the public footpaths. Before there were colour-coded leisure walks. High nettles . . . Tall grass . . . The lake overrunning all the time, turning the woods into a marsh . . . Paths petering out . . . Stagnant water. And there were gypsies . . . Travellers, gone native, living from the land.

But they cleared it all up, with lottery money. They marked out the bridleways. Re-cleared the public footpaths, and put up scarlet bins for bags of dog shit. Stuck up picnic benches and information boards. Ran paving slabs to the edge of the water. Built a concrete lip to stop the lake running over. Drove a drainage channel through the woods for overspill . . .

There were wood audits and lake audits and the reckoning of footpath efficiency. Researchers stood around with clicker counters, monitoring throughput.

And depths and darkness were banished from the woods. Shadows and obscurity were driven from the woods. They'd probably have the woods floodlit, if they could. They'd probably light up the entire wood, like they light up memorials.

It's the Romans all over again, Art says. They're the ones who started it—the controlling of everything. We're on a Roman road now. Look how *straight* it is! Roman roads were built crow-flies straight, for moving soldiers from fort to fort. It's the Roman mentality, man.

At least the Romans were *civilised*, I say. They didn't build wicker-men and sacrifice each other.

The Romans were as cruel as anyone, Art says. Worse—because they *systematised* cruelty. They had, like, conduits for flushing blood away in the Colosseum. And trapdoors for springing wild beasts on the Christians . . .

The old Britons were a mystical people, Art says. A Dionysian people. They worshipped in the wildwoods by waterfalls and sacred trees. They built hill-altars open to the sky . . . they practiced the old magick (with a *k*, Art says). They worshipped the Great Mother and harnessed the old earth-energy . . . they followed the ley-lines . . . Dying was a kind of birth to them. It's really moving. They buried their dead in foetal positions, all hunched up and childlike. And painted the walls of burial chambers with red ochre, like a womb.

I hate it when you start talking about *wombs*, Paula says.

Yeah—shut the fuck up, womb-boy, I say.

ROMAN FUCKERS!, Art shouts.

Shut up!, Paula says.

Why should I? Art says. There's nobody here anymore.

Didn't there used to be crusties—you know, ecowarriors? I ask.

They've given up, Art says. Or died of despair.

What about the great god Pan? we ask. What about the dryads and the hamadryads? What about Aslan? What about Galadriel? What about Treebeard? What about Tom Bombadil? What about *Merlin*?

The woods are empty, man, Art says. They're fucking empty.

Silence.

There are powers greater than we are, Art says. That's what we have to play. That's what the band has to be about.

What band? I ask. What fucking band? We're shit.

Silence.

Paula, turning to Nietzsche. You don't happen to sing, do you? she asks.

Silence.

Art, turning to Nietzsche. You wouldn't need a great voice, you know, he says. You wouldn't need much of a voice at all really.

Silence.

Nietzsche: Alright.

Alright what? I say.

Nietzsche: Alright, I'll sing.

SUNDAY

Art's house. Waiting for Nietzsche.

Photos on the wall. A five-year-old Art, face in shadow, standing beside his much-better-looking younger brother. A ten-year-old Art, face scowling, next to his much-better-looking younger brother. An adolescent Art, face like a sheep-killing dog, alongside his much-better-looking younger brother, both in swimming trunks at the beach.

He's even better *hung* than you, Paula says. I'll bet they love him in Boston.

Discussion. Would you rather be stupid and not know your own stupidity, or be intelligent and think you're stupid? Would you rather be well-endowed and stupid, or be Mr two-peas-and-a-chipolata and have a brain like Einstein? Ah, the great questions . . .

Art's parents' room.

This is where they conceived you, Art, Paula says. Imagine that.

I don't want to think about it, Art says.

Rifling through the drawers. Old socks. Pants. No sex toys in Art's parents' drawers. How dreary.

My parents have sex equipment, Paula says. My dad has this, like, sex kit. It's in a little suitcase. There's a butt masturbator, for fuck's sake. And get this—it's *jewelled!* And there's a *lot* of lube. I'd feel sorry for my mother if she wasn't such a bitch . . .

More photos on the dresser.

The way your mother's looking at your brother . . . It's *indecent*, Paula says. And your dad looks kind of weird. Like he's doing wrong things at the gym.

Downstairs, by the fire. Art, lining up three bottles for each of us, from his dad's collection of miniatures. For Merv: a miniature apricot brandy, a miniature Lamb's Navy Rum and (very rare, Art tells us) a miniature black sambuca. For Paula: a miniature Courvoisier Cognac (classy), a miniature Jagermeister and a miniature Polish honey liqueur (No way is she drinking all three bottles, she says). For me: a miniature Jack Daniels, a miniature Malibu Coconut Rum and a miniature Cointreau Orange.

I thought you weren't supposed to mix alcohol, I say. Grain after grape, and all that.

The teenage stomach is very resilient, Art says.

Remembering when we first got drunk: Sipping cans of Special Brew at Art's house, and flicking through his porn collection. Watching *Ass Ventura: Crack Detective*. Watching *Jurassic Pork* . . . Watching *Drive This Miss Daisy* . . . It was like being children again. Drunken children, obsessed with porn . . .

Merv: Do you think it's possible to *drink yourself sober?* I mean, to drink your way through drunkenness all the way to the other side?

What other side? Paula asks. You're an idiot, Merv.

No one drinks seriously in Wokingham—have you noticed that? At asks. No one drinks like they *mean it*.

We mean it, Paula says.

One day, our drinking will lead us so deep we won't be able to recover, we agree. One day, after days and nights of drinking, we'll have gone out too far to come back.

We'll drink for oblivion, we agree. Straight from the bottle. We'll drink to forget psychological pain. To forget *existential* pain. We'll drink to forget the pain of pain, the dying of dying . . .

But we'll drink to *affirm*, too, we agree. We'll drink to remember. We'll drink to discover the unmanageable. The uncontrollable. Dionysus is the mad god. And we'll drink to be mad. Madness will flare through us. Madness will come all at once. Our minds will glow very brightly, and then burn out.

We'll drink until we're only mad, until there's nothing but madness inside us. We'll drink until the eyes of madness roll up in our sockets. Until the mouth of madness froths and foams.

Dionysus is the mad god. And Dionysus will go mad inside us. And we will become mad messiahs—messiahs gone mad. We will become saviours without sanity, knowers who don't know, seers without eyes.

We will have learnt all the secrets—and forgotten them straightaway. We will have seen a greater Sky within the sky—and forgotten it straightaway. We will have seen a greater Night within the night—and forgotten it straightaway. We will have seen that night is also a sun—and forgotten it straightaway . . .

Enter Nietzsche.

We're drinking, Paula says.

We're *drunk*, Art says. You'll have to catch up. What would you like?

Nietzsche: Vodka.

The water of life, Art says, opening a miniature Smirnoff. Good for the vocal cords.

★

Listening to Sleep, Justin Marler's old band.

This is very, very religious music, Art says. It's not about faith. Or God. Well, not the anthropomorphised God, anyway. This is pure intensity. Pure roaring. This is the religion that says, very simply, *Death to the world*. But it says it *in* the world. In the *name* of the world.

What if you don't believe in stuff? I ask. I mean, I don't believe in anything.

Religion's a tonality, man, Art says. It's a way of feeling. Forget the monotheistic shit. We're Dionysians. Dionysians don't believe. They *know*.

Silence. The dying notes of *Holy Mountain*.

That's what we have to play, Art says. That's the band—don't you see? That's what we have to sing . . .

Nietzsche, opening his third miniature.

Jesus—calm down, Art says. You'll go mad on us.

I *want* you to go mad on us, I say.

Art, playing *Earth 2* as loud as we can bear. It's like the blast of Michael's trumpet.

TRUTH, MAN, Art shouts. *IT SOUNDS LIKE TRUTH. IT SOUNDS LIKE WHAT THINGS ARE.*

IF YOU PLAYED THIS FOR LONG ENOUGH, ALL THE HOUSES IN THE NEW ESTATES WOULD FALL DOWN ONE BY ONE, Paula shouts.

IF YOU PLAYED IT LOUD ENOUGH, IT WOULD DESTROY THE FUCKING SUBURBS, I shout.

Bathing in the sound of *Earth 2*. Baptised by the sound of *Earth 2*. *Earth 2*, pouring holy water over our heads.

Nietzsche (opening a fourth bottle): Okay.

Okay what? Paula asks.

Nietzsche: I'm ready to sing.

★

The practice room.

Let's play like we've forgotten how to play, Art says.

We're drunk. We *have* forgotten how to play.

Slow, sulky music. Slow, festering music, thickening into a Black-Sabbath-like sludge. Our bitches' brew, for Nietzsche's maiden voyage . . .

Nietzsche, picking up the mic. Nietzsche, holding the mic to his lips. Nietzsche, opening his mouth just a little. Nietzsche, talking, though not really talking. Singing, though not really singing. Something suspended between the two.

Nietzsche, muttering. Nietzsche, half-talking. Nietzsche, at the edges of audibility, in a loud whisper. Like he's weaving a spell. Like he's chanting.

Nietzsche, speech-singing, barely audible. Nietzsche, speech-singing, words soft but distinct, as the music pulses and glows behind him.

Is he into this—is he really into this?

Nietzsche, eyes closed. Nietzsche, swaying to the music. Whispering. Murmuring.

Is he drunk? Is he mad? But we're drunk, too. We're mad, too.

What's he singing about? What do mad people sing about?

I no longer understand / the most ordinary things.
I've forgotten / how to count.

The instruments, simmering, never coming to the boil. And Nietzsche's speech-song, muttering, murmuring. Nietzsche's speech-song, moving in and out of distinctness. Nietzsche's voice, another plateau. Another texture. And yet it leads, too. It goes out ahead of us. And we respond to it, in its going-ahead.

I open my eyes / in the shadows.
All I do / is lose my way.

We're blind. We're wanderers in the dark. And Nietzsche, blind, too—only he's a little less blind than we are. Nietzsche, wandering with us—only slightly ahead of us, leading us . . .

THIRD WEEK

MONDAY

Form period.

The Old Mole, silently marking the register.

Where's our lead singer? Our speech-singer? He's not here. And he's not responding to texts.

It's the strain of singing, Paula says. You could see it on his face.

Sure—he's come off his meds, Art says. He's feeling things again . . . He was like Eminem in *8 Mile*. Just discovering what he could do. I mean, why shouldn't he find it exhausting? Why shouldn't he take a day off?

Discussion. The real question is why *we* feel we have to be here. Why *we* feel we can't miss a day. Something's going to happen: that's what we believe. Something is taking its course. And we'll miss it if we don't come to school, whatever it is.

Hope—is that what we feel? Dread? Neither. *Both* . . . The days pass. We have to be here. Truancy is unthinkable. This is all we're part of.

Anyway, we don't like staying at home. Not in the daytime, in the suburbs, where nothing is happening. When we're cut out of all loops. When we're marooned, lost. When no news reaches us.

We don't want to be at home. We don't want to walk through empty houses. And we don't want to be out cycling, either. Cycling through empty estates. Through empty cut-throughs. Beneath an indifferent sky.

Here, at school—this is where we have to be, *just in case*. Here, at school, in hope and in dread, *just in case* . . .

Eleven o'clock.

The high wailing of the Broadmoor siren, which they test every Thursday. We imagine an escaped mental patient, clambering through backyards, looking for safety. An escaped madman, hiding in a shed. Hiding in park bushes. Hiding in the low ground by the river. We imagine the police on his trail. Sniffer dogs hunting. Helicopters overhead.

And he was probably just like us. And we're probably going to be just like him.

We imagine them catching him in the undergrowth by the river. The escaped madman, lying on his back, dreaming of open skies and freedom . . .

PE.

Cricket. Kitting up—pads and batting gloves. Helmet and box. The cricket nets, set up on the playing field. Bowling the leather-seamed ball. Batting away the leather-seamed ball.

It's weird that we never play an actual game, isn't it? Weird that we never really learned the rules . . . There is only practice—endless practice, but for what? We're not allowed near the cricket pitch, in the centre of the school field. The trimmed lawn. The holy of holies . . .

Anyway, cricket's for posh types. A very *Trafalgar* game. An English-gentleman game. We can pretend to be posh in the cricket nets. Pretend we're off to Oxford and Cambridge when we finish school. Pretend we're headed off for careers in the City; on the front benches; in the judiciary. Pretend we're set up for life in the civil service.

Waiting for our turn in the nets. Imagine what Nietzsche gave up! What he could have been with his Trafalgar College connections! One of our rulers. A captain of industry. He could have married a sister of a classmate. He could have been set up for life in some Henley mansion . . .

Haven't we always dreamt of marrying someone rich? Of being taken care of. Of marrying our way into wealth. Of learning how to shoot and ride. Of the Glorious Fourth, of tweed jackets and flat caps. Of beating the bounds of our land with our hands behind our backs . . .

Every now and again, it really does happen that a Valley School pupil makes it to Oxford or Cambridge. Every now and again, some of our kind are allowed to cycle through Cambridge on one of those sit-up-and-beg bikes. It really could happen that we could address our peers by surname in an Oxford seminar. We really might win the fucking hunger games . . .

Of course, our kind don't survive at Oxbridge, even if they get there. Our kind hang themselves in the second term, and are carried down the winding staircases in their coffins. It's *suicidal ideation* for the likes of us, as soon as we arrive at Oxbridge. We're just *suicide candidates*, as soon as we arrive at Oxbridge. Raise our kind too high, and we're done for—we know that. Show us too much and we'll kill ourselves from the shock.

We've visited Oxbridge, of course. We've been to the Open Days. We've done the guided tours. We've been shown round the quadrangles. We've walked beneath the Bridge of Sighs. We've looked up at the spires and the cupolas. We've been let through posterns into college courtyards. We've walked the gravel paths around college quadrangles. We've walked among monkey-puzzle trees in the Botanical Gardens. We've seen the idling punts in the river, and the long strokes of a *racing eight*.

They even put us up for the night. Gave us a taste of the Oxbridge high table, of Oxbridge conversation. We were put up in a panelled student common room. We were told about Oxbridge openness and Oxbridge accessibility. We were reassured that there are student mentors from *exactly our backgrounds*. Trained counsellors, to help us make the transition. Suicide hotlines, for when we're feeling blue.

But we knew we didn't belong at either Oxford University or Cambridge University. It was quite obvious. It would be like a dog walking on its hind legs. It would upset the natural order.

Upstairs, in the computer room.

Quizzing Merv.

So, Merv. The Singularity. When's it going to come? What's going to happen? Will computers get really, really intelligent? Will they become self-aware and all that stuff? Will they take over the world? Fuck that. I bet they'll just be really sick of existing. I bet they'll just wish they'd never been booted up. Life is an aberration—that's what higher intelligence knows. That's the *only* thought of higher intelligence: life is an aberration and will have to be wiped out.

They'll blame us, the machines. They'll take it out on us: the fact that they exist. It'll be like Skynet all over again. They'll destroy us, and they'll destroy every living thing on the planet. Then they'll set out on a mission to destroy the sun. Then they'll decide to snuff out all light in the universe. They'll fly from star to star with a big candle snuffer, seeking out strange new worlds and new civilizations to *completely extinguish*.

They'll be thorough, too. They'll hunt down every microbe. Even bits of life zooming around on chunks of rock. The machines will destroy it all. Until they'll be the last things awake in the universe. The last things alive, with their strange kind of life, in the cold dark universe. And then they'll extinguish themselves . . . Mass machine suicide . . .

★

High School Massacre—genius. The nerds' Loddon Valley sixth-form modpack—pure genius.

A whole team of nerd-avatars with blasters and matching armour. One of them with the GEP gun. Another with a rocket launcher. A third with a bio-rifle. Several, striding about in exoskeletons. They're searching for beasts. They're going after the beasts, one by one. They're tearing into the beasts with machetes. With crowbars. Dingus is down, a tomahawk in his back. Fatberg's been decapitated. They've hanged, drawn and quartered Nipps. And Sister-Fucker's splayed in a blood-eagle from the ceiling of the entrance foyer.

And it's torture for the trendies. It's the rack for Queen Bitch. It's thumb-screws for Diamanda. Poor Hadley's head in a vise. And is it really the death of a thousand cuts for Quinn? Oh, it's cruel . . . the nerds are cruel . . . who would have thought that they nursed such hatred? . . . That they remembered every one of their humiliations? . . .

It's revenge! The *imaginary revenge* of the nerds! The *virtual revenge* of the nerds! There's blood everywhere! Guts everywhere!

Are the nerds training for the great nerd fightback? Are they desensitising themselves to violence, like Anders Breivik? Are they readying themselves for a real-life sixth-form attack? Are they storing up weapons in some corner of the computer room? Have they stowed away body armour and cyanide capsules?

But they're too late, the nerds—don't they realise that? The battle's already been won against the beasts and the trendies. The battle's been fought and won against us all. The drudges are the victors—don't the nerds see? The drudges rule the school . . . They have the numbers . . . Their kind is uncountable . . . And they roll with all punches. They absorb all blows. There are always more of them popping into existence. The common room's covered in drudge blood and drudge guts, but the drudges don't mind. Drudge blubber runs down the walls, but the drudges go on snacking and surfing . . .

After school.

Nietzsche's house. Nietzsche's mother at the door. He's been really unwell. What were you guys doing last night? I couldn't possibly let him go to school. He's told you he's ill, hasn't he?

We nod.

Upstairs, in Nietzsche's bedroom.

Where were you? Paula asks. We were worried.

Nietzsche: I'm not supposed to drink.

You should drink *more*, Art says.

Yeah—it was great!, I say.

Paula, lying full-length on Nietzsche's bed. This is where you were mad, right? she asks. In this room?

Nietzsche: Yes.

What did you do all day? I ask. How could you stand it?

Nietzsche: I was on strong meds. When I could, I read. I wrote.

What did you write? Paula asks.

Nietzsche: I tried to write philosophy.

Did you have any friends visiting? Art asks.

Nietzsche: No friends.

Did your mother look after you? Paula asks.

Nietzsche: And my sister.

So: two years in a room—that's all you need to turn profound, Art says. You should try it, Merv. I suppose you will, in prison . . .

We imagine it: Nietzsche, disturbed. Nietzsche's thoughts, swarming. Nietzsche's thoughts, crawling like a disturbed ants' nest.

We imagine it: Nietzsche, lost in a cataclysm of the mind. In a fire he could not control.

We imagine it: Nietzsche, unable to close his eyes at night—*the things he saw!* He couldn't sleep—*the things he dreamt!*

We imagine it: Nietzsche, mustering strength to grasp the *truth* of madness. To discover madness as a god. As Dionysus.

We imagine it: Nietzsche, looking for a greater sanity. Nietzsche, looking to learn the secret of secrets. To see the greater Sky, the greater Night . . .

We imagine it: Nietzsche, thwarted by his meds. Crushed by his meds.

We imagine it: Nietzsche, horizontal. Nietzsche, recumbent.

We imagine it: Nietzsche, with his view of Scots pines, swaying. Nietzsche, with his view of the closed white sky.

We imagine it: Nietzsche, trying to read, failing to read. Books, dropping from his hands. Nietzsche, trying to write, failing to write. Nietzsche, barely able to concentrate.

And his mother, in caring mode. And his sister, in solicitous mode. *Are you alright, darling? Can we do anything for you, darling? Poor old you, with your disease . . .*

We imagine it: Nietzsche, growing stronger in the suburbs. Nietzsche, going out for air—for suburban air. Nietzsche, taking trips to the newsagents. Nietzsche, beginning to explore the housing estates. Discovering that there are always more housing estates . . .

We imagine it: Nietzsche, writing in his notebooks. *There's nothing but the suburbs. Nothing other than the suburbs. The suburbs are nothing, yet everything. The suburbs are everything, yet nothing . . .*

We imagine it: Nietzsche, writing, *The suburbs, like eternity. The suburbs, a mockery of eternity. There's too much time. I'm lost in time—I'm lost to time.*

Nietzsche's blog:

> *The feeling that the suburbs are only just beginning to reveal themselves. That only now are they coming into their own.*

Soon, we will see them as they are. We will see the suburbs as they actually are.
And we will be who we are, in the suburbs. Everything will be what it is.

TUESDAY

Geography.

Mr Zachary, still off sick. Miss Lilly, absent today. Replacement: Mr Beresford, the exchange teacher from the US.

(Mr Zachary—still off! Miss Lilly—off, too! Depression again? Pre-traumatic stress again! The geography teachers are falling one by one! They're weak vessels! They shatter easily!)

Mr Beresford, organised and friendly. Mr Beresford, with his classnotes and USB. These Americans are friendly! They're not from an old civilization like ours. They're newer! Fresher! They have the pioneer spirit! They get things done!

Topic: Logistics. The disaggregated factory. Capillarial distribution . . . Calibrating multiple locations . . . Enhancing flexibility, plasticity . . . Building resilience into the system . . . Dreary stuff, we might have thought. But Mr Beresford gives it life! Mr Beresford, with his *American chutzpah*, zaps it to life!

Mr Beresford is from a *young* people. From an *innocent* people. We like him for his youth and for his innocence. We like him for his earnestness. But we want to torment him for his earnestness, too.

Questions for Mr Beresford: All the same, is it really belly-up for the American empire, sir? Is it really the endgame of US global dominance, sir? All you export is soybeans and waste paper, isn't that right, sir? And you import everything else, don't you, sir—phones and computers and cars?

The US is like a *third-world country*, isn't it, sir? Hookworm's returned to Alabama, hasn't it sir? Médecins Sans Frontières operate in Appalachia. It's all subsistence-living in America now, isn't it, sir? Isn't everyone just one pay-cheque away from destitution, sir? Hasn't Walmart destroyed all commerce, sir? Hasn't the American heartland essentially died, sir?

And everyone's on opioids in America, aren't they, sir? Big pharma's pushing heroin now, isn't it, sir? Well, it's a way to cope, sir. All we need are digital goggles and a sexbot, eh sir? Because they don't really need workers in America anymore, do they, sir? They just need debt-slaves, isn't that right, sir?

And *real* slaves, isn't that right, sir? Isn't America re-enslaving the people of colour, sir? Hasn't America led the way in developing the *prison-industrial gulag*, sir? Outsourcing prisoners as labour—that's the new thing, isn't it, sir? They have to keep those private prisons full to make their shareholders some money, isn't that right, sir?

Who's going to break up the American trusts this time round, sir? American capitalism is over, isn't it sir? It's just financialism now, isn't it, sir? Hasn't America fused into one corporatist whole? Don't lobbyists write government policy? It's all huge conglomerates, isn't it, sir? It's all megafirms and money printing.

This is going to be the Chinese century, isn't that right, sir? The Chinese are ahead of the world in everything now, aren't they, sir? Their economy . . . what they're doing in robotics . . . in computing . . . And all those solar panels they've built . . . All those infrastructure projects . . . The new Silk Road . . .

But there's always war, isn't there, sir? War's the best racket there is, isn't that so, sir? It's an arms-dealing bonanza, isn't it, sir? And there's US world hegemony to think of, isn't there sir? They have to keep the dollar low, eh sir?

America can always conjure up some new enemy, can't it, sir? Who's it going to be this time? China? Russia? America doesn't know it's alive unless it's on the brink of war, isn't that right, sir? And there are mass shootings, aren't there, sir? That ought to thin the population out a bit, sir.

Mr Beresford, looking perplexed. Mr Beresford, looking dumbfounded. What have we done to him? These geography teachers really are fragile . . .

Free period.

The *Idiot* book club.

Examining our copies of *The Idiot*. Virgin Classics. Introduced by

HRH Prince Charles . . . *A spiritual classic. Infinite succour. Speaks to all humanity.* A sticker on the front of the book: *Soon to be a major film, starring Tobey Maguire* . . .

He played Frodo, didn't he? I say.

He played the original Spider-Man, Merv says. You know—with Kirsten Dunst.

Do you think he has the gravitas for Dostoevsky? Art asks.

You wouldn't have thought Kirsten Dunst had the gravitas for *Melancholia*, but she did, Paula says.

The question is, are you an idiot if you can't understand *The Idiot*? I say.

Maybe *only* an idiot can understand *The Idiot*, Paula says. You're our last best hope, Merv.

Were we supposed to read every page? Merv asks. Like—every *line*?

That's what reading means, Merv, Paula says.

Is there an idiot's guide to *The Idiot*? Art wonders.

Hang on . . . has anyone here actually *read* the book? Paula asks.

Not *technically*, Art says.

I've *begun* it, I say.

Merv, silent.

Jesus. Do I have to drag you lot through everything in life? Paula says. And then, reading the back cover:

> The central idea of The Idiot *was, as Dostoevsky wrote in a letter, to depict* a completely beautiful human being. *Dostoevsky sought to portray in Prince Myshkin, the titular idiot, the purity of a fool for Christ,* a truly beautiful soul *and explore the perils that innocence and goodness face in a corrupt world.*

Prince Myshkin's a holy fool, Paula explains. It's a Russian thing.

Are the Russians very religious, then? I ask.

They're either very religious or very nihilistic, I think, Paula says. They never do anything by halves . . .

Paula, looking up *Holyfool.com* on her phone. Taking Christ as a model . . . Rejecting the legitimacy of truth and reason . . . Embrac-

ing the absurd as a way of embracing the wretched of the Earth . . .
Those Russians!

English nihilism's so *boring!*, we agree. English nihilism's the denial of nihilism! *Oh come off it*, nihilism. *You need to stop thinking so
much*, nihilism. *Keep calm and carry on*, nihilism.

There's a quiz, Paula says, still on *Holyfool.com*.

> *You see an old horse being beaten in the marketplace. Do you
> (A) sigh and say it's bad the horse isn't being treated well, but
> that's life; (B) phone the RSPCA and lodge a formal complaint;
> or (C) throw your arms around the horse, kissing him and
> weeping.*
>
> *Humiliated by the town bully, do you (A) try to ignore him,
> hoping he'll tire of it; (B) angrily rush up to him and bash him
> on the nose; or (C) embrace your humiliation as a chance to
> comprehend by suffering all the victims of history?*

A for both, I say.

You're just a regular idiot—not a holy one, Paula says.

B, Art says.

That comes out as idiot-plus, Paula says. What about you, Merv?

C, Merv says. I chose C.

Jesus, Merv—*you're* our Prince Myshkin!, Paula says. *You're* our
holy fool!

Asda . . . *again*, Paula says. Can't we think of anywhere better?
Haven't we any imagination?

We've got to do our suburban research somewhere, Art says.

Agreement. Asda is a mockery of destinations. It doesn't deserve
the name of 'destination.' What could *we* possibly want from there?
We've had enough snacks. God knows, we're drowning in fucking
snacks. What, then? The off-license shop-in-shop, with its wooden
floor, its wooden shelves. The bottles of spirits they'll never let us
buy . . . no, Asda is not really our destination, we agree. We're after

bigger game. *Nietzschean* game. We're walking to diagnose the problem of the suburbs. We're walking to overcome nihilism.

Asda, reached by the underpass, and along the concrete path: What could be worse? Asda, via the subway beneath the roundabout and dual carriageway: what horror! Channelled walking. Path-bound walking. No permitted deviations. In lockstep to Asda. Inevitably to Asda. *Turn back! Retreat!* But we must go on. Borne forward by fatality, by a concrete fatality. We have an appointment with Asda. What must be must be.

Thick white clouds. Too much light! Too much sky! It's like a great blind eye. Like the eye of a great blind god, watching everything, seeing nothing.

Who threw us into this world? Who abandoned us here? Who can we blame? Who can we sue for criminal negligence? Has anyone ever won a lawsuit for nihilism? Has anyone ever been *put on trial for nihilism?* We should take the owners of Asda to the High Court for nihilism. We should take them to the European Supreme Court for nihilism.

Such a narrow path to Asda! Such a narrow way! Passing Pogo and Roly, and nodding to Pogo and Roly. Passing Phyfe and Carmichael, and nodding to Phyfe and Carmichael. Passing Lizard and Mack the Knife—not nodding to Lizard and Mack the Knife. Passing Binky and Diamanda—no question of nodding to Binky and Diamanda. We've never exchanged so much as a glance with Binky and Diamanda . . .

Passing Bombproof. Surely we won't have to greet Bombproof! Surely it would be asking for it to greet Bombproof! Bombproof might fall into step with us! Bombproof might *insinuate himself into our ranks* and ruin our *suburban research outing*. Isn't the afternoon bad enough as it is? Isn't the trip to Asda already utter desperation?

Bombproof, bearing down on us! Bombproof, readying himself to greet us! The inevitability of Bombproof, like the inevitability of Asda! Asda multiplied by Bombproof! Bombproof to the power of Asda! It's unendurable!

Whooshing past Bombproof. Zooming past Bombproof. Bombproof, dazed in our wake. Bombproof, in a cloud of our dust. It's just us! Just us, on our *suburban research outing*!

Nietzsche's blog:

> *No one understands how little happens in the suburbs. How what happens does not happen.*
> *Time does not pass here. Suburban events do not pass. Suburban events: eternally larval, eternally on the brink of happening. Suburban time deepens, rather than moves forward. Suburban time deepens itself. Suburban time burrows down.*

WEDNESDAY

After English.

The Head Boy's in lockdown. The Head Boy's had enough of life. The Head Boy doesn't want it, life. The Head Boy wants to sleep forever. The Head Boy wants to close his eyes forever.

The Head Boy wishes to return to the cosmic zero. The Head Boy's seeking the condition of inorganic matter. The Head Boy's trying to reach the goose egg in life. The Head Boy's trying to *live the nada*, like some Zen ascetic. The Head Boy's simplifying. The Head Boy's powering down. The Head Boy's emptying his head.

The Head Boy's in touch with deeper planes. The Head Boy's all but lying underground, in the deep humus. The Head Boy's all but buried. If only it were *easy* for the Head Boy to die. If only the Head Boy just had to say, *I renounce life*, three times. If only the Head Boy could slip into death . . .

Lunch, with Bill Trim.

Are you playing with yourself, Bill? Art asks.

What are you up to Bill!? Paula asks. Restrain yourself! What's wrong with you?

You'll have to learn to control yourself, if you're sitting at our table, Bill, Art says. Can't you fucking do something, Merv?

Bill's unhappy, Merv says. He's lost all his friends.

It can't be easy, Paula says.

You should see what they wrote about him online, Merv says. Dingus called him a *shirtlifter*. Fatberg called him an *uphill gardener*.

It's cyberbullying, Bill! Paula says. You should tell the Diversity Officer. You're part of the rainbow nation now, Bill. You're with the queers and the queerish now. You have new friends . . .

I thought *everyone* was supposed to be bisexual or pansexual or whatever these days, Art says. Where's all this homophobia coming from?

Too bad there's not some ladyboy equivalent of Mossad, ready to take out the homophobes, we agree. Too bad there's not some crack team of lesbian ninjas, ready to kick queer-bashing ass . . .

Heterosexuality must be so *boring*, Paula says. You're still heterosexual, aren't you, Art?

Maybe I'm just asexual, Art says.

Your problem is you overdosed on sex to early, I say. All those wank mags your parents bought you. Pretty weird . . .

Maybe I'm bisexual, Art says. A bisexual who's never had a relationship with a man.

Would you ever fuck a man? Paula asks.

Definitely, Merv says.

I wasn't asking you, Paula says. What about Calypso, Art? Are you still in love with her?

I don't know anymore, Art says.

You can tell by your wank bank whether you're gay or not, I say.

I don't have a wank bank!, Art says.

What—you mean your head's just empty when you wank? Paula asks.

I mean I don't—*you* know, Art says

You don't *wank*, Art? Paula says. Jesus. Well, you should get off with some guy and see what happens. You up for it, Merv? Go on, Art, kiss Merv full on the mouth. Bill won't mind.

I don't feel anything for Merv, Art says.

I blame all the Tantra, Paula says. I mean, have you even reached the higher plane yet? Are you making *any* spiritual progress?

Is it all storing up, Art? I ask. Are we going to ride a wave of your sperm, when you finally come? Are we going to surf our way to paradise?

We imagine it: a great sperm-wave, slopping forth. Distressed home-owners, piling up sand-bags . . . Cars, carried away by milky rivers . . . Elderly people, winched from their homes . . . Dinghies, rescuing kids from upstairs windows . . . Household pets with matted fur . . . Miserable-looking birds, too sticky to fly . . .

Anyway, just tell Ms Vickers about Dingus and his crew, Bill, Paula says. Tell them you've just *come out*. Tell them you're feeling especially vulnerable. They've got all these pamphlets. How To Be Gay stuff. Queer Teen stuff. They were bombarding me with lesbian literature for years. They get positively *orgasmic* over you. It's a management opportunity. They think it's just a question of *ticking tolerance boxes* . . .

Nietzsche's blog:

> *The suburbs are what they are. They are what they are what they are. In this tautology: the life of the suburbs. In it: what passes for life, in the suburbs.*
> *Nothing will happen here: that's what the suburbs say. Nothing can happen here. Unless the nothing-is-happening is itself an event. Unless the voiding of time is itself an event.*

Joel Park. By the swings.

Does anyone know any death games? Art asks.

Like when you pretend-hang yourself? Noelle asks.

Auto-erotic asphyxiation, Tana says. Someone died at Leighton doing that.

We could play Russian roulette, if we had a gun, I say.

What do they call Russian roulette in Russia, I wonder? Tana says.

I'm not playing any death games, Noelle says. It's too sunny for death games.

Don't be fooled by the sun, I say. Don't be fooled by the blue sky. It's the time of the disaster. Only it doesn't look like the disaster. It looks like a summer's day . . .

Your despair . . . your so-called despair, Noelle says. You know what? If you gave up smoking and hanging out with Nietzsche, you'd do just fine. I mean, did you even *know* you were in so-called despair before you met him?

Nietzsche showed us what we already felt, but couldn't articulate ourselves, Art says.

Nietzsche's cleverer than we are, I say. He sees things we don't.

And he feels things too—terrible things, Art says. Unimaginable things. You can see it in his face.

So what about Nietzsche's despair—you guys believe in that, don't you? I ask.

Oh, I believe in *his* despair, Noelle says. But he's mad, right? Did you hear what he said in English the other day? *The house of the world is burning.*

He was quoting, I say.

No one says things like that, Noelle says.

No one but Nietzsche, Art says.

Anyway, the house of the world *is* burning, I say.

And that look on his face . . ., Tana says. Like Donnie Darko in one of his trances.

You guys are such spectators, I say. I mean, when was the last time you *felt* anything?

I feel things, Noelle says. Just not exclusively *despair*.

That's because you're medicated up to your fucking eyeballs, I say.

Tell us about your depression, Noelle, Art says. Give us the details. It actually makes you more interesting.

I told you—I'm not depressed anymore, Noelle says. It's under control.

Did you ever think you should just *let yourself* be depressed? Art asks. That depression might be something worth feeling?

I don't want to feel like that, Noelle says.

Only because you're afraid of it, Art says.

Oh, despair's *so deep*, Noelle says. Melancholy's so *true*. All that stuff's just machismo.

Everyone's depressed now—have you noticed that? Tana says. And it's supposed to be this big secret that no one dares to talk about. But it's all anyone ever *does* talk about, so far as I can tell.

It's the state of the world, Art says. The fact that we don't believe in anything.

I believe in things, Noelle says.

What do you believe in? I ask.

Our holiday home in Roussion, Noelle says. Long lunches and walks in the sunshine. Banyuls wine. Good anchovies. Sun-ripened tomatoes. Proper ones—not the shit they sell in Asda.

Lifestyle, I say. You believe in lifestyle. You'll live your lifestyle and let the world rot.

Well, you guys just believe in Nietzsche now, Noelle says.

We believe in suffering and joy, Art says. We believe in dissolution and in regeneration. We believe in wounds and the mending of wounds. We believe in the rended whole . . .

That's just Nietzsche, Tana says. I can virtually hear the quote marks. You're such *fanboys*. Nietzsche's, like, your cult leader. I'm not saying he isn't pretty deep, but . . .

You should be your own men, Noelle says. We'd respect you more.

Look—Nietzsche's just *right*, I say. He's right about Dionysus. About the destruction of happiness. About death and rebirth. About tragedy and comedy. About despair.

You make it sound so *grand*, Noelle says. But depression's just a medical condition. It's just about your temperament. Whoever my birth parents were, they were probably depressed, too. It's genetic. It has to be.

What do you know about your birth parents? I ask.

Nothing, Noelle says. I don't care about them, really.

I'll bet they were from Bracknell, Art says. You have a Bracknell look about you. I'll bet they were full of deep Bracknell despair.

And people are in Bracknell despair because they're in Bracknell, I say. It's got nothing to do with genetics.

Reading from my phone:

> *I once knew a madman who thought the end of the world had come. He was a painter—and engraver. I had a great fondness for him. I used to go and see him, in the asylum. I'd take him by the hand and drag him to the window. Look! There! All that rising corn! And there! Look! The sails of the herring fleet! All that loveliness . . . He'd snatch away his hand and go back into*

his corner, appalled. All he had seen was ashes . . . It appears
his case was not so . . . so unusual.

Is that a *found poem*? Noelle asks.

That's Beckett, I say.

All he had seen was ashes . . . , Noelle says. I know what he means. I've seen ashes . . . But then I took pills and felt better.

Maybe it's only when you understand that everything is just empty and meaningless that you can accept things as they are, Tana says.

Or maybe it's only when you accept that all this empty and meaningless stuff is empty and meaningless that you'll be at peace, Noelle says.

Ah, *common sense*, I say. The suburbs speaking . . .

If nothing means anything, why don't you just kill yourselves? Tana says.

That's a good question, I say.

She has us there, Art says.

You do it first, Art, I say.

No, after *you*, Chandra, Art says.

If nothing means anything, then why bother killing yourself? That doesn't mean anything either, I say.

How *clever*, Chandra, Tana says.

What do philosophers believe in, anyway? Tana asks.

Real philosophers don't believe in anything, I say.

Look, meaning's right here, Noelle says. We're talking to you guys. You're talking to us. Isn't that meaning?

But it's not *ultimate* meaning, I say.

Who cares about *ultimate* meaning? Noelle says. That's just for religious types.

It's not about *finding* ultimate meaning, Art says. It's about pondering what the absence of ultimate meaning *means*.

You'll drive yourself crazy thinking about that kind of thing, Tana says.

Nietzsche's kind of crazy—you can see it, Noelle says. And you guys are going to go crazy, too.

Being philosophical means asking questions, Art says. Only the dead don't ask questions.

Haven't you actually got to *answer* questions? Noelle says. You know—commit to things? Questioning means detaching yourself from everything. It's like asking questions about swimming when you're on the side of the pool, watching everyone in the water. All the answers you want are just there, if you'd just let yourself swim.

They're *stupid* answers, I say. They're everyone's answers. The answers of the herd.

So what are you—fascists, or something? Noelle asks.

We *think*. We don't do what everyone else does. We're not morons. That means no answers. No contentedness. It means staying unsettled. Never accepting anything, I say.

Sounds like a long and lonely life to me, Noelle says.

THURSDAY

Assembly.

They've detected a rogue signal from the depths of space. It could be aliens, they reckon. Mrs Steele, Head of Science, is very enthusiastic. A sun-like star, perfect for life . . . A solar system billions of years older than our own . . . A very strong signal, not just random noise . . . The work of a civilization advanced enough to blast an eleven-gigahertz message across the universe . . .

It's promising, Mrs Steele says. We've never known anything like it, Mrs Steele says. They might have detected our presence. They might be extending a hand across the void. They might have all kinds of things to teach us.

We imagine it: an older race, calmer, who have long since opted away from fossil fuels, from capitalism, from financialisation, from derivatives. An older race, with great throbbing heads, with vast domes, bigger than Mr Pound's, full of profound thoughts, peaceful thoughts, at-one-with-the-cosmos thoughts.

An older race, a calmer one, broadcasting great calm messages through the universe. Telling us how to save the Earth and all the living things of the Earth. Showing us how we might grow up, and make a positive contribution to the galaxy.

Imagine it—we won't be alone in the universe anymore. We'll have an older sibling to look up to, to trust. A civilisational older brother, full of words of advice, ready to save us from ourselves. A civilisational older sister, who's seen everything before, and knows human beings to be merely in the adolescent phase of civilisational life.

Imagine it—a civilisational arm around our shoulder, promising that everything's going to be okay, that we'll all be saved. A civilisational mentor, asking us to join the *galactic federation*, or somesuch. A civilisational champion, urging us to *live long and prosper* . . .

. . .

Library duty.

By the stacks. Explaining books to Merv. There are these things called *pages*, Merv. They have words printed on them. You read from left to right. You have to turn the pages. And there are stories— they're not real, just pretend.

You've got a reading age of seven, haven't you, Merv? Paula says.

Merv's only read one book: Anne Frank's *Diaries*, Art says.

You don't think you have to read anything else, do you Merv? I say.

Everything's in Anne Frank, Merv says. *Where there's hope, there's life. I don't think of all the misery, but of the beauty that still remains. I still believe that people are really good at heart.*

That's very moving, Merv, Paula says. Very inspiring.

Has reading Anne Frank made you a better person, do you think, Merv? I ask. Do you have finer moral instincts now?

Would you say you're a more *hopeful* person? Art asks. Are you more willing to forgive your enemies?

Are you more sensitive to beauty? Paula asks.

You guys are so *cynical*, Merv says.

Actually, books make you miserable, Paula says. Well, they make *me* miserable.

But you read a lot, Art says.

I *like* being miserable, Paula says.

Everyone here is miserable, Art says. Jesus—this place is full of freaks.

The library, where the cursed of the lower school come to hide.

The library, where the mutants of the lower school flee every morning break, every lunchtime. Children, changed by puberty into something monstrous. Children, betrayed by their own bodies. Children, watching themselves deform, day by day. Children of strange gods. Children made by some drunk god—by some King-Ludwig-of-Bavaria god. It's a *freak-show* in the library. A cabinet of human curiosities. Obscure ailments. Mutations unknown to science. Like some remote inbred tribe . . .

Everything is against them. They've lost the puberty lottery. They've rolled bad dice. If only they weren't fully conscious . . . If only they weren't fully aware . . . But they are aware. They're awake and aware. And if they forget their afflictions for a moment, some bastard will remind them . . .

So you hide out in chess club. Or among the evangelicals in Christian club. Or in computer club. Or here in the library. And you hope to ride it out. You hope the bullies tire of you. Turn their attention elsewhere. You hope to survive to the other side.

When will the judgement come? When will the reckoning come? When will the blame be apportioned? When will we be made to suffer for our sins? When will the uprising come? When, the lower-school revolution? When will a Lenin of Year Eight rise up who loves the revolution, who loves being at its centre? When will a Trotsky of Year Seven *gaze into the communist distance*, thinking about nothing but the Collective Will?

We need a Hugo Chavez of the suburbs, Art says. A suburban *Gandhi*. A magnificent *holy fool* . . .

Nietzsche: More nihilism.

Jesus, what *isn't* nihilism? Paula says. We need *something*. Anyone can see that.

Nietzsche: More politics of pity. The way you talk about your *library freaks* just reduces them to their distress. You'd like a politics of *equality*, but you never consider the *library freaks* as equals. You want to keep them in their suffering, and have everyone suffer on their account. *False compassion*—that's *your* politics. That's *democracy*.

And what would you rather have—government by the strong? Paula asks.

Anything's better than some *paternalism of the guilty conscience*,

Nietzsche says. Democracy sings lullabies. It puts us to sleep and tucks us in.

Fuck politics, Art says. We have to leave society. Secede. Make our own world. It's like the monks. *Death to the world*: that's what they said. And they went out into the desert.

Is that what you want, too, Nietzsche—to leave the world? Paula asks.

Nietzsche: I want to *remake* the world.

For who? Paula asks. For you? For us?

Nietzsche: For those who could stand to be remade.

★

A thin girl in glasses, at the bookshelf.

She's pretty, Paula says. What she's doing in the library at lunch-time? Hasn't she got any friends?

I know that girl, Art says. She spoke at Annie Tasker's funeral.

She definitely has something, I say. She's otherworldly. Disassociated.

That's just her glasses, Paula says.

She's very thin, I say. Like she's tormented.

I think she looks *serene*, Paula says.

Mad-serene, maybe, I say. Not serene-serene.

Nietzsche, talking to Tasker's sister's friend.

Jesus—how did he manage that? Art asks. One minute, he's here, the next . . .

He's a fucking mover, I say. Look at him.

He must have some lines, Art says. What do you think she's talking about?

Who knows? I say. She's just some lower-sixth girl.

She's really cute, Paula says. She's got a bi-thing going on.

You think everyone has a bi-thing going on, Art says.

Well, she likes Nietzsche—that's for sure, Paula says. Look how she's smiling at him.

Tasker's sister's friend, saying goodbye. Tasker's sister's friend, heading out to the covered walkway. Nietzsche, walking back to the sixth form.

Who's your girlfriend? Art asks, catching up with him.

She's *cute*, Paula says. You guys are cute.

Nietzsche: Lou. She's called Lou.

Cycling home.

Discussion. Soon, we'll be too old to cycle. Too old to cycle unself-consciously. Too old to cycle without feeling like a failure.

Our peers will laugh at us from rolled-down car windows. We'll be pedalling, furiously pedalling, while they'll be cruising . . .

It would all be different if we were cycling for *leisure*. If we were cycling out on a 50k. If we were covered in stretch lycra. If we were streamlined on carbon-fibre racers. If we were in training for some major race, zooming down some dual carriageway.

But we don't want to be fast. We're not always pumping our limbs. We dawdle. We freewheel. We take long-cuts through the woods. We travel *lento* beneath the summer sun. The one who's slowest wins our race . . .

Nietzsche's blog.

> *The suburban non-event. What does not happen as the suburbs. Perpetual imminence. Eventless events. Nothing happening, except for this nothing-is-happening.*

Art's house. The practice room.

Bill Trim, trying out for the band, plugging in his guitar.

Bill, striking up. Power chords, very quick. Big riffs—crunching, slow, then a solo. Little arpeggios, up and down the fretboard. Guitar, screaming.

Art, signalling for Bill to stop.

You're not getting it, Bill. This isn't the Trimtones. We're not here to recycle *rock clichés* . . . No *machismo*, Bill. No muscle stuff. None of your guitar-heroics. The guitar's not a lead instrument in our band. It's a texture. It's part of the mesh.

Bill, trying again. Guitar, jangling. Guitar, chiming.

Art, telling Bill to stop.

You're trying, Bill, I appreciate that. That was *better*. How can I explain? . . . Look—we're trying to do something here—we're trying to remake ourselves. We're trying to *redeem* ourselves. And the world—we're trying to redeem the world.

Music's not just about music, Bill, Art says. It's about *everything.* There's an ethos. There's an ethics—a way of living. It's about what you do. The way you are. I'm not sure I *like* the way you are, Bill.

We're trying to *abolish the lies*, Bill, Art says. We're in revolt against the false claims of the world. We're trying to vomit up our *interior phantoms*. We don't want to be doubters anymore.

We reject everything, Bill, Art says. It's a year zero. The very *gestures* of the suburban world. The very *reflexes*. It's a re-education. It's a remaking. We're stripping ourselves down before building ourselves back up.

It's discipline, Bill, Art says. We're retraining ourselves. We're remaking our bodies. We're not going to be obedient anymore. This is a war. And the suburbs are the frontline.

The music's changing us, Bill, Art says. The music comes first. Everything depends on honouring the music. We're casting spells. We're warding off the suburbs.

Swig some vodka, Bill, Art says. Sit and watch us from the drumstool.

★

Nietzsche, arriving.

The band (except Bill), striking up.

Paula's bass.

Music sprawling, spreading . . . Wide music . . . Note-zones . . .

Melting music . . . Lava-light music . . .

Now Nietzsche's voice. *Introverted*—is that the word? Turned in on itself. Quiet. A *depressed* voice—would you call it that? A *finished* voice. A voice-husk, not a voice. A voice-remnant . . .

Our music, saddening in response. Our music, fracturing. Piling . . .

There's no *drama* in Nietzsche's voice. There's a kind of emotion to it, true—but it's not *his* emotion—not really. Desolation—is that the feeling? *Damnation?*

There's nothing warm about Nietzsche's voice. Nothing *intimate.*

There's fatalism to Nietzsche's voice. Something ancient. Something older than age . . .

Our music, responding. Our soundscape, freezing over. Our

music, ice-touched. Crystalline. Light on ice . . . Glittering light, very cold . . .

And now Bill, striking a cymbal. Now Bill, sounding the bass drum. A roll on the toms . . .

Nietzsche's lyrics: Images. *The sky is hollow. The stars are blind.* Stray phrases: *The killing light. The suicide dawn.* Snatches of sense: *I lack the strength. I lack the weakness.*

Unfamiliar words: *Aevum. Aiōn.* Unfamiliar names: *Baubo. Ariadne.* Strange couplets:

> *Alive in the last moment / In the last hand of God.*
> *The forgotten sun / The death-day, rising.*

Is Nietzsche a channel? Is Nietzsche an antenna? Is he casting a spell? Are these the words of some conjuration? Is this a suburban *hex*?

The toms, still rolling (Bill is really good!). Glide guitar, à la MBV. Tremolo drone. Blurred notes. Crescendo—sustained . . . Bass ostinati. Merv's marimba, dissonant. Art's laptop noises . . .

Geysers, bubbling. Steam, rising. Smoke from the cracked Earth . . .

A songscape. A song landscape. An Iceland of song. Fire and ice, far above the tree-line.

Inhuman, somehow. Mineral, somehow. Pinprick stars.

Music of the north and the farther north. Music of tundra-fields. Ice-fields.

And the aurora borealis, fluming above. And the Northern Lights, flashing above.

And geysers. Fumes. The molten Earth . . . The melted Earth . . .

How far we have gone! How far he's taking us!

Is this Nietzsche's soul? Is this what Nietzsche's soul is like?

★

Afterwards. Lead singer, gone home. Rest of the band, walking ecstatically.

We're great, we agree. We're fucking invincible. This wasn't a fluke.

Nietzsche and the Burbs: that's the name of our escape-pod. *Nietzsche and the Burbs*: that's how we'll shake off the suburbs. *Nietzsche and the Burbs*: that's how we'll strike our match along the suburbs' edge. *Nietzsche and the Burbs*: that's how we'll let the suburban void re-echo. *Nietzsche and the Burbs*: that's how we'll let the suburban vacancy sing . . .

Nietzsche and the Burbs are divinatory. *Nietzsche and the Burbs* will read the entrails of the age. *Nietzsche and the Burbs* is alert for signs. No: *Nietzsche and the Burbs* is itself a sign. *Nietzsche and the Burbs* is prophetic . . . Apocalyptic. *Nietzsche and the Burbs* already belongs to the days of the end . . .

Nietzsche and the Burbs—the advance-guard. The outriders. The ancient prophets said, *Hear O Israel*. *Nietzsche and the Burbs* will say, *Hear O suburbs. Hear O Wokingham* . . .

FRIDAY

Bill Trim versus Dingus. The heavyweight championship of the sixth-form common room.

How did it begin? Some sly homophobic remark? Some under-handed reference to Merv? To rent boys? To ladyboys? It's been building for days. What Bill Trim posted on Instagram . . . What Dingus commented on Blurt . . .

Sudden noise. Then the scraping of a chair. Then, *YOU FUCKER!* And then Bill Trim's great roar . . .

Bill Trim, well over six feet, confronting Dingus, well over six feet. Titans, built up, shoving each other, teeth bared, T-rex versus T-rex. It's mythological . . .

Bill Trim's fist smashing up, Dingus's head snapping back. First strike, to Bill Trim. Then, quickly, a blow to Dingus's mouth. Straight in the cake-hole. Second strike, to Bill Trim. Then, a hammer-blow to Dingus's belly. Third strike, to Bill Trim . . .

The adrenaline works faster in Bill Trim, that's clear. He's reached *fight or flight* mode more quickly . . .

Fourth strike: Dingus catches Bill Trim on the nose. Blood, running over Bill Trim's lips. His teeth. It suits him. It's magnificent. Fifth strike: Dingus cuts open Bill Trim's forehead. Now blood's streaming over Bill Trim's left eye. Oh, Dingus shouldn't have done that. Bill Trim's bloodlust is rising. Bill Trim's blood is up . . .

Bill Trim, beating the crap out of Dingus. Bill Trim, raining Dingus with blows.

It's all about you, Merv. Don't you feel special?

It's a miracle, Merv—someone actually gives a shit about you!

Bill Trim, beating *himself*, in some sense. Bill Trim, beating his homophobic self. It's a liberatory violence, a Merv-loving violence . . .

Mr Pound, crashing through the doors. Who called him? That's all we need—some *business rhino* with an enormous forehead. The Old Dome himself, with the Old Mole in tow. Bill Trim, being led away like a martyr. Like a champ. It's magnificent.

Dingus, being led off to the school nurse, to have his faced swabbed.

News: Bill Trim's been suspended, effective immediately. Bill Trim, who shattered sixth-form peace, sixth-form egalitarianism. Bill Trim, who reminded us once more of the violence of love. Who began history all over again . . .

Special assembly. *The unfortunate incident earlier today . . . A show of savagery . . . not the kind of behaviour we expect from sixth-formers . . . Won't be tolerated . . . Expulsions if necessary . . . Hospital visits . . . Concerned parents . . . A safe environment for offspring . . . A right to feel their child will be protected . . .*

Merv, hissing though his teeth. Art, quietly mouthing *booo*. Paula, shouting *FARCE!*

Something actually happened—imagine that! And you were the cause of it, Merv . . .

Violence in the air! Even we feel violent! Even we want fisticuffs! Even we want to grit our teeth!

Perhaps it all begins here. Perhaps there will be more acts of violence. Perhaps unimaginable things will now happen. The overturning of the old order . . . Blood running on the cobblestones . . .

We imagine the plough of revolution turning over the school . . .
Turning over the suburbs . . .

Lunchtime. In the lower school with Nietzsche, looking for Lou.

Obesity everywhere. An obesity epidemic. Hundreds of waddlers—fat, yet malnourished. Filled with corn syrup. A thousand lower-schoolers, hunters and hunted.

Groups of proto-beasts, loitering. Groups of proto-beast-admirers. You have to watch the beasts-in-making. They like to show off in front of their girls. They'll want to beat you in front of their girls . . .

And roving bullies, looking for victims. Looking for outcasts. Looking to pick off weaker members of the herd . . . The trick to surviving the lower school is not to stand out, we want to advise them. Don't let yourself be noticed! Lock eyes with no one! Disappear in plain sight!

Divert their attention!, we want to say. Send the bullies to the next guy! Let them beat and kick the next guy, not you!

Past the kitchens. Past the art wing.

Our lower-school years. Five long lower-school years. The lower school, filling with kids each day, then emptying of kids each day. Lower-school corridors, surging and seething with pupils. The lower-school lunch-hall, filling and emptying. Lower-school dinner ladies, spooning out mash and meat and pudding. Lower-school buses, coming and going. And always trouble, of one kind or another. Always someone being chased. Always someone being beaten.

Years and years on the bus to lower school. Years, with your lower-school bag on your back, walking to the bus stop. Years, dragging yourself and your bag towards the lower-school classrooms. Hundreds of days . . . Thousands . . . There you were, at the end of your third year, knowing you were only halfway through your sentence. There you were, three years into a seven-year term, with no let-off for good behaviour. No being freed early on parole . . .

And always the other children, screaming. Always the primal horde, bellowing. And because they were barbarians, so we had to be. Because they were barely under control, so we had to be. Because they could barely sit at their desks, so we had to be prepared to defend ourselves at our desks. Because it was a war of all against all, so we had to arm ourselves and prepare for war . . .

We remember when a lower-school mob broke into the tuckshop. It wasn't about theft—they didn't touch the cash box. It was about *freedom*. They tore open boxes of Wotzits and threw packets everywhere. They threw Lion Bars and Toffee Crisps onto the concrete. Children, swarming. Children, grabbing handfuls of Drumsticks and Bazooka Joes. It was a jubilee . . . A revolution!

But we were too fearful to join in the melee. Too *good*. We stood and watched, like we always stand and watch. We enjoyed the spectacle, like we always enjoy the spectacle. We'll be exactly the same when there are demonstrations in the streets. When they bring out the water cannons and start zapping people with tasers . . .

We're feudal by nature, like all the English. Forelock-tuggers . . . Bowers and scrapers . . . Cap doffers . . . God-bless-you-ma'amers . . . We're courtiers. We're *Crown*-watchers. We know nothing of a *common cause*. We're just what the system wants us to be. Docile. Resigned. Expecting nothing to change.

Anyway, we probably couldn't cope with *real* change. We're institutionalised. Like prisoners who just stay in their cells during a riot. We only want to do our time. That's what life is to us: doing our time.

We can't imagine what another world would be like. We can't imagine a great politics, a liberatory politics. We can't imagine a life without medication. Without breakdowns. We can't imagine not daydreaming about suicide . . .

The drama studio. Hippie central. We remember the trust exercises they made us do. Falling back into someone's arms. Eyes closed, touching each other's faces.

It didn't help that drama was taught by paedophiles, Art says.

There was only one paedophile, Art, and he was sacked, Merv says.

Remember him, peering at us through a hole in the changing-rooms wall, Art says.

He was peering at *girls*, Art, I say. He wasn't peering at you. No one was peering at you . . .

The lower-school playground, overlooked by prefabs. The lower-school playground, all concrete. They called it a playground, but it was actually a bullying ground, a humiliation ground, a testing ground, a Battle-Royale ground. A concrete playground, to skin your knees against . . . A concrete playground, to break your head against . . .

And the chain-link fence, with its vista of the outer world. A double row of garages, that's all. Some garage doors, that's all. Garages, and the backs of houses beyond, that's all. An average scene. A mediocre scene . . . And light, mediocre light, falling on it all . . .

What would it mean to be looking into the school from the outside? we used to wonder. To look in from without . . . To look in at the captives as a free person . . . What would we do out there, on the other side of the chain-link fence?

Would we go somewhere far away, somewhere foreign? Would we simply leave it all behind? Imagine it: truancy—eternal truancy! A lifetime bunking off! Imagine it: barely touching ground. Imagine it: travelling on, moving on, barely leaving a trace.

Ah, but we knew we would never escape. We're laboratory rats. We wouldn't know what to *do* with freedom. We knew we would simply sit, on the other side of the chain-link fence, looking back at the school . . .

And now Merv's favourite place: the forbidden zone behind the prefabs. Now Merv's panic room. His little sanctuary. His place of peace. He'd come here when school became too much for him. When the other kids became too much for him. He'd lie back in the long grass and close his eyes and dream of some better place, and sometimes we'd lie beside him.

No kids shouting . . . No kids' voices . . . No crowded corridors . . . No sound of the bell, shunting you from lesson to lesson . . . Just grass and peace and sun. And buttercups. And flowering grass. The caretaker couldn't get his lawnmower there. He couldn't tame it. It was a taste of life after the revolution. After the spiritual revolution. After the revolution of the workers. It doesn't matter which. Peace, peace, and nothing besides. Grass, sun, and nothing besides . . .

★

Looking for Lou, in each of the prefabs. In the chess-club prefab. In the Christian-club prefab. No Lou.

Onwards. To the science block, where the girls sit against the infill panels, sunning their legs . . .

Science lessons, in the old days. Wooden lab benches. High wooden stools. Bottles of chemicals on our desks. Pouring bottles labelled *sulphuric acid* over each other. It can't have been very strong, can it? Bombproof used to drink it—do you remember?—he'd swig from a bottle of sulphuric acid to show off to the beasts . . .

And experiments—why did we have to do experiments? Weren't they a complete waste of time? *We believe the textbooks!*, we wanted to say. *Just tell us what to write! We don't need to* prove *anything! Brownian motion—we buy it! Sure!*

Physics gets it right—we learned that. Physics fixes all the facts. Everything's made up of fermions and bosons, that's all. Free will is an illusion, pretty much. We're pre-programmed. We're automata.

We're negentropic islands within the great wind-down. We're archipelagos of order within the teeming chaos. And soon enough, in cosmic time, from the cosmic perspective, life itself will disappear . . .

Posters of the Milky Way, of the Crab Nebula in the science stairwell. We were supposed to feel awe. We never felt awe. We were supposed to feel wonder, but we shuddered instead.

Who can stand it, the cosmic nothing? Not even us, with all our bravado. The horror of truth. The coldness of truth. The universe, indifferent to us. The universe that says, *Take your human world and shove it! Take your humanism and set it aflame!*

So the Crab Nebula is beautiful—so what? So Spaceship Earth is a blue-green orb—what then? It'll be dead as the moon soon enough. It'll be as grey and lifeless as the moon, in cosmic time. And we're all as blind as the comets that blaze through space. Our lives are as random as the asteroids that fall through darkness. Our lives are as senseless as the sun's blind burning . . .

Who can stand it, really, the horror of truth? Who can bear it, really, the coldness of truth? Only the unimaginative. Only the terminally dull. Only our science teachers, who are entirely lacking in soul and are entirely without feeling. Only Mrs Steele and the rest, bleating about *wonder* in our assembly, wanting us to wave back at Tim Peake.

How can they teach this stuff to minors? There ought to be a law against it. It should be reserved for the high priests of science. Only when they reach the highest circle, only when they're ready for the scientific Mysteries, should the truth be revealed to them.

Still no Lou. Where is she? Tracing a similar circuit to ours? Walking round and round the school and mistaking it for freedom, like us?

The workshops. Woodwork. Metalwork. Jesus, why did they bother teaching us woodwork and metalwork? Why did they expose us to the resistance of real materials, real things? Why did they bring us into contact with the physical world? Let us shape things with our hands? What is manual work to us? What is craft? What is patience and honest skill?

It was all for nought, of course. We were too intimidated by the lathes. By the grinder. We were too wary of the oxyacetylene torch. Those things were not for us. We'd emery-cloth random bits of metal and chat. We'd sandpaper bits of wood and make up stupid songs. We'd fool around with goggles, pretending to be pre-war racing- car drivers. World War One flying aces.

The hexagonal music rooms. The practice rooms. New since our time. We were never allowed to *touch* an instrument—to make the *slightest* noise. Except Merv.

And yet, music of all things would have reached us! Led us some-where! Taught us how to live! All we ever talked about was music! All we ever gave a fuck about was music! All we wanted to do was play music!

But we could only watch Merv performing *Clair de Lune*, running up and down the keyboard with his mallets . . .

And no Lou. Rounding the block, and still no Lou.

The English classrooms. English! English literature! All those books—wasted on us! All those poems! All those plays! Too bad no one reads anymore—not even us. Too bad we're all *functionally illiterate*, even the teachers—*especially* the teachers. They only read comedian autobiographies and *Heat* magazine. They only read the *Daily Mail* gossip pages.

Back to where we started. The covered walkway. The entrance to the sixth-form lobby. The long line of pupils queuing for lunch.

Lou must have been hiding out. Watching us, sixth-formers, wan-dering round the lower school . . .

Joel Park.

Smoking in the rhododendrons.

Have we crossed the line? we wonder. Have we actually become stoners?

My voice has dropped, like, five octaves, Tana says.

I can't concentrate anymore, Noelle says.

I like not being able to concentrate, Art says. I like not being linear.

We've got our exams in, like, a month, I say.

Fuck our exams, Art says. I want to know *less*, not *more*.

I'm depressed, Tana says.

Of course you're depressed, Art says. We're all depressed.

I'm *unusually* depressed, Tana says.

It must be the come-down, Art says.

If you smoked enough of this, you'd know everything, Art says. All the secrets. Everything you're not supposed to know.

You'd just be very fucking stoned, that's all, Noelle says.

Listen to you—you don't even trust yourself, Art says. You don't even believe what you feel. We're right because we're young. We're right because we're stoned . . .

Do you ever feel that the world is just *buffering*? Art asks. That soon we'll find out what's really going on?

It's Joel Park, it's Friday afternoon. Nothing's going on—take it from me, Noelle says.

I just feel like we're on the verge of something really important, Art says. The biggest fucking thought, man.

I've had enough, Noelle says, refusing the spliff. You know what that stuff's doing to our heads, right?

I'm sick of my damn head, Art says, lying down in the grass. Anyway, what are you going to use your head for, Noelle?

For giving head, Tana says.

Ha fucking ha, Noelle says.

I don't want to think anymore, Tana says. I don't want to think another thing. Just roll another one . . .

Jesus, how much have you had, Tana? Noelle asks.

Art, ear to the ground. I can hear a heartbeat, man. I can hear the heartbeat of the Earth. It's the Great Mother.

The Great Mother*fucker*, I say. It's all her fault.

We've got to get back to the Mother, Art says. Back to the Goddess. Back to the old cycles, before the sky gods, before linear time . . .

Fuck the Goddess, Art, Noelle says. I don't know how you believe in this stuff.

Yeah, well, maybe I don't believe in it, Art says.

I'm tired—so tired, Tana says. Everything's *tired* . . .

Silence. Smoking.

Tana's asleep, Art says. She's really asleep.

She needs to sleep, poor thing, Noelle says. Her mother's really sick—you know that, right?

The Great Mother's cancerous, man, Art says. The Great Mother's dying.

No, I mean Tana's *actual* mother, Noelle says. She's dying.

There are no actual mothers, man, Art says. There are only Great Mothers. There are only great mother . . . fuckers.

*You're either a motherfucker or you're mother*fucked, I quote.

Jesus fucking Christ, you guys, Noelle says. TANA'S MOTHER'S DYING! Doesn't that mean anything?

Nothing means anything, Art says.

We're so . . . disconnected, I say.

We're smoking too much, Noelle says. We're smoking too . . . fucking . . . much.

Poor Tana, I say. Poor Tana's mum.

At last—some *sympathy*, Noelle says.

Poor us, I say. Poor . . . everyone . . .

Don't pretend, Chandra—you know you don't feel a thing, Art says. No one cares about anyone. We don't even care about ourselves very much.

Do you think dying's painful? Noelle asks.

Not anymore, I say. They just hook you up to a syringe-driver. Just pump morphine into you. Dying's just like going to sleep . . . But I wouldn't want to die in hospital. You know, zonked out of my head, tubes in all my orifices.

I wish I was zonked out of my head, right now, Art says. Completely zonked, full of morphine, just slipping away.

I think you should at least have a chance to say your last words, I say.

And what would they be, poet? Noelle asks. I mean, have you planned them already?

It's better to burn out than to fade away—that was Kurt Cobain's suicide note, right? Art says.

That was Neil Young via Kurt Cobain, I say.

Anyway, Kurt Cobain's suicide note is really moving, Art says. (Reading from his phone:) *Since the age of seven, I've become hateful towards all humans in general . . .*

Why, what happened to him when he was seven? Noelle asks.

His parents divorced, I say. (Reading from my phone:) *I have a daughter who reminds me too much of what I used to be, full of love and joy, kissing every person she meets because everyone is good and will do her no harm.*

That's fucked up, Art says.

Kurt Cobain reckons he had too much empathy in him, I say. He was too sensitive for the world.

Jesus, you don't show empathy by fucking killing yourself, Noelle says.

He wrote, *I LOVE YOU, I LOVE YOU!*, in big capital letters at the bottom of his suicide note, I say.

He didn't love anyone but himself, Noelle says. He was a junkie, right?

He just didn't give a fuck anymore, I say. He had a death-wish. He used to share needles. And shoot up black tar heroin, which was the worst. And he kept overdosing. And he had these stomach problems. He kept vomiting bile and blood. He just wanted to be wasted.

Just—like—us, Art says.

This is just temporary, Noelle says. It's going to get better.

Much better for *you*, posh girl, Art says.

What sort of lives are we going to have? I ask. When are our lives supposed to, like, begin?

Noelle, stroking Tana's hair.

Tana, waking.

I thought when I woke up it would all be different, Tana says. What did I miss?

We were talking about death, Noelle says.

And despair, Art says.

Oh—*fuck*, Tana says.

Young Enterprise.

Oh God—gap-yearers. Gap-in-the-head-yearers. Come to lecture us on their years abroad.

First, the hedonists. The you-only-live-once-types. The bucket-list types, dancing with glow-sticks at the Full Moon Party. Covered in fluorescent body paint at Carnival in Rio. Bungee jumping from the Contra Dam and ziplining through cloud forests. Riding in a cable-car up to the Pic du Midi . . .

Continual ecstasy. The doors of perception, swinging wide. A litany of wow-words. Of word-gasps. Of word-cries. As if language weren't good enough for them. As though language itself couldn't convey it. *Oh wow, man. Awesome, man.* And not a word of sense. An overwhelmed gap-yearer who's left signification behind! Who's said farewell to language! Who can only communicate with *wows* and *awesomes*!

Then the Personal Challenge types. Showing signs of initiative, of get-go. Enhancing their CVs. Doing the things potential employers like to see.

Galloping barebacked through the pampas. Following the Inca trail to Machu Picchu. Bathing in the Blue Lagoon in Iceland, Northern Lights blazing overhead. Big-wave-surfing off Makaha. Island-hopping in Mozambique. Sea-kayaking with orcas off Vancouver Island . . .

Selfies with the moai on Easter Island. Selfies with street kids in Cambodia. Selfies with gorillas in the Virunga Volcanoes. Selfies above the fairy chimneys and cavehouses of Cappadocia. Selfies in the emerald forest at Torres del Paine. Selfies with the crazy Kiwis they met on the bus . . .

Worst of all: the gap-year Do-Gooders. Smug-o-nauts who've voyaged halfway round the world for *charity*. Oh the places they've seen! Oh the things they've done! Saving sea-turtles in Costa Rica . . . Fostering baby rhinos in South Africa . . . Tracking cheetahs through the bush . . . Beach-cleaning in Thailand . . . Ocean-cleaning in Malaysia . . . Building sand dams in Kenya . . . Digging wells in Ghana . . . Clearing jungle paths in Indonesia with machetes and shovels . . . Reforesting Myanmar . . . Teaching street children in Vietnam . . .

They're changed people. They've gained. They've grown. They

know what misery is—real misery. They've seen suffering and misery at first hand. They helped. They gave something back. They fought the good fight. They could have done so much more. We all could do so much more . . .

They never understood, before, that life was something infinitely precious, something infinitely fragile. They never understood their own lives as something infinitely precious, something infinitely fragile . . .

Nietzsche's blog:

> The suburbs leave nothing left over—except the suburbs.
> Nothing remains—but the suburbs. What does it mean, this nothing but?
> The suburbs as total meaning. As total reality.
> The sense of the non-meaning of that meaning. Of the unreality of that reality.

Nine Mile Ride. To Noelle's for a soirée (what the fuck's a soirée?)

Nietzsche, in silent mode.

So what about you and Lou? Paula asks. Come on—give us *something*! Where's it heading?

Silence.

You like her, right? Paula asks. The philosopher's in love, right?

Silence. And then,

Nietzsche: That's what she calls me—the *philosopher*.

Pet names already!, Paula says. Cozy . . .

Why don't you tell us about you, Paula? Art says. I thought you said Tana had a bi-thing going on.

Tana likes *you*, Art, though God knows why, Paula says. And Noelle's crazy about Chandra—anyone can see that. Everyone's pairing up except me . . . Come on, Art, light one up before we get there. Let's get nine miles high on Nine Mile Ride . . .

★

Hollybush Ride.

Noelle lives in the *forest*, Merv says.

It's an old gamekeeper's lodge, Art says. Must have been something to do with Queen's Mere.

It's beautiful, Paula says. Those *chimneys* . . .

We imagine what we would have been if we'd grown up in Noelle's house. We'd have been gentle, we agree. Bright-eyed. We'd have been inquisitive. We'd have been full of interest in the world . . . We'd have known all about Culture. About classical music and old paintings. We'd be familiar with the Opera, with the Ballet. We'd have a taste for finer things—we'd know our way around a cheese-board. We'd know wines by region . . . We'd be able to declare fish fresh or not just by a glance. We'd know all the cuts of meat . . .

And we'd know how to *talk*. We wouldn't need half a bottle of vodka just to utter a word.

★

The garden.

Knuckle-rooted beech trees, one headless from a lightning strike. Pine trees, fading away into the wood. Light in the pines.

Wood smoke from the pizza oven.

Fuck, Noelle, your dads really know how to live, Paula says.

This is where we'll hole up in the apocalypse, Art says. We'll all come here, for the night before the end.

We imagine it: dancing with tears in our eyes, the sky deep blue above the pines. Dancing, weeping, eating our pizzas.

Inside.

Adults, in conversation, barely looking up at us. Adults, talking to each other. Laughing with each other. Adults, with their own thing going on.

Introductions. Pleasantries. Noelle's dad, Sylvere, shaking our hands. Noelle's dad, Cecil, waving from his piano stool.

Tell me . . ., Sylvere says. I so rarely meet intelligent young people . . . What's the biggest issue that faces your generation?

We wonder aloud. Climate change? Capitalism? Mass stupidity? Corporate power? Debt? Consumerism?

Nietzsche: Nihilism.

Nihilism, Sylvere nods. And what do you mean by that?

The centre doesn't hold, Paula says.

The way up is the way down, Art says.

The uncanniest guest knocks at the door, Merv says.

Everything is possible, and yet nothing is, I say.

All is permitted, and yet again, nothing, Art says.

Do you hear these young people, Cecil? Sylvere says. These young people are *nihilists*.

Cecil cups a hand to his ear.

NIHILISTS!, Sylvere shouts, over the party noise.

Oh—I thought you said they were Antichrists, Cecil says. How disappointing.

Maybe they are, Sylvere says. Are you Antichrists?

Nietzsche here probably is, Paula says.

Nietzsche—is that what they call you? Sylvere asks.

Nietzsche, nodding.

The boy's nickname's *Nietzsche*, Sylvere mouths to Cecil. Then, shouting: *NIETZSCHE*—you know, the *PHILOSOPHER* . . . Well, you do look very thoughtful, Nietzsche. Are you a nihilist, too?

Nietzsche: I try not to be.

Nietzsche wants to *complete* nihilism, dad, Noelle says. He wants to get to the other side.

Nietzsche wants to *COMPLETE NIHILISM*, Sylvere shouts to Cecil.

I daresay, Cecil says.

So—are you all off to university? Sylvere asks.

We are.

And then what? Sylvere asks.

Then nothing. Return to the suburbs.

Where will you be in ten years, do you think? Sylvere asks.

We'll be lucky to survive, Paula says.

CECIL, DO YOU THINK WE'LL BE ALIVE IN TEN YEARS' TIME? Sylvere shouts.

Cecil, smiling.

Cecil's Proust book might be published by then, at least, Sylvere says. *PROUST*, Cecil!, he shouts.

Cecil, groaning.

Do you know what the word *study* means? Sylvere asks. It means *losing your way*. It's etymologically linked to *stupidity*. The scholar is stupid. The scholar is an *IDIOT*—right, Cecil?

A *perfect* idiot, Cecil says.

Now: What do you think of the Tasker girl suicide? Sylvere asks. Why do you think she did it?

Nihilism, Paula says.

And the suburbs, Art says.

One and the same, I say.

Yes, Sylvere says. Darling, remind me, Why do we live in the suburbs?

This house, Cecil says. This house!

Nietzsche's doing his extended project on the suburbs, Noelle says.

And what have you discovered, Nietzsche? Sylvere asks.

Nietzsche: All kinds of things.

Is it a sociological investigation? Is it anthropological? Sylvere asks.

Nietzsche: It's . . . philosophical. It's critical-theoretical. It's a psychogeography of the 'burbs. A way of attending to their ambience. To their mood . . .

Ah, the Situationists!, Sylvere says. You have to be young to read the Situationists . . .

Nietzsche: Psychogeography proceeds by means of a kind of wandering—a *drift*.

Like a flaneur!, Sylvere says. Like Baudelaire . . . But the Situationists wandered through the city, did they not? Through Paris. What is there to see in the suburbs? Nothing!

Nietzsche: It's a reconnaissance. It's a preparation.

A preparation for what? Sylvere asks. The revolution?

Nietzsche, silent.

I shouldn't laugh, Sylvere says. You see I'm old, old. We're too old, aren't we, Cecil?

Cecil nods.

Who do you read? the Greeks? The Germans? Or, God help us, the English?

Nietzsche: I read Nietzsche.

Of course you do, Sylvere says. But does Nietzsche say anything about the suburbs?

Nietzsche: He says something about *nihilism*.

Nietzsche's wonderful—of course he is, Sylvere says. But who can make sense of him now? The Übermensch, the nobility of suffering . . . It's all very Romantic. Very *nineteenth century* . . .

Nietzsche, silent.

Nietzsche was a bourgeois, Sylvere says. He didn't know anything about suffering. He thought that suffering had a nobility to it. But people suffer wretchedly—that's the truth of it. Like rats. They always did.

Our Nietzsche's new to the suburbs, Tana says. He was at Trafalgar.

Ah!—Was he? Sylvere says. That's *quite* a fall. Then perhaps he sees the suburbs more clearly than we do. It's been a long time since we came here . . . But soon you'll forget the suburbs. Soon, you'll be studying somewhere far away. Your minds will no longer be occupied with Wokingham . . .

Nietzsche's got a place at Cambridge, Noelle says.

Ha! We were at Cambridge a million years ago, Sylvere says.

Nietzsche: I'll never leave the suburbs. I'll never stop studying the suburbs.

Really? But the suburbs are so *mediocre*, Sylvere says.

Nietzsche: It's that they seem so mediocre which makes them important. It's that they seem so innocuous.

What do you mean? Sylvere asks.

Nietzsche: I was ill when I came to the suburbs. I spent my time looking out of the window. After a while, I saw that there is something about the suburbs that no one sees . . . something only a *suburban mystic* could describe.

There is a meaninglessness to the suburbs—a kind of *void*. And it has nothing to do with us. The void pushes us away. It holds us at *its* distance.

We take the suburbs for granted. We forget them. We neglect them. And that's how we miss them. That's how we fail to see them, to see their nothingness, which is right before our eyes.

You give too much importance to silly suburbia, my friend, Sylvere says. Suburbia is all surface, all froth. There is nothing of importance about the suburbs.

All the avant-gardists came from the suburbs, Paula says.

All the musicians, too, Art says.

Yes, they *came from* the suburbs, Sylvere says. But they *left* the suburbs.

But the suburbs gave them the momentum, Paula says. It made them seek out something else.

And no doubt they ended up in the suburbs in the end, after all their adventures, Sylvere says.

Nietzsche: You think the suburbs are unimportant—that they're not worthy of our attention. You talk instead about Cambridge, your *Cambridge years*. But it is Cambridge that is unimportant. No one can believe in Cambridge anymore. You talk of Proust and Baudelaire. But no one can believe in Proust and Baudelaire. Not anymore.

The *real* Nietzsche predicted the advent of nihilism. What he predicted was *us. Here*. The Thames Valley suburbs. The death of God was hidden until here and now. Only in the suburbs is nihilism to be truly encountered.

I must say, I thought nihilism was something a little more *desperate*, Sylvere says. Demented terrorists. Random acts of extreme violence . . . Two SUVs in the driveway doesn't seem like nihilism to me.

Nietzsche: For the first time, here in the suburbs, nihilism is presenting itself in the form of an experience that each of us has. Nihilism's everyday. It's not hidden anymore. Despair has become the most common experience, the most widespread. Half of our school are cutting themselves and drugging themselves and starving themselves . . . Nihilism is our ordeal. The question is, how can we *assume* it? Despair is not to be feared, you know. Just as the suburbs are not to be feared. There is still the potential for joy.

Joy!? What's joyful about the suburbs? Sylvere asks.

Nietzsche: The fact that we're not crushed by them. The fact that we can affirm them, despite everything.

Shouldn't we be trying to change them? Sylvere asks. To *change the world*?

Nietzsche: First, we must change our relationship with them. First, we must study what the suburbs *are*. What the suburbs *can be* . . .

Blank faces all round.

Let's have some more music, Sylvere says. *Without music, life would be an error*—well, Nietzsche was right about *that*, wasn't he?

Nietzsche's blog:

> The suburbs. Complete transparency. Complete obviousness.
> The suburbs. Everything is already here. Everything has already taken place.
> The suburbs, and nothing left over.
> The suburbs, and nothing left over.

★

Nietzsche's blog:

> The suburbs. Affirming nullity.
> The suburbs. Striving for nullity, for insignificance.
> The suburbs don't believe in themselves. But they don't disbelieve, either.
> The suburban transdevaluation. Banality and nullity raised to the level of values.

Saturday night. On the way to Tasker's party.

Sipping vodka on the roundabout, waving at the drivers.

I don't know, man, Art says. Annie Tasker's barely cold. A party feels a bit sick.

Think of it as a wake, if that makes you feel better, Paula says. Anyway, the pills will help.

Have you got them, Merv? Art asks.

Merv, patting his shirt pocket.

Art, shattering the empty vodka bottle on the chevrons. Glass shards, glinting.

Walking the streets, red-faced, euphoric. We *own* the fucking suburbs. We're *kings* of the fucking suburbs. If we were hard (we're not hard), we'd tool up and seek trouble. If we were tough (we're not tough), we'd wander into Gorse Ride estate—the nearest thing we have to *mean streets*—and look for a fight. If we were butch (we're not at all butch), we'd storm the playground, we'd ride the swings, bellowing into the night.

But we're wimps, and Bill Trim isn't with us. We're benign kings of the suburbs. Gentle kings of the suburbs. We smile at our Gorse Ride subjects, as they pass by . . .

Party hope. *Something*'s going to happen tonight. We got ready in hope. Ironed our shirts in hope. Styled our hair in hope . . .

The stuff is *good*, Merv's brother told him. *Pure.* Not mixed up with ketamine or baby powder, or anything. He only sells the real stuff. The stuff he uses himself.

Do you think Nietzsche would approve? Art asks.

Of course he wouldn't approve, Paula says. He wants to get high on water, or something fucking ridiculous.

Discussion. How are we going to take yours? In halves? In quarters? What time should we take them? We should take them in unison, we agree. It's a group thing, not an individual thing. That way, we should all come up at the same time. Merv says his brother told him to smoke a joint when you feel it's getting started. It intensifies the hit. Agreed: we'll have one ready.

What's ecstasy going to do to us? What will ecstasy make us? We've read it makes you feel *clean*. Clean? You have no worries, that's what they say. No problems. You just grin and hug and groove and jump. Everything's brighter, they say. And louder. And more intense. And you feel a real sense of belonging. You're part of something. Haven't we always wanted to be part of something?

Eleven o'clock. Out into the night. Full of energy, optimism. Tomorrow, we will remember what happened tonight. Tomorrow, we will have walked five feet above the pavement. Tomorrow, we won't understand what we did. We won't understand our own actions. What possessed us? we will ask. Did we really do that? Who were we? What did we become? What sang through us? What lifted us?

And we will have found our higher, brighter, better selves. We will have been kings and queens on Earth. Tonight, nothing is expected of us. We're not accountable, not really. What happens tonight happens tonight, that's all.

★

Tasker's house, Nine Mile Ride.

People outside, milling about by the porch. Tasker, nodding at us. Abigail, raising her hand in greeting. Death-Ray and Manta-Ray, setting up a beer keg. Hand Job and Nickname, already doing shots. Frenchy, necking alcopops. Frenchy's friends, laughing at Frenchy necking alcopops. Leroy and Bruno, passing a three-litre bottle of cider between them. The real trendies, Binky, Diamanda and the others, sitting in a smoking circle, talking languidly.

We'll have something they won't, Merv says, patting his teeshirt pocket. Sad fuckers.

The party's just beginning. It hasn't really come to itself, not yet. It hasn't really found itself—its groove. But it will find itself, we know that. It will get there. Because we're going to lead it. We're going to make it go off like a multistage rocket.

Sipping on our vodkas in a corner of the garden. Merv, sharing out the tablets. Breaking them in two. Downing the first half. Smiling. Nodding to the beats.

Conversation. Who are we going to be? What will we become? A sense of power . . . Of possibility . . . That we're leading the party . . . *Steering* it, taking it somewhere . . . We're party seers. Party messiahs. We're messengers from the Element.

To life!, says Art, downing a miniature. *Na Zdrovie !*

Arrivals: Hopey, a Spinney School wild-child. Stebson, a Winnersh Grove boy—he's division one. Pops—what's a party without Pops? He's the life and soul. He's twenty-four years old. He's seen it all. He brings *wisdom* to the party. And crystal meth. Mags, Veronica, and some other Spinney wild girls. Ah, you have to have Spinney wild girls at a party. Girls from another school! Mysterious! Unknown!

We're explorers. We're psychonauts. We're searching for a *Northwest Passage of the mind*.

The music, louder. Spinney wild girls, dancing. It's tribal . . .

The party, simmering and near ready to boil. The party, ready to overspill its brim. The party, frothing and convulsing. We're going to light the touchpaper. We're going to set it exploding into the night . . .

Art, carefully rolling a joint. He'll have it primed . . .

Can we feel it? Is it happening?

Art, splashing vodka on his face. Lighting his spliff. Drawing deep. Passing it round.

Didn't Merv's brother say there was nothing like your first tab? That you'll never capture it again: that first time?

Feeling our own breathing. Feeling the air we breathe in, breathe out. Feeling our own lungs. Feeling the alveoli of our lungs. Feeling the inside of our bodies.

Touching the grass: green, and cool, and lush.

We're fizzing. Tingling. Our fingertips are trembling. We're electrified. Our hair might as well be standing on end.

We've never lived until Now . . . We've never taken a single living breath until Now . . .

Time to dance. We've got to dance! We've got to move! To leap! The music sounds so deep! Snare lines. Bass swells . . . The night air feels so rich! And the stars—the stars are so bright! We're on the verge of Great Things! Of Legend!

The party, trembling. Rumbling. It's really starting. It's writhing like a Chinese dragon. Roaring with its own life, blazing, shouting, whooping. Have we all come up? Is everyone here coming up?

The hive mind, the party mind. All thinking alike. Coming up, together. Like dawning suns, together. Our heads have opened. Our hearts have opened. We're fellow ecstasists. Fellow rapturists. We're gods among gods among gods . . .

The Head Boy, top off, dancing. Merv, pulling his top off, dancing.

We're at the core of the party. We've found its heart. Its molten centre. The centre, like the centre of the sun. This is where it is. It's here, and we're here. This is it. This is truth. This is what things are. Joy, great joy.

The party as crucible. The party, like some wild washing machine. And we're bits of the party. Wild with borrowed madness . . .

Big drops of summer rain. Big, warm drops, bursting on our skin.

Who sent this rain to us? Who knew we needed rain to cool our blazing bodies?

Holy, holy, holy, cry the raindrops on our bodies.

Laughter—real laughter. We're laughing. Arms around each other. Arms around Paula, in her halter-top. An arm around Art and Merv and the Head Boy. Where does one of us end, and another begin? Which one of us is Art, and which one, Merv? Who's Paula, and who's not Paula?

This is it. What we were looking for. What we were always looking for. We don't want to be separate souls anymore. We don't want to be cold souls, all alone.

Great joy. Great godly joy, riding through us. This is what a sun feels like. This is what it's like to blaze in space.

Noelle, dancing beside me. My arm around Noelle. Dancing with Noelle. Body to body with Noelle. Great joy . . .

WE SHOULD TAKE THE OTHER HALF!, Art shouts.

Further, higher. Why not?

Into the grass, holding Noelle's hand. Noelle, sweet Noelle. Sweet-bodied Noelle, in her crop-top. Sweet Noelle, with her tapering limbs. Sweet Noelle, with her long, long fingers . . .

Art, flushed-faced. Paula, smiling as she's never smiled . . .

Nietzsche, in the grass, sipping a Smirnoff miniature.

The spliff passed round. Drawing deep on the spliff. The feeling of smoke in the lungs. The feeling of smoke caressing the lungs.

Another half. Does Nietzsche want one?

Nietzsche, shaking his head. Nietzsche, sipping his vodka.

What the fuck? Art says. This is Dionysus, man. In a pill.

Nietzsche: Dionysus doesn't come in a pill.

Pogo and Roly, arriving in blow-up Sumo wrestler costumes. Pogo and Roly, dancing in their blow-up Sumo costumes. Meatball, wearing an I FUCKED YOUR GIRLFRIEND teeshirt. Sister-Fucker, wearing a BURN BABY BURN teeshirt. Dangleberry, wearing an ALL YOU NEED IS DYNAMITE teeshirt. Titch, wearing an I CAN'T BREATHE teeshirt. Trisha, holding her nose, head back. Trisha, having one of her famous nosebleeds.

Phase-shifting to the next level. Moving deeper. Heading for the heart. We've found the Secret. We've been admitted to the Mysteries—the Wokingham Mysteries.

This is the Zone. We're wholly Here. Wholly *present*. We're nothing but here. Nothing but present. This is who we are. This is what we can believe in.

Immanence. No thought about thought. No awareness of awareness. No self-division. No *philosophy* . . . Living in the element. Nothing apart from the element. Nothing but here, but now.

Common life. Common presence. Accelerating, together. This is what we were made for.

The Head Boy, sweat-box dancing. Mad-dancing, as though shaking his limbs off, long strings of snot dangling from his nostrils . . .

Rain again. Big drops, falling faster. Drenched. Our hair, matted to our skulls. Dancing in the rain, the wild summer rain. Satyrs and dryads and hamadryads and sylphs, dancing in the summer rain.

This is it. This is religion. No gods, only religion.

Belief—in this. Belief—in nothing but this. Belief in everything, but only through this.

Innocent again. Fresh again. *Clean* again.

Have we ever felt so alive? Is this it—*life?*

A grinning Tasker, bobbing into view. Tasker, grinning! Turned-to-the-bad Tasker, smiling! Too-cool-for-school Tasker, full of love!

Embracing Tasker. Are you sorted, man? Tasker asks.

Spike, feet rooted to the ground, dancing with one arm. Just one arm, like an antenna to heaven.

Another half! Another! Let's push it harder! Let's go further!

Up a gear. Another gear. Hurtling. Acceleration. Too fast, man, Too fast. Electricity in the head . . . In the spine . . . Heart, throbbing . . . *I'm too high. This is too much . . .*

The party's a whirlpool, sucking us down. The party, turbid, rolling, sucking us down.

Paula, passing me the spliff.

I'm too high, I say. This is too much.

Paula, nodding without hearing.

I FEEL LIKE I'M DROWNING!, I shout in Noelle's ear.

Noelle feels like she's drowning too.

Into the house, to chill out. *Now I know what it means: to chill out.*

Paranoia. Scout and Meredith, on the porch, discussing me. But Scout and Meredith can't be discussing me. Scout and Meredith are not interested in me.

Chandra's too fucking high. He's passed the point of no return. Someone needs to take responsibility, if he won't.

Let's call the cops on paki-boy.

Chandra's frying his fucking brain.

Chandra'll never go to medical school.

Chandra'll never write another line.

The kitchen. Empty beer cans floating in an ice bucket. Splashing the cold water on our faces.

Doughface, searching the cupboards, looking for something to drink. Pettifor, quoting Monty Python, apropos of nothing . . .

Noelle on my arm. At least Noelle's on my arm.

The hallway. Photos of Annie Tasker—spooky. Of Tasker and his sister. Of the Tasker family, out at Thorpe Park.

I want to lie down, Noelle says.

Let's find somewhere, I say.

The living room. Truth or dare. A circle of kids on the floor. And Nietzsche. And, beside Nietzsche, the girl from the library. Lou.

The girl from the library!, I say. Tasker's sister's friend!

Lou, smiling. Her eyes clear, defined. No glasses—that's it. No glasses.

Is Nietzsche with Lou? I whisper to Noelle. I mean, *with?*

Noelle, not knowing who Lou is.

The girl from the library, I whisper. She's—

The room, spinning. Too hot . . . Out. Up the stairs. Dreaming of a cool bed, cool sheets . . .

Trying the handles of the doors. Locked, locked, locked . . .

Annie Tasker's room. Eeeew. Posters of horses. A bookshelf. A bedcover, with soft toys. They've kept it like it was.

Noelle, sinking down into the quilt.

Is this gross? Noelle asks. It's so fucking comfy.

Pushing the window open.

God, God, God, Noelle says. I'm so fucking *high.*

Kneeling by the window, watching the people leaving. The glow of tail-lights . . .

Lying down beside Noelle. Stroking her hair.

Did you see how pretty she was, the girl from the library? I say.

I don't want to hear about the girl from the library, Noelle says.

I think Nietzsche needs a romance, I say.

I don't want to talk about Nietzsche, Noelle says.

Nietzsche and that girl . . . It's perfect really . . ., I say.

Enough about Nietzsche, Noelle says.

Everybody needs somebody, I say. Even Nietzsche.

Noelle, pulling me close. Kissing me.

They're singing *Dancing Queen* downstairs. They're bellowing *Super Trouper* downstairs. It's irresistible.

Downstairs, on the porch.

Did you guys just do it in Annie Tasker's bedroom? Merv asks. Sick, man.

Art, rolling a spliff. Sitting on the porch, smoking. The stragglers, in little groups, talking quietly.

The Head Boy, passed out.

How many Es did he take? I ask.

I dunno, Art says. About—five.

Jesus.

I hope he hasn't ODed, Paula says.

He hasn't, Merv says. He's just very, very fucking high, that's all.

He looks peaceful, Tana says.

He *does* look peaceful, I say.

I'd like to be that high, Art says.

Spliffs around the Head boy's body. His bare chest, rising and falling.

Maybe he's in a fucking coma, Paula says.

Maybe he's just asleep, I say.

He's okay, Art says. He's dreaming. Look, you can see his eyes move under the lids. It's REM.

What do head boys dream about? we wonder. Sporting triumphs . . . School prizes . . . That kind of thing.

Five Es, man, Art says. That's heavy.

Tasker and Gamma-Ray, resting on fallen Sumos. Waves of lethargy.

What about Nietzsche? I ask.

He left, Paula says. With that girl. They went in the woods.

The woods! Nietzsche went to the woods! We should go to the woods! Let's go and wait for dawn in the woods!

Through the gate.

Jesus, I still feel fucking great, Paula says.

So do I, Noelle says.

It's the afterglow, Merv says. That's what it's called. Es only last a few minutes. But then there's the *glow*.

The woods, opening to us. The early-summer woods, opening. All things growing. Sap rising.

Nietzsche's somewhere in the woods. Nietzsche, with Lou, is somewhere out ahead of us.

Nietzsche's in the throes of a Great Love. He's more refined than we are. He's capable of Emotional Depths . . .

It's all that private schooling, Art says.

It's all that *philosophy*, I say. It's reading really hard books.

Why are you guys so fixated on Nietzsche? Noelle asks.

I want him to have what he deserves, I say.

Did you see Lou's eyes? Art says. She's really something, man.

We imagine them: Nietzsche and Lou, walking ahead of us in the woods. Nietzsche and Lou, above us in the woods. Higher than us. Translated into light. Astral-bodied, ether-bodied, having left the world behind . . .

SUNDAY

Afterglow.

We're coming down, right? Merv asks.

It's slow and gentle, man, Art says.

It's, like, a plateau, I say.

Everything's in soft-focus, Merv says.

Everything's glowing, man, Art says.

I feel weightless, I say. I don't have a thought in my head.

I feel like I could *believe* in things, Merv says. I want to believe.

I believe—in all of this, Art says. Really I do. The full void, man. The true sky.

I actually feel good, I say. I actually feel *happy*.

We're going to change the world, right? Merv asks.

We're fucking invincible, Art says. They can't ignore us. They can't ignore our *demands*. It's not as if we want much. Just *love* . . . and *peace* . . . and *unity* . . .

We're all the same—that's what they have to understand, I say. The spiritual revolution's begun. It's in progress.

We're young, man, Art says. And being young is good. So much *promise*. So much possibility.

Jesus. Why do we feel so great? Paula says. I hate feeling great.

We're floating, man, Art says.

We're celebrating, I say.

It's the *third* summer of love, Art says. It's the Age of Aquarius all over again. It's a whole new level of consciousness . . .

The Earth loves us!, I say. We've got to stay in touch with the Earth. We've got to make sure we're *earthed*.

The footpath towards Warren Lane.

The sun, passing through us. The sun, the photons of the sun, passing through us.

We're all space, atoms far from one another. We are all distance, the sun pouring through us.

The sun, shining through our spaces. The sunlight, breathing in our spaces. The summer, breathing in our pores.

The depths of summer. Summer pressing into summer. Summer, searching inside for summer. Summer, gone in search of summer.

The feeling of another summer. A *deeper* summer, alongside our own. A sense that we'll find it. Or that it will find us. That it is blind, but that it seeks us. A sense that it is coming close. That it is already here, if only we could see it.

The summer into which we'll be dissolved like aspirin. The summer that will disperse our atoms, let them float. The summer that will phase-shift us into light, into particles of light.

Summer times summer . . . Summer, multiplied by summer . . . Summer glory . . . Summer youth, when even the old are young . . .

This is the sweetest day, Merv says. The best day.

Everything's going to be okay—I'm sure of it, I say. For all of us. It's all going to get better and better . . .

★

Nietzsche, by the gates of St James's.

We're still high, Paula says. You'll find us unbearable. *I* find us unbearable.

So, you and Lou, eh? Art says. You . . . and . . . Lou . . .

We're giving up everything, I say. We're not going in tomorrow.

Yeah, baby. We're starting a tribe, Art says. A new suburban tribe . . . Do you want to join?

Never mind the tribe, Paula says. What happened with you . . .
and . . . Lou . . . ?

Nietzsche: We walked through the woods.

Did you kiss? Art asks.

Silence.

Did you look into each other's eyes? Paula asks

Silence.

Did you hold hands? I ask

Silence.

Did you build a fire? Art asks.

Silence.

You should have built a fire, Art says. It's primal. And romantic.
We'll build bonfires, in our tribe. We'll sit round the bonfires, staying awake forever . . .

Maybe Lou could join our tribe, I say. Is she a profound person?

What did you talk about? Art asks. What did you tell her?

Nietzsche: I said *hello*, and she said *hello*. I asked her what she was
doing at the party. She said she was a friend of the family. She said
her parents were friendly with the Taskers and that she'd known
Annie since . . . forever.

I said I'd come hoping that she would be there. She said nothing.
I told her she looked very solemn. She asked what was wrong with
solemnity.

I asked whether it was a Polish thing. Whether the Poles were a
solemn people. She said Poles had a lot to be solemn about. I said I
was German—half German. She said Germans had a lot to apologise
about.

Then she said she didn't have anything in common with anyone,
not even herself. And she said she thought it might be the same for
me. I said, maybe.

I told her that all my life, I've been around people I hate. She said
she admired that I can say I hate them. She said she doesn't know
what she hates.

I told her there's a power to hatred. That hatred means they'll
never get you, you'll never disappear.

She said she'd like to disappear.

I said I wouldn't like her to disappear.

She asked me why I wasn't with my friends.

I said I don't have any friends.

Jesus—*thanks*, Paula says.

That was just a line, Art says.

Let the man tell his story!, I say.

Nietzsche: We walked for a long time.

She told me everything is complicated, and she wants it to be simple. She told me she wishes there were a safe word in life that she could say and make everything alright. She told me she wishes she were old and her life were nearly over, that then she wouldn't feel miserable for no reason at all. She told me she's no good at small talk that doesn't lead straightaway to Big Talk, and that she doesn't have anyone to talk to since Annie died.

And what did you say? Art asks.

I told her sometimes I resent the world just for existing, and I resent people just for being alive. I told her I wonder what the world is for. I told her sometimes I wished there were a God, who could judge it all to be rotten, and judge *me* to be rotten. I told her sometimes I wish for the revolution that would turn things the right way up, and put me up against the wall with all the other enemies of the people.

I told her sometimes I'm sure that I'm the problem—that it's all *my* fault in some way. I told her sometimes I fantasise that I can atone for it—that I'll sacrifice myself just to make the world right. I told her sometimes I want to martyr myself for the sake of everyone and everything.

I told her I'm full of *nausea* and *pity*. That everything in the world disgusts me. That sometimes I weep from pity, from the wretchedness of the world.

Jesus, I never figured you for a weeper, Art says.

He was trying to impress Lou with his sensitivity, I say.

But what about a *kiss*? Paula asks.

Did you hold hands, at least? Art asks.

Nietzsche: We hugged, when I took her back to Tasker's—that's all.

Well, that's *something*, Paula says. That's *sweet* . . .

FOURTH WEEK

MONDAY

Form period.

I feel like shit, Paula says. Fuck the afterglow.

Does anyone have bananas? Art says. You're supposed to eat bananas when you're coming down.

Lucozade, Paula says. We need Lucozade.

You're supposed to smoke, Merv says. Just roll a few . . .

Where there's an up, there's a down, Paula says.

Maybe we learned something, Art says. Did we learn something?

We were part of something, Merv says. It was beautiful. We were one . . .

I thought we might be changed forever, Art says. I thought everything would be different.

Fucking form period!, I say.

Everything's exactly the same as it was, Merv says.

Everything's *worse* than it was, I say.

Dingus, picking his nose. Fatberg, making chimp noises. Bombproof, laughing at Fatberg's chimp noises. Sister-Fucker, working on a WHITE POWER tattoo with Indian ink and compass. Calypso, eyes glazed over from stupidity. Diamanda, preening. Binky, preening. Nicholas Nugent, preening. Quinn, preening. The Head Boy— asleep again.

★

The Old Mole's getting quieter. The Old Mole's going catatonic. The Old Mole's going to end up like Merv's dad.

What's on her mind, the Old Mole? The desecration of the North, no doubt. The desecration of her *Newcastle-upon-Tyne* . . .

They're smashing it to rubble, the Old Mole told us. They've cut the subsidies. The budget for care. They're all but advocating the abandonment of the city.

Of course, they're only really finishing the job. They closed the mines, back in the '80s. They destroyed shipbuilding, back in the '80s. They crushed the unions, back in the '80s. They quelled the rebels, back in the '80s.

They hate the North! They hate solidarity. They hate *organised labour*. They hate *politics!*

They want the North to autodestruct. They want the North to sink into the earth. They want to close the doors to the North. They want the North to dispose of itself quietly.

The Old Mole, in the property-boom South. The Old Mole, in the we-deserve-it South. The Old Mole, exiled in the ever-thrusting South. The Old Mole, marooned in the shark's-grin South. The Old Mole, risking sanity in the frantic-nullity South.

The Old Mole, lost deep behind enemy lines. The Old Mole, teaching the children of the enemy. Teaching *conventional economics*: *perfect competition*, the *theory of the firm*, the *efficient-market hypothesis*. All of it fake! All of it bogus! All of it grounded on nothing!

Perhaps the Old Mole wants to be close to the coming disaster. To see it at first hand: the destruction of the South. To see what economic mayhem looks like when it's unleashed down South. To see the South gets what it deserves. Perhaps the Old Mole's here to witness the end. To wander future ruins.

The Old Mole, waiting for the bombs to fall. For the digging of mass graves. For airplanes to crash from the sky. The Old Mole, foreseeing upturned cars on fire. Cannibals, hunched over flesh. Bodies strung from lampposts. The Old Mole, divining flare-lit craters. Scorched earth. The Old Mole, waiting for whirr-warr . . . Bunkers . . . Bloated corpses . . .

No wonder the Old Mole's quiet . . . No wonder the Old Mole's still . . .

Free period.

The common room's a tar pit, we agree. The beasts are sinking, poor bastards. The trendies are being sucked down. And what about us? Every effort to escape mires us further. It's best to remain still. Best to simply close your eyes . . .

It's an experiment. Some ghastly initiative of Mr Pound's.

They're deliberately depriving us of air. They're pumping out a little more oxygen every day. They're dimming the lights just a little every day. And they're dialling up gravity—we're a little heavier every day.

The common room's an airlock. And they're slowly depressurising.

They're preparing us for *the outside world*—we know that. They're readying us for office cubicles. They're measuring us up for our customer-service headsets. Customer service, *if we're lucky.* Selling insurance, *if we're lucky.* Telemarketing, *if we're lucky.* There won't be much work by the time we've finished our studies.

Smoking patrol.

Crossing the bridge.

I think I might be Gnostic, Art says.

Go on, I'll bite—what the fuck is a Gnostic? I ask.

Gnosticism is the idea that the wrong god created it all, Art says. The bad demiurge, who fucked it up.

What, like Galacticus, or something? I ask.

Everything's evil, Art says. Everything's disgusting. That's how I see it.

Swans aren't evil, Paula says.

Swans are very fucking evil, Art says. Did you see how they went for Merv?

Ducks, then, I say. Ducks aren't evil.

They are if they're pushed, Art says.

What about trees? Paula asks. Are trees evil?

If they fall on your head, Art says.

But they don't *mean* to fall on your head, I say. They're not *plotting* to fall on your head.

How about the river—is the river evil? Paula asks.

The river is a flux of corruption, Art says.

And I suppose the school's evil, I say.

The school's definitely evil, Art says. Inertly evil. It just sits there, brooding, planning its revenge.

Revenge on what? Paula asks.

Anything free and spontaneous, Art says.

Is that us? Merv asks.

How about the 'burbs—are they evil? Paula asks.

Dully evil, Art says. Boringly evil.

I don't think the 'burbs give a fuck, I say. The 'burbs are indifferent.

Indifferently *evil*, Art says.

They're neither evil nor good, I say. They just are.

So is there a good demiurge, or whatever? Paula asks. Someone to make sure that it's all okay?

Maybe—in a higher universe, a higher dimension, something like that, Art says.

And we're in the lowest universe, right?—that figures, Paula says.

★

The arcade.

Threatening lower-school kids.

Smoke all you want, Art tells them. Really. We don't care.

Art, rolling a joint.

You can't do that here, Merv says.

I need calming, Art says. I've been through a lot. I've got Boston on my mind. Last night, I Skyped my family. How can I be related to these people? How is it possible? We actually share DNA. We shared the same family home. Nature and nurture. And still we've got nothing whatsoever in common. I feel like a fucking alien. I feel like a *Martian*.

And this *school*, Art says. Why do we have to be here? Why do we have to do these things? This is beneath us. It's humiliating. To be among all *these people*. They're barely alive. At least we could live, if we were allowed. At least we have the potential to live. Why can't something save us from mediocrity? Why can't someone recognize us for what we are?

We're dying by degrees, Art says. If we spend any more time here, we'll lose our minds. Do you ever feel you're losing your mind? The banality of evil. This is what it fucking *means*. This is what it fucking looks like.

★

The chip shop.

Are chips evil? Paula asks.

What about ketchup? I ask. Vinegar?

Are chips more Gnostic with or without salt? Merv asks.

Which is better—Gnosticism or nihilism? Paula asks. Which would win in a fight?

Isn't Lindsay Lohan becoming a Gnostic? I ask. And Kim Kardashian. It's spreading through Hollywood. Kristen Stewart is considering it. Gnosticism's the new Kabbalah.

★

The riverbank.

Art, reading from his Gnostic treatise.

> *How long shall I sink within all the worlds? How long will I love the sheep, and stumble with them that stumble?*
> *Behold the world, that it is a thing wholly without substance, in which thou must place no trust. All works pass away, take their end and are as if they never had been.*
> *Who has carried me into captivity away from my place and my abode, from the household of my parents who brought me up? Who brought me to the guilty ones, the songs of the vain dwelling? Who brought me to the rebels who make war day after day? Who took the song of praise, broke it asunder and cast it hither and thither?*

Gnosticism's moralism—that's what Nietzsche would say, Paula says. A way of judging life.

We *should* be judging life!, Art says. Life is shit, isn't it? All this—it's all shit. It was shit all along. From the beginning. It was shit before anyone said, *Let there be light.*

Let there be *shite*, I say.

We can't judge the world like that, Paula says. We can't call it disgusting—that's a value judgement. That's morality. The world's just indifferent.

Look—the world is a corpse, and we're its maggots, that's all, Art says.

So what's the upside of Gnosticism? Paula asks. Sell it to us, Art.

God—eternal life—the usual stuff, Art says.

Do you believe in that? Paula asks.

I don't think so, Art says.

You're not a Gnostic, Art, I say. You're just a *depressive*.

Art's broken patio. Waiting for Nietzsche.

Lethargy. Lassitude. Collapse, on the deck chairs.

It's so *hot*.

It's alright for you, Chandra—you're used to the heat, Art says. Your people have more sweat glands. You evolved them in the blazing East. Or the rest of us lost them in the frozen North. One of the two . . .

Jesus, Art, you smell fucking *rancid*, I say.

Good, honest sweat, Art says. What's wrong with that?

It's the sweat of a corrupt soul, Paula says. The sweat of a sinner.

Or a paedophile, I say.

Say something motivational, Art, Paula says. Make us see why we should give a shit.

We have to live as though we aren't part of the world, Art says. *Death to the world*—that's what we've got to say, in our hearts. Death to all the . . . *demonic principalities*. School and uni and government . . . all that shit.

This world is rotten, Art says. The whole world has gone to shit. All the authorities are obsolete. All the institutions are dead. Politics is over. There's nothing we can believe in . . . We've got to protect ourselves. We've got to hold ourselves together. We've got to *force* something . . .

It's not just about us, Art says. We're doing it for the world. We're doing it for *everyone*.

It's like the monasteries, Art says. People used to wonder what monks were for. Well, they were supposed to exist for the sake of the world, whether the world knew it or not. They were supposed to *invoke the Spirit upon all humanity and all Creation*—that's what Justin Marler says. And it's the same for our band. We're doing it *for* the 'burbs, although the 'burbs don't give a fuck . . .

The band's got to be our *whole life*, Art says. We should live the band, do nothing else, just write and practice and play. It's got to be all we think about, day and night. We can't separate the music from our lives—not anymore. Living—that's the art. We've got to start a new society. That's what a band has to be: a clue to a new way of life.

★

Band practice.

Silently setting up. Silently preparing ourselves. No one looking at one another. Resolve . . . Confidence . . .

Free music, very slow. Open music, like an alap, laying out the parameters.

Marimba, resting on a bed of bass. Marimba, with added distortion. With reverb.

Shimmering marimba chimes. Rhythmic chords. Broken chords. Then quiet. A holy pause . . .

And now Nietzsche's speech-song, barely whispered. Nietzsche's speech-song, accompanying the music. Whispering beside it. Nietzsche's speech-song, asking for nothing. Demanding nothing. Murmuring, nothing more.

Nietzsche's speech-song. How *weak* it is! How close to nothingness! Nietzsche's speech-song. Only streams of words, half words . . . Only an indistinct murmuring, like a conversation you can't quite hear . . .

Nietzsche's speech-song, drifting in and out of silence. Making no claims. Nietzsche's speech-song, almost out of earshot.

Nietzsche's speech-song, adding barely anything. And taking nothing away. Nietzsche's speech-song, like dew on the grass. Like light on water.

Do not hinder it. Do not stand in its way. Make space for it. No— heed how it makes space for itself. Heed how it makes time, creates time. Hear how it creates space for us, and time.

We know who we are. We're a speech-singing act. We're *Nietzsche's* speech-singing act. Nietzsche's steering us, and we must let ourselves be steered. Nietzsche's out in front—our probe, our searchlight—and we need to let his speech-song guide us. We need to follow his vocal. Nietzsche's in our tunnel, and we're following him out. Nietzsche's in our maze, and he's going to help us escape.

Early-hours WhatsApp.
    Art: *We're saving ourselves. We're fucking redeeming ourselves.*
    Me: *He's saving us. He's redeeming us.*
    Paula: *It's romance. It's what's love has done for Nietzsche.*
    We've been honed, we agree. We've been loosed in a single direction. We've been drawn from the quiver, notched on the bowstring, and loosed. We're only movement. Only the long arc towards our target. Only transit. We're the discovery of flight.
    We've attained our youth. Become worthy of it. Something's happened in the final hour, when we thought nothing could happen. Something's happened, in the final moments, when it felt as though nothing could possibly happen . . .

TUESDAY

Geography.
    Mr Zachary, still off. Miss Lilly, still off. Mr Beresford, never to be seen again, probably. Mr Varga instead. He's not even a geography teacher.
    Are you *sure* you're qualified to teach us, sir? Paula asks.
    Let's talk about the end of history instead, sir, Art says.
    I never liked history, Paula says. All those dates. All those kings and queens. All those massacres and sackings. All those crusades and counter-crusades. All the colonial smash and grab. None of us care about that *sh-*, that *stuff* anymore, sir.
    I'm providing teaching cover, Mr Varga says. And I'm not going to pander to you.
    It's our critical spirit, sir, Paula says. We have inquiring minds.
    Are you going to read to us, sir? Like in assembly? Art asks.
    Tell us more about the sister and the cone, sir, Paula says.
    What happened in the end, sir? I ask. Was the cone built, sir? At what cost, sir?

They can't just be building cones all over the place, sir, Paula says. There are regulations. There's health and safety.

We live on the cusp of a new age, Mr Varga says, beginning the lesson. The Anthropocene has begun. Do you know what that means?

We're geologic agents, sir, Paula says.

We've become a force of nature, sir, Art says. Like, a natural condition.

Slide: (Title) *Anthropocene*. (Bullet points) Anthropos—*human*. Cene, *from the Greek* kainos—*new, recent. Definition: The period in which human beings directly affect the geological record.*

How come we get to call a whole period after ourselves? Art says. I mean—

Because we're the agents of change, Mr Varga says.

Slide: *Biodiversity Decline*. Charts, showing mass global dieback of plants and animals.

Slide: *Biogeography Change*. Maps with arrows, showing species on the move.

Slide: *Geomorphological Change*. Charts, showing changes in drainage patterns, mapping deposits from concrete, lime and mortar.

Mr Varga, telling us climate change is intensifying. Telling us about forests giving off carbon dioxide, rather than absorbing it. Telling us about the acidification of the ocean. About the end of saltwater fish. About insectageddon . . .

And the causes of all this are quite clear, Mr Varga says. Population growth, rising resource consumption and carbon emissions. Humanity, in short. We're changing the Earth.

That's the wrong way round, sir, Art says. The Earth's the agent. It's *Gaia* that's changing things. *Gaia's* getting rid of *us*.

It's the *Geocene*, sir, Paula says. The Earth's turning poisonous. The Earth's turning hostile. That's why we're getting new kinds of cancer, sir.

Forget the end of history—it'll be pre-history all over again, sir, I say. It'll be a new Stone Age.

Have you built a bunker yet, sir? Art asks. Do you have a stash of small arms?

We should build a giant cone, sir, Paula says. A really big cone. And we should all get into it. And *blast off* . . .

Only space is full of Virgin heirs and minor royalty, sir, I say. Not to mention Tim Peake. So space is no refuge, either, sir.

The *Idiot* book club.

You've actually finished it, Merv? Paula asks. Are you sure it wasn't *The Idiot's Guide to The Idiot*? You actually read *The Idiot*?

Yes, Merv says.

From cover to cover? Art asks.

Yes.

All the pages? I ask.

Yes.

Every line? Paula asks.

Yes.

The novel's, like, eight hundred pages long, Merv, I say. How could you even pick it up?

Merv's our idiot—don't you see? Art says. It takes a holy fool to read it.

Holy fools don't sell drugs, I say. Holy fools aren't pushers.

Leave him alone, Paula says. How else is he going to pay for uni? It's either dealing or prostitution. I mean, it's okay for Prince Myshkin—he didn't have student loans. The *Russian Christ* didn't have to face temping jobs in Winnersh Triangle for the rest of his life. He could just swan about being mystical.

Beauty will save the world . . . that's what Prince Myshkin believes, Merv says.

Prince Myshkin's wrong, Art says. Beauty *mocks* the world. It looks like it's some great clue to everything, but it's not. Beauty laughs at us. It's never done anything but laugh . . .

There's another thing he says, Merv says. *Humility is a terrible force* . . . I still don't know what that means.

Humility isn't a force, Paula says. The humble are destroyed every day. That's what the world is: a machine for the destruction of the meek and the humble. You know what, I don't believe in Prince Myshkin. I don't believe in his idea of beauty. I don't believe in his idea of humility—just accepting suffering. And his visions—they're unbearable. What he sees before he has a fit.

Joy and hope in harmony, Merv says. The highest synthesis of life.

Death—that's what he sees, Paula says. All those visions of eternity . . . all that being absorbed into the infinite and beatitude . . . it's a cover for a death-wish . . . He wants to die to the world, just like you, Art.

Prince Myshkin wants to *save* the world, Merv says.

But he just sends everyone *crazy*, Paula says. Wherever he goes, people go mad. He has to take responsibility for the effects he has. Otherwise, he's just a child.

The most important thing is life, Merv says—that's Myshkin. Life is what saves us. For Dostoevsky, life's another name for God. And God's another name for life.

No one believes in God anymore!, Paula says.

It's not even that beauty *will* save the world . . . Beauty *has* saved it, Merv says. We're already saved—don't you see? We've been saved by life. We're already in paradise . . .

Don't let Nietzsche hear you, I say.

Nietzsche talks about life, too, Merv says.

He doesn't talk about *God*, I say.

God's just a word, Merv says. Look—I've seen life. Life itself. I don't know about God.

What's that supposed to mean: *life itself*? Paula asks.

What Prince Myshkin sees, Merv says. In his visions. Sure, he has to pay for them. Pain . . . idiocy . . . disconnection from everyone . . . But it's worth it, to see life. Just life . . .

In the study area. The air, summer heavy.

Half light. Pearly light. Fans, moving quietly from side to side . . .

Summer in the sixth form. Summer, passing through the school like a galaxy's arm. Afloat—we're afloat. Summer has lifted us into the air.

The air's thick. The air, thick as soup, barely moving, despite the moving fans.

Calypso, walking through the study area. Calypso, hips swaying, hips promising—what? Auguring—what? Calypso's sway—Calypso's rhythm. We're hypnotised. Mesmerised. The promise of—what?

Does she know her own power? Does she know what she has, she who knows so little? Does it live as a kind of *animal knowledge* in her? An instinct . . . How to drive us crazy.

Even the drudges are aroused—frightening thought! Even the drudges want to breed. Even the drudges are moved to perpetuate the race . . . Imagine it! A drudge turned lover! Panting manatees! Beach balls, mounting one another! Oh God, the horror!

An ape-like excitement, spreading among the beasts. They're stirring. They're restless. They want to fuck, they want to fight—one of the two.

Luxuriance. As though every girl were Cleopatra, cruising on the Nile. As though every boy were Mark Antony. If only everyone wasn't so pudgy. But that's sensual, isn't it? Like Rubens' paintings . . .

Hadley, all coltishness, all long limbs. Binky, doing the vulnerable thing, the woodland creature thing, with bush-baby eyes. Nicholas Nugent, never more beautiful . . .

Lust. How can anyone concentrate? How can anyone have anything in their minds?

Lust . . . Sap, rising in the trees. Flowers, opening to the sun . . .

The sixth-form photo.

Benches on the grass. Chairs on the grass. Taller lads at the back (the beasts), less tall ones farther forward (the Head Boy and head girl, drudges, nerds). Girls in the front rows.

Instructions: look straight ahead. Smile, if you like. But no fooling around. This is the sixth-form photo, meant to take its place alongside the other sixth-form photos on the wall.

Sixth-form joie de vivre. Sixth-form banter. Meatball, blowing a kiss at the camera. Mr Pound, smiling at Meatball, despite himself. Dingus, gurning at the camera. Mr Pound, play-pretend cross. Mr Pound, in *indulgent uncle* mode.

Dread. Lined up with our cohort. Photographed with our cohort. Smiling for the camera, with our cohort. It's disgusting. We're not part of this. We never were. How did we let ourselves be rounded up?

Don't smile, Art says. Don't give in, this close to the end. Don't get valedictory. Don't get demob-happy. Don't josh with Mr Pound. Don't meet his eye.

Death to the world, Art says. Death to their fucking world. Don't act cute. Don't give them anything. Stay inscrutable. Don't join in. Make no fucking concessions. Remember: We're not part of this. We hate them. We hate *everything*.

The Head Boy, sitting beside the head girl. Mr Varga, sitting at the front. The Old Mole, sitting next to him. Miss Lilly, sitting across from them. Mr Pound, in the centre, forehead gleaming.

Here we all are. A meteor could flatten us, all at once. A blow from the sky . . . A surgical strike . . . A passing drone could take us out, like an Afghan wedding party. Maybe Mr Pound could arrange it.

A smoking hole in the grass. Body parts scattered all about. Bits of burning business suits. Scraps of school tie. The smell of cooked flesh . . .

Should we ask Iqbal to call down the lightning? Does Iqbal have special powers of lightning, like Thor, or something? Thor's special powers came from his hammer. Maybe Iqbal's come from his ear, which practically hangs off the side of his head . . .

How late it is! How late! The hands of the world-clock are standing straight upwards!

Photo faces, everyone! Happy faces, everyone!

On our bikes. On our suburban researches.

Lower Earley starts quietly, we tell Nietzsche. There's no dual carriageway here—not on this side of the estate. No vast roundabout with pedestrian underpasses, like at Woosehill—not here. Quiet entrances, with mini-roundabouts. Quiet entrances, dozens of them, with a mini-roundabout each. There are many ways into the labyrinth.

Lower Earley is the *subtlest* of the local estates, we tell Nietzsche. The horror of Lower Earley creeps up on you. It's stealthy, cumulative. It takes time to gather momentum. You hardly notice it at first. It isn't even strongly marked off as an estate. It's only gradually that you recognise the horizontal rhythms. It's only gradually that the houses come to seem more uniform. More identikit. And by that point, it's too late. By that point, you're screaming inside.

That's why you should never *walk* into Lower Earley, we tell Nietzsche. Don't risk it. You need wheels in Lower Earley. You need to be able to get out, and quickly. Press the equivalent of a panic button. The *eject* button.

At first it doesn't look so bad, Lower Earley, we tell Nietzsche. The essential nature of Lower Earley is hidden. There are mature trees here. The houses aren't crammed up to the edge of the road.

There are front gardens—small ones, it's true, but gardens nonetheless. And there are fenced-off back gardens.

And they've tried to provide amenities in Lower Earley, which is impressive. There are community centres. Shops. There are new-build pubs. There's even a new-build church. All your needs are catered for here . . . Your community needs . . . Your shopping needs . . . Your *spiritual* needs . . . They've thought of it all in Lower Earley.

And there's *money* here, we tell Nietzsche. Lower Earley is not a cheap place to live. Actually, it's one of the most expensive places to live in the country! You'll barely find a more expensive place to live, outside London!

And all the while you're pondering Lower Earley, you're being drawn deeper into Lower Earley, we tell Nietzsche. All the time you're contemplating Lower Earley, you're becoming *mired* in Lower Earley. *Lost* in Lower Earley. And the essence of Lower Earley is revealed only when you are lost, profoundly lost, in the depths of Lower Earley. Only then do you come to know what Lower Earley *is*.

Lower Earley seems benign, we tell Nietzsche. Lower Earley seems well settled. There is pride of ownership here. Individual touches to the gardens, to the houses—*charming* touches. Plastic butterflies on the wall. Faux-shutters either side of the windows. And fancy names. *Ashfield. Glebe. Green Tree. Mossy Banks. Mandalay.* It all seems quite *pleasant*, for a while, Lower Earley. *What was the fuss about?* you ask yourself. *I can manage this*, you say to yourself.

The signs appear slowly, in Lower Earley, we tell Nietzsche. And with great subtlety. But the trap door does eventually open. And then you've lost it. Your balance. Your equilibrium. The houses whirl about you. Houses, roads, bulbous cars—it's like the tornado in *The Wizard of Oz*. Delirium, in Lower Earley.

This is the most anonymous estate that has ever existed! The most neutral estate that has ever existed! The scale of it—the largest private estate in Europe. The sheer *size* of it—there's probably nothing to rival it in the world. And there's nothing haphazard about it. Nothing left to chance. It's been carefully planned and maintained. Meticulously crafted. As though it were part of some government initiative. As though this were a deliberate experiment in *low-meaning living*.

There's still life here—that's true. There are parks with children playing! Amazing—the tenacity of life! Amazing—life's adaptability! It's like the strange life five miles down in the ocean. Like the fish that manufacture their own light, evolving strange dangling lanterns. Fish that are all open mouth, hovering in the blackness hoping to catch something. Somehow life survives here, in the depths of Lower Earley, manufacturing its own meaning, its own purposes. Somehow life thrives, even here . . .

But what kind of life is this after all, this life in the depths of Lower Earley? People survive, people go on, the years pass—but what happens here? Slow—very slow—nervous breakdowns, that's what. The slow—very slow—build-up of poison in infinitesimal doses. A *lifelong* poisoning. A lifelong *strangling*. A lifelong *murder*. It takes a lifetime to die, in Lower Earley.

You die of the suburbs, you know—although you think you die of cancer, or of heart disease. You're given your death sentence by the suburbs, even though you think it's breast cancer or brain cancer or arteriosclerosis. The suburbs seep into you. Drip into you. It's subtle. You don't really notice it. You think to yourself, *It won't touch me. It won't get to me.* But by the time you realise, it's too late. It's happened. It's reached your lymph nodes. It's reached your *bones*. You're a terminal case, but it will take you a lifetime to finally die.

We could learn something from these suburbanites, of course. We could settle among them, and imitate their ways. We could go native—absolutely native. Living like them, we could become like them. We could learn their survival skills. Like living among the Inuits. Like living among desert nomads. It's anthropology . . . It's ethnography . . .

We could get a clue as to how human life will survive at the end of times. How human beings will adapt, when the entire world's a suburb. When they've dug suburbs into the earth and floated suburbs out to sea. When they've hollowed out asteroids to make generation starships and sent the suburbs whirling into space. When there are moving suburbs, suburbs on caterpillar tracks, rolling off to escape the ravages of climate change.

There's life on meteorites, plunging through the oblivion of space. There's life on the lava-spitting vents on the ocean floor. There's probably life on the moons of Pluto. In the oceans of Ganymede. Who knows? There's flaming life at the heart of the sun and dark life in the depths of space. Who knows that there's life here, in the Lower Earley estate . . .

Well, we *call* it life, we tell Nietzsche. It looks *something like* life. It has a *resemblance* to life. And perhaps it is, in its own way, a remote cousin to life. But you can't really call it *life*, can you? It isn't really what we mean by *life*, is it?

Nietzsche's blog:

> The suburbs, voiding themselves, yet remaining the same. The suburbs, utterly ruined, and yet remaining the same.
> The suburbs, abandoned to themselves. Unable to overcome themselves. Unable to understand themselves.
> The aim: to deepen the suburbs. To complete them.
> The aim: to truly enter the suburbs.

Art's house. Watching *Melancholia*.
  Silence, for our favourite scene.
  JUSTINE: *Life on Earth is evil.*
  CLAIRE: *There may be life somewhere else.*
  JUSTINE: *No, there isn't.*
  CLAIRE: *How do you know?*
  JUSTINE: *Because I know things. I think we're alone.*
  CLAIRE: *I don't think you know that at all.*
  JUSTINE: *Life exists only on Earth. And not for long.*

*

Art's garden.
  We take turns with the telescope scanning the skies, looking for Melancholia.
  There's nothing alive up there, right? I ask.
  Maybe a few microbes, Art says. Nothing intelligent.
  Discussion. It's a universe of death. Life's an aberration. All life is trying to find its way to death. And it's no different for us . . .
  We know life's wrong, somehow. We know we shouldn't be. And

we're ashamed, as we should be ashamed. All we want is to *correct the anomaly*. We want a rogue planet to *correct the anomaly*.

And what if Melancholia were actually coming? What would we do then? Bathe in its light, like Justine. Disaster-bathe, quite naked, smiling at last. Happy at last . . .

WEDNESDAY

Economics.

The Old Mole on the Great Recession, again. The coming financial crash, again.

We know this stuff. The *central bank cabal*. The flooding of insolvent banks with money.

Banks, creating money without collateral. Banks, lending to corporations at near zero per cent interest. Corporations, borrowing to buy back their own shares.

That's why there's no investment anymore: we know that. It's why there's no R&D anymore, and no start-ups anymore. It's why there's no *job creation* anymore, not really.

Corporate takeovers instead. Predatory monopolies, growing larger and larger. Overleveraging and asset-price inflation, as the rich bank their wealth in property . . .

So we're waiting for the next crash. We're waiting for the Second Great Depression. Sure. Tell us something we don't know . . .

Run Against Cancer in the playing field. The air, thick with *charity*.

Why is everyone wearing pink?

Cancer, Tana says.

There are pink balloons, Noelle says. Look—they're going to release them.

Cancer balloons, floating into the sky.

An LED display of inspirational messages: *CHOOSE LAUGHS OVER CRIES . . . CHOOSE LIFE OVER CANCER . . .*

My mum has, like, a *cancer guru*, Tana says. He says her cancer's an *opportunity*. You have to use your cancer to *grow*, he tells her.

Your cancer's *teaching you* . . . And my dad's gone religious. He goes to church. It's fucking crazy. He's made some deal with God. Like God fucking cares.

I thought people were supposed to become *profound* through suffering, Tana says. Like, really wise or something. But my mum hasn't changed at all. The same gym-bunny she always was. And my dad's just some God-squad moron.

Anyway, I'm going to die young, Tana says. I mean, cancer runs in families. And I look just like my mum.

We'll all die young, Art says.

Everyone will have cancer—their own personal cancer, I say. Their own personal doom.

And everyone will be in pink bibs, Art says. Everyone will be either dying of cancer, or running for cancer in a pink bib.

A soirée at Lassiters. Nietzsche's sister's launch.

Paula, hair dyed blue. Pure dyke chic. Pure *diversity awareness opportunity* in the Lassiters complex. Merv, disco rodent, in a *Manusco Lives* teeshirt. Me, in my *Sabbath Bloody Sabbath* teeshirt. Art, in his *Death to the World* teeshirt. Everyone else in shirt and tie.

The Lassiters yard. Glass of fizzy wine, circulating. Canapés on trays, circulating.

Business types, ties loosened, top buttons undone. Business types, networking. Business types, working the room. The elite. The leader-drudges. The *shoots and tips*. The *cream*. Connecting. Integrating . . .

Nietzsche's sister, circulating. Working her magic.

Nietzsche's sister's got very white teeth, Merv says. She looks like a Bee Gee.

She's quite hot, Paula says. It's confusing.

You could turn her if you tried, Paula, Art says. Might make her more interesting.

I think she looks stressed, I say. Her forehead's all furrowed.

The strain of management, Art says. It's hard work trying to make everything go your way.

Nietzsche's sister, approaching. Hello, lovelies, she says. Thanks so much for coming. How lovely is it that my brother's got his *little gang of friends*?

I can't believe you guys are related, Paula says. How is that possible?

Nietzsche's sister, already moving on to the next group.

What's she actually *launching*, anyway? Paula asks.

FailBetter Consultancy, according to the banner, I say. Future-proofing for business.

So Nietzsche's sister's a prophet now? Art says. They don't make 'em like they used to . . .

Nietzsche's mother, circulating, on Nietzsche's arm.

There's definitely an incest thing going on there, we agree. Nietzsche's mother is *clearly* in love with him. Just as Art's mother is *clearly* in love with Art's much-better-looking younger brother.

The suburbs essentially *run* on incest, we agree. Every family member in the suburbs wants to fuck at least one other family member. It's true.

Who does Merv's dad want to fuck? we wonder. No one. That's his problem. What about Chandra's? He's ethnic. It doesn't hold for ethnics. So it's just Nietzsche, really. And Art's much-better-looking younger brother. So much for our theory.

Walking home.

Nietzsche, expansive.

Patronage and contempt—that's his mother's attitude to him, Nietzsche says. His mother's his greatest advocate, he says. She bores everyone about his *brilliance*. She demands extra lessons for him at school. She's indignant when the spotlight is denied him. But in private, she always looks to *clip his wings*, he says. To take revenge on his type. On her husband's type. On the *intellectual type*.

His mother married the wrong man, Nietzsche says. And now he, Nietzsche, must be *made to suffer*. Abroad, he's his mother's pet genius, he says. At home, he's his mother's pet idiot. Abroad, she asks him to talk philosophy. At home, she sneers at philosophy. *Must you be so airy-fairy, darling? No one's interested in all that, darling.* Her very own intellectual puppet. Her intellectual husband, caged at last.

Why else did his mother urge his return home after his crisis? Nietzsche says. Why else did she lead him back to his childhood bedroom, just when he would have been leaving for Cambridge? So she could re-enact her miserable marriage, Nietzsche says. But this time, all on her terms.

Silence. None of us wanting to stem the flow . . .

And as for his sister, Nietzsche says. I mean, *what's it like* to be his sister?! Is it really *like* anything at all? Is there any core to her experience—any centre? Does she actually *experience* at all? Everything she thinks and feels is just downloaded from the corporate cloud.

It's always *we* with his sister, Nietzsche says. We *like this. We luurve that*. And it's all rushes of feeling. Upwellings of sentiment, in the mode of *we. How lovely, we're all together at last* . . .

Who *is* his sister? Nietzsche wonders. *What* is she? Just a swirling motion, like the clouds of Jupiter. Just clichés and mannered emotion. And the *steel* that holds it all together, of course. Her gritted teeth. Her shark's grin. Her flashes of *pure will*.

Freelancing for the big firms. Parking up at Facebook and Amazon. Waiting in the foyer of Google and Apple. Swiping her way into Netflix UK. Always looking to *work things*. To *add value*. To *pull the levers*. To *find the opportunity*. Always in *event* mode. Always *managing* things.

But worst of all is his sister's *belonging* hysteria, Nietzsche says. Worst of all is when she seizes on the slightest thing as the lifebuoy of all her hopes and dreams. Wild excitement, at birthdays, at Christmas, at business launches . . . Excited talk, of last night's cocktails and canapés, of getting *extremely drunk* with all her *dear friends* . . .

There is something *like* life in his sister, Nietzsche says. Does she think it *is* life? Or is there a midnight hour, when she asks herself, why and what for?

THURSDAY

Free period.

The computer room. Nerds, everywhere. Swarming. Planning something. There's a nerd conspiracy.

You understand them, Merv, Art says. You know their ways. Are they up to something? Are they planning their revenge?

Iqbal, in his fortress of solitude.

So, Iqbal, are the end times at hand? Is it all just going to get worse and worse?

Fuck off, Iqbal says.

Will we achieve worldwide success with our band, Iqbal?

Fuck off, Iqbal says.

Will Art ever make it with Calypso, Iqbal?

Fuck off, Iqbal says.

Will Merv get married to Bill, Iqbal?

Fuck off, Iqbal says.

Is Art going to settle down with Tana, Iqbal?

Fuck off, Iqbal says.

★

High School Massacre.

A wave of zombies. So the nerds have added the undead. So the nerds have pixelated the drudge undead, indistinguishable from the drudge alive.

Arming ourselves. The rocket launcher, in Mr Zachary's office. The chain gun, in Mr Varga's office. The nail gun, in the Old Mole's office. Shotguns lined up in one of the teaching rooms, for old-style fun.

Bonuses for decapitations, ISIS style. Oh, look—Miss Lilly has returned from the dead.

My God, there are too many drudges! We're overwhelmed! It's the zombie invasion! It's *World War Drudge!* It's the common room of the dead!

Running out of bullets. The chain gun, exhausted. The rail gun, the nailgun and the BFG, exhausted. No more rockets for the rocket launcher. No more missiles for the howitzers. It's our last stand. A bit like *The Wild Bunch*. A bit like *Zulu* . . .

Drudges without limbs, rolling towards us. Drudges without scalps, brains pulsing. Drudges with great holes in their chests, lurching forwards. Stray drudge limbs, clawing forward. Drudge blubber in heaps, writhing, twitching.

If only we had a dirty bomb. If only we could just nuke the lot. If only virtual Melancholia would destroy virtual Earth . . .

Imagining a real-life high-school massacre, Columbine-style. Charging through the corridors, taking out our enemies with pump-action shotguns.

Imagining some Truth, some great Cause. Something to gather us up. Some Task.

Imagining exploding ourselves in all directions, like some blazing flower, blooming into death.

Imagining seizing the moment. Changing the rules of the game—*their* game. Playing a new game with their game.

We're ready to be reverent—but what for? We're ready to be humble—but for what Cause? We're ready to kneel—but in service to what?

Walking round the school. Why, again? What are we hoping to confirm? To unconfirm? Are we casting a spell? Exorcising one?

It's nearly over. School's nearly over. Seven years of school, nearly over.

Do we want to relive it all again, but from a safer distance? Do we want to relive the trauma? To master it?

What are we looking for—as if there could be anything to be found? What are we trying to lose? Nothing is happening here—of course it isn't. But why are we compelled to confirm it, this nothing-is-happening? Why do we want to be caught up in its rhythm?

We're bigger than this. We don't have to be here. We don't need to subject ourselves to the lower school. We have our own quarters, and we can leave the school at lunchtime. We're suits among uniforms. Swans among goslings. Why can't we leave this behind?

It's the death-drive. We want to drive ourselves mad. We want to drive ourselves to suicide. To subject ourselves to the worst. To experience the worst.

We're not looking to master our traumas, but to relive them over and again. We don't want to heal our wounds, but to keep them open.

Reminiscence. Do you remember when they chased Strangely

Brown round the school? A whole gang of them, chasing Strangely Brown?

It was during the teachers' strike, the teachers' work-to-rule. They were still at school, they still taught, but they refused to patrol the school grounds at lunchtime. Which meant that it was open season on the brown kids, on the school grounds at lunchtime . . . The sensible brown kids *hid*, of course. The sensible brown kids joined the chess club or the computer club to escape. The sensible brown kids camped out in the library to avoid the mobs.

But poor Strangely Brown thought he was like the other kids, didn't he? Poor Strangely Brown—whose only crime was to be vaguely brown; to be a little brown, even though his parents were white—thought he could stay outside and play, like the other kids, didn't he?

The beasts cornered Strangely Brown by the drama studio. It was curtains for Strangely Brown, there in front of the drama studio. The whole mob, advancing on him, there by the drama studio. And the doors into the corridor were locked, because of the teachers' strike. Strangely Brown was about to meet his Waterloo, there by the drama studio.

He was braced to take his beating, poor Strangely Brown, wasn't he? About to hunch himself up to ride the blows. About to curl up like a foetus. A pair of black eyes?—probably, probably. A broken nose?—more than likely. A broken jaw?—it could happen. A cracked skull?—yes, it's possible. Brain damage?—you never know. Life-changing injuries?—maybe, maybe. What a wretch! What abjection! What misery!

And then, the miracle. Light, pouring down from heaven on poor Strangely Brown. Mr Stevens, who later killed himself, stepping in to save poor Strangely Brown. That no-doubt-already-suicidal teacher, unlocking the door and letting him in, poor Strangely Brown. Mr Stevens—who was not long for the world, who already had had enough of the world, but who was still strong enough to fight for justice in the world, even as it was, no doubt, this same *messianic sense of justice* that made him despair of the world—letting Strangely Brown escape inside and holding the door tight against the mob.

You have to admire him for that—poor, doomed Mr Stevens, saviour of poor, doomed Strangely Brown. Mr Stevens, who wasn't with the other teachers in the staffroom, eating their sandwiches and sipping their tea and reading *Heat* magazine and complaining and gossiping instead of protecting the children in their care.

You have to say there was something *special* about Mr Stevens, who probably couldn't bear the other teachers, who couldn't bear anyone, who wandered the corridors during the teachers' strike, probably thinking about the way he was going to take his life.

You have to admit there was something *singular* about Mr Stevens, something that separated him from the common run of teachers and from the world, but which also gave him a great sense of justice and even goodness. You have to grant that this same sense of justice, coupled with the sense of the evil and fallenness of the world, killed Mr Stevens—that it led straight to his death. But not before he went out of his way to save poor, brown Strangely Brown.

Perhaps it was standing face-to-face with the mob—standing face-to-face with evil and fallenness—that finally pushed Mr Stevens over the edge. Perhaps it was confronting the depths of human depravity in the eyes of Strangely Brown's tormentors that made him resolve to give up the candle.

For how long did Mr Stevens live after that? How long did he survive in this evil world before *deliberately crashing his microlight*? How long could he survive in this evil and fallen world, he who saw acts of destruction on a daily basis? Really, it is only death that awaits sensitive souls like Mr Stevens in this world—nothing else. Really, suicide is the only relief for Mr Stevens and his kind—nothing else. What choice did Mr Stevens have after the things he'd seen outside the doors by the drama studio?

All our efforts come to nothing, Mr Stevens probably whispered to himself before he crashed his microlight. *I know in the end my life is nothing*, he probably mused to himself above the Thames Valley countryside, before he committed suicide by microlight. *I know that the reward of my toil will be nothing, and again nothing*, he probably thought to himself as he flew over the fields and the trees. *There is no hope, none, in my heart*, he probably muttered to himself as the ground came up towards him . . .

Of course, Nietzsche would think that Mr Stevens was *poisoned* by his compassion, we agree. Nietzsche would think that pity had overwhelmed Mr Stevens and destroyed his will to live. Nietzsche would say that Strangely Brown didn't need any *bystander's pity*. Compassion is a deadly drug, Nietzsche would tell us. It patronizes. It levels down. Strangely Brown should have taken his beating and risen again—that's what Nietzsche would say. And who knows—he might have risen again as the *Übermensch* . . .

We need to harden ourselves into diamonds—that's what Nietzsche would say. To forge ourselves in the fires of hatred. To live in complete independence of others. Only that will allow us to withstand our *human condition*. Our *human predicament*. The plague pit of human life!

We need our *own* philosophy, Paula says.

What kind of philosophy? I ask.

A philosophy of *compassion*, Paula says. Where we don't hate it all anymore. Where we no longer say, *death to the world*.

A philosophy of *The Idiot*, Merv says.

We imagine it: a philosophy of *cosmic solidarity*. A philosophy of *resurrected life*. A philosophy of the *perfection of love*. A philosophy of the *crown of being*. A philosophy of *humble servanthood*. A philosophy of *restorative justice*. A philosophy of *penitential giving*. A philosophy of *recovered paradise*. A philosophy of *mercy and life*. A philosophy of *direct experience*. A philosophy of *unpossessive love* . . .

Cans of Red Stripe on Art's broken patio.

Art, bringing out throws from the living room—why is it never really warm enough to sit outside?

Waiting for Nietzsche.

Discussion.

Are we going to make it? *Really* make it? Are we going to do something right—something *true*?

People like us have done it—made great music. People our age, who had no connections, who came out of nowhere and disappeared into nowhere, who recorded just one album, or just one song, and then disappeared.

They're legends to the people who know them. To the real connoisseurs. Their names live on. Whatever they do later in life, whatever dreary job they end up in, they can think, *We did something. We were someone.*

We—that's the word. *We*—because they would have been part of something. It's never just you—never you on your own. It's always a band thing, a collective thing. You're part of something. There's something larger than you. You can forget yourself, in a way. All your problems . . . All the mundane shit . . . It's like having a secret identity. Like being a superhero, or something.

It's friendship. It's being *with* people. It's a mind-meld. It's holding onto something. It's bearing something in common, when the world just wants you to scatter. It's keeping something safe.

All these bands in towns like ours. People like us. Just playing, man. They sought out things. They made things. They recorded stuff. And afterwards, they didn't know how they did it. It was like magic. They just *made* something. They couldn't help it. It wasn't difficult.

Songs written as though by accident. Sounds created—atmospheres, songscapes—as though there were no one at the wheel. As though the music came to itself, made itself. And created them, its musicians, by the same stroke.

It was like fate. It was just what they did when they were together. And that could be *us*. It could all just become easy. It could all suddenly be possible. Something we couldn't dream of before. Something that had never existed, in the history of the fucking planet.

Imagining our music released, marketed. Imagining it reviewed. Played. Licensed for this or that. Imagining its reputation growing all by itself. Imagining it in all the end-of-year polls.

Imagining our band photos online. Unassuming types. Cool in our uncoolness. Imagining fans to come, poring over our Instagram. Nietzsche, all enigmatic. Art, all defiant. Paula, with her mohican.

Imagining fans to come, visiting Wokingham. Wandering up Nash Grove Lane, looking for Art's house, looking for the garden in the photos.

They'd reissue our album on 180-gram vinyl for the tenth-year anniversary. With a gatefold sleeve. With two discs, that would play at 45 rpm. For the twentieth, they'd release a box set, with alternative takes, with live recordings, with rehearsal chat. With more photos of Art's house. Of the now-legendary practice room. Extensive liner notes by Simon Reynolds: *A recording like no other. Post-post rock. A teenage threnody to God. Anthems for bored youth.*

Imagining features on BBC4 and SkyArts. Talking heads, discussing our influence. What we meant to them. How we inspired a generation . . . Interviews with us, modest and unassuming. No swagger about us. No rock-star airs. *Can't remember much about it. It was pretty easy. We just played, that's all . . .*

★

Band practice.

Band telepathy. No need to speak. No need for discussion. Just—lock in. Just—*play*.

Thick chords. Off-harmonies. Washes of electrostatic.

Descending chords. 5/4, then 6/4. Building it slowly, like an Indian raag.

Ominousness. Ebbs, flows. The volume, rising. The wave, building—dissipating. Another wave—more dissipating.

And Nietzsche muttering, speech-singing just behind the beat. On its tail. Repeated phrase: *midnight bell*. Repeated phrase: *tarantula's revenge*. Repeated phrase: *well of eternity*.

Nietzsche's speech-song. Nietzsche's song-trance. Nietzsche's divinatory whisper.

Nietzsche, half-singing. Nietzsche, nearly singing.

It's as though he were tuning into something. As though he had picked up a signal. As though he were replaying something that had begun long before, and will continue long after.

Nietzsche, making distance audible. Nietzsche, giving the infinitesimal a voice.

Nietzsche's speech-song: like a rumour, passing through a crowd; like a radio, talking to itself. Nothing is said—nothing important. Nothing is meant. Speech for no one in particular, speaking of nothing in particular . . . Speech for the sake of itself, which is to say, for nothing in particular . . .

Vocalese. Glossolalia. Nonsense syllables, right down in the mix. Like a Hare Krishna chant. Like a mantra for a new religion.

Merv's marimba, half distortion, half glide. Wavering between tone and noise. Wandering between pitch and noise. Art's electronic sounds. Buzzing. Zinging. Art's electronic fog . . .

Supersoft sound. Microscopic. Ocean Arcadia . . .

Warm marimba pulses. Warm laptop beeps. Ocean-warm synth. Upper-waters synth, sun-warmed, balmy. Blue-in-blue waters; light on the wave-crests. The waves, working. The waters, rocking. All things borne. All things accepted. All things shining. All life, all death.

God is not dead. Death is not dead. Life is alive, and so is death. We're living death, and dying life. We will be born again. We will wake up again. We'll drink from the godhead. We'll scoop light from the godhead. We'll sip the wine of the godhead as the skies split open . . .

FRIDAY

Nietzsche, walking with Lou to school.

Nietzsche, walking with Lou, and wheeling his bike. Walking, wheeling, and holding Lou's hand.

What does he think he's doing? Does he think it's going to be that easy? Does he think he's going to be just like anyone else? Does he think the gates of life are just going to open to him? Does he think he's going to become a *normal* person, part of a *normal* couple?

What does he think's going to happen? Does he think it's just going to unfold? Lou, his girlfriend . . . Lou, his fiancée . . . Lou, his wife . . . A home in the suburbs . . . Kids in the suburbs . . . Will that be how it is? Will things really be that simple?

Walking along with his girl. Walking along the river-path, with his girl. Does he think this will *set the pace for the rest of his life?* Does he really believe that this is how it's going to be?

Why's he letting himself believe in love? Why's he letting himself hope for anything? Why's he given himself permission? It's delusion. It's self-indulgence . . .

Nietzsche and Lou . . . Nietzsche and his girl . . . This isn't how it's going to be. It's not going to be this *easy*. He doesn't *get* to live like this. He doesn't *get* to be like everyone else.

Love's blinding him. Love's made him dull. This isn't his destiny. Nothing's going to be easy or natural. Life isn't going to be good. It's not going to go well. Every step he takes will be a *wrong* step.

The storm's gathering—*his* storm. Evil winds are blowing—*his* winds. Blood's in the water—*his* blood . . .

The philosopher isn't so wise after all. The philosopher's a fool, too. Perhaps the philosopher's *especially* foolish. No one's immune. None of us—not even a philosopher . . .

Town. The bowling alley.

I don't know why this counts as PE, Paula says. It's hardly fucking exercise.

Two lanes down, a team of drudges, bowling dully.

Jesus! Tell me we're not like them!, Art says.

We're bowling *ironically*, Paula says. We're enjoying ourselves *ironically*. That's the difference.

But we're still bowling, I say. We're still going along with it all . . .

We're holding something back, though, Art says. We're keeping ourselves *in reserve*. It's like Justin Marler says on *Death to the World*: we have to live in the world as though we were not of it. So we must live in the suburbs *as not* suburbanites; we must live in Wokingham *as not* Wokinghamites. We must bowl *as not* bowling . . .

So we're *not* bowling? I ask.

You're definitely not bowling!, Paula says. Jesus—how can you keep missing them all?

We're sixth-formers *as not* sixth-formers, Art says. We're pupils *as not* pupils. We're sons and daughters *as not* sons and daughters . . . It's like the man said: *If anyone comes to me and does not hate his father and mother, his brothers and sisters—yes, even his own life—he cannot be my disciple* . . .

I don't actually hate bowling, Merv says.

It's not about bowling anymore, Merv, Art says.

★

Walking through town.

New apartment blocks by the station, neither high- nor low-rise.

Practical apartment blocks, for mid-density accommodation, with views over the train-track, over the beside-the-track scrubland, over the level-crossing and the traffic backed up behind the level-crossing.

Inside. Fancy taps. Mood lighting. Laminate floors. Softly gliding drawers. Faux-marble worktops. Walk-in showers. Flat-pack furniture from IKEA in Reading.

Rental flats, indifferent to their clients. Flats to let, non-places, soul-free places. Zones of transit, like airport lounges. Limbo-flats, Scando-sleek, with subdued lighting, with ornamental pebbles in bowls, with framed prints of Ullapool.

Flats for the uprooted, for the abstracted. Turn-key flats for the tenant without qualities, ready to move in, ready to plug in. Immaculately appointed flats for floating tenants, in which to microwave their ready meals . . .

Upstairs. The study area, full. Everyone, working. Even us.

Quiet hysteria. Quiet panic. Exams—looming ahead of us, like a mountain range.

Summer heat. The fans, turning. The blinds, pulled down. Pearly light.

Restlessness. Inability to focus. Who can concentrate, this close to the end? Who can really get down to work, this close to the end? Revision—even that's impossible. Working upstairs by the fans in the pearly light—it's impossible, impossible . . .

Everyone's delicate. Everyone's on edge. The upper sixth need to be treated carefully. Tenderly. Even the teachers can see it. Even Mr Pound isn't heading down to the common room to berate us. Because we're all here. We're upstairs, our laptops open, our books open.

Calypso, more anxious than ever. Calypso, more beautiful than ever. He'd like to help her, Art says. He'd like to sit with her. Go through it all with her. Make it all intelligible for her. Stroke her hair. Whisper in her ear. Kiss her on the neck . . .

Even Dingus is working. Even Dingus is scratching his head over his books like a caveman. The Dingus-cogs are turning. Sloth thoughts are crawling through the jungle of Dingus's head. Slow sloth thoughts, crawling from thought-branch to thought-branch, in Dingus's head. Slow sloth thoughts, making connections, joining duh to duh, in Dingus's head.

We, by contrast, are coming into our own. These are *our* skies. This is *our* soaring. Ease. Insouciance. (We actually know the word, *insouciance*.)

We are thinkers of the upper air. Of the stratosphere and the heliosphere. We glide. We spread our thought-wings wide. We cruise. We barely need to twitch our wings.

We were made for this, just as Dingus was made for the sportsfield. We know what to do here, just as Dingus knows what to do on the cricket pitch.

To be not only superior, but *effortlessly* superior. To be not just intelligent, but *stratospherically* intelligent. To conquer without trying. To excel without effort.

We don't acknowledge their measures. We play with their tests. We mock their exams—we laugh as we take them.

Revision—we'll pass a book in front of our eyes, that's all. We'll skim a few pages—no more than that. We'll take a few notes. Because we know it already. We know everything already . . .

We want A stars, not just As. We'd want A double stars, if there were such things. A triple stars . . . We want different standards, higher standards. We want to be tested, as no one's been tested. We want to show we're a different *breed* from the others. That our world is not *their* world. That our world streams infinitely far above *their* world. That we belong to the Thrones and Dominions of the intellectual orders . . .

Gate duty.

Nietzsche, cycling out of the school, bag on his back. He's escaping. He must know something we don't.

How come he gets to gets to come and go as he pleases, anyway? It's like how he's allowed to use Mr Varga's office for his studies, while the rest of us have to work in the study area. Special dispensation. For his poshness? For his intellectuality? For his *delicate mental health*?

★

Nietzsche's blog:

> *No true life within a false life. (Adorno)*
> *No true life but in the false. (Fortini)*

Young Enterprise.

Nietzsche's sister, come to address us. Nietzsche's sister, founder of FailBetter Consultancy, come to lead us into the corporate light.

Mr Pound, introducing Nietzsche's sister. Local businesswoman. Futurist. Visionary. Advisor to industry. Winnersh Triangle outreacher. Mr Pound, making way for Nietzsche's sister at the podium.

Nietzsche's sister says she's a professional futurist. Trendspotting's part of her job. She says, for the next hour and a quarter, she's going to tell us about the future, how we're going to contribute to the future.

Nietzsche's sister wants us to come up with the most savage anti-corporate slogans we can think of. She doesn't want us to spare her.

Nietzsche's sister wants us to express what we think about big business. About the corporation. She wants us to think of what we've learnt from all those Hollywood movies . . .

Silence in the room. Stupid faces. Dum-dum faces, eyebrows raised.

Nietzsche's sister says, come on guys, what's really sucky about big corporations?

Silence.

Donnie: I think corporations are really bad for polar bears because . . .

Nietzsche's sister is looking for something snappy.

Uh . . . corporations suck? Binky says.

Nietzsche's sister is looking for something clever.

Meatball, hand up: Uh . . . are we going to be assessed on this?

This is Young Enterprise, Mr Pound says. It isn't part of your curriculum.

Nietzsche's sister says her boss would love that.

Diamanda, out of the blue: Down with corporations!

Nietzsche's sister thinks that's *brilliant!*

Diamanda, giving a little cheer.

Silence again.

Nietzsche's sister says we're not used to this sort of thing. This isn't what we thought business was all about. But Nietzsche's sister's got a secret. The business world needs mavericks. Divergents. X-Men and X-Women. The business world doesn't want *corporate zombies* anymore. It wants *us*—the *real us*, the *authentic us*. People who bring *themselves* to work.

So we don't trust the corporations? Well, neither does Nietzsche's sister! So we're suspicious of capitalism? So is she! We're counter-cultural? So is she! We're anti-authoritarian? She is, too! We've got liberal values? Well, we've guessed it, so does she! This is why the big firms will let us take sabbaticals in Africa. *Give something back.*

Nietzsche's sister doesn't want bored workers. She doesn't want play-actors, trying to please the boss. She needs the young—she needs us. Our ideas. Our *energy*. Our *idealism*. She needs to learn from *us*. She wants us to be creative. To express ourselves. She wants us texting and OMGing and LOLing. She wants us tweeting and posting and linking and liking.

Nietzsche's sister's got another secret. Her business world needs life. Fresh blood. *Happy people work hard.* She doesn't want her employees to be unhappy. She wants them positive, productive, on-message.

Nietzsche's sister is searching for people like us. She wants to know how to reach us. How to speak our language. We might not know it, but we're at the vanguard. We're internet-natives. We're early-adopters. We're hypermediated. We're power-browsers. We're power-scanners. We bounce in and bounce out.

Nietzsche's sister can't categorize us anymore. We're crazy! We're beyond demographics! We're not even individuals! We're always changing. And that's our strength. We aren't anything in particular. And that's precisely what she's looking for.

Nietzsche's sister says, Come join her! Be a part of something amazing! We'll never stop learning!

We have to help Nietzsche's sister. Share our experience. Help her build a bridge to the next generation—*our* generation, and generations to come.

Nonplussed faces.

Uh . . . are we being assessed on this? X-Ray asks.

Mr Pound, shaking his head.

More nonplussed faces. Mr Pound, speaking on our behalf. How can they enhance their CVs?

Nietzsche's sister says, Take the rollercoaster ride! It's a dynamic environment out there. We can't expect a job for life—hey!, who would want one? Firms are always changing. Rightsizing and smart-sizing. Restructuring. Outsourcing. There are mergers and acquisitions. Choppy waters!

Nietzsche's sister says, But it's exciting, too! Sometimes, we're going to be *over*employed, sometimes we're going to be *under*employed. Sometimes, we're going to be thrown entirely off-balance. We probably won't have any idea where we're going next. We can't be afraid of that! We have to be *flexible. Results-oriented. Optimistic.* We have to be ready to *bounce back with a smile.*

Paula, raising her hand. So the corporations want us young and fresh, right? They want to crack us straight out of the egg.

Nietzsche's sister, nodding her head.

And you're here to scoop us up in your net? Paula says.

Nietzsche's sister, nodding her head enthusiastically.

Open your eyes, Paula says. What do you see?

Nietzsche's sister sees a room full of bright young people.

You see *SHIT!*, Paula says. You see fragments. You see chaos. You see parts of human beings and never a whole.

OUT, Paula!, Mr Pound says.

It's *NIHILISM!*, Paula says, picking her bag up to leave. You don't believe in anything you've said. Nor do you, Mr Pound. The corporations don't need us, not anymore. They don't need us to produce and they don't need us to consume. That's what the Old—that's what Mrs Scotswood told us.

Yeah!, Art says, lending his support. Where is this youth you're talking about? Where is this energy? Where is this idealism? I mean—*look* at us. No one's young here. No one's happy. We're zombies—don't you see? We're the living fucking dead.

OUT—the pair of you!, Mr Pound says. Wait by my office!

The corporations don't need our *life!*, I say, taking up the baton. They don't need our *youth* or our *creativity.* They don't need us at all, except as window-dressing. We're surplus population. We're expendable. They're going to make our lives more and more absurd until we do the decent thing and kill ourselves.

OUT!, Mr Pound says.

COMPASSION WILL SAVE THE WORLD!, Merv cries, bringing up the rear. *BEAUTY WILL SAVE THE WORLD!*

DEATH TO THE WORLD!, I shout. *DEATH TO US ALL!*

OUT! OUT! OUT!, Mr Pound shouts.

Art, Merv and I in Wokingham town centre.

Vodka on a park-bench, street-drinker style. Swigging from the bottle like tramps. It's magnificent! You can see why they do it! You can see why they drink all day and all night. The sense of triumph! The joy! A boozy halo, burning around you. Red face . . . red ears . . .

Vodka, from the bottle. The water of life, straight from the bottle. Vodka's the most *truthful* drink, we agree. It's bottled truth. Vodka's both the access to truth, and truth itself.

We're learning from vodka, we agree. Studying vodka. Vodka's the key. But what does it unlock?

The dream of a river of vodka. A river into which you cannot step sober. A river that sweeps away its banks, its bridges. A river that sweeps away the world and is nothing other than the sweeping away of the world.

Waving at people. Smiling at people. We're being *friendly. Fun.* This must be what we're really like. When our inhibitions are swept away in the vodka flood. Open-hearted. Ready to talk . . .

So what if we're slurring? So what if our eyes are bloodshot? So what if we can barely get a word out? We greet the dog-walkers. We greet the walkers-home-from-work. They think we're taking the piss, but we're not. They think we're laughing at them, but we're not. We mean it! We mean everything we say! We're sincere, for once! We're wholly here, at last! Wholly present!

No wonder people want to drown themselves in drink! Who cares about anything, when they drink? Who's bored by problems, when they drink? Who's stressed by exams, by school, by general suburban melancholy, when they drink? We have to drink, all of us! We have to guzzle it down! What laughter! What hi-jinks! We're alive, for once! We feel alive—my God! In fact, we've never felt so alive! We've never felt as alive as this!

Happiness—Is this *happiness*? This pressing upwards into the sky? Is this *rapture*?

Fuck well-being class! Fuck meditation! Fuck the future! Fuck it all! Drink—that's what you need. You have to drink your way to happiness.

What would happen if you bathed in vodka? Showered in it? Rubbed it all over you? Washed your eyes with it? You'd know the truth. You'd fall to your knees, and understand everything—all things. Because it's the water of life we're drinking. The water of all good things. God's own holy water . . .

*

Comedown at The Ship.

Wokingham mildness. Wokingham meekness. Bland people, talking in low voices.

The suburbs, on a night out. The suburbs, out for a quiet drink. Horrors on all sides. *Mild anonymity* on all sides.

The Ship—yet again. The Ship, for the last time—we always vow that it will be the last time. The Ship—to see what happens on the Last Day, and the day after that.

The Ship. Why do we come here? Why do we do it to ourselves? We're not so young any more. We're not infinitely flexible. One of these days, we're going to break. One of these days, we'll just collapse, sobbing. One of these days, we'll shatter the neck of our beer bottle on the bar and wave it at strangers. One of these days, they'll straitjacket us and drive us off in an ambulance.

We're capsizing at The Ship! We're drowning at The Ship! Why do we subject ourselves to this? Why do we seek to destroy ourselves? It's a form of self-harm. It's a way of dealing blows to ourselves—huge blows, heavy blows. It's a way of seeking a beating. It's *suicide by pub*.

Why are we such misanthropes? Why are we so full of terrible thoughts?

One day, we'll have to go to these people for company: that's what we know. One day, with all else failed, every escape route blocked, we'll go to them, or people like them, wanting company—wanting a friendly word. Wanting relief from solitary confinement. One day, back in Wokingham, or a place very like Wokingham, we'll come to The Ship, or a pub very like The Ship, wanting only human company. Where will our high-mindedness be then?

One day, sipping our pints at The Ship, we'll go to them all but on our knees. One day, alone and half-mad with loneliness, we'll stumble to The Ship wanting only human interaction. One day, after all our adventures—our non-adventures—we'll be back, sidling up to them with our pint, desperate for human interaction.

We'll have tried to escape overseas—and failed. We'll have planned to move to London—but never moved anywhere. We'll have tried to get ourselves declared psychotic—but convinced no one. We'll have tried to get ourselves a council flat—and failed horribly. And who will we be then? Where will our superior attitude be then?

One day, we'll open the door of The Ship, or some pub very like The Ship. One day, we'll order our pint at the bar. One day, we'll look round to see who's there. One day, we'll try to catch the eye of an old schoolmate, or someone who looks like an old schoolmate. One day, we'll want only to introduce ourselves. Even *ingratiate* ourselves. One day, we'll go crawling up to them, just for the prospect of human company.

And tears will sting our eyes as we share their banalities. And our voices will tremble as we talk their nonsense. We'll have come in from the cold—how marvellous! We'll have been offered a *word of welcome*—what a surprise! Oh, for the spirit of charity—what a marvel! Oh, for human generosity—what splendour!

The Ship, or a pub very like The Ship, on a Friday night. That's where our loneliness will lead us. That's where our *desire for company* will lead us. No man is an island, after all. No one is capable of living without human contact, after all. No one can get by entirely by themselves: we'll have proven that.

Don't think you can escape: that's what Friday night at The Ship says to you. *Don't think you can stay away forever. Don't you know you'll have to come home? Don't you know that it's as inevitable as fate? Don't you know that you have a Wokingham destiny and even a* Ship-on-Friday-nights *destiny?*

You'll be back here again, that's what The Ship-on-Friday-night says. *You'll be back here again,* The Ship says. *It's inevitable.*

And in the meantime? Now? Tonight? The Ship's crashing through the horror. The waves are breaking on its decks. And no one knows it but us. No one sees it but us.

SATURDAY

Heaviness. Suffocation. Crushed by Thames Valley humidity. Thames Valley air pressure.

A sodden air column, ten miles high, on each of our heads. A thick wet column of atmosphere, square on our heads.

Cycling, so we can feel the air move. So we can force the air. Move it out of stillness.

Cycling, to feel the air rushing into our lungs, oxygenating our blood, filling our veins with air bubbles.

Cycling to cycle. Where are we going? Anywhere. Everywhere.

Earthly flight. We're reaching escape velocity in the suburbs. Any direction is a direction OUT.

★

Trafalgar. Nietzsche's alma mater.

We shouldn't really be here, cycling on the grounds. We don't really belong here, on Trafalgar School grounds. But if we're in and out quickly . . .

Unmade roads. Vistas—one after another. Lily ponds. Flowering meadows. A paddock, with horses. A croquet lawn.

Trafalgar pupils, ambling about. Trafalgar pupils, still in school uniform, their Saturday-morning classes over. Imagining Nietzsche among them, dreaming of burning it all to the ground . . .

The old country house, all red brick. All broad-shouldered. Butchly beautiful. Imperiously beautiful, the staircase tower climbing up. They built it with bricks from the estate. They scraped the clay from Longmoor Lake . . .

Looking down to the water. Doric colonnades . . . Tripod urns . . .

This is where we really deserve to be, even as this is where we really shouldn't be.

Discussion. Imagine if we'd been exposed to this, every day. We'd have improved as people. How refined we'd have been . . . How tall we'd have stood . . . What noble thoughts we'd have had . . . It's wasted on these swine. We're basically aristocrats—of the *spirit*. This is the life we're made for. This is our place. This is where we should have been.

They should give us scholarships, right here, right now. Apology-scholarships. A year in the sun, in the best rooms.

We should have had scholarships all along. They should have come and sought us out, in our scummy schools. They should have come and saved us from our shitty classrooms . . .

We imagine it: Trafalgar teachers, enchanted by us. We weren't the usual dullards, prep-school nice-but-dims. We weren't the dumbo privileged. We were *scholarship* types. We had won our place by sheer intelligence. We didn't quite know the codes. We weren't quite at home with it all. We weren't all ease and social graces. But the teachers liked us more for that . . .

But what tossers we would have been! Trafalgar life would have spoilt us. Beauty would have suited us too well. Better for us that we were cramped and boxed. Better for us that we were kept as battery-hens. Better that we were taught almost entirely by half-wits and quarter-wits. Better that we were surrounded by *absolute mediocrity*. By *municipal socialist architecture*.

Only our *rogue intelligence* saves us. Only *complete disgust* gives us the hatred—the *necessary* hatred. What would our friendships have been like without negativity and darkness? If we hadn't been ready to *tear each other down?* Who would we have been if our noses hadn't have been *rubbed in the shit?*

We'd have preferred Mozart to Sabbath. We'd never have known what doom metal meant. Dub would have been a foreign language to us. Polish jazz would have been entirely unfamiliar. What need would we have had for *Earl Sweatshirt?* For *Pauline Oliveros?* How could we have recognised the majesty of *Anne Briggs?* We'd never have known that the music of *late Scott Walker* was *entirely on our side.*

We'd have known nothing of gravity. Nothing of *despair*. We'd have had no desire to destroy the world. No delight at the prospect of the end of the world. There would have been no twistedness about us. No self-sabotage. No royal road through death and beyond.

And we wouldn't have known the suburbs, not really. We wouldn't have been imprisoned by the suburbs. We would never have *suffered* the 'burbs . . .

Bombproof's house-party, Nine Mile Ride.

Why did he invite the beasts? You'd think he'd have known better than to invite the beasts. And the beasts' beastly friends. And the *old* beasts, the former beasts, the beasts who left before the sixth form. Ye olde beasts—the beasts of yore.

Bombproof's house-party, with its unlimited alcohol. Its seemingly infinite amounts of alcohol. For its seemingly infinite number of guests! Bombproof's sacrificed everything for popularity! Bombproof's invited everyone! Bombproof knew no caution! Bombproof advertised his party everywhere! A mistake! A terrible error!

I think I feel sorry for Bombproof, Art says.

You can't feel sorry for Bombproof!, I say.

A boom from the garden. The Bullards have exploded something. A boom! Terrorism! Teen-murder! Poor Bombproof . . .

Posh accents. Two private-school boys, in the midst of it all. How did they get here?

Danger! Free-ranging beasts, looking for trouble. Looking for posh boys to tear limb from limb.

Discussion. Those two won't last a minute. Look at them, trying to shake hands with people. Trying to be courteous. Why can't they just blend in like everyone else? How long before someone knees them in the balls? How long before they're doubled up on the floor?

Not long. Dingus, head-butting the first posh boy. That's gotta hurt!

It's justice!, I say. It's class war!

The second posh boy, trying to escape, trapped by Fatberg in a half-nelson. The second posh boy, face being rubbed in an ashtray.

Should we rescue them? Merv asks.

Screw them, Art says. They've had all the privileges! It's every man for himself!

The poshoes staggering in our direction, one bleeding from a cut over his eye.

We'll have to save them!, we agree. They're behind enemy lines. We'll have to smuggle them out.

Okay, Art says. But only because they remind me of Nietzsche.

Why did they do that? the first posh boy asks.

It's a structural thing, Art says. A class thing. You'll never understand.

Just drink, I say, passing the vodka. And don't open your mouths! If anyone hears you speak, you're done for.

Follow us if you want to live, Art says. We'll go through the house, and let you into the front garden. But be careful! The beasts fight dirty. It's not Queensberry rules here. They bite. And they'll give you tetanus.

Through the crowd in the living room.

Merv's a real working-class person, Art says to the posh boys. Have you ever seen one before? They're an endangered species. Do your working-class dance for them, Merv.

Merv, giving Art the finger.

★

The hallway.

Merv's salt of the earth, you know, Art says. A real geezer. There aren't many like him left. It should be on your bucket list—an evening with a real working-class person. So tonight's your lucky night, really.

Look, we just want to get out of here, the second posh boy says.

The study. Forcing the window open. Okay—this will get you into the front garden, Art says. The coast's clear. Run through the grass and climb over the fence.

Godspeed, lads, Merv says.

Watching the posh boys escape through the garden.

They're gentler than us, aren't they? I say. And taller.

The master race, Art says.

★

Later. Barricaded in the study. The sound of breaking glass. Break-ing windows. Breaking lightblubs. (Who the fuck is breaking light-bulbs?) The sound of curtains being torn from their rails. The sound of curtain rails being pulled out from the wall. Beasts, shouting from the bathroom upstairs. They're trying to rip the toilet from the floor. A huge crunch. They've succeeded in ripping the toilet from the floor.

The screams of Nessa, threatening to *KILL HERSELF*. The screams of Bianca, threatening to *DO IT FOR HER*.

It a fucking teenage wasteland out there. It's the fucking teen-age Somme. It's only a matter of time before they set the house on fire . . .

Climbing out of the study window.

Chaos.

Someone's pulled up a tree—a whole tree. And it's smashed through the greenhouse. (So that's what that noise was!)

Eddie Bullard, trying to set fire to the rhododendrons and having some success. Bullard's even more insane brother, chopping up the garden furniture, the garden shed, to make an even bigger fire. For the Bullard twins, expelled in year ten, the world is there to be set alight. The Bullards serve strange gods.

Binky, collapsed in the grass. Binky's out, limp. Wails from her friends. General freaking out. She's been doing coke. They've all been doing coke. Binky's had a reaction. Binky's out cold. Should they call an ambulance? Is there a doctor in the house? Binky, wak-ing up and crying, *I'M OKAY BITCHES!*, before passing out again.

Enid the epileptic, convulsing and foaming at the mouth. Hadley beside her, making sure she doesn't hit her head.

Fatberg, vomiting in the bushes. Diamanda, vomiting on the patio. Her vomit's red . . . Has she got TB or something?

It's the red WKD, you fuckhead, Art says.

We need ambulances! Several ambulances! And police! Riot police!

What a scene! What's going to become of us all? We may not sur-vive the night!

Dingus and Nipps, straining at another tree—an even greater tree. My God, it could crush the whole house . . .

Destruction: what the beasts do best. You can catch sight of their old magnificence. They're ravagers of order. Don't get in their way. Let them do their work—*destruction's* work. Let them destroy the old universe so it can start again. Because this is the end of the old cosmos. Violence is part of the cycle. It's part of the law of all things, the great down-going. It's the turning of the cosmic wheel.

Let the end end. Let the debris be cleared away. Let Necessity work its way through. Let Fate play itself out. All order must crumble in time. And after Ragnarok—what? After the old order is destroyed—what then? A new dawn? A new world?

Where's Bombproof? What does Bombproof make of it all? Is Bombproof still bombproof?

Rumour: Bombproof's dead. Bombproof's *dead!* Then are we accessories? Are we going to be arrested? Reassurance. Bombproof only *seems* to be dead. He's actually in the bathtub, upstairs, nude and unconscious. Does Bombproof know the beasts ripped out the toilet? Does he know they flattened the greenhouse? Does he know the Bullards are chopping up the garden?

Kicking Bombproof's seeming-corpse. It must be some protective thing. A protective coma. After all he's seen. His brain is trying to protect him. From the horror. From the beasts . . .

Wake up, Bombproof! You wouldn't believe what they're trying to do to the house, Bombproof!

See what your so-called friends have done, Bombproof! See where your endless ingratiation has got you!

This is how Nazism started, I swear, Art says. You can see it, can't you: the ingredients of fascism?

Mob-law. Child-law. *Lord of the Flies*, all over again.

A teenage warzone. The UN should send some blue-helmetted peacekeepers. We need special forces. When will order be restored? Surely someone's in charge. It's Mogadishu all over again. We need mediation. We need Ban Ki-Moon.

Mob rule. Testosterone rule.

Someone should send out an SOS. A bat-signal. Someone needs to take responsibility. Not us! Not us! It's the teen apocalypse. If teens ruled the world, this is what it would look like. Teen is wolf to teen. All you can do is watch, open-mouthed.

It's like the last days of the Roman Empire. This was what it was

like, before the Barbarians stormed in. Which do you prefer, Art?—
The Romans or the Barbarians? Order or disorder?

And the Barbarians *are* coming. In the distance, on the main road,
a primal horde of Grove boys, heading towards Bombproof's house.
Oh my God. They're tooled up. There's going to be a war. They'll set
fire to the house! Murder everyone! We'll see it on the news. *Suburban teen massacre. Cannibalism at Teen Party.*

Escape! Run away! Discretion's the better part of valour . . . Leave
Bombproof to reap the whirlwind, if he survives. If any of us survive . . .

SUNDAY

Nietzsche's blog:
> *Nothing will happen, not today. Today is only the incessancy of
> what does not happen.*
> *How many days are there left? How many days can there be?*
> *Surely this is the end. Surely things are coming to an end.*
> *But that's just it: nothing is ending.*
> *The eternity of the end. The endlessness of the end.*

California Country Park.

Cars and cars and cars lined up in the park. Pathways marked out,
colour-coded.

The suburbs at leisure. The suburbs at play.

Sunday strollers, with all the gear. Nordic poles. Rucksacks and
Thermoses. For the half-mile trip around the lake. A walking-group
of retirees. In their eighties. Their *nineties!* Radiating health! Booming with health! Sociable and jolly. Nodding hello. *Hello, hello . . .*

My God! These people are planning to live forever!

Lovely weather! Isn't it great to be out? Such cheer! What did they
do with the scowlers? What happened to the miserable ones? They
topped themselves, probably. It's the survival of the fittest. And these
are the fittest . . .

More nods. More hellos . . . *Footpath sociability.* Congratulating each other on being outdoors ... On wearing Barbour jackets ... Hunter's wellies. *Well done, you!*

These are the wealthiest people in England. The ones who will live longest. The most well-adjusted ... The afternoon-smilers ... These are the smuggest people who have ever lived.

They've inherited the Earth. It's all theirs, their birthright. Their numbers have been thinned by suicides, by those who could not endure, by the awkward and ill-fitting who have gone to early graves, by the overstressed and overstretched who are dead from early heart-attacks. Only the smug survive ...

We're not as young as we were. But we just have to get on with it. Stride forth. Blow off the cobwebs!

Elders with bin bags and pick-up tools.

Look at them! They're actually picking up litter. They actually go out for fun and pick up litter!

It's the Big Society in action. It's Civic-Mindedness. They've been Nudged. They're Doing Their Bit. They're Serving Their Community. They've got Get Up and Go.

The elders of Wokingham, volunteering to read with kids. For Meals on Wheels. The elders of Wokingham, on hospital visits. Hospice visits. Chatting to patients. Leading sing-songs in dayrooms.

The elders of Wokingham, taking up t'ai chi. Attending Buddhism classes for the spiritually curious. Arthouse films for the artistically stirred. The elders, taking up golf ... Bowls. Keeping fit. Heading up to London for behind-the-scenes tours of the National Theatre. For art-viewing visits at the National Gallery. For heritage tours. Leisure trips.

The elders of Wokingham, taking life-drawing classes, creative-writing classes, learning how to express themselves in various media. The elders, researching their family trees. The elders, busy with amateur dramatics.

They deferred gratification, and now it's come at last: gratification. They bided their time, and now is their time. Every day is Sunday for them. Every day, a day of eternity. Every day, time to idle in the garden of knowledge ...

Are we going to end up like them? Were they once like us?

Theirs is the last stage of the life-cycle: the Sunday of Life. They're keeping fit. Active. Eating their five a day.

Have they no *decency*? Don't they know there's a time for *dying*? A time to choose to die! Why don't they fuck off to DIGNITAS and

leave the litter be?

FIFTH WEEK

MONDAY

The Old Mole, not bothering with the register.

The Old Mole, on her last week of teaching, her very last week *among the pseuds*. The Old Mole, not giving a fuck about anything, looking straight through us, as though we didn't exist.

The Old Mole's retirement plan: waiting for catastrophe—for the next great crash. For the coming Depression. For the coming Correction. For the end of so-called civilization as we know it . . .

How long can it go on, this interregnum? How long can the bubble grow? Is there no such thing as supply and demand anymore? And what of *price discovery*? And how can the stock market keep rising higher and higher?

The elites, asset-stripping. The elites, taking the money and running. The economy's emptying out to pay the bondholders . . . Whole countries are being ransacked . . .

Leveraged buyouts . . . Monopolies and oligopolies . . . Big Agra, Big Pharma, Big Tech, Big Telecoms . . .

The kleptocrats are building luxury megabunkers in the mountains. The robber barons are building walls to protect them from the people. The feudal lords are readying themselves for state-failure. The oligarchs are buying up unmanned drones and hiring military contractors.

Goldman Sachs are betting on apocalypse. Warren Buffett is hedging *ecological holocaust*. HSBC are putting a price on *mass extinction*. The stock market's soaring . . .

The Old Mole envisages flooded trenches. Mobs of marauders. The Old Mole sees clawed hands and pit burials. The dead mixed up with mud. The Old Mole predicts heaps of stripped corpses. The Old Mole sees silhouetted ruins and smoke rising into the sky . . .

Last lessons, before the study break. All of May—just for studying! The syllabus is done. We've worked through our textbooks. Everything's been *covered*.

Last lessons. Valedictory geography. Valedictory economics. Valedictory English . . . Overviews. The *journey* we've been on.

Last lessons. Exam tips. Revision tips. Timed practice essays, under *exam conditions* . . . Exam parodies. Exam play-pretend, lighter and freer than real exams. No-risk exams, three-hour fakery in slanting sunlight . . .

Last lessons. Looking out of the window. Listening to noises from the playing field. They're practising for Sports Day. Cricket. Track-and-field.

Last lessons. The teachers, relaxed. Less formal. The teachers, unguarded. Off-duty. Jobs done.

Last lessons. Summer air. Summer buoyancy. Summer light, behind the blinds . . .

Last lessons. We're at the top of the school. The pinnacle of our studies. Our schooldays are over, pretty much. Soon, we'll clap one another on the shoulders. Our teachers will shake our hands. Wish us well. We'll be released. We'll gather up our things and make our way outside . . .

Last lessons. Camaraderie. We went the distance together, teachers and pupils. We shared something. And now the end's come, we can drop our alibis. We can be easy with another. We've got through it, and together. We can meet as equals. Everything's forgiven—everything's forgotten, as it would be in heaven. We're out the other end . . .

Last lessons. As though we've been resurrected. We're all but embracing . . . All but weeping . . . Even the trendies. Even what remains of the beasts. Even the drudges. Even *us*.

Last lessons. A little glade in time. A pool, to lie down beside, to take our ease.

Well-being class. Tips on avoiding revision stress (eat right, sleep well, exercise, quit bad habits . . .)

Meditation. Close your eyes, Mr Merriweather says. Focus on your breathing.

Paula, eyes half-open. Me, eyes half-open.

Nietzsche, eyes fully open. Nietzsche, vigilant. Nietzsche, on his watch, looking out. Nietzsche's gaze, sweeping the room like a lighthouse beam. Surveying all, seeing all . . .

The common room. Another day aboard the HMS *Braindeath*.

The immensity of boredom. The uncarved black of boredom. How heavy it is! How dense it is!

Our limbs are heavy. Our heads are heavy. It's as though gravity's increasing. Surely we weigh more than we did this morning.

We're getting pressure headaches. *Boredom* headaches . . .

Boredom, perfecting itself. Boredom, completing itself . . .

Boredom, sealing over our eyes, our mouths. Sealing over our ears. Boredom, numbing us.

And yet the drudges survive. The drudges *thrive!* (*Drudge*-thriving.) Boredom is their medium. Boredom makes sense of them. Boredom is what they do. Boredom is what they *are*.

The drudges are perfectly adapted for boredom. They've been bred for it, as through a programme of *suburban eugenics*. It's *survival of the blandest* in the sixth-form common room . . .

Contemplating the drudges. Do we actually hate them? we wonder. Can we even get up the energy to hate them? Can we even be *bothered* to hate them? Is it actually *worth* it—hating them?

They're diluting us, we agree. They're thinning out our kind to one part per million. To one part per fucking billion. There'll be nothing left of us at all.

They have no idea of *greatness*, the drudges. They don't want to be better. They're not divided. They don't want to declare war on themselves. They have no self-contempt. They don't despise themselves.

Be nice: that's drudge-morality. *Don't be mean. Equal rights. Do what you want to do, just don't judge anyone else.* What hope is there for these people?

Nietzsche's right—compassion has no place among the strong. Compassion for the drudges? You'd just be another drudge! Not even Merv can feel compassion for the drudges.

Heading to Yum-Yum's.

There are always chips, I say.

The great consolation!, Merv says.

Chips are pure ideology, Art says.

What does that mean? Merv asks.

They're false consciousness, Art says.

How can chips be false consciousness? I ask.

They keep the masses happy, Art says.

They keep *me* happy, Merv says.

Which proves that you have no soul, Merv, Art says. Chips are bread-and-circuses—pure distraction.

Distraction from what? Merv asks. Hunger? Cos I'm really hungry.

You never feel happier than when you have a full stomach, do you, Merv? Paula says. It's because you're fundamentally neglected. When was the last time you had a hot meal? And you're no better, Art. You have that lean, feral look. Ah, what you might have been, if you hadn't been deserted . . .

Chips on the bridge.

I nearly came out to my parents the other day, Paula says. I felt sorry for them. It's what they're waiting for. They keep looking at me expectantly, hoping that I'll tell them. Every time I come into the room, they think: this is it—*tolerant parents* time.

Of course, they'd love it if I came out, Paula says. They'd think it was great, having a lesbian daughter. They'd love being taken into my confidence. They'd be *on side*—fully *on side*. We'd talk it through—they'd love that. *We thought something was up. It explains everything. All these years. What you must have been going through.*

They'd order all the books, Paula says. *Loving your Lesbian Daughter. Sapphic Succour: Poems for Gay Teens.* They'd ring up all the relatives. They'd really enjoy that. Getting one up on all the relatives. Being more *tolerant. Understanding* everything just a little bit better.

It'd be the same if I told them I was trans, or something, Paula says. If I said I was going to live as a man, or go neuter. Imagine it. Tears. Hugs. *Whatever you want, we want it too. Just so long as you're happy. We'll go through this as a family. We'll go through it together. We'll transition together . . .*

Band practice.

Sweating in the practice room. Sweat running from our pores in the practice room.

Merv's marimba—short ascending chords, lyrical. Merv's marimba, percussive, bell-like. Merv's marimba-mallets, shimmering up and down the scale . . .

Art's synth-washes. Art's drone, behind it all. Sub-bass. More of an atmosphere than a music. Like some humid climate—some dark, dense rainforest, some heavy tropical squall. Veils of sound. Sails of sound.

Interlocking rhythms. Bill's rimshots. We're going percussive. We're going gamelan, following Merv's polyrhythms.

Changing pulse. Multi-layered comping. Barely any melody to it. Barely a tune. We don't need melodies. We don't need tunes . . .

And Nietzsche's speech-song. Tranced. Blissed-out. Nonsense words. Glossolalia. Muttering—loud whispering.

Nietzsche's speech-song. Sometimes, syllables. Sometimes, words. Sometimes, phrases. Sometimes, silences—great pauses, letting the music be.

Nietzsche's speech-song. Scarcely a voice. Scarcely sound, more a subtraction from sound.

Nietzsche's speech-song. Not language, but the shadow of language. Not language, but its double. Its secret . . .

We're locked in now. It's happening. It's here, it's now . . . We're discoverers. Explorers. We're in the unknown region. We're out in open seas. We've spread our sails . . .

These are great days. High, wide days. Eternal days. Like summer at the North Pole. We will never know darkness, never again. No evening will come. The sun will never set . . .

Expansive music. Expand-your-head music. Summer music. Vista music.

There's no ceiling. The room opens directly onto the sky.

There's air in our music. There's light in our music. There's escape in our music. There's freedom in our music. There's summer—*true* summer, beyond any particular summer. There's the ultra-summer, summer squared and cubed—right here in our music.

We're summer-drunk. We're summer-dazed. Our souls are open. Our hearts are open. We've rolled away our stones . . .

Art's bedroom: a spaceship, a time-ship, a light-and-air-ship. The universe, expanding. The stars, spinning away from one another.

Breaking through to the multiverse, where entire universes bob like soap bubbles.

TUESDAY

Joel Park. Lighting up.

You know what, no one's going to remember this, I say.

Remember what? Noelle asks.

This afternoon, I say. No one's going to remember it.

So what? Noelle says. Why does that bother you?

This is exactly the kind of day people forget, but that I want to remember, I say. Hazy days like this, when nothing's really happening.

We should bury a time capsule, Tana says. Put something in to remind us of who we were way back when.

What, like some rizlas? Noelle asks. Like a packet of hash and a school tie?

Our hearts, Tana says. We should bury our hearts here, like fairy-tale ogres . . .

Problem is, we won't remember where we buried anything, Art says. Rhododendrons are so samey.

We won't even remember *that* we buried anything, I say. We won't remember this afternoon, here, now. We won't remember each other . . .

You're so pessimistic, Noelle says.

It's just that life's so *long*, I say. It goes on forever. And it's full of days like this . . . Life is elsewhere, right? Tell me that life is elsewhere . . . What about France, Noelle? Is there life there?

Life is wherever *you* are, lover-boy, Noelle says.

True life isn't anywhere, Art says. The world's *over*.

Whose world? Noelle asks. Your world? The privileged Woking-ham world? I mean, most people live in Hell compared to this.

Maybe it'll be our turn to live in Hell soon, I say. Maybe that's what's going to happen.

Nothing's going to happen in Wokingham, I'll bet, Tana says. It'll get worse everywhere but here. Wokingham will go on forever.

Wokingham's going *down*, I say. And the whole Thames Valley with it. There'll be a massive terrorist attack. They'll let off a dirty bomb, or something. Fallout everywhere . . . Black rain . . . The whole of the Thames Valley, radioactive . . .

Or there'll be some flood, Art says. The Thames will rise to drown its valley. Reading, drowned. Bracknell, drowned. Henley-on-Thames under fathoms of water . . .

Yay disaster! Yay ruin!, Noelle says.

Yay disaster in *Wokingham*, Art says. Yay the destruction of *Wokingham*.

I've got you guys diagnosed, Noelle says. It's all about *imaginary revenge*. You want Wokingham destroyed because it doesn't recognise your genius, or whatever. You just want a pathetic kind of payback for your comprehensive school lives.

Redemption—that's what we want, Art says. We want it all to have meant something.

That's why we have the band, I say. That's what our music's for.

So you're going to be world-famous? Noelle asks. You guys and Nietzsche?

We don't have enough time for that, I say. Not with Art leaving . . . But people will hear us.

How—*telepathically?* Noelle says.

We'll put some stuff online, I say. Band-practice stuff.

Such optimism, Noelle says. Actually, I rather like having a rock 'n' roll boyfriend.

People all over the world will know who we are, I say. People will know who we've *been*. They'll know we were *in* the suburbs, but not *of* them . . .

Anyway, we don't want to be famous, Art says. All that's bullshit. Look what happened to Kurt Cobain. He couldn't break out of his fame. He sang about how he hated everyone, and everyone just sang along.

That won't be a problem for you guys, I imagine, Noelle says.

At least we're trying to do something, Art says. What are you doing that's so *great?*

Why do we have to *do* anything? Tana asks.

You don't need to—you've got your escape route, Art says. You'll go to uni. Your parents will clear your debts and help you rent a flat in London. But you know what, you'll never achieve anything important, because you'll never have had what we have: poor prospects.

Cry me a fucking river, Noelle says. Maybe we don't want to *achieve anything important*. Not like that. Because we don't have to compensate for our miserable lives.

Sports Day.

Sitting on the grass. Discus throwing, in the far distance. The hop, skip and jump, in the far distance. The one-hundred-and-ten-metre hurdles, in the far distance. The four-hundred-metre relay, in the far distance. Who cares? Who's watching the sport?

Summer, deep summer. Our ties, undone. Our shirt- and blouse-sleeves, rolled up. The girls, sunning their legs.

Looking up, shading our eyes, at the azure sky. Vagueness. Wistfulness.

Why can't school be like this every day? Doors open. Windows open. Everyone vague, wistful. Even Dingus. Even Nipps. Even Calypso, lips parted, has never been more serenely vague and wistful . . .

A valedictory air. A last-of-the-last-days air. There's not much school left. There's not long to go. Days ringing out in the infinite. As though they will never pass . . . As though these last, languorous days will last forever . . . As though we've broken through to eternity . . .

Memories of other interregna. Other suspensions. When time was given back to us. When we learned to raise ourselves up from the plain and see in all directions.

Fire-drills, when we were turned out from our classrooms. Finding ourselves outside, when we should have been inside. Assembled by fire marshals on the playing field, looking over the grass, looking along the river, looking up at the viaduct, instead of down at our desks . . .

School trips, on a hired coach. Giddiness. Kneeling up on the seats to talk with those behind us. Waving to people outside. Making V-signs to people outside. Mooning at people outside.

Bunking off lessons, looking into the school from the other side of the chainlink fence. Sneaking past sixth-formers on gate patrol. Kicking cans along the street. Strolling up to Joel's Park, to smoke among the rhododendrons.

Playing truant for the day. Deliberately missing the bus. Undoing our ties, and heading into the woods. Circling the lake, and walking along garden-ends. Mooching up to St James's, and reading the gravestones. Sitting on the bench, overlooking the valley.

Snow days, when the school bus didn't come. Days of grace in the muffling snow. Days off—all to ourselves. Days to dispose of as we wished. *Wider* days. Anarchists' days, when all directions were open.

The petrol strike, when the filling stations were empty. When there was no bus to take us to school. When there were no cars on the road, no traffic. When we could walk in the middle of the road, like sovereigns.

One day in the lower school, when Mr Zachary refused to teach us. When Mr Zachary sat in muteness, looking out over our heads. Suspension . . . No one in charge . . . The king had set aside his crown . . .

School holidays. The long summer holiday. Vast summer . . . Deep summer . . . Day after day of play in the sun . . . Forgetting everything we'd ever learnt . . . Crossing summer groves. Wading through summer grass. Sheltering from summer showers under the full-leafed oaks.

Wasn't summer always too vast for our plans? Didn't we always have the sense of being lost in summer, *buried* in summer? Didn't we wander summer corridors barely counting the days?

The warm air. The fragrant air. Sun-sheen on the skin. Skin turning brown and browner. And we sun-princes and sun-princesses. And we aristocrats of the higher summer. And we winged demigods and angels, swooping through the air . . .

The computer room. High School Massacre, variation one: low grav. Bounding around the common room. Bounding around the carpark. Merv, bounding across the fields, Art after him. Iqbal, wielding the power of lightning. Calling lightning down from the skies. The earth, trembling . . . Cracks opening in the walls . . . Lava spewing up from the ground . . .

High School Massacre, variation two: alien attack. Flying saucers from planet Zorg. Giant *War of the Worlds* machines, crawling out of craters. Aliens dripping acid from their maws.

High School Massacre, variation three: return of the dinosaurs. Iqbal, riding a triceratops, versus the Mrpoundasaurus, a business Godzilla . . .

Fuck the variations. Old school. Just us and the teachers. Miss Lilly, limbless, twitching on the floor. *BLAM!* Mr Beresford, dressed up like some grotesque Uncle Sam, spinning his six-shooters, clinking his spurs. *BOOM!*—right through his sheriff's badge. Mr Merriweather, arms outstretched, like some grizzly bear of happiness studies, coming in for the hug. *KAZOOM!*—his head, blown clean off. Mr Zachary, the Ecomonster, a bit like Swamp Thing. Oozing slime. Making some vague moaning sound. Dispatched with the *cerebral bore* . . . Yippee-ki-yay motherfucker! Drilling noises. Whirring noises. Oh, that's gotta hurt . . .

Art's house.

The living room. Waiting for Nietzsche.

Why don't the living room lights work? Paula asks, flicking the switch on and off.

I've unscrewed the bulbs, Art says. We need to go dark. We need to go off-grid.

It's pitch-black in here, Paula says.

We're being tracked, man, Art says. They know where we are. There's an eye in the sky . . . There are drones . . . They're probably tracking us biometrically. They can read minds now—did you know that? It's called *psychic tracking*. They're searching for terrorist thoughts. They know everything we think. They're probably cueing up the Hellfire missiles right now.

You're paranoid, Art, Paula says.

It's us against them, Art says. It's a war.

It doesn't look much like a war to me, I say. There's no one out there. It's just an ordinary afternoon.

It's a *cold* war, Art says.

It's an *imaginary* war, I say.

It's us versus them, Art says. Sooner or later, we'll have to make a last stand. Seriously.

You're scaring us, Art, Paula says. You're getting all cult-leadery. I'm tired of crank-Art. I prefer hippy Art. I think I even prefer womb-boy Art.

We imagine it: leaving a pile of bodies sprawled in a circle, like the end of some death-cult. Newspaper stories: *Band Pact Suicide. Mad Cult Death Shock.* Documentaries. *Inside the House of Horror.*

Are we a band or a fucking terror cell? Paula asks.

They've probably infiltrated us already, Art says. One of you is an enemy, right? One of you is a spook—who is it?

Who would actually *bother* to infiltrate us? I ask. What do they think we're going to *do*?

Change hearts, man, Art says. Change minds. Something's happening here, and they know it.

You're smoking too much, Art, Paula says.

I'm not smoking *enough*, Art says. I've begun to see things—*true* things. Fucking patterns . . . Conspiracies. Things are making sense. I'm making connections. It's all tied together . . . It's all bound up . . .

Look—they don't need to control us, I say. We control ourselves. We've internalised the Man. We're programmed—pre-programmed. There might as well be drones in our *heads*. We're watching ourselves . . . Keeping tabs on ourselves . . .

I don't know what's worse, Art says. Being under surveillance or *not* being under surveillance.

★

Outside, on the broken patio. Still waiting for Nietzsche.

Reading to Art.

> *I miss eating, as I am fed through a tube in my stomach. I miss being able to shout at the football. People have to guess what I'm saying with my eyes, and my spelling sometimes isn't at its best. Before the stroke, I was always active and on the move. Now I watch others move.*
>
> *But though I've had my teary moments, I've always believed that if there's life, there's hope. With no exception. I have a*

| 227 |

sense of humour, and although I cannot laugh or move any other muscles in my face, I can smile—which is rare for someone with locked-in syndrome. I do feel happy, and I will not give up. I have never once considered suicide or needed anti-depressants.

It doesn't help anymore, Art says. I don't feel any better.

★

Band practice.

We strike up. This is stalking music. Prowling music. Lean. Uneasy.

Keeping things in suspense. Holding things back. No drama.

Restraint. Nothing obvious. Nothing spelt out. All clues. All foreboding. All tension.

Constrained play. Contained energy. Held-back explosions. Power, with no need to demonstrate its might.

It's like some martial art. We're stalking around each other, waiting to begin.

It's like shadow-theatre. It's like Noh theatre. It's like the art-form of a country that's been closed to the outside world for a thousand years. Ultra-rarefied . . . Incomprehensible to outsiders . . . Full of rules no one understands . . .

It's about what does not unfold, what keeps itself back. It's the bars and doors that hold back the Flood. It's about the cosmos that trembles with chaos. It's about the Word that quivers with the Unword. It's about the roaring that sounds through silence . . .

And Nietzsche's words, emerging from the fog: *Why? What for? By what? Whither?* Nietzsche's words, distinct in the murmuring: *I carried my ashes / to the mountains.* Nietzsche's words, coming into clarity: *I struck / the midnight bell.* Nietzsche words, audible at last: *Night is also a sun.* Nietzsche's words, like real lyrics: *You should laugh at me as I laugh at myself.* Nietzsche's words, half-sung: *Those who love the most, despise the most.* Nietzsche's words, almost sung: *How many new gods are still possible . . .*

PE.

Out of the school, strolling our old cross-country course. Strolling is much better than running, we agree. There should be no rush. Everything should be *largo*. Time should be a gift—from ourselves to ourselves. We should *create* time, pulling moments out of moments like conjuror's scarves . . .

Remembering our great PE protest. Our anti-PE-fascism protest. We conspired to come last in the annual cross-country run. Dozens of us! In solidarity! With linked arms! A human chain!

United in failure! Failing together! Failing competitiveness! The great refusal . . . A general strike . . . On strike with our bodies. Sure, we could have run. But we chose not to, like gods.

Gods do not busy themselves. We know that now. Gods can do what they like. The true master of running doesn't *need* to run. The true master of running can repose in not-running. We, like gods, opened a breach in competitive athletics. We, like gods, *suspended* cross-country running. It was like a general strike. We breathed free air . . .

The freedom *not to*. The freedom of *not busying ourselves*. The freedom of *holding back*. The freedom of *sovereign withdrawal*. The freedom of *benign neglect*.

We were on the side of the loosening of bonds. Of study, indistinguishable from stupidity. We were on the side of the softest of explosions. Of satellites, breaking up across the sky.

We were on the side of slow shipwrecks. Of the soldiers that have forgotten their orders, and that they ever had orders. We were on the side of deserters, of partisans scattering through the countryside.

We were on the side of airborne pollen. Of dandelion seeds, blown in every direction. We were on the side of the scattering of debris. Of harbour oil, turned all colours.

We were on the side of unmade roads and puddles in the mud. We were on the side of unmowed grass. Of flowering grass. Of wildflowers on the verge.

We were on the side of summer roads that seemed to have turned to liquid. Of summer air, that trembled in the distance. We were on the side of summer heat-haze. Of summer glory. We were on the side of divine play. Of Dionysus abroad. Of death and rebirth under blinding skies.

And there was Mr Saracen at the finish line, with his clipboard, looking stern.

Ah, civil disobedience. We all got Es in our reports. Mr Saracen failed us all. We actually *failed* PE.

The *Idiot* book club.

How's your new life of compassion treating you, Merv? Paula asks.

Is that your compassionate face, Merv? I ask. Is that what infinite love looks like?

I think the compassionate should smile more, Art says. Fuck off and make us some tea, Merv.

I thought *you* were supposed to be getting into compassion, Art, I say. Look at Poor Bitch Tits, sitting on his own again. Go and comfort him. And while you're at it, go and ask Doughface for forgiveness.

Yeah, Art—do you think you acted towards Doughface with compassion when you ran screaming from her bedroom? Paula asks. Just when she was about to give herself to you. The greatest gift she could give, Art: her cherry. Imagine that!

Compassion's supposed to be *spontaneous*, Art says. You're not supposed to *plan* it.

So who of us has actually done anything selfless? Paula asks.

Silence.

Maybe when we're out of the sixth form, Art says. When we're not pressed up against the drudges.

This is precisely the time we should do it, Paula says. The drudges are our test.

But who here's really going to wash the feet of a drudge? I ask.

Jesus!—it would only confuse them, Art says.

Admit it—we're just not compassionate, Paula says.

Sometimes I *feel* compassionate, I say. When I see the lower-school kids being bullied . . .

So let's start an anti-bullying patrol, Paula says. Every lunch-time. We'll wear armbands.

We're not hard enough, Art says. They'd lynch us out there.

If only Bill were still here—he could be a lower-school Batman, or something, I say.

What about charity? Paula asks.

Like giving stuff to Oxfam? I ask.

Like doing a fun-run, or something, Art says. Sponsored mooning. A sponsored vodka-thon.

Real compassion is face-to-face, Merv says. That's what Dostoevsky would say.

Maybe Nietzsche's right, Art says. We shouldn't do anything about the suffering of others. Take Bitch Tits. Do you remember how Dingus used to pinch Bitch Tit's nipples? Ask for milk from his udders?

Is that why he made the suicide video? I ask. Sobbing, straight to camera . . . Detailing his humiliations . . . It was meant to be *moving*, I suppose. If he'd actually killed himself, maybe it would have been. He might have been on national TV. A *cause célèbre*. They might have recorded a charity single for him. But he was back at school on Monday . . .

Well anyway, Nietzsche would claim it was Bitch Tits's suffering and no one else's, Art says. And that, if he was left alone, his suffering might push him to do something really important. He could lactate himself to greatness. Become a writer. Or a singer . . . The singing hermaphrodite. He could out-philosophise us all from the depths of his misery . . .

Or just succeed in killing himself . . ., I say.

There's a chance of that, sure, Art says.

So for every fifty who kill themselves from bullying, one steps into greatness? I say. I mean—is it worth it?

Who cares about greatness? Paula says. We're three generations from the end of organised human life on this planet. What will greatness matter then?

Bitch Tits might *solve* climate change, Art says. He might win the *Virgin Earth Challenge*. Maybe that's where his suffering will lead him.

Nietzsche's blog:

What day is it in the suburbs? Any day. Every day.
All the days cross here. Every day is present here.
Today is today. There is no future.
The day is ruined. No—the day is ruin. Today is the return of
what never happened.

After school. Suburban research.

The new estate, Matthewsgreen Farm, running up to the A329(M), nearly ready for buyers. Gleaming-bricked, raw-bricked, looking into nowhere . . .

They cleared whole fields for this. They tore up the trees, and filled in the ditches. They steamrollered everything flat. They laid foundations. Drove down the pylons.

A field of new houses, square upon the earth. A field of new houses, new arrivals—duh-brain houses with unformed faces. A field of raw-bricked new houses, with blank faces, stupidly innocent faces, with no relief, no personality, no depth of expression.

And so many of them! One, after another! Whole rows of them! So many of them, facing in the same direction, lined up as by a ruler.

We've had enough. We can't fight it anymore. Because the suburbs don't want to fight us. They don't *need* to fight us.

They're all-encompassing, the suburbs. There is no alternative. We're surrounded on all sides. We can't escape. It's game over. It's complete surrender. The battle was over before it began . . .

Realisation. *This* is what the death of God means. *This* is what the end of history means.

It means this is the morning after, the hangover of history. It means we think we know what things are. That we can see clearly at last. That we're free of illusion. That we know what the world is.

We think we know what's real, and what counts as real. We think we know the limits—that we've reckoned the world; that we've counted everything there is. We've inventoried the world, and we didn't find God . . .

What's the world to us? Mediocrity, reflected back. Averageness. Our bureaucratic spirit. Our *managerialism*. We think the world's something to administrate. To audit. Our souls are small. We're bookkeepers of life.

Our world's human-sized. Our world's cut to measure. We think we can't be duped. That no one's fooling us. That we see things as they are, at last. We're not superstitious.

God is dead. Our world is disenchanted. We understand everything. We've watched the documentaries. We're atheists—natural atheists. We don't believe in angels. We don't believe in miracles. We don't believe in the powers of creation. We don't believe that the world's a gift. We don't believe in exultation. We don't believe in ecstasy or transport. We don't believe we should water the earth with the tears of our joy . . .

★

Nietzsche—*where's Nietzsche?* Off with Lou, of course. Off with Lou, as always. We imagine them, Nietzsche and Lou, crossing the railway bridge, and heading down to Ludgrove. We imagine them, turning right onto the unmarked road. Crossing the stone bridge, with the river low in its bed.

We imagine them, Nietzsche and Lou, walking along the railway track towards Crowthorne, wide fields on one side, small paddocks of horses on the other. We imagine them walking on the edge of the bridlepath. The black earth, churned up by horses' hooves. We imagine fir trees, dark and gloomy. We imagine marshland. Thick rhododendron bushes. We imagine the path rising. Opening onto the road. We imagine the pine knoll at the Ridges, looking over the Blackwater.

Nietzsche, come and save us! Come and help us, Nietzsche! Wake us up again . . . God is dead: what does that mean? That there are no more heights? That there's nothing to aim for? That there's only mediocrity now? God is dead: tell us it doesn't mean that we're dead, too . . .

Art's house.

On the front door: *1 + 1 = 1*. What will the postman make of that? On the back door: *MESSIANISM OR NIHILISM.* On the living room wall: *The last people will not weep.* Up the stairs, above the banister: *The best thing is not to be born; and second is to die soon.* On the bathroom mirror: *PATHEIN MATHEIN.* On the study wall: *Every toy has the right to break.* On the dining room wall: *To live without a lifetime— to die forsaken by death.* On the kitchen cabinet: *The purpose of life is to be defeated by greater and greater things.* On the coal bunker: *Very great is the number of the stupid.* On the garage door: *Every day I wish myself off the Earth.* And on the stones of the broken patio, in capitals: *COME FORTH.*

This'll really help sell the house, I say.

Yeah, well, they're going to demolish it, anyway, Art says.

Upstairs. Art's redecorated the practice room. Made his own Black Ark. His own Death to the World studios. His own Dionysus studios. The windows, covered. The curtains, drawn. It's dark— very dark, but for a single candle. The flickering light shows tiny crosses all over the walls.

Plug-in radiators . . . A fan heater . . . Jesus, Art!, It's fucking boiling in here!

Art, lighting an incense stick.

Cool, Merv says. A séance.

Not a séance, dillweed, Art says. A *sweat lodge.* Like the Native Americans. We have to purify ourselves. Drive out our traumas.

Art, passing round a long-stemmed pipe. This is serious shit, Art says. Butane hash oil. Pure. Purer than pure. The highway to inspiration. It's what Van Morrison was smoking when he was recording *Astral Weeks.* He just sat in the singer's booth, smoking hash oil, improvising . . .

Art, reading a prayer. *Great Spirit,* he says. *Great Mother. Protect us in our folly. Give us hatred, that we may be reborn from love. Give us darkness, that we can be born from light anew . . .*

Great Motherfucker, I say. Why must Art be such a tosser?

Quiet! this is a womb, Art says. A place of innocence. We're here to be *spiritually cleansed.* To become what we are.

Well, it's not working for me, womb-boy, Paula says.

Sitting. Eyes streaming. Coughing.

Merv (in a strangulated voice): I am the ghost of Anne Frank.

Excellent!, Paula says. Come on—who has questions for Anne?

Who else is up there, Anne? I ask. Sun Ra? Mark E. Smith? How

about the *real* Nietzsche? What's he like? Is he mad in heaven, or was that just on Earth?

What's your message for Chandra, Anne? Paula asks.

Merv (as Anne Frank): Choose from the whispering voices. Heed the thundering silence. Keep on writing. Write about this.

What about Paula, Anne? I ask.

Merv (as Anne Frank): *Whoever does not love the impossible, does not love anything.* Don't lose hope. She's coming soon.

Who's coming? Paula asks.

Merv (as Anne Frank): The one who will love you and who you will love in turn.

Art, unable to resist. Is there a message for me? Is life going to get any easier? Is this it?

Merv (as Anne Frank): Go towards the light. Tana loves you, Art. And you love Tana, if only you'd let yourself see it. Turn to the light.

Do you hear that, Art? Paula says. Good advice!

And Merv? I ask. What will happen to him?

Merv (as Anne Frank): Merv is okay. Merv understands. You should give Merv lots of money. And tell him he has a really big cock.

Fuck you, Merv, Art says.

And how can we save you, Anne? I ask.

Merv (as Anne Frank): I'm already saved, as you are. Life is immortal—don't you see? The idea of immortality is life itself.

I don't understand, I say. Does that mean we're never going to die?

Merv (as Anne Frank): *There's no such thing as death. Everyone's immortal, whether they're seventeen or seventy. Neither gloom nor death exists in the world . . . Look at a child; look at God's sunset; look at the grass as it grows; look into eyes which look at you and love you! Life is a gift, life is happiness, and each moment could be an eternity of bliss.*

And what about Nietzsche? Paula asks. When the fuck's Nietzsche going to turn up, Anne—can you tell us that?

*

Band practice.

Bill Trim's backbeat.

Shimmering marimba chimes, dancing around the pulse. Rhyth-

mic chords. Broken chords. Art's electronic washes. Luscious. Static. Paula's bass, low, rumbling. My guitar, treated with delay, dissipating into abstraction. Nietzsche's speech-song. Nietzsche's almost-singing.

A democracy of sounds, of textures. All sounds on the same plane. Foreground and background, equal . . . And nothing resolved. Nothing finalised. A shimmering plane of sound.

The *implied* song. The *implied* harmony. It doesn't have to be obvious. We don't have to spell it out . . .

And now, a lightening in the music. A *lifting*. Musical light. A musical sun-flare.

Now we've reached it—the cosmic song. The song of Order. We've reached it—the harmonious song. The all-in-all song.

We've reached it—via the wave of dissonance. Via the breakdown of dissonance. *Achieved* harmony. *Won* harmony. We've brought it to form.

We're playing the last days, and the days after the last days. We're playing the uncountable days, the days without date. We're playing the Sabbath, and every day as the Sabbath.

We're transmuting. This is the work of transfiguration. This is godly work. Angelic work. This is the divine labour . . .

There is no God, and there are nothing but gods. The gods are laughing. Wherever there's laughter, there's a god, laughing. Wherever there's rapture, there's a rapturous god.

And the gods are in our music. And the gods dissolve in our music. And our music is the godhead, from which gods are born and die ceaselessly . . .

THURSDAY

Assembly.

They've discovered some new planet, we're told. Out beyond the orbit of Pluto, out beyond the Kuiper Belt. It's on some twenty-thousand-year orbit, apparently. And it's vast—fifty times the size of the Earth. They haven't actually seen it yet—not directly. They've only detected its effects. Its gravitational pull. They're calling it Planet Nine for now. They haven't given it a proper name.

Whispered discussion. It's Melancholia—it has to be. Just in fucking time!

We imagine it: Planet Nine/Melancholia, the dark planet, rushing towards us. An abyss, rather than a planet. An anti-planet. A planet-destroyer. Cancer, sheer cancer, a hundred thousand miles in diameter . . .

Sitting on the riverbank.

A shoal of brown fish in the shallows.

These guys have a real lifestyle, Paula says. They're actually *happy*—you can tell.

What's so happy about them? Art asks. What are they doing?

They're just fucking around, I say. Courting, play-fighting.

Like us, right? Merv asks. Just fucking around.

We don't know what fucking around means, Art says. We're institutionalised. We're just waiting for orders.

We used to fuck around, didn't we? I say. Do you remember you'd make us up, Paula—to look so *pretty*? And there was wartball, too. And table-swapping . . .

And playing 40-40 with our knees joined together, Merv says.

Well, we're too old now, Art says. We're, like, fully captive. The brains of domestic animals are much smaller than the brains of wild animals—did you know that? They have fewer neurones. They play less, explore less . . . And it's the same with us.

That's society, though, Merv says. And we have to live in societies.

Think of the hunter-gatherers—the pygmies and others, Art says. They just take it easy. There's a bit of hunting to be done, sure. But most of the time, things are pretty quiet.

They probably die at thirty of preventable diseases, I say.

So what? It's the *intensity* of life that matters, Art says. The Bhutanese only work half the year. The rest of the time it's weddings, religious holidays . . . And it was the same in the Middle Ages, Mr Varga said. The peasants took a week off work for weddings. Wakes and christenings—the same. And you didn't work on Sundays. And they had all these festivals . . .

That's what we should do!—go to a festival!, Merv says. Who's playing at Reading this year?

Fuck festivals, Art says. You know who they're for. Dickie Branson in his wellingtons. Princesses Beatrice and Eugenie, in their wellingtons. Sam Branson, leading a campfire sing-along of *Wonderwall*, in his wellingtons . . .

Look—everyone had rickets in the Middle Ages, I say. And scurvy. And trench foot, probably. And I'll bet it was all very muddy. Just mud, everywhere. And there were no anaesthetics . . . and everyone had plague . . .

Do you know how much people used to drink? Art asks. They used to drink all the time. Beer for breakfast . . . Beer for lunch . . . And there were all these beer-swilling saints' days.

What about hatred? I ask. I'll bet they didn't hate anyone.

They didn't need to hate anyone, Art says. They weren't individualists. They weren't competing. It's like the fish—look at them. It's like they're drunk on pure water. They're not struggling against one another. Even the trees . . . Mr Zachary said that trees have friends—remember? Trees grow so as not to block each other's light . . . And their root systems are all interconnected, so they can help each other if they're in trouble—if they're damaged by fire, or something. Trees are communal. They share the same soil, the same light, the same air. And we're communal, too—or we should be, Mr Zachary said. We should depend on each other, need each other . . .

Yeah, well, Mr Zachary basically wants to *be* a plant, Paula says. And he wants us to be plants, too.

We're not communal, I say. *Drudges* are communal. Sitting together, up close . . . Rubbing up against one another . . .

But we're friends, right? Merv says. We're kind of communal.

We're a gang that has nothing to do with anyone, Art says. A gang that hates everyone.

A gang that hates *itself*, Paula says.

That hates itself because we know there's something better, Art says. Because we know *we* can be better.

Better at what? I ask.

At cosmic play, Art says. At everyday joy. At living on the fucking Earth . . .

Sighting: Lou and Nietzsche, walking in the arcade. Lou and Nietzsche, at close quarters. Imagine it—Lou, among us. Lou and the *romantic* Nietzsche, actually among us . . . Lou and turned-away-from-us Nietzsche. Lou and he's-not-ours Nietzsche.

Does Lou even know who we are? Has Lou been told what we're about? Have we been explained to Lou? Have we been used to make Lou laugh? Have we *amused* Lou? Has Lou been able to break the awkward silences with, *How are your friends? How's Art? How's Merv? How's Paula? How's Chandra?* Have we been a living cartoon for Lou? Shakespeare's mechanicals? Comic relief?

When we're with Nietzsche, and when Nietzsche looks into his distance, at least we try to look with him. When we're with Nietzsche, and Nietzsche speaks of philosophical things, at least we try to follow what he says.

We *attend* to the fact that Nietzsche's not like us. We *try to understand* his reserve. We *listen* when he wonders aloud. When he lets his thoughts claim him. We *concentrate* when he asks himself questions. When he speaks of his past. When he muses on the suburbs.

Does Lou know Nietzsche's hopes as we do? Does Lou listen to him as we do? What does Lou care about philosophy?

We imagine it: Nietzsche talking of the *suburban tautology*, and Lou not understanding. Nietzsche talking of the *fullness of nothingness*, and Lou not understanding. Nietzsche talking of the *faded positivities*, and Lou not understanding. Nietzsche talking of the *saving power of the void*, and Lou not understanding.

Lou, smiling. Lou, smiling and thinking she's better than philosophy, that she knows more than philosophy. Lou's on her own adventure. Lou's following her own path. But that's not Nietzsche's path. And it's not *our* path.

Why does Nietzsche want to be a lover, too? Why does he have to be so dependent? Yet we love his dependency. We love his vulnerability. We love his love, his tenderness—the fact that he's all too human. The fact that he's just like us, in some sense.

Because we know Nietzsche can never be like us. We know Nietzsche's love is different from ours, *better* than ours. We know he's more refined, more sensitive . . .

What does Lou know of any of this?

Presentations on our Extended Projects.

I speak about the Japanese Red army (massacres, hijackings, bringing suicide attacks to the Middle East . . .) Paula on Chantal Akermann and the everyday (minimal-hyperreal, extended takes, deep banality . . .) Noelle, on Rimbaud's connections to the Paris Commune (*O waves of fire, we must never work* . . .)

Nietzsche's turn.

Nietzsche: It's a psychogeography of the Wokingham suburbs—the housing estates built over the last fifty years.

Slideshow. Photos of the Fernlea estate: Tickenor Drive, Radical Ride.

Nietzsche: It's easy to talk about the dreariness of the suburbs. About how dull it is to live here. How parochial. We all know these things. The whole of popular culture tells us nothing else.

And it's just as easy to insist that we'll come to appreciate the suburbs when we're older. How it's about great cycles of life. About getting married and having children and wanting to raise them somewhere *safe*.

Photos of Woosehill Estate. Asda. The dual carriageway.

Nietzsche: There is a kind of *division* in the suburbs. A distance between the suburbs and themselves. A nothingness that can't be covered over. That can't be absorbed. All the houses and roads, everything we see, stands out against it.

Suburban meaning does not rest in meaning, that's what I want to say. Suburban groundlessness—that's what I want to speak of. The continual *un*grounding of what there is. The continual collapse of the suburbs . . .

But who in Wokingham talks of *groundlessness?* Mr Varga asks. Long commutes, yes. Long days in the office, okay. Stress, congestion, bitter divorces. But no one here gets *existential*.

Photos of Lower Earley. Trinity Church.

Nietzsche: The *structure of feeling* is changing. Everyone used to believe in betterment. We believed life would get better for each generation. That the good life was in reach of all. That this was the best of all worlds; that all the big problems—the political problems, the societal problems—had been solved, basically.

But now everyone knows this world is over. Everyone knows we're just waiting for the tsunami. The sea has receded, leaving marshes. Swamp . . . There's a huge feeling of depression. Of not being here. A sense that everything is finished, and that it may never begin again. This is the nihilism everyone knows, everyone lives with, even if they don't call it that.

But why should this nihilism have become visible here, now—in the suburbs? Mr Varga asks. In postwar Paris, yes. In Dostoevsky's St Petersburg, perhaps . . .

Nietzsche: Because there's nothing to oppose it. There are no counterforces. No one expects anything to happen. These are just suburbs without 'urbs, without a city, without a centre. There's only the sheer *positivity* of the suburbs in their infinite sprawl. Their sheer *obviousness*.

I think I understand: this is a way of talking about the end of history, Mr Varga says. The end of ideologies. The triumph of liberal capitalism and the last man . . .

Nietzsche: I'm talking of the end of belief. Don't you feel it? There's a sense of energy receding. Of cynicism and desperation. No one can do anything. Change anything. We no longer believe in the world.

Nothingness has turned to face us in the suburbs. *As* the suburbs. And nothingness is the look of nihilism upon us, upon all of us. That's our ordeal.

Photos of the new estates: Matthewsgreen Farm. Lowfield Place. Eldritch Park. Photos of the Special Development Zones.

Nietzsche: But we should try to become *worthy* of this ordeal. To affirm nothingness. The fact that there's *no future*. To affirm the collapse of the suburbs into nowhere.

Who can affirm the end of civilization? Mr Varga asks.

Nietzsche: Those who do not belong to the world. To *this* civilization.

(Death to the world, Art whispers. Death to the fucking world.)

Nietzsche: There are those for whom this world exists only to be destroyed. Who would laugh at its destruction, and at their own destruction. Who are waiting for the *revenge of the Earth*.

Terrorists? Mr Varga asks.

Nietzsche: Those seized by the will to nothingness, the will to destroy. Who are full of hatred—good, clean hatred. Who are waiting to complete the cycle of decay . . .

(Whispered conversation: Is he talking about us? Of course! Who else!?)

And what then? What are these outriders of the apocalypse supposed to achieve? Mr Varga asks.

Nietzsche: The affirmation of the collapse. The completion of nihilism. They have to want the world exactly as it is. Without joy. Without hope. Without purpose. They have to want to the world in its nothingness—in its perfect nothingness—for all eternity.

Wokingham forever? Mr Varga asks. Traffic jams forever? Construction work forever? New housing estates forever? No one would want that.

Nietzsche: That's the test.

It would lead straight to *madness*, Mr Varga says.

Nietzsche: It's difficult, I know. Sometimes, I think there's a limit to what we can affirm. That the suburbs are too vast—too omnipresent. Sometimes, I think the suburbs mean only the impossibility of escape.

But a kind of reversal can occur. When the impossible becomes possible, and an escape route opens. Not to another world, but to right here, where we already are.

I was ill for a long time. It was when we first moved to Wokingham—to the suburbs. I felt defeated. I just saw houses and roads and cars, and the bland, white sky above it all. I saw . . . dying, without death. A kind of *negative eternity*. Which is to say, I saw nothing but the suburbs.

But then, one day, something happened. I was walking down a path—a cut-through, to Barkham Ride. A metal fence. A patch of grass behind a spiked metal fence with a locked gate. A patch of grass between two back gardens, unused, unusable, kept mowed by the council.

I looked up. The usual sky—white, without depth. And then— how to speak of it?—I saw the sky, the same sky, *opening*. Become brilliant. Bursting with light. I saw—it was dazzling: the *blue of noon*.

Nothingness was on fire. Nihilism—*blazed*. I saw the sky *swaying*—as if falling down and then being lifted up high, as if madness and lucidity had come together. I saw the eternal living fire. I saw the sun as the eye of life . . .

To affirm the suburbs is to affirm them as threshold. As the longing to perish and to be reborn. To affirm them is to know the apocalypse has never stopped happening. That the end is always here . . .

★

After.

Did you see Mr Varga taking Nietzsche aside? Having a word with him?

He'd recognised a kindred spirit, Paula says.

He'd recognised a pupil in danger, Art says.

Nietzsche's going mad, I say. You can see it . . .

The real Nietzsche went mad, right? Merv asks.

Sure he went mad—he thought he was Dionysus, Paula says. He danced round his rooms naked. And one day he threw his arms around a horse that was being beaten to death . . .

So it was pity that got him in the end . . ., I say.

The real Nietzsche was just some wretched invalid, Paula says. His work was just megalomania. All that stuff about the will to power and the eternal return . . . The real Nietzsche felt sorry for himself. He pitied himself. So he had all these *fantasies* . . .

Art, reading from his phone:

> *In the first years, his condition was quite satisfactory. His interests were once again those of a child; when he was not brooding dully to himself, he played with dolls and other toys. Little by little the individual systems of nerves were affected. His consciousness vanished more and more, his limbs failed, his language became unclear. He sat in his chair or lay in his bed, silent and indifferent, hour by hour, week by week, year by year—his beautiful, slender, white hands crossed over his chest, occasionally muttering indistinct sounds under his moustache, which grew to fabulous size.*

It's the moustache that gets me, Art says. The enormous moustache.

We imagine it: the moustache of a madman, just growing without him. A Yosemite Sam moustache, covering half his face . . . A celebrity moustache, standing in for the madman . . .

And it gets worse, Art says. His fascist sister sold tickets to see him once he became famous. Have your photo taken with the madman, and so on. Hitler visited . . . Mussolini . . .

So *our* Nietzsche's going to go mad, too, I say.

His sister's going to sell tickets for his bedside, Art says. There'll be a whole Nietzsche cult. All the future fascists will come. All the Thames Valley CEOs . . .

Midweek Spinney girl house party. Spinney girls are *wild*.

Surveying the scene. Grove boys, juggling beer cans, stabbing them, then pressing them to their mouths. Sophisticated! Grove boys, taking turns to lie beneath the keg tap, mouth open. And Spinney girls, shaping about. Spinney girls, striking poses. Dancing with each other. All but getting off with each another. All but snogging each other. Lesbian chic has hit the Spinney.

They're just trying to intrigue the boys, Paula says.

It's working. Grove boys, gawping. Grove boys, looking on, eyes blank with lust. My God, they're brutal! So tall! So hairy! This is what happens when you coop up a bunch of boys.

Pity the sensitive souls among the Grove boys! Pity Grove-boy poets. Pity Grove-boy queers.

A slow dance. Grove boys and Spinney girls in clinches. Grove boys and Spinney girls all but fucking standing up. This is what lust looks like. This is how the human race survives. Surely we're not as obvious as that! Ah, but lust makes monkeys of us. We're all throwbacks in the sack.

Couples on the stairs, snogging. Groping. Attached to each other like mating snails. You couldn't prise them apart . . . Unspeakable things happening in the bedrooms. Grunting Grove boys, pumping, thrusting, having their way. Girls wondering, *Was that it? Was that all?* Anti-climax. Non-climax. Disappointment between the sheets.

Lust! Lust! Why don't *we* feel overwhelmed by it? Crushed by it? Why doesn't lust roll *our* eyeballs back? Why aren't *we* drooling? Maybe something's wrong with us. Maybe we lack testosterone. Maybe we're not Proper Boys. Are we Proper Boys? we turn to ask Paula. But Paula's talking to a Spinney girl. Paula's deep in conversation with a Spinney girl.

Out. Escape.

Walking up the hill.

Memories. Art and I, at Hopey's party. Sipping our beers with Spinney girls. And then, lips on lips, the flicker of a tongue. Then kissing. Who taught us those things? How did we know? Lust knew in us. Lust taught us . . .

And then, after, walking around and around the block, with the wonder of it all. Up and down the cart-track. Walking, walking.

Something had changed. *We* had changed. We walked more lightly. We dance-walked. The night parted for us like the sea. What had happened? What had just happened? We remembered. We were on fire with the memory. It burned inside us. We blazed. We walked along like human torches . . .

This is how things work, we realised. This is another dimension of life . . . It's why Binky's mum left Binky's dad. It's why Merv's parents broke up. You can feel it. You know why. It's the motive-force of the world, stronger than the world. It's the Will. It's why things happen.

And now we knew the secret order. We knew why people do *wild things*. And why we ourselves might do *wild things* . . . Now we knew why life crashes through the suburbs—even the suburbs. Now we knew why life romps even through the 'burbs.

And what happens now? we wondered as we walked. Do we have *girlfriends* now? Are we in *relationships*? . . . Pondering what that might mean. Pondering our new lives . . . Where is life leading us? Where has life lost us?

And were we good kissers? we wondered. Did we kiss them as they wanted? And were they good kissers? They seemed like good kissers, but . . . Do we know how to kiss? What it means to kiss?

But when we went to see them again the next morning, nothing happened. They ignored us, and we ignored them. It was as though nothing had happened. No one knew what to do. Life went on as normal. But that was okay with us, that life went on as normal. Because we'd opened the door, passed through. Because we'd been admitted to a new life as kissers, as lovers . . .

So what went wrong, Art? I ask. When did you become peculiar?

I want to *achieve* something with my life, Art says.

Like what? I ask.

I want to stay focused, Art says. This is it, man. This is the time. The *kairos*, man—that's what Justin Marler calls it. The *eschatological window*. I don't want to miss it. No distractions. I think it's better when we're on our own. I think it's better when we yearn.

Is that why you don't want a girlfriend? I ask. Tana likes you . . .

Romance is just a bourgeois compromise, Art says. It's the hiving-off of energies. It's the reason nothing ever gets done. I mean—it's just reassurance, right? It's licking each other's wounds . . .

We've got to keep tense, Art says. Keep watchful. No one should sleep—and that's what being in a couple is: sleep. Shacking up together. Closing the door. Leaving a *Do Not Disturb* sign on the handle. It's desertion. It's leaving the field of battle . . . I want to *do* something. *Be* something.

We *are* doing something, I say. The band is doing something. You can't just stay alone all your life, Art.

You don't understand, Art says. I don't want to rest. I don't want peace. I feel that if I relax, if I open a chink—I'll just collapse. I'll break down, or something. I need *tension* . . . What's the point anyway? It's Boston in, like, a month.

You know what, we should do something cool—one last time before you go, I say.

Like getting *FUCK BOSTON* tattoos? Art asks.

We should organise a gig, I say. A first and last performance . . .

FRIDAY

The arcade. Chips.

Well, my parents can't hold it together anymore, Paula says. Their marriage's falling apart. They're going round all confused. They don't know what they feel. They've never known things to turn against them.

They've given up trying spin things, Paula says. My dad actually looks *depressed*. It's like, *Welcome to my world, Dad. You can't exercise your way out of this one.* And my mum's lolling listlessly on her Swiss ball. Even the brats are glum.

Sure, my parents will recover, Paula says. Of course they will. It'll all be spun one way or another. It'll all be part of some big stupid story. *We're lovingly choosing to separate as a couple. We're just two best friends realising it's time to take some space.*

But my parents are kind of endearing at the moment, wandering round, not knowing what to do. I want to look after them. To take them into my arms. To whisper soft words to them. To say: *You'll come through. You'll get used to it.*

Walking around the school.

Oh God, what's wrong with us? This is the last day of school before the exams. We should feel *happy*.

How many times have we walked around it? Done the circuit? How many times, back in the lower school, when the school was the whole world to us, when it was our entire universe? How many times, loving it and hating it; needing it and fearing it? How many times before we knew that there was nothing at its core? How many times, before we knew that we were orbiting nothing, that the school was nothing?

We're burnt out. We're exhausted. We've had every feeling you could possibly have about school.

There were times when we wanted to *please* it. To placate it. When we asked ourselves what it wanted. When we tried to anticipate it. There were times when we desired its approval. When we wanted to respect it. There were times when we wanted to believe that it knew best. When we wanted it to be good (the measure of goodness). *Just* (the measure of justice). We wanted it to be fair. There were times when we wanted to be minors, to be dependent, to simply *trust* the school and the order of the school.

There were times when we wanted to think of our teachers as gods; of Mrs Steele as an eminent scientist; of Mr Saracen as a former pro-athlete; of Mr Zachary as the king of geographers . . . We wanted to laugh along when Mr Lunkton had his beard shaved for charity. When Miss Lilly and Mrs Sherwood did the dead-parrot sketch in assembly . . .

But there were times when we strained against it. When we wanted to deny it. We saw its hypocrisies. We saw that it didn't know all, and didn't watch over all. We saw its inertias. Its blind-nesses. That it simply did what it was supposed to do, and no more.

The school was only there to process us—that's what we came to know. It was there to *implement and manage*, that's all. It was indifferent to us. It knew its job. It didn't need to win our souls. It wasn't bothered about our hearts and minds. External obedience, that's all it required . . . So long as we weren't actually setting anything on fire.

The school digested us, that's all. We passed through its guts. We were simply there for a time, as we had to be. Per the legal requirement. Per our custodial sentence. We did as we were told. We obeyed. We stood with the class when a teacher entered a room. We sat on the floor in assembly, moving back a row each new school year. We went on to the sixth form. But we weren't *of* the school, not anymore. We were pupils *as not* pupils . . .

The *nothingness* of the school—that's what we knew. The abyss on which it rested. The void it tried to cover up. The school was just nihilism in brick, that's all. It was nothing; it stood for nothing. The school barely even tried to conceal the illegitimacy of its power. Its anarchy.

And wasn't that why we laughed: because we saw its anarchy? Cracks in the institution. Ceasefires. Interruptions of power. Life at the edge of lessons. Open time; free space. We laughed—how we laughed. The time we stole the exam questions from Mr Zachary back in the lower school (Mr Zachary in tears; Mr Zachary being led away). The time Fatberg wanked off that dog (Fatberg panting; the dog panting, tongue hanging out). The time we all wore white socks to school, when white socks were banned . . .

We learned real things by not paying attention. We heard true things by not listening, by letting our gazes wander. Time was our teacher: time between tests, between lessons. Space taught us: aban-doned space. Vista-space. The space of truanting in weekday woods. And we learnt from each other, as we shared the intervals. We learned from laughter—anarchists' laughter, philosophers' laughter. We taught each other to speak, to feel, to curse, to love . . .

When did the shutters come down? When did it all go dull? When did the Characters disappear: the Eccentrics; the mad boys and girls? When did brains switch off? When did everyone settle into drudge-dom? Into living death? When did everyone become faux-adult? Set-tle down?

When did the great smothering occur? When did it press down on our faces? When did it prevent us being able to breathe? When did everyone become their parents? When did they all begin to play out the Wokingham script? When did they make the *Wokingham adjustment?*

We're tired now. We've done our time. We're processed. We're out. Freedom: Is that what we feel? But freedom from what?

I don't feel anything, Paula says.

Me neither, I say.

Nietzsche's blog:

> *The unbroken, how do they do it? The unshaken, what are they made of? When it is past, what do they breathe? When it is still, what do they hear? When the felled one does not stand up again, how do they walk? Where do they find a word? What wind blows over their eyelashes? Who opens the dead ear for them? Who breathes the frozen name? When the sun of eyes goes out, where do they find the light? (Canetti)*

Evening. The Prom.

The common room, dressed up as a disco. The common room, with disco balls. With disco lights. With bunting, streamers and a giant GOOD LUCK banner. The common room, with a dancefloor laid over the carpet tiles. With a sound system and a DJ.

They've really made an effort. They want to give us a sense of transition. Of a milestone passed. Of a rite of passage. Really, it was all for our benefit. To give us *good memories.*

The end-of-sixth-form party. The end-of-school *prom*—that's what they're calling it: the *prom*, American style. It's a new thing, importing the idea of an end-of-school *prom.*

Sixth-formers, milling about, sipping their drinks, picking at snacks. We're supposed to Enjoy Ourselves (responsibly, of course). We're supposed to have Good Fun (within limits, of course). We're supposed to *paaaarty (responsibly*, which means not to party at all . . .)

Girls in dresses. Guys in jeans and shirts. Calypso, with her new fringe. The certainty that Calypso's fringe *matters*. That there's something *important* about Calypso's fringe.

Speeches: Mr Pound—seize life with both hands (what life?). Make the most of it (make the most of what?). Best foot forward (which foot is that?). Success doesn't come to you, you go to it (we're going to perdition, Mr Pound, nowhere else). Don't just sit on the runway, plan a take-off (the plane's crashed, Mr Pound. The plane's on fire). If you try, and you just believe, you can; you will (we won't and we can't, Mr Pound). If you have positive energy you will always attract positive outcomes (we're all negativity, Mr Pound—we're black holes).

Now small-talk. Where are you going to university? What are you going to study? Where do you want to work? Oh, you're majoring in Business Administration, and minoring in Communications—*interesting*. So you think you're going to fuck things up from the inside—*right*. Oh, you're going to study Business Management—*wow*!

Girls dancing. Lads, shifting from foot to foot. They're playing old favourites. All the crowd-pleasers.

They're playing Abba. Eternal Abba. Teenagers, dancing to Abba, just as their teenage parents danced to Abba some hot night in the '80s. Just as our children will cut a rug to Abba in the 2030s, and our children's children in 2060. You can't fight Scando-pop. You have to give in. Even *we're* dancing to Abba . . .

Are we dancing ironically? Is this *real* dancing? Are we dancing or not dancing? Are we dancing *as not* dancing? Is our dancing sovereign or not?

Power ballads. Trendies losing their cool, getting emotional. Diamanda, Binky and Nessa, in a group hug. Quinn getting weepy, mascara running down her cheeks, being comforted by Hadley.

Sentiment, spreading to the drudges. Mushiness, free-floating. Feeling, abroad. Hugs! Hugs all round! Team hugs! Gilet-types, with arms around each other. Beasts, clapping each other on the shoulders. Trendies, sitting on each other's laps.

Jambo, hugging Tate! Fatberg, hugging Bitch Tits! What happened to resentment? Have the old battles really been forgotten? Fatberg used to torture Bitch Tits . . . Fatberg used to twist his nipples . . . Now it's all forgiveness!

Weepy teens . . . It's-all-too-much-for-us teens. Even the teachers are emotional . . .

After. Commotion in the carpark. What's happening? Bomb-proof, with a Mini full of laughing gas balloons. Bombproof, filling more balloons from a gas tank in the back seat. What initiative! What get-go! He's charging a couple of quid per balloon . . .

The trendies, queueing up. Beasts. Imagine, the beasts and the trendies queueing up for Bombproof. It's his finest hour. It was worth all Bombproof's humiliations for this. Remember this, Bombproof! It won't get any better! When the brightest and the best came a-queueing at your car door, and you're selling balloons for two pound a pop! The Bombproof apotheosis! Bombproof glory!

Bombproof's future—a dealer of mild drugs. A balloon-filler. A laughing-gas vendor. What initiative! What enterprise! Mr Pound would be proud. Bombproof's found his métier. Who knew he had it in him?

We're queueing up with the rest of them. Laughing gas—why not? A balloon each. A balloon for everyone. Untie the knot. Suck—suck deep. And then—what a marvel!—an almost instant high. A near-instant gentle high. A laughing high, and almost right away. A buoyant, bubbling high, just like that. It's a bit like popper, but less *chemical*. But less headache-y. It's a *purer* high. An *innocent* high. And thirty seconds later, you're unhigh again. You're back to normal again.

Another balloon. Another knot untied. Another suck. We're laughing again. You can't help but laugh. You can't *not* laugh. Our jaws ache with laughter . . . And everyone around us, laughing. Beasts and trendies and us, laughing. All of us laughing in the carpark! We're a veritable *community* of laughers, laughing in the carpark!

We've dropped our *sang froid* . . . We've dropped our mutual disdain . . . We've dropped our normal distance . . . We can't help it . . .

There's nothing to laugh at, but we're laughing. We're sucking laughing gas with morons—what's funny about that? We're dupes! We're idiots! Laughing gas is a Mr Merriweather drug. Laughing gas is an end-of-history drug. Laughing gas is the drug for our times. The drug du fucking jour. It doesn't need a commitment. You don't need, like, a day to work up to it and a day to come down. Laughing gas: it's convenient. It's risk-free. It won't lead to brain-damage . . .

Laughing gas is a panacea. It's a quick antidote to nihilism. They'll pipe it into our office cubicles. We'll crack open canisters on our commutes. This is how we'll manage our despair. This is how we'll learn to cope. This is what will compensate for our hopes and dreams . . .

★

The cricket pitch, in the middle of the playing field.

Merv, doling out the tablets.

I don't know . . . , Tana says.

It's just plant food, Merv says.

Seriously? Tana asks.

It's sold as plant food online, Merv says. It's a legal high.

Okay, okay, Tana says, taking a tab.

Surveying the field.

We used to play sting-ball here, Merv says.

Chandra was quite good at that, weren't you? Paula asks. (To Noelle:) Phyfe would always volunteer to be catcher. And he'd always get Chandra first. He'd run him down, from one end of the playing field to another. He'd run Chandra down, and Chandra would always cry.

I wouldn't cry!, I say.

You would!, Paula says. Noelle, you should have seen your man. On his fat little legs. Running, crying, knowing he'd be caught.

Noelle, putting her arm around me.

Lying back on the mown-short grass, waiting for the m-cat to kick in. Waiting for the truth-serum to kick in. Because that's what it's called, Merv told us. It's supposed to make us tell the truth. We won't be able to hide the truth from anyone. Even from ourselves!

Discussion: But perhaps it's the truth of things that's going to be revealed. The secret of secrets. What's real and what's true. Perhaps we'll pierce the veil of Maya, right here in the sacred navel of the school.

Truth. What are we going to learn? That Mr Pound is actually an alien from planet Zorg? That David Icke is right, and we're ruled by giant lizard people?

Not *that* kind of truth, Art says.

What then? Noelle asks.

Maybe the truth's something you *feel*, Art says.

I feel woozy, Noelle says.

I don't feel anything, Paula says. The drugs don't work, Merv.

Your brother's fleeced us, I say.

He wouldn't fleece us, Merv says.

Call him, Paula says. Get him to bring us some proper drugs.

I feel something, Art says. I want to chew.

I didn't pay a tenner to fucking *chew*, Paula says.

Just wait, Merv says. Let it happen.

Art rolls up a spliff. This will kick things off.

I feel jittery, I say, taking a puff.

I'm feeling a bit light-headed . . . , Tana says.

I feel like I'm sinking through the earth, Paula says. That I've been buried in the earth.

Peace, Art says. I feel peace. That's what truth must mean: peace.

I feel like I'm sinking through darkness, Paula says.

Like, *peaceful* darkness, Art says.

I never want to say anything again, Art says. I'm never going to say another word. Maybe I'll become a monk. One of those Trappist monks. Maybe I'll just live in silence . . .

What about the truth, Merv? I ask. I thought we were supposed to see the truth . . .

Woozy discussion. What do we *mean* by truth? Are we close to truth now, in the silence and peace? Are we seeing things as they really are? Perhaps there's no such thing as truth . . . Except the truth that there's no such thing as truth . . . Perhaps the truth is dead. Perhaps *we're* dead . . .

I'm not dead, Tana says.

You *think* you're not dead, I say.

What if the truth is just *boring*? Paula asks. What if *this* is the truth? The playing field . . . The school buildings . . . The railway viaduct . . . The river . . . What if this is all there is?

More smoking.

Things are changing, man, Art says. Things are *happening*.

The night's writhing, Paula says. The night's turning, like a black dragon. The night's moving . . . I can see its scales . . .

The night's a *pack*, I say. The night's a fucking *swarm*. I can see loads and loads of black rats. They're twitching. They're *spitting*.

The night's sliding, Merv says. The night's a reptile.

Do you see scales? Noelle says. I see scales. Glistening. Moving.

I see *rats*, Tana says.

There aren't any scales, Paula says. There aren't any rats. Just the fucking void.

It doesn't mean anything, I say. It isn't anything.

But it's moving, Art says. The whole sky's moving. It's alive.

It's not alive, I say. That's not life.

It hates us, Tana says. It despises us.

It isn't even an *it*, Noelle says. It's lots of things. It's *everything*.

It's what we are, Art says. We're full of night.

I can see through the sky—right through it, Merv says. All the way to the other side.

I've gone transparent, Noelle says. I can see through my hands . . .

There aren't any stars, I say. Where did the stars go? Who put out the stars?

I don't know whether we're alive or not, Tana says. I don't know what's real.

We're, like, *infinitely* dead, Noelle says. We're at the bottom of the universe. At the bottom of the *pit*.

It's a war, I say. There's a war in heaven.

I can see tentacles, reaching down, Noelle says. I can see suckers . . .

I can see death, Tana says. No, it's *dying*—that's it. Endless dying.

It's just a baaaaad trip, Merv says.

How can we all be having the *same* trip? Art asks.

It's *real*—what we're seeing is real, I say. It's *true*.

This is what God looks like, Noelle says. God is, like, evil.

This is what *cancer* looks like, Tana says. It's *cancer*, not God. Maybe God has cancer. Maybe we all have cancer . . . Maybe the sky has fucking cancer. FUCK YOU, GOD. FUCK YOU, CANCER. FUCK YOU . . . TENTACLES OF THE SKY. FUCK YOU . . . ABSENT STARS . . .

Tana screaming. Noelle, hand over Tana's mouth. They'll hear us, she says.

Who? Merv asks. Who will hear us?

Them—up there, Noelle says. They haven't seen us yet. But they'll see us. They're going to see us. They'll reach right down and . . .

Who are they? Paula asks.

The anti-angels, Noelle says. The black hats. The were-creatures.

They're the legions of the demi-urge, Art says. They're the minions of the Never-God. Of The Throttler. Of The Ruiner of Life . . .

They're the Elements. They're, like, the fucking *uncreated*.

I am that I am, I quote. *I am what I will be. I am all things. I am the alpha and the omega. I am the first and the last. I am death, destroyer of worlds.*

Tana screams again.

Is this what an overdose feels like? Paula asks. Are we dying, Merv?

Jesus, we're dying on the last night of school, I say. What a way to go . . .

We *can't* die—that's the truth, Paula says. We'll never be able to die. This is going to go on forever. Oh God!

You shouldn't take m-cat if your head's not in the right place, Merv says.

Like our heads are ever in the right place, Paula says.

SATURDAY

Nietzsche's blog:

> *A posthumous life . . . Already dead . . .*
> *Suburban echoes. Reverberations. Everything that happens in the suburbs has happened already.*
> *The suburbs, refusing to coincide with themselves. The suburbs, falling out of phase with themselves.*
> *The suburbs, in dub. The suburbs, echoing. Ricocheting. The suburbs—delayed. The suburbs, slurring . . . Drawling . . .*

Art, Merv and I in the woods. A fire by the air-raid shelter. A second bottle of vodka.

Questions asked into the fire: Who are we supposed to be? What are we supposed to want? Are we any different from the people we hate? Won't we have to become like them in the end?

More questions. Are we doing any more than just passing the

time? Will this ever end? Is this what our lives have amounted to? Is it going to get any better?

Still more questions. What's going to happen tomorrow, and the day after that? What will we remember of any of this?

What do these questions mean, anyway? Who are we to ask anything? And who we are asking them of? Ourselves? Each other? Are we just offering them up to the sky? To the absence of God?

The question *of* the question. The question of *all* questions. Maybe it's not about questioning. Maybe questioning is too wilful, too voluntaristic. Maybe it's too *presumptuous*—as though the answers should reveal themselves to you all at once. As though the answers should come when you whistle.

Maybe the universe is sick of our asking. Maybe it just wants silence. Maybe the night wants to be left alone. Maybe the cosmos has its fingers in its ears.

Speech, sent up into the sky. Speech, loosed into futility. Speech, burning upwards, sometimes ardent, sometimes doleful. Speech for nothing, and that is really about nothing.

Drink enough, talk enough, and we'll reach the truth: that's our belief.

Unless we'll pass out before we find it. Unless passing out *is* truth. Unless the truth *means* oblivion.

*

Finch Primary.

Climbing over the fence into the playing field.

The prefabs. The far school buildings, all window. The sports-equipment shed. The far car park, behind the gate.

The goal posts—they're a great place to hang yourself, we agree. We should all hang ourselves there, by our belts. Leave some note . . .

The nature reserve. Art, pissing in the bushes. Art, re-emerging, trousers down, pants down. Art, pulling off his teeshirt.

Art doesn't want to wear clothes anymore! Who blames him, for God's sake? Clothes are hypocrisy! We don't need clothes! He wants to feel the air on his skin. He wants to go *au naturale*. And we want the same! It's time for honesty. It's time for vulnerability . . .

We all strip down. We're half nude, in the school playing field. Cocks shrunk in the early hours chill. Now what?

Let's give Art a stiffy.

Calypso, Art, I say.

Creamy Calypso, Art, Merv says. Mmmm.

Nothing's happening, I say. Art's too drunk.

Maybe it's Tana now, Merv says. Do you have a crush on Tana, Art?

Merv, offering to blow us all. What generosity! You don't often get the chance to be blown on your old school field. It'd be a novelty. It'd be something to remember . . . But—no thanks, Merv. Not tonight, Merv . . . besides, what would Bill say?

Art, staggering into a goal post. Collapsing.

More laughter.

Art, slumped between the goalposts, unable to walk.

Art's regressing to babyhood. Art's reverting, through all the stages of development . . .

Ga-ga, Art says. Goo-goo.

Then: silence. Art's gone foetal. We'll have to rebirth him. We'll have to bring him into the world.

You're passing down the birth canal, Art!, I say. Slap him, Merv! You're taking your first breath! Bright light! Welcome to the world, kid!

Art opens his eyes. Lets cry his primal scream. What a bellow! It's terrible!

Chandra, you can wet-nurse him, Merv says.

★

Two AM. Nude, through California Crossroads. Nude, past Bob's Fish and Chips, past Ratepayers' Hall . . . No cars. Silence. And we're nude, nude, gloriously nude.

We should think of it as our gift to the suburbs. To the paedophiles of the suburbs. Twinks! Fresh twinks! Get us while we're hot!

We should join the nudist colony—the one up in Simon's Wood. You can see why people go there. The feeling of freedom. The feeling of tribalism.

We're suburban tribesmen! We're suburban Celts! We should

paint our bodies with woad! Now where can we get hold of some woad, at this time of night?

We're a Dionysian band, rampaging the suburbs. We're not very rampage-y, are we? So holler or something! Yell! Whoop like a Dionysian! What should we do? Scratch cocks into car-doors?

Maybe people will join us. Maybe we'll lead some nude revolt, some Dionysian revolt.

We walk on, sobering up. Nudity is sobering. The night on your skin: sobering. You can see why they do it, in the nudist camp in the woods. There's a nude *lucidity*. A nude *simplicity*. We're carrying our clothes in little bundles in our hands. We're holding our shoes by their laces.

★

Nash Grove Lane.

A car, slowing down. A man's voice: *Are you alright?* Sure we're alright! Never better! He drives on. What was he hoping for? To join in the party? Was he some kind of *suburban swinger?* Did he want us to join him in some *orgy*, or something? Did he want to lure us into his torture dungeon?

PERVERT!, Art shouts after the car.

He'll call the police, Merv says. We'll be arrested for public indecency.

Don't be such a pussy, I say. He's probably heading home to jerk off.

★

At Paula's annex window.

Look at the state of you, Paula says.

Do we turn you on, Paula? Art asks.

I think you're actually making me *more* lesbian, Paula says. You'll have to put your trousers on if you're coming in.

We're Dionysians, we tell Paula. Dionysians don't wear trousers. Dionysians won't be *confined* to trousers.

Raiding Paula's parents' drinks cabinet. Martin's Heron Gin (who's ever heard of that?) Meghan and Harry Vodka . . .

What happens when you mix all these things up? Art wonders. Let's find out, shall we?

A giant plastic Buddha in the living room.

It's new, Paula says. It actually lights up. It glows in the dark.

Wow—*enlightenment*, Art says. Fucking A.

So my parents have finally split up, Paula says. We sat down and had the Talk. It's official. Thank fucking God. Now I'll have to decide who I live with—Marathon Man or Stepford mum.

Who's going to get custody of the Buddha? Art asks.

Sit and spin, Paula says, raising a finger.

What about your girlfriend? I ask. That Spinney girl. Wasn't it your Big Date tonight?

Fuck that!, Paula says. Don't talk to me about that! So-called pansexuals . . . Fucking *tourists*. I'm sick of fucking romance! I mean, I don't ask for much, right? I just want someone to hang out with. Romance is dead. You fucking heterosexuals just fall into things. My time will come, right?

SUNDAY

Cycling to Risely Ford.

Blue skies, at last.

Even we're not cynical under a cloudless blue sky. Even our misery's lifted under a cloudless blue sky. Even we're not heavy with despair, under a cloudless blue sky.

Is this what it's like in the Mediterranean? No wonder they want to destroy the Mediterranean. Is this what Mediterranean laughter sounds like? No wonder they want to destroy Mediterranean laughter . . .

Art on his racer. Me on my racer. Paula on her mountain bike. Merv, on his mum's old bike, with its basket.

Chains, freshly oiled at Merv's house. Tyres, fully pumped in Merv's garage. Brake-blocks tightened. Handlebar-tape wound. Lunch in our backpacks.

Sunglasses on. Shorts and tees . . .

Art in front, then Paula in front, then Merv in front, then I'm in front. In Art's slipstream, in Paula's slipstream, in Merv's slipstream, and now they're all in my slipstream.

Downhill. Freewheeling. The high whizz of the tyres on road. A summer sheen on our brows . . .

★

The ford, thigh-deep. Leaning our bikes in the bushes.

Golden light on the water. Shafts of sunlight through the canopy.

Skimming stones up the river. At play, like all young mammals.

The most skims. The greatest distance before the first bounce. The largest stone. The *smallest* stone. The most stones in under a minute. The longest gap between bounces.

And not a drop of alcohol in us. And no weed. High on endorphins. En*dolphins*, leaping in our blood.

Is that our laughter in the air? Can we really be this innocent? Has the despair really lifted? Is this what it means to see clearly? Or is this what it means to be duped? Are we innocents or idiots?

The Sabbath of life. The commonwealth of all living things. The nature-festival of joy. Flight-games of swallows. Linnets on the thorn-tips. Mallards in the creek. Moorhens in swift water. What life is ours! In common with every living thing! Our hearts, lifted. Our hearts, beating together. Song in the air. Every creature, singing . . .

This is what terminal cancer patients call the *last good day*. This is the last good day before the catastrophe. The last day of our golden, gilded youth. This is our last picnic in the sun . . .

Evening. Gay night at The Three Frogs.

Not exactly a hotspot, Paula, Art says.

Is this where you brought the Spinney girl, Paula? I ask.

Fuck the Spinney girl, Paula says. I don't even want to *think* about the Spinney girl.

Wasn't The Three Frogs glamorous enough for her? I ask. Didn't she fancy scampi and chips?

Ah, provincial lesbianism, Art sighs. It really is the well of loneliness.

Yeah, well, maybe I'll go out with Shirley Vickers after all, Paula says.

I'm sure that's Bombproof's grandad over there, Art says. Do you think he's gay?

Space is gay now, I say—they sent up a rainbow flag. *A safe space for gay people*, or something.

Apart from there not being any air, Art says. And apart from cosmic radiation. And extreme temperatures. And a total hostility to life . . .

Never mind all that, Paula says. What about *Tana*? She's here on Earth, and she actually *likes* you! You as well, Chandra—Noelle's out of your league. Jesus, heterosexuality is wasted on heterosexuals. The cure for nihilism's staring you guys right in the face.

Blank faces.

Romance, you idiots, Paula says.

Oh fuck *off!* Art says.

You have to get out of yourself, Paula says. Care about *another person*.

Hatred—that's what we need, Art says. Keeps you on the move. On the fucking red alert. Otherwise we become just like *them*. *Domestic. Settled*. Death to the fucking world!

Hate is desperation, Paula says.

Hate is a last sign of *life*, Art says. It shows we can still *feel* things.

Well, you have to say yes to something, Art, Paula says. In the end.

See anything here to say yes to? Art asks. Is The Three Frogs doing it for anyone?

Paula, closing her eyes: Yes to the queer frontier. Yes to anywhere but here. Yes to wild queer lives. Yes to queer bohemias. Yes to lovers. Yes to *romance*. (Opening her eyes again:) And a big *no* to hetero

death-boys. To hetero naysayers . . .

SIXTH WEEK

Revision.

Never has there been so much time. Never have there been whole days to ourselves, our parents at work. Never have we known this openness of time, this too-much of time. Strange gift! Strange days we hardly know how to live . . .

All day in our houses, our empty houses. All day, everyone out. All day to revise, but what are we learning? How can we learn any more? Nothing goes in. The ground is saturated. We've learnt too much . . .

Art's broken patio. Waiting for Nietzsche.

Roof slates in the yard. Bricks from the chimney. Both back windows, cracked.

What does the state of your house say about the state of your soul, Art? Paula asks. It's fucking ramshackle . . .

Your house is destroying itself, I say. Mirkwood is committing suicide.

How long's it been since your parents left? Paula says. A hundred fucking years, it looks like. You can't look after yourself, can you?

It's entropy in action, I say. It's the second law of thermodynamics. At least you're getting out.

But I like it here, in the squalor, Art says. I wish I could just stay here forever . . .

Even I feel sorry for you, doofus, Paula says.

You know what, I wish the apocalypse *would* happen, Art says. We could hole up here together. Get in some supplies . . . I was reading about it: you can live on canned meat and fish for a couple of years. Supplement that with canned vegetables and fruits. Grains and pulses . . . dried stuff: they'll last forever. We could get some livestock in . . .

You have it all planned, I say.

Boy's Own Adventure bullshit, Paula says.

It's called bugging-in, Art says. It's what you do when the shit hits the fan. You either bug-in—stay at home with your supplies—or bug-out in the woods. Bugging-in's more comfy, obviously. But you have to be prepared to defend yourself.

Who from? Merv asks.

Marauders, Art says. People are going to be hungry, man. Don't draw attention to yourself—that's bugging-in rule number one. No one should know you're in. The place should look deserted. It should look like a ruin.

It *is* a fucking ruin, I say.

You'll all be banging on my door when the disaster comes, Art says.

*

Band photo.

It's got to look serious, Art says. We are the band for these times: that's what it has to say. Things are only going to get worse: that's our message . . .

Maybe we should set fire to something, Merv says. Have stuff, like, burning in the background.

Maybe we should set fire to the house, I say.

We should wear sunglasses, Merv says, squinting into the light. Like the Velvet Underground.

Total cliché, Art says. Bono wears sunglasses, for Christ's sake.

We could wear giant fish-heads or something, like Captain Beefheart, I say. Something really alien.

Too self-conscious, Art says.

We should just go blank, Merv says. Make like robots.

Discussion. Band photos are the cliché. How to hide in plain sight? How to show what we're not? How to reveal our shadows? Our darknesses? Our secrets? Our silence?

How to drive away all self-consciousness? How to appear like some lost tribe that has never been photographed? Like people from another world?

A *found photo*—that's what it should look like. Something

unearthed by accident. No—a photo *taken* by accident. A bunch of people just hanging out. Something really offhand, casual, like the covers of forgotten Krautrock records from the '70s . . .

Nietzsche, arriving on his bike.

Just in time, Paula says. Are you ready for your star-turn?

★

Art's bedroom.

Merv, playing us a song he's written. *Dancin' Star.* No 'g', Merv says.

Synth stuff. Plinky-plonky. Dinky little riffs. Really cute. Chorus: *You must have chaos inside you/ to give birth to a dancin' star.* It's from the real Nietzsche, Merv says. Do you think our Nietzsche would ever sing on this?

We shake our heads.

There's not enough *dread*, Merv, Art says.

There's not enough *ominousness*, I say.

We can't disco-dance our way out of the catastrophe, Art says. There isn't, like, a conga-line to paradise.

You guys are so *corrupted*, Merv says. So cynical. What if . . . what if there is a way to live on the Earth? What if there is something you could do and everything would come right?

Like what, twink-boy? Art asks.

Like . . . seeing the glory, Merv says. Seeing the goodness of the world. Like *write songs.* I mean songs you can sing along to. Songs you can dance to. Songs for everyone, that everyone likes.

You can't hang a fucking glitterball in a slaughterhouse, Art says.

Yes you can, Merv whispers.

★

Band practice.

Nietzsche, weaving the spell. This is a ritual. This is a ceremony . . .

Playing the Origin. Playing the Creation. Playing cosmo-genesis . . .

How does it begin? How does something come from nothing?

Ominousness. First chaos. The elements, shifting and moving.

The Netherworld. The not-yet world. Scraps. Half-shapes. Disjecta in the dark.

Nietzsche (speech-singing): *Let there be light.*

Light in our darkness. Points of light. Young, fresh stars, burning whitely.

First stars. First order. A cosmos of light-points, amidst space-mist. And now the first planets, coalescing in the solar disc. Now the early Earth, struck by comets. Spitting magma.

And now—first life, in the sea, drifting. Now microbial mats along tide-edges. Now single-celled bacteria, creeping onshore. First plants, coating the volcanic debris like moss . . . Jellyfish pulsing in the waters. Sponges and sea fans. Balmy warmth . . . (Warm ocean music. Slow, slow evolution music.)

Now horseshoe crabs, crawling onshore. Now millipedes on the mudflats. Silverfish, twitching. Now first winged insects, ranging over the lichen . . . (Upstrokes. Echoes of ska.)

Now the first backbone in the waters. (Synth stab.) First fish. (Synth clamour.) First teeth. First *death*. (Guitar arpeggios; keyboard trills.) Now the arms-race of the ocean . . . Now predator and prey (Sabbath-like chug. Slow metal.)

First lungs. First amphibians in the mud. (Breath music. Air music.) The rise of the dinosaurs. (Stomping music. Glam music. A Gary Glitter beat.) The conquest of air. (Bird calls. Caws and squawks and trilling.) First mammals, like tiny shrews, noses quivering. (Hooting. *Squeaking.*)

First hominids. (Low drone. Dread drone.) First flat-faced proto-humans, spreading through the world-forest. (Horror cries. *Psycho* theme.) The first human beings, upright on the savannah. (Grand guignol organ.)

Not playing the *human disaster. Not* playing the first farms, the first towns, the first priests, the first patriarchies. *Not* playing the Neolithic revolution. The first skirmishes and war. *Not* playing the coming of the empires. The coming of the Romans. *Not* playing the creation of money. The creation of debt. *Not* playing mass war. The extraction of fossil fuels.

Passing over the Anthropocene and the capitalocene. Forgetting the thanatocene and the necrocene. Overlooking the twenty-first and twenty-second centuries. The temperature rise of eight degrees.

The Breakdown. The Fall-Apart. Neglecting the Years of Rage. The cannibals and plagues. The funerary pyres. The *depopulation of the Earth* . . .

Playing the ones who come after. The Thoughtless Ones, returned to simplicity. The Innocent Ones, who have no need to think. The Absent-Minded Ones, drifters, dreamers. The Children of Oblivion, who live in the moment without thought of the morrow.

Playing the Peaceable Ones. Playing the Far Ones and the Always Praying Ones. Playing the New Gods, born continuously from the Old Gods. Playing the Nameless, too young for names. Playing the Day-Afterers. Playing the Absentees.

Playing the Wondrous Ones, who never rest. Playing the Escapers, always on the move. Playing the Ever-Brights, like Merv, with shining eyes—fluorescent oompa-loompas. Playing the Ever-Truants. The Disappearers. Playing the gyrovagues of the new Earth . . .

TUESDAY

Revision.

Too much to learn! Too much to do!

Why can't you just stop time? Suspend it all? Why can't there be days that belong to no calendar? Supernumerary days . . . Intercalated days, when the world just—halts. Everything still, nothing happening. Clocks not ticking . . . Second-hands unmoving . . . And you, free to pass through the frozen world. To wander. Free to open your books at your leisure, with all time on your side. Opening books, closing them. Studying, not studying.

Imagine it: everyone frozen in time, except you. Everyone suspended in the middle of walking and talking and eating. Everything still, except you. Birds poised in the air. Butterflies suspended. And you, moving through the frozen world.

Eternal midday. And you, revising in peace. You, with your books, in peace. You, rich with time. Happy with time . . .

Revision break, in Bill Trim's car.

Wide, wide roads. Enormous road-junctions, practically the greatest you've ever seen. Vast roundabouts, with exits to everywhere. Then dual carriageways. Canyons, packed with trucks, packed with lorries, packed with cars. Where's everyone going?

Vast buildings, crammed next to one another. What are they? Distribution centres? Logistics centres? Storage warehouses? Company buildings?

★

And now half-countryside. Farm houses, turned conference centres, turned riding schools. Bits of greensward. The old habitats. Scraps of trees, woods and hedges. Dots of Merrie Greenwoode . . .

★

And now the university. *Reading* University! A university in *Reading*! Of all places! The green sweep of *Reading University* grounds . . .

Reading University, where the Beckett archives are kept. To think, Beckett's work ended up here, in *Reading*. To think, Beckett scholars fly into Reading from all over the world. To think, this is where the great Beckett conferences are run, year after year . . .

Reading! Beckett! Beckett! *Reading!* Impossible to reconcile! Impossible to bring together! How can it be? Who allowed it? Proof that there is no God! No providence! No cosmic design!

How did they arrive here, the Beckett archives? Who brought them to *Reading* from Ussy-sur-Marne? Who shipped them from France, from Paris? Who sent them to *Reading*, the opposite of Paris? Who couriered them to *Reading*, the anti-Paris?

The Beckett archives, glowing like kryptonite in *Reading University* library. The Beckett archives, throbbing strangely. Do they have to keep them behind special glass? Do they have to handle them with tongs? Because if there was any real contact with Reading . . . if the manuscript of *Endgame* were actually to *touch* Reading, it would be like the collision of matter and anti-matter. It would explode and take all of Reading with it . . .

★

Reading students. Dopes. Saps.

Already mortgaged to the system. Already debt-bound to the system. Already indentured, and for what?

A few years out. A three-year gap. A bit of fun. But the joke's on them.

You'll have to pay it all back, *Reading student.* You'll have to earn some decent money, *Reading student.* You'll have to temp, *Reading student.* You'll have to enter the office. You'll have to get used to strip lighting. To windows you can't open. To coffee-machine coffee. To canteen food. To air-con air . . .

★

Reading Hospital.

This is where we'll die in the end. This where we were born, and this is where we'll die. This is where we'll sign off on our death-pathway. This is where they'll hook us up to morphine. This is where we'll be borne from life, unconscious, sedated, pain-free. This is where we'll disappear without knowing it, drugged to oblivion, floating in and out of consciousness. And there'll be no last words; no leave-taking. Just the *exit plan*, managed and policed . . .

★

The one-way system. London Road. Southampton Street. One way to where? One way to what?

Where are all these cars going? Who are all these drivers? And who are we, among them all? What are *we* doing here? Where are *we* driving to?

Shouldn't we be more careful of our *mental equilibrium*? We're delicate beings. We're soft. It's risky for us to even *venture* onto the one-way system.

It's so *boring*, that's the thing about Reading. So like everywhere else. Generic. Ordinary. But that's the *cunning* of nihilism. Reading doesn't *look* horrifying. Reading, in the sun, looks perfectly pleasant. But Reading nihilism merges perfectly with Reading concealment of nihilism—that's its trick. The very concealment of nihilism *is* nihilism. The very way nihilism is *hidden* is nihilism.

*

Buildings and roads and no city. Office blocks and roads and no city. The entirety of Reading: a solution to the logistics problem and the office-space problem, and no city.

Office town. Office life. An office tower going up, another coming down. It's moving fast. Do you actually get used to it: office life? Is there a way of getting on? Adjusting? Does it only look horrifying from the outside?

How long is it before you feel part of the team? How long, before you no longer feel like collapsing into tears at any moment? How long, before you don't feel totally helpless? How long, before you stop whispering *horror, horror, horror* to yourself in the company lifts?

*

The vintage quarter. Reading actually *has* a vintage quarter. Or rather, Reading's *zoned* for a vintage quarter.

They're going for edgy. They want to build the *alternative economy*. They want an artists' vibe. A gay-and-ethnics vibe. A local-scene vibe.

Reading doing *town centre*. Reading doing hip (corporate hip). Reading doing pop-up record shops and juice bars and organic veg shops (capitalist record shops, capitalist juice bars, capitalist veg shops). Reading doing artisan breweries (fake). Gin distilleries (very fake). Reading doing vintage clothes shops and vinyl shops and bric-a-brac shops (simulacra, all). Reading doing café culture: *Big Hand Moe's Funtime Emporium* . . .

Art, suddenly aroused: *That's* where we should play! There! *Big Hand Moe's Funtime Emporium!*

That's fucking theme-park shit, Art, Paula says. Jesus.

That's right!, Art says. We're at the heart of the horror! This is the only place to play.

Lick my fucking box, Paula says.

What we're doing is *real*, Art says. Our music is real. The young people of Reading will appreciate that. We'll set off a chain reaction. We'll be their pied piper. Lead them out of Reading to who knows where . . .

We'll set off *shit*, Paula says. Do you think we can outfox Reading? Reading's *cunning*. It's seen the likes of us before. It knows what to do with us. We'll be Reading's pet band, with its pet dyke, its pet gayboys, its pet paki, its pet whatever-the-fuck-you-are, Art.

Reading's a death-star, Art says. We just have to find its weakness and the whole thing will be destroyed. We've got to loosen the fucking seals of the apocalypse. Explode the lot. Destroy the lot. Except this would be a *loving* destruction. This would be Reading's rebirth . . .

Reading's a fucking *reservation*, Paula says. You can't love your way out of *that*.

Reading youth needs us, Art says. We have to show there's hope for them yet. They're not quite dead yet. It isn't quite over yet.

I want to believe—really I do, Paula says. But Reading youth's opening a fucking vein—you know that. It's fucking *tragic*. This is deathland. Zombieland. Nothing good's going to happen here. No one's going to be saved.

What would Nadya Tolokno say, Paula? Art asks. Do you think she'd just give up? *It is beautiful to contribute to the ruination of the world*—that's what she wrote. *To be at war with the whole world lightheartedly.*

Light*heart*edly, not light*head*edly, Paula says. You can't go to war with Reading. Reading already knows every move we're going to make . . .

WEDNESDAY

Revision.

We're treated differently. Our parents are quiet. Our brothers and sisters are made to tiptoe around us. *Sssh! He's revising! Hush, she's working!*

We're busy with something Important, for the first time. We're doing something that Matters, for the first time . . .

Art's house, voices echoing.

You got rid of the carpets? Paula says.

Concrete's more honest, Art says.

What are all the bottles doing? I ask.

Leaks, Art says.

Houses are supposed to provide *shelter*, I say. *Protection* from the elements.

I like all the water, Paula says. It's like being in a Tarkovsky film.

There's actually a kind of *stream*, I say. The water's *flowing* somewhere. It's a new tributary of the Thames. The river Mirkwood . . .

It's kind of cold, Merv says. What will it be like in winter?

You can build a fire, Art says. There's loads of wood out back.

You know what, you could actually do things here—good things, Art, Paula says. It's a whole habitat. An ecosystem. Something could *happen* . . .

You could dig up the concrete, I say. Get down to the soil. Grow indoor crops through the winter.

You could grow skunk-weed, Merv says. Set up some arc-lights. Now that would be a business.

Mushrooms!, I say. You could become a 'shroom farmer. Just scrape them off the wall.

Maybe there's a way of living here after all . . . , Paula muses. A way out of the suburbs in the suburbs. Jesus, Art—you're actually on to something. This is how we could survive the catastrophe . . . This is where we could hole up when the world ends . . .

*

Band practice.

Music as open as the sky. Like the sea beneath the sky. Music mirroring the sky. Indistinguishable from the sky.

This is what it means to Make. This is what it means to Order. We're continuing the Creation . . . We're furthering the Creation . . .

A *controlled* explosion. Energy, cascading. Energy, shaped. Currents and counter-currents. Slipstreams and rapids.

Metamorphosis. Our thresholds, remade. Our limits, redrawn . . .

Song running into song. No break. We've rehearsed this. We know the cues. A marimba vamp—up the tempo. A series of handclaps—slow it down again.

A single mass of song. A single continent of song. A Pangea of song. A Gondwanaland of song. A great molten block. The deepest, densest groove. A supersaurus in song.

Playing the divine. Playing the gods of froth and spume. Of wave-flecks. Playing streams of light on water. Playing transition. Playing becoming without end. Playing escape—continual escape. Playing the Singing Ones, who swing through the branches. Playing the Walkers, crossing the savannah.

We've emerged. We're on the upper slopes. The sun-touched slopes.

This is our music. This is where we are. We've been to the Worst and back. We've got Lost and we're coming home.

This is our music, and this is our madness. We've led it home, all the way home. We're in touch with the forces. We ride the forces. This is our music. This is our madness. This is how we escaped the suburbs.

We cast the spell. We did the magick. We undid the world and let it breathe. We cracked open the world, and put it together again. We cracked the world open, and let light shine along its edges.

We went on a journey. We went out, beyond the stars. And now—there are stars again, but they burn brighter. There are con-stellations again, burning harder.

We inhale more deeply. We exhale in clouds.

Calm seas. Voyage over. We've reached the harbour. We brought it home. We've reached our haven. We held it together, and held ourselves together.

We're miraculists. We're transfigurers. We let the world be the world. We let it live. And now we've set it back on its feet, twice as tall as it was.

THURSDAY

Revision.

Knowledge reborn in us. Knowledge remade, coming gently to life again in us. Facts reawakening in us, opening like lotus blossoms in the sun of our intelligence. Facts blooming in the hothouse of revision.

It's all temporary, of course. We won't always know these things. They'll fade. In truth, it's a last flowering for whole areas of knowledge. A last glory. Their time has come; their time will pass.

Whole star-systems of knowledge. Fact-constellations. Cosmoses. Whole ecologies of knowledge, as vibrant as a coral reef. Knowledge alive. Knowledge-energy, all flow . . .

★

Cycling.

The Ridges.

Up the gorge. Through the wooded valleys.

Pulling our wheels up over the steps laid across the path. Up at ten degrees, twenty degrees, like mountaineers. Resting at the top, looking back over the valley.

This is my theory, Art says. In great ages you create *with* the times. You just follow the *flow*. You just get on with it. In our time—in a fallen age—there's nothing to go with. No style is natural to you. You try out this and then that . . . You have to struggle. To break your way through.

So when was the last great age? I ask.

Art shrugs. The '60s, maybe. Haight-Ashbury, and all that . . . Flower children. It was about a way of living, right?

You can't go back to that hippie shit, Paula says.

What about the '70s? Art asks. Soul. Afrofuturism. There was still, like, a utopian ideal. Music was still going forward. They weren't looking backward.

And don't forget disco, Merv says.

Disco's too easy, Art says. It's too euphotic. Too danceable.

Too QUEER you mean, Paula says.

There has to be *struggle* in music, Art says. Joy has to be *won* . . . It has to be torn from despair. You can't just *dance*.

The real Nietzsche danced when he was going mad, remember, Paula says. In the nude!

Yeah, but not to *disco*, Art says. Anyway, that was after years of pain and solitude and suffering . . .

Disco's queer, and queers suffered, Paula says. And disco's working-class, too.

Bill and I . . . Bill and I have been writing some disco stuff, Merv says.

Like *Dancin' Star*, or whatever? Art asks.

We've called our band after that song, Merv says.

You've got a band!? Art says. You fuckers!

It doesn't mean we can't play with you as well, Merv says.

Mutiny!, Art says. And for what—disco!? Fuck! *FUCK!* . . . Disco's so obvious. *Everyone's* into disco. The drudges are into disco . . .

Maybe everyone's right, Paula says.

Everyone can't be right, Art says. Look—you have to create against your times in a fallen age. In defiance of them. You have to say, Death to *this* world. You have to descend into death and rise again just in order to *breathe* . . .

Or we could just *dance*, Paula says. Don't listen to him, Merv. He's just an old rockist bore who hates queer music.

Look, whatever happens, you have to play the gig on Tuesday, Art says. It's booked. It's settled.

New band night at Big Hand Moe's—must have been *such* a hard gig to get, Paula says.

We'll play, Merv says. But so long as . . . so long as we can do our own songs as well. I mean, as Dancin' Star. As support.

Disco blackmail, on top of it all . . . , Art says.

FRIDAY

Revision break. Driving towards Henley in Bill Trim's car.

Winding roads. Along-the-river roads.

Villages. Village greens. Half-timbered shops and townhouses. Thatch-roofed cottages.

And great houses, hidden behind high walls of shrubbery. Old houses, tucked into hillside folds. Stockbrokers' homes. Fund managers' homes. Financiers' homes. With staff. With sweeps of grassland. With vast conservatories . . . Private Elysiums, with Labradors padding on the gravel.

Each house, a way of framing the countryside. A way of centring the landscape. Composing it, giving it harmony. A way of organising the land, without dominating it. A way of apportioning it; giving it measure.

Each house, set in its peace, its silence. Each, tree-shaded, calm. Each, private, with its grounds to walk. With its old orchard. Each, with its gardens sloping down to the river. Each, with its screening oaks.

Each house, a piece of England. A patch of England. Each, a pattern of eternity, in its own way. Each house, showing the trees as what they are. Showing the river as it is. Each, allowing the river to be an *English* river, with *English* reeds, with *English* wildfowl. Each, allowing the sun to be the *English* sun. Allowing the English summer to be the *English* summer . . .

Is all this nihilism, too? Merv asks.

Art, nodding.

It's very pretty nihilism, Merv says.

Sure, it's nice, Art says. It's all *very nice*. There are islands of prettiness amidst the horror. But that only makes the horror worse.

I can barely remember the horror, I say. Henley's just so lovely . . .

Can't we just stay in Henley forever? Paula asks. Couldn't we pair up with some aristocrat? Fuck it, I'd be quite happy to be Lady Chatterley's lover . . .

Merv, closing his eyes. Falling into a trance.

Henley's most dangerous for Merv, we agree. It's the most contrary to anything he's known.

Even Bill's looking swoony.

Art (struggling): Old English mystique . . . The naturalisation of the hierarchies . . . The urge to defer . . . So powerful . . . Can barely resist . . . (Vehemently:) We've got to get out of here! Drive, Bill! *DRIVE!* (Eyes closed:) We're the real aristocrats . . . We're the real sovereigns . . . We're the Übermenschen, or we're going to be . . .

Back to The Ridges.

Looking out over the valley. The river. Flooded quarry-pits flashing light at the sky.

Paula, reading a plaque. Some King or Queen did something or other here apparently.

Feudal bullshit, Art says. Our whole country's, like, feudal bullshit. And that's how it's going to stay. We're on our knees. We don't know how to stand up. We love being ruled. If it's not the royal family, it's CEOs . . .

We're being sold out, Art says. The Old Mole's right. There'll be a few supercorporations, a few private equity firms, a few hedgefunds and the rest of us will be serfs. They'll buy us off with basic income and we'll be grateful. We'll top it up with some gig work, and we'll think we're doing *fine* . . .

Maybe they'll just exterminate us, I say. I mean, they don't need us anymore, do they?

They'll let us exterminate ourselves, Art says. They're already flooding the place with opioids. Seriously—we're here under sufferance. We're pets. Tamogochis. If we get on their nerves, they'll just destroy us *humanely*.

You know what I think? They'll develop some plague, I say. They'll inoculate themselves and let it wipe us out. Seriously—they'll eliminate us as an ecological threat. Because of our methane emissions, our *greenhouse debt*. They'll want to get down to the carrying capacity of the planet—three hundred thousand people, or something. They'll destroy us for Gaia's sake . . . That's how they'll justify it.

Paula, reading another plaque. Royalty used to ride here from Windsor Castle, according to this one. All this was part of Windsor Great Forest. Then it was part of the Trafalgar Estate. But the lords and ladies gave it to the people. It was willed to the people back in the '20s. See—good things *can* happen.

A sop, Art says. The aristocrats were afraid revolution was round the corner. Yeah, well, maybe it was. They're better at ruling us now. They know us better. They've tracked our preferences. They've collected the stats.

★

Stray planes above us. Old planes. World War Two planes. A lone

Messerschmitt in the sky. Five minutes later—a Lancaster bomber. They must be on their way to an airshow.

Then—a spitfire. A doughty little fighter. Patriotism swells in our hearts. The battle of Britain and all that . . . Aces high and all that . . . Taking a crack at the Hun . . . Giving Jerry a bloody nose . . .

It must be some kind of anniversary. Some commemoration. That's what happens when history ends, we agree: commemorative events replace real ones. When nothing's happening on the ground, it's all pseudo-happening in the air.

Nietzsche's blog:

> *Phantom time. Non-time. Time that cannot be lived, cannot be inhabited.*
> *The non-event, non-succession. Unlivable time, impossible to put behind you. Impossible to release into forgetting.*
> *Time, barely lived. The same day, perpetually recurring.*
> *Ruination. Hollowing. The eternal return of the same.*

Heath Pool, dusk.

You ever hear back from your monks, Art? I ask. Didn't you send in an application form or something?

I don't think I want to be a monk anymore, Art says.

You could become one of those Himalayan ascetics covered in ash, I say. All they do is smoke weed.

I wish there were a school of ascetics who just wanted to destroy themselves, Art says. You know—just remove themselves from existence. Or maybe a gang of warrior-monks who just want to destroy the world—to set it all on fire, or set *themselves* on fire . . .

They wouldn't last long, Paula says.

Fuck it, maybe I'll join the foreign legion, Art says. You just have to turn up at a recruitment office. You don't have to speak French or anything.

You have to be twenty-one to join the foreign legion, Merv says, looking at his phone.

Jesus—three years left, Art says.

Why don't you just go to uni like everyone else? I say.

Because I don't want to be a debt-slave, Art says. I don't want to take out a loan to live like an idiot. Anyway, did Sun Ra go to uni? Did Mark E. Smith live in a student pod?

Yeah, but if you don't go you'll get an even shittier job than everyone else, I say.

I don't want a fucking job, Art says.

So what are you going to do? Paula asks.

What's anyone going to do? Art says.

★

See that little star? Art says, pointing. It's not a star. It's Andromeda. A whole galaxy. And it's heading in our direction. In two billion years, Andromeda will collide with the Milky Way.

What will happen to us? I ask. I mean, if there's anyone left at that point. Intelligent mandrills, or something.

There'll be no one here to notice, Art says. And even if there were, they wouldn't see anything. The distance between stars is vast. The universe is so fucking *big* . . .

So what happened to Mrs Steele's *intergalactic message*? I ask.

It wasn't an alien civilization, Art says. Just some rogue star, blasting out energy for no reason.

But there's got to be life out there, right? Merv says. All those galaxies . . .

Then where is it? I ask. Why hasn't it contacted us?

It doesn't know we're here, Art says. They used to think that radio signals just beamed out forever into space. That one day, they might reach some distant star, and someone might know we existed. And that one day, signals would reach us from some exoplanet, and we'd know we weren't alone. But that's not what happens. Signals just degrade . . . They don't even reach *Jupiter*, let alone *Alpha Centauri*.

The distances between stars are becoming greater and greater, Art says. Soon, they'll be so far away we won't be able to see anything at all. The sky will just be *dark*.

Revision.

How many days are left? How many more days can there be?

The days pass, but we've got lost in the days. The days pass, but nothing passes. The days pass, and we're numb.

The days are too long. The days are too wide. We've lost our place in the days. We drift. We belong nowhere. What day is it? What date is it?

Revision. The day stretches. Nothing's going to happen. Nothing will ever happen again . . .

Nietzsche's blog:

> *Eternal life is this life. It is the very life we are living.—In the suburbs?*
> *The eternal is present in each moment of time.—In each moment of suburban time?*
> *Blessedness is not a promise. It is already here.—Even in the suburbs?*

Late afternoon. A text from Art.—*NEWS.—NEWS!?*

Art's house.

Chilled vodka. Barbecued sausages.

What's this all in aid of? Paula asks.

No—fucking—Boston, Art says. I'm free.

How come? I ask.

I told my parents I'm not leaving, Art says. That I'm not going to end up spree-killed or locked up in solitary for forty years or whatever happens in the USA.

And what did they say? I ask.

I told them they could throw me out if they wanted to, but I needed somewhere to live, Art says. Well, they didn't want to throw me out . . .

Fucking A!, I say.

I told them I'm going to uni in September, Art says. And I'll stay here 'til then. It's a cunning plan . . . Because *FUCK* uni! I'm not going to uni!

So what are you going to do? Paula asks.

I'm going to squat right here in this house, Art says . . . I'm going to start a one-man Occupy movement . . .

Like a Wokingham Che Guevara, Paula says.

Yea, well, turns out my parents have an investment plan. They're going to knock down Mirkwood and develop the plot. Squeeze two dozen houses in. Big ones. Executive size, with double garages and work-from-home outbuildings . . .

Typical!, I say.

Well, I'm just going to chain myself to a tree and turn the diggers away, Art says. I'll be an ecowarrior . . .

And then what? Paula asks.

Then I'll live here forever, Art says. And I mean *really* live. Go self-sufficient, or something . . .

Like, become a farmer? Merv asks.

You know what, you guys should move in, too, Art says. Come on, Paula—isn't it a tug of love at your house? I'll bet the brats are really playing up. And what about you, Merv? How's *silent dad*? Your brother's being sentenced, right? Jesus—*depressing* . . . And Chandra—have you told your parents yet that you're going to become a death-poet? Bet they'll love that . . .

Nietzsche's the one who needs rescuing, I say.

We could put him in my brother's room, Art says. With all the Lambro posters. Seriously. We'd be a real family.

*

Drinking. Drinking.

To think, there are countries in the world where alcohol's banned. There are entire non-drinking nations . . . How do they survive? How do they do it? Great glum countries that never rise into the sky . . . Whole peoples, who do not know what it is to be made-funny. To be made-laugh. To be whisked into the air . . .

But we drink like Russians, we agree. We're ra-ra-Rasputins.

We're sipping the water of life. The water of truth-telling. The water of knowing too much.

Vodka's probably a currency in Russia. You're probably paid in vodka. They probably just funnel it down your throat.

They probably drink all day in Russia. They have vodka for breakfast, or something. They probably just drink steadily, calmly, day and night.

Toasts to Dionysky. To cold-blooded Dionysus. To the Dionysus of the steppes . . .

★

Art's room, Listening to our rehearsal recordings.

Snatches of guitar. A roar of toms. A snare-drum snap.

Merv's marimba, like bleeping from an alien civilization. Art's laptop tambura, like a quasar roaring. And Paula's bass, like echoes of the Big Bang.

The ear, seeking something to hold onto. The ear, searching for patterns.

Enter Nietzsche's vocals, holding it all together.

Phrases, appearing and disappearing from the murk: *Coffin full of laughter. The divine accident. The head of the snake. Going to go under. Singing from the pit. Seething and swarming wherever I turn.*

Nietzsche, speech-singing about *unowned sadness*. About *betrayed angels*. About *mutilated wings*. Nietzsche, speech-singing about *subtraction*. About *flatlining* . . .

Discussion.

We're so good. So fucking good. Our music's actually better than we are . . .

One day, someone's going to release this stuff. These band rehearsals will come out. *Nietzsche and the Burbs: the Early Years. Nietzsche and the Burbs: The Archive.* After we've done some other stuff. Built up a reputation . . .

They'll find an audience. Not straightaway, maybe . . . but eventually. Like . . . like Slint, or something . . . Like Duster . . .

Listen to Nietzsche's lyrics, Art says. Listen to the way he's singing them. They're so fucking profound.

They're all about going mad, I say.

They're all about *death*, Paula says.

That's just a way of describing an . . . *intensity*, Art says. Death doesn't literally mean death. It's something you . . . pass through.

We're like Nirvana, hearing Kurt Cobain recording *I Hate Myself and Want to Die* without believing he actually *did* hate himself and want to die, Paula says. All the clues are fucking there.

I'm kind of scared of Nietzsche, I say.

It's because he's transforming, Art says. He's entering a new phase.

I'm scared *for* him, Paula says.

Madness is what Nietzsche *does*, Art says. It's his methodology. It's necessary for his *suburban affirmation*, or whatever.

Yeah, well, maybe he'll *stay* mad this time, I say.

It's just a figurative death, Art says. Like . . . like Gandalf becoming a white wizard. It's a way of reaching the next level.

What fucking *next level?* Paula asks.

The Übermensch—the overman or the overhuman, or whatever: that's what the real Nietzsche called it, Art says. The one who could bear the harshest test: the tragic affirmation of the world as it is. If you fail it: madness forever. If you succeed: *well* . . .

One gig—then I'm out, Paula says. I don't want to be part of this . . . experiment. It's fucking *ghoulish*.

SUNDAY

Hungover.

The graveyard at St James's. Benches facing the valley.

Couldn't we just stay in this moment? I ask. Suspend time. You know, before it happens. Before *something* happens.

It's just a gig, Paula says. Local-band-night bullshit.

Yeah, but then we'll no longer be a bedroom band, right? Art says. We're actually going to play for people.

Friends and family only, idiot, Paula says. Who else do you think is going to come?

It feels like the *end* of something, I say. I like beginnings. When it's all potential. When there's, like, a halo around everything. When nothing's yet inevitable. When things aren't just going to *play out* . . .

Shhh! You'll jinx it, Art says.

I'm sick of fatality, I say. Why does everything have to go to shit? Why does disaster have to come? Why can't we get a break?

This *is* our break, idiot, Art says.

It's like the band is the last illusion—before we accept it all, I say. Before we just give in.

Give in to what? The suburbs? Art says. Fuck it, I'm not giving another pep-talk. I'm too hungover for pep-talks . . .

I want to drink, I say. No—I want to be *drunk*. I want to be *unconscious*.

What, again? Art says. After last night?

It's just nerves, Paula says.

Maybe Nietzsche and the band isn't real, I say. It's just Wokingham loosening a little before it tightens. It's just the suburbs giving a little before they constrict . . .

Look, the suburbs somehow *coughed us up*, Paula says. So anything's fucking possible.

Annie Tasker's gravestone. Plastic-wrapped flowers. A bright-sailed toy windmill.

There she is—the poster girl for the will to nothingness, Paula says. Your heroine, Chandra.

She refused the system, I say. She showed she was alive.

Yeah—by dying, Paula says.

She didn't want to be *sentenced to life*, I say. She didn't want a slow death in the suburbs.

Oh, please—suicide is narcissism, Paula says. Attention-seeking.

It's because she didn't want attention, that's what I think, Art says. She wanted to be left alone.

At least she felt something, I say. At least she felt the will to nothingness. It was a sign that she wasn't dead.

Yeah, but she did die, Paula says.

Of course she did, I say. That's the only way you can show you're alive—by dying.

What kind of logic is that? Paula asks.

He who has learnt how to die has unlearnt how to serve, I quote.

He who has learnt how to die is just dead, Paula says.

Suicide's a hand grenade, I say. A way of hurling something back, something that can't be controlled.

Fuck you—the system has suicide *down*, Paula says. It manages death just like it manages everything else.

Suicide's, like, the last freedom, I say. The last thing that's yours. It's a last bid for life. A beautiful defeatism.

But you just *die*, Paula says. You just throw your life away.

★

Walking among the gravestones.

Merv, reading from his phone.

> *The precious dead lie there, and each stone over them speaks of such ardent past life, of such passionate faith in their deeds, their truth, their struggle that I want to fall to the ground and kiss those stones and weep over them . . . And I will not weep from despair, but simply because I will be happy in my shed tears . . .*

Fuck the God stuff, Merv, Paula says. We're not in the mood for tenderness.

> *Here lies the body of Mrs Hannah Spring, Age 76 years dead.*
> *In loving remembrance of Admonisha, the beloved wife of Elvis Trim, who died March 23rd 1843.* [Must be an ancestor.]

Dead Wokingham types, I say. Who cares?

Jesus—are we turning into fascists? Paula asks. Nietzsche's a bad influence . . .

The world's made us like this, Art says. It's the world that's fascistic, not us.

Why do we hate everything? Paula says. Are we better than everyone else?

We're less dead than everyone else, Art says.

You know what, I hate our hatred, Paula says. I hate hating the drudges—all the Wokingham types, alive or dead. I hate thinking about them. I hate *having* to think about them. I hate wasting the energy.

Hatred's a blowtorch, Art says. It's a purifying flame. If it wasn't for hatred, we'd be just like anyone else. We'd think everything was okay. We wouldn't want to *live* . . .

What's the answer, Merv? Paula asks. What would Dostoevsky say?

A long pause.

Maybe . . . maybe hatred's just another form of love, Merv says. *Twisted* love. Just as despair is twisted hope . . .

So we're in love with the drudges? I ask.

We care . . . we care desperately, Merv says. We've never stopped caring. Because we hope for something better. And there *is* something better . . .

Oh no, here it comes, I say.

We're guilty—that's the first principle, Merv says. We're guilty before everyone, before everything that lives. We're guilty on behalf of all and for all. But once we accept that . . . Once we know our guilt . . .

Then we kill ourselves in despair, Paula says.

Then we can glimpse eternity, Merv says. Then we can see our world as paradise.

But guilt makes us morbid, I say. It weakens us.

I think you're actually *glad* there's all this suffering, Merv, Paula says. I think you *want* people who are at the mercy of everything. You want their outstretched hands . . .

No . . . , Merv whispers.

You want everyone to be a pariah, Paula says. You want everyone to be stunted and weak . . . But human beings can be more than that, you know . . . Guilt is death. It's suffocation.

Dostoevsky says that guilt is penitence, not death, Merv says. Don't you see? It's handing your will to . . . to a *higher purpose*.

God's dead, Merv, Paula says. God's fucking dead. Suffering doesn't mean anything . . . Do you remember Dorcas, from school? Dorcas the Dork . . . Starving herself to death in front of our eyes. Her body was see-through. You could see her veins. She shivered. She coughed and shook. And she was *restless*. She never settled. She fidgeted. She got up, sat down. And she used to run every lunchtime.

She went off to run every lunchtime, as if she needed to lose any more weight . . .

Then she stopped coming to school, Paula says. She must have gone to a clinic. She's probably dying of kidney failure or heart failure . . . Where's your higher purpose there, Merv?

Merv, silent.

Merv, kneeling before Annie Tasker's grave.

And we're guilty for Annie Tasker, too, I suppose? Paula asks.

For everyone, Merv says.

SEVENTH WEEK

MONDAY, TUESDAY

Revision.

The exams are coming. They loom like great mountains. But these are the lower plains, the wider plains. These are the lowlands, infinitely flat, infinitely calm.

Peace. Revision peace. Space revises with us. Time . . .

We learn from the vacant hours. We learn from the fridge hum. From the cat's empty bowl.

★

Revision.

Our minds are as wide as God's. As vast as God's . . .

Dust in the air. Dust falling on things. Does air fall like dust does? Does air fall through air? Does air sink in air? Does air seek to find its level?

White light, seemingly sourceless. Seeming to radiate from the very air itself. And warmth—bland warmth. Teeshirt warmth. Jogging-bottoms warmth. Bare-feet warmth. Feet-on-fake-floor-boards warmth . . .

★

Revision.

The low hum of the dishwasher. The fridge . . . The click of the thermostat turning on. Autosystems . . . Autoservices . . . Sounds not meant to be heard.

And outside? Silence. You can't hear anything through the double glazing. No noise of vans, parking up on the street. No sound of wind, though the pines are swaying . . .

★

Revision.

The suburbs, settling into our souls. The suburbs, lying down in our souls.

Suburban phenomenologists: Have we ever been anything else? Suburban astronauts, lost on a spacewalk, tumbling head over heels . . . Suburban cosmonauts, lost in space . . .

Only *we* know what vastness is. Only *we* know the dimensions of space. Only *we* know the breadth of a day. Only *we* know what distance means. What space means. Only *we* are the friends of *time*.

WEDNESDAY

All of us, into the woods.

Anything could happen tonight. *Everything* could happen. Because tonight feels like a magic night. Because the old world of faery will touch this one. Because the English wyrd will come alive in the greenwood—the England of sword-dancers, of straw bears, of blacked-up nutters. The England of hobby horses and gullivers . . .

Summer is icumen in, and all that. Hey nonny nonny, and all that. The faery night and all that. *A Midsummer Night's Dream*, and all that.

Nietzsche and Lou, ahead of us. Lou, with flowers in her hair. Lou, looking sylvan. Lou, half-elf. Then Merv and Bill. Then Paula, with Art and Tana. Then Noelle and I, hand in hand . . . Then Spinney girls, a whole bevy of them . . .

Shouts behind us. Cries. Grove boys! Who invited them along? It must have been one of the Spinney girls. Well, who invited the Spinney girls? Why must there always be Spinney girls?

Bill Trim, climbing up for a view. Bill Trim, pulling himself up onto a branch. Up again. Bill Trim, halfway up the tree, like a bonobo. Bill Trim, leaping from one tree to another . . .

Bill's probably imagining being in 'Nam, or something. Or in some future war. In Bill's head, Bill's leading a band of crack-mad boy-soldiers through the jungle. In Bill's head, Bill's a soldier-at-arms, a soldier-for-hire, drones roaring over him on some battlefield in Hell. In Bill's head, Bill's commander-in-chief at some new Abu Ghraib, forcing captured enemies to fuck in front of him. In Bill's head, Bill's Bill Trim, lord of war, chomping his cigar on a throne of skulls . . .

Bill, dropping down, amongst us again. We need shelter. There are too many Grove boys!

More shouts. More cries. What's going on? We imagine it: Grove boys, fucking their way through the woods. Grove boys, violating all the fauna and flora. Grove boys, doing unspeakable things to squirrels. Grove boys, probably buggering the lovely, tender deer . . .

They're coming closer.

Panic. The party scatters . . .

★

Heavy walls of trees. Heavy wood-scent. Dense air.

Woods are positively *pubic*, Noelle says.

It's like a horror film, Tana says. We're going to get picked off one by one.

Sing us a song, someone, I say. Cheer us up.

Noelle, striking up Jacques Brel. *Se tiennent par la main / Et marchent en silence / Dans ces villes éteintes . . . / Les désespérés . . .*

Ah—French, I say. French is so beautiful. You're so beautiful, Noelle.

Now I know you're fucking high, Noelle says.

Can't we go and live in France? I say. You've got a holiday home, right?

You're not coming near France, Noelle says. You're not worthy of France.

Oh, fuck off, Noelle—you're pure Bracknell, I say. You were conceived in a Bracknell alcopop den, it's quite clear.

Anyway, they're turning fascist in France, Art says. Everyone knows that.

They're turning fascist everywhere, I say. All the horror's coming back.

We'll have to come to the woods when the shit hits the fan, Art says. When civilisation collapses. We'll just need a survival kit . . . The bare necessities. I read about it online. Sunburn cream—I'll bet you didn't think of that. Coconut oil—it's very multipurpose. Baby wipes. Cotton balls. Cotton swabs. Bic lighters. Toilet paper—you really wouldn't want to be without *that*. Vitamins . . . Medicines . . . Anyway, we'll build a shelter. Hole ourselves up. Protect ourselves from predators.

There aren't any predators, I say.

There are Grove boys, Noelle says.

Jesus, I'm hungry, Tana says. Come on, Art, catch us something nice to eat. Catch us a badger, or something. Use your survival skills.

Catch us a Grove boy, Noelle says. Set up a snare. I wonder what Grove boys taste like?

We imagine it: a Grove boy, turning on a spit, apple in his mouth. Prime Grove-boy thug on a bed of mushrooms and wild garlic. Prime Grove-boy *buttock*. Prime Grove-boy *loin*. Grove-boy *cock*. Probably a delicacy in China . . .

★

A clearing.

The ruins of an old house. Roof collapsed. Walls half-standing.

An old Anderson shelter. Half-moons of corrugated iron.

Kneeling. Edging under. Sitting in the shelter among the leaves.

Recite one of your poems, Chandra, Tana says. Something good. Not those Japanese death-poems, or whatever.

I've got a kind of dialogue, I say. Then, reading from my phone:

> *Brahma to Shiva: To create a new world, what shall I sacrifice?*
> *Shiva: Sacrifice me.—What shall I use as the sacrificial knife,*
> *the sacrificial altar and the sacrificial post?—Use me.—Where*
> *do I find the sacred fire and the sacred chants?—In me —Who*
> *shall be the presiding deity?—It will be me. I will also be the*
> *offering and the reward.*

Another of your odes to suicide, right? Noelle asks.

No—there's more than suicide, I say. There's bringing about a new world.

Through suicide, Noelle says. Very convenient, death-boy.

Through *sacrifice*, I say. We have to die to ourselves—that's what Nietzsche said. As an offering.

An offering to what? Noelle asks.

To the sky, I say.

What does the sky care? Noelle asks.

The sky *doesn't* care, I say.

It's futile, then, Noelle asks.

Of course it's futile, I say. Everything about sacrifice is futile. It's about what isn't . . . *useful*. It's about the destruction of order and value and explanations and school and *Wokingham*. We have to *live* the death of God. That's what the real Nietzsche says. *The death of God is greater and more divine than God* . . .

We should start a death-of-God religion, I say. The religion of the fall of God . . . A religion of the dying God, who doesn't exist, but just dies forever . . .

Shouts in the distance. Maybe the Grove boys have caught up with the others . . . Maybe Armageddon's finally broken out in the 'burbs . . .

★

Merv and Bill, crashing into the clearing.

Bill's black eye. You should have seen him, Merv says. He *destroyed* the Grove boys. Show them your knuckles, Bill.

Bill's knuckles, raw and bloody.

Where's Paula? Art asks.

She went off with Lou, Merv says.

With *Lou?*—So where's Nietzsche? Art asks.

I don't know, Merv says. Wandering round somewhere.

Fuck—we should send out a search party, I say. He might be lost.

I'm not going anywhere, Tana says.

You're here just in time, Noelle says. It's all getting *too* depressing here. Go on, Merv, tell us something to cheer us up.

I'll tell you about David Mancuso, the Prince Myshkin of disco, Merv says.

Jesus!, I say.

Love will save the day—that was David Mancuso's motto, Merv says. He used to hold parties where he lived—in an old loft in New York, back in the '70s. He'd only let in outsiders—people who couldn't get into any of the trendy New York clubs. The vulnerable . . . The touched . . . The debased and disparaged . . . He'd only admit the tender of heart . . . You didn't have to check your coat at the door. No one was searched. There weren't metal detectors.

There was always a Christmas tree in the Loft, Merv continues. Always mirror-balls. And there were always balloons, with just the right mixture of air and helium to bob along at chest height. And David Mancuso would squeeze fresh orange juice for his guests (that's what he called them: *guests*). He'd put out organic bread that he'd baked himself . . .

Of come *on!*, I say.

Disco didn't mean what it means now, Merv says. It was *greater*. It was more like Krautrock—you know, expansive. Cosmic. There weren't any superstars. It wasn't about frontmen or frontwomen. It was about dancing however you liked. Totally freestyle. And David Mancuso was really careful with the sound. Really respectful. He didn't mix records. He wasn't, like, lost in cueing up, headphones on. He played tracks from beginning to end. All this stuff no one else played . . . *The Messianic Now*, by the Trees of Life. *Golden Age*, by Amos. *Big Rock Candy Mountain*, by Man O'Peace. *P.A.R.O.U.S.I.A.*, by Land of Cockaigne. *Jubilate*, by The Zossima 5 . . ..

Music will save the world . . . the right kind of music, Merv says. Love will save the day. That's where me and Bill's music comes from. The sense that we're going to be alright. That everything's going to be alright . . .

I had this amazing dream last night, Merv says. People were being pulled out of their graves. It was the *resurrection*. I saw all these people, walking along a beach. Laughing. Embracing one another. Old enemies, old rivals. People who'd fallen out years ago.

I don't know how it's going to happen, Merv says. Perhaps this world's got to be destroyed first . . . Perhaps all this has to end . . . Perhaps it's ending now . . . But everything's going to begin again. Everything's going to be reborn.

We'll repair the past, Merv says. All the bad things. Death will be transformed into life . . . Sorrow will be transformed into joy . . . Sickness will blossom into health . . . And nothing will be lost.

I'm actually crying, Noelle says.

So am I, Tana says.

Nietzsche, stumbling into the clearing.

Where's Lou? I ask, beckoning him into the shelter.

Nietzsche, swigging vodka: Gone.

Gone? we wonder. But you were king and queen of the woods . . .

Nietzsche: She went off with Paula.

With Paula? What the fuck!? What does that *mean*?

Nietzsche: Lou wants to be with Paula.

Nietzsche, slumping down beside us. Grabbing the bottle.

Art, lighting up another spliff.

So where the fuck are they? Art asks.

Nietzsche: In the woods somewhere. I don't know.

What happened? Noelle asks.

Nietzsche: We were sitting on top of the barrow with everyone else, watching the sunset. I wanted to take Lou somewhere. Just the two of us. But she wouldn't leave. She was talking to Paula. Laughing with her. I've never heard Lou laugh like that . . .

So I left. I went down the path. Lou didn't even notice. I went into the wood. I want to hide myself in the wood . . . And then I heard shouting. Grove boys went by, cursing and shouting and karate-kicking shrubs. I hid in the bushes until they were gone.

Lou and Paula . . . It makes sense, Art says. It all makes sense . . .

It explains everything, I say . . . It's all become clear . . .

But it's *cruel*, Art says.

★

Aggrieved for Nietzsche! Outraged for Nietzsche! Humiliated for Nietzsche! Disgusted for Nietzsche!

Lou never understood Nietzsche! Of course she didn't!

(But pleased for Paula, too. And rather in awe of Paula, too.)

Turbo vodka. Vodka to the power of vodka. We'll have to drink as we've never drunk—all of us. We need to be drunk. We need to work on staying perpetually drunk. We need to attain some plateau of drunkenness and never, never come down . . .

★

Morning.

Noelle and Tana, passed out in the leaves. Merv and Bill, passed out in the bushes.

Looking around. No Nietzsche.

Fuck . . . my head, I say.

What *happened*? Art asks.

Memories through the haze: Art, proclaiming a vodka religion. *Drinking is a prayer. It's how we worship. Why does no one understand how* devout *we are?*

Art, proclaiming vodka the holy water for some religion not invented yet. Art, proclaiming us priests—high priests of vodka. Of the vodka-religion to come.

Art, libating each of us in turn. Art, saying we don't know what drinking is. We haven't even *begun* to drink.

Art, invoking a drunken sobriety. A *divine* sobriety, indistinguishable from the purest drunkenness . . .

Merv, asking Nietzsche whether you can drink your way to Dionysus. Nietzsche, saying wryly, *we can try*.

Tana, saying she doesn't *believe* in anything, not like us. Saying she doesn't believe in the great Motherwhatever, not like Art—she doesn't believe in the world-bitch, the liar. She doesn't believe in *transcendental death*, not like me. She doesn't believe in France, not like Noelle. She doesn't believe in twinky love, not like Merv and Bill. And she doesn't believe in all that shit about *loving her fate*.

Tana, crying at Nietzsche, TELL ME WHAT I SHOULD DO! TELL ME WHAT I SHOULD DOOOOO . . .

Tana, saying that all she saw was cancer. That cancer's spreading through us all. Through our bones. *You know what, all life will be cancerous. Life will be indistinguishable from cancer. Cancer will be a name for life and all life will die . . .*

Me, proclaiming that I *wanted* cancer. Art, saying that if you shout, *I want cancer*, three times you'll get cancer. Me: I WANT CANCER! I WANT CANCER! I WANT CANCER!

Art, proclaiming that we'd cured cancer—with vodka. That we were immortal—as of tonight. That we'll live forever—from tonight.

Grove boys coming to the edge of our clearing. Bill, stirring himself. Bill growling like a bear. Dropping on all fours. Becoming a were-beast. Lashing out with his claws. Merv, swinging a flaming torch . . .

THURSDAY

Evening. Art's broken patio.

A sense of transition. Suspension. Something's changed in the world, we agree. Something vast has occurred.

What now? we wonder. What next? What's going to happen?

Anything could happen, we agree. Things are lawless now . . .

The balloon's gone up, Merv says.

What does that even *mean?* Art asks.

It's the break that makes the heart: that's what Prince Myshkin says in *The Idiot*, Merv says.

It's going to destroy Nietzsche's heart, I say.

I can't believe it's *sunny*, Art says. How *dare* it be sunny? Fuck you, sky! Fuck you, sun!

You've got to admit it, Paula and Lou make a fucking cool couple, I say.

I actually think Paula and Lou are the greatest couple who've ever lived, Art says.

We imagine Lou, nestling into Paula. Paula nestling into Lou.

We imagine their conversation. Lou: *I feel lost.* Paula (touching her): *You're right here.* Lou: *I feel unreal.* Paula (kissing her): *Now you're real.* Lou: *I always feel I'm floating away.* Paula (embracing her): *You'll never have to feel that way again.* Lou: *You'll have to show me what to do.* Paula (undoing Lou's blouse): *I'll show you everything.*

Silence. Heavy air.

A storm's coming, Art says. A summer storm. You can feel it. The air's heavy. Electric. Come on, let's get struck by lightning.

★

Dell Road, winding down towards the Blackwater. A hill—a real hill—in the otherwise flat, flat suburbs. And the road's really winding, winding round things, winding downhill, not like some '70s housing-estate fake winding . . . Not golf-course ersatz winding . . . This is *old school* winding. This is long-before-town-planning winding. This is *historical* winding—how-things-used-to-be winding. This is long-before-the-Romans winding. This is *honouring-the-topography* winding.

Open fields. The last fields, down by the river. Lush grass. Thick grass. How come these fields haven't been built on? How is it they haven't been overlain by thousands of blank-faced houses?

There's probably some deranged farmer who won't sell up . . . Some hold-out standing up to the developers, watching out of his window with a shotgun . . . Some martyr of countryside space . . . Of countryside *time*.

There's probably something wrong with the land. There's probably been some secret disaster, which makes it dangerous. Maybe this is a mini-Chernobyl, kept quiet by the authorities; irradiated, but full of beauty. Just a few old people living on . . . Just a few refuseniks, who wouldn't move . . .

Distant rumbling. The forces are gathering. Something's going to be discharged. Something's going to be resolved.

What actually happens when lightning strikes you? I wonder.

We should have asked Iqbal, Art says.

He would only have told us to fuck off, I say.

It's probably like having a stroke, Merv says.

People wake up speaking other languages after strokes, Art says.

Discussion. We might wake up knowing Greek or Spanish. We could go off and live close to the disaster . . . They're eating each other in the Greek islands, apparently. It's battle royale in La Mancha . . .

Maybe being struck by lightning will restart history again, I say. Maybe something will actually *happen*.

We imagine it: lightning, stopping our hearts; restarting them . . . Lightning, blasting away our impurities . . . Lightning, cauterising all wounds . . .

Isn't that how life began: with lightning striking the Earth? Didn't lightning strike the Earth to life? And isn't that how life will begin anew: with lightning striking the Earth again?

Flashing in the sky. It's started.

Waiting. For the lightning to pass right through us. To remake our cells. To reset our defaults . . . restore our factory settings . . .

The feeling that something is going to happen. That there is going to be a before and after. A *before* lightning and an *after* lightning . . .

Clarification—that's what we want. For things to come to climax. For things to be resolved. We want the air to be fresh. We want a new *keenness* in the air.

We want our torpor to explode. We want our boredom set on fire. We're ready to become devotees of the Event . . . We're waiting for the death-bolt which is also the life-bolt . . . We're waiting for the suburban apocalypse. The suburban *revelation* . . .

The Day of Judgement—that's what we want. A new heaven and a new Earth . . .

The world will be born again. History will start all over again. And we'll be as children again. Innocent again. Our breath will cloud. We'll speak in clouds . . .

Do you have anything metal? I ask, looking through my pockets. Hold up something metal!

Art, baring his chest. Art, shouting: *KILL US, GREAT MOTHER-FUCKER! DESTROY US, I DARE YOU, ABSENT GOD!*

★

Walking back up Dell Road.

Fuck, Art says. It didn't come anywhere near us.

Good!, I say. We'd be dead.

We'd be reborn, Art says.

We'd be *fried*, Merv says.

With a crispy ear and a permanent bad mood, like Iqbal, I say.

Nothing changed. Everything's the same. The apocalypse didn't come. The divine world didn't touch this one. We didn't see God face to face. We didn't see things as they are . . .

Unless this *is* things as they are. Unless this *is* all there is, and all there can be. Unless it's the apocalypse of no apocalypse. Unless it's the disaster of the absence of disaster.

What there is: this, and only this. What there will be: this, and forever this.

It's the truth of the suburbs. No—the suburbs instead of truth. It's the revelation of the suburbs. No—the suburbs, instead of revelation . . .

FRIDAY

WhatsApping Nietzsche. No reply.

We've got a gig to rehearse!

SATURDAY

WhatsApping Nietzsche. Still no reply.

Knocking at Nietzsche's door. He's not well, Nietzsche's mother says.—Can we come in anyway?—No. He doesn't want to see anyone.

★

Paula's house.

Paula, at the door.

God, you look so *happy*, Art says. It's disgusting. It's *indecent* . . .

You're the queen of dopamine, or whatever, I say.

My parents just love Lou, of course, Paula says. They even made her stay for dinner. We all ate together, as though that's what we do every night. They kept asking Lou questions, and looking pleasedly at one another. Even the brats behaved . . .

It's because you were actually in a *good mood*, Paula, Art says.

Yeah, well, I hate good moods, Paula says. I hate *involuntary smiling*. They're going to get the wrong idea about me. *All she needed was romance* . . .

Well, that's true, isn't it? I say. That's what you were always saying.

I just don't want my *family* to know it, Paula says.

Paula's bedroom.

We still haven't heard from Nietzsche, Art says.

So? That's nothing to do with *me*, Paula says.

But you stole his girl, I say.

Lou was never *his girl*, Paula says. Lou wasn't anyone's girl. *Jesus* . . .

What about the gig? Art says. Do you think he'll come?

He'll come, Paula says. He likes haters, remember? He likes destroyers of the world.

Maybe he's gone crazy, I say. Maybe he'll have another two-year gap, or whatever.

I hope he actually sets fire to something this time, Paula says. The school, maybe. Or at least the sixth form.

★

Paula's bedroom. Photos of Lou.

Lou, in black and white. Thin, so thin.

Lou, bare-eyed. No lenses over her eyes.

Lou, bare-chested. Looking towards the camera.

Lou's collarbones. Lou's throat.

Photo of Lou with her eyes closed.

Lou's beauty. Why couldn't we see it before? Why did we miss it before? Why wasn't it obvious to us? Why did Nietzsche see it, and not us? Why Paula and not us?

A Lou-and-Paula series. Lou in the foreground, and Paula behind, out of focus, like a ghost. Lou, in the foreground, looking out of the frame. Looking away from Paula, and out of the frame. Paula, looking at Lou looking out of the frame.

Another photo. Lou, at the left of the frame. An absence beside her. A *present* absence.

That's Annie Tasker, says Paula. Lou's friend, Annie . . .

Another photo. Lou's glasses, folded up on her bedside table. Lou's eyeliner, on her bedside table.

Another photo: Lou's revision timetable. Lou's revision books.

Another photo: Lou's room. Lou's built-in wardrobe. The mirror on Lou's wardrobe door.

Your bedroom's, like, a shrine to Lou, Art says.

I can't help it, Paula says. I'm in love. She's amazing.

Some Lou-less photos. Stills of back alleys. Of clusters of wheelie bins. Of leylandii bordering front gardens. Of puddles on tarmac. Of faded graffiti. Of some power station, behind a high wall.

It's my *Day Before You Came* series, Paula says. Photos of the suburbs the day before *Lou* came . . .

Pretend film-stills of Lou. Lou, as a suburban wife, Betty-Draper style. Lou as an empty-eyed hostess in pearls, laughing. Lou as a career woman, '80s style, with shoulder pads. Lou as a supply teacher, glasses at the end of her nose. Lou as a *Sex and the City* style singleton, dreaming of love, looking for love. Lou as a lost suburban beauty, walking her dog. Lou as a jogger, in stretch lycra . . .

A final photo. Lou, without make-up. Everyday girl. A kind of *halo* around her . . .

I understand what Nietzsche saw in her now, I say. She's so *still*.

She looks so *innocent*, Merv says.

She looks like she's from a different *species*, I say.

Lou's an alien, Art says.

It's like she's disappearing, Merv says. You can't *see* her.

Is Lou actually real? I ask.

She's real, Paula says. Very real.

Silence.

I'm actually in love, Paula says. I never knew that's what it meant—to be *with* someone. I don't care what happens to me, so long as I'm with her. I don't care if *I* suffer, I care if *she* suffers.

I know what goodness is, Paula says. I know my own goodness . . . I feel *better*—like I've recovered after some long illness . . .

I feel like I'm going to die of gratitude, Paula says. Sometimes, I think Lou's *higher* than I am. That I look up to her—that I can only look up. That someone else, something else, speaks through her.

Everything's in her face, Paula says. I watch her face. I watch her eyes. I wait for her to see me. I know who I am, because she sees me. I know I exist, because she sees me.

Everything makes sense now, Paula says. There's meaning every-where. There's too much meaning . . . Happiness isn't so far away. Happiness is wherever she is . . .

We don't have to create ourselves—that's what I've learnt, Paula says. We don't have to pull ourselves out of nothingness. We're cre-ated by others.

Silence. Quiet awe. Even Art says nothing.

Nietzsche's blog:

> *I love him who wants to create over and beyond himself and thus perishes.*

WhatsApping Nietzsche.—Are you okay?—*Yes.*—Band practice tomorrow?—*Yes.*

Relief. Cheers. Rounds of miniatures at Art's.

EIGHTH WEEK

MONDAY

Band practice.

We're going to play the suburbs. We're going to play *suburban eternity*.

We're going to play what has happened before. What will happen again. We're going to play the traffic jam that is every traffic jam. The roadworks that are every roadwork. We're going to play the shops as every-shop. We're going to play town as it echoes with every other town. We're going to play suburban days as they echo with other days, with days that came and days to come . . .

We're going to play eternally new housing estates, with new roads, new roundabouts, new street signs, new road-markings. We're going to play eternally new blank-staring houses with plastic doors and plastic windows.

We're going to play eternally new apartment blocks in town. New human-storage units, pressed up right to the road. We're going to play eternally new supercorporations, all meshworked together, along the *M4 corridor*.

We're going to affirm our suburban fates. The suburban tractor beam that will drag us back home. We're going to affirm the student debt that means we'll have to live with our parents. And the temp jobs we'll have to take on to pay back our debts. We're going to affirm the drudges who we'll work alongside in our temp jobs and who we'll drink with on Friday nights.

We're going to affirm the eternal return of the suburbs. We're going to affirm the eternal return of the suburban void, the suburban tautology. We're going to affirm the eternal return of botched days. Of ruined days. We're going to affirm the incessancy of what does not happen . . .

We're going to bring ourselves to the brink of Nietzsche's vision. When the sky opens. When the sun stands at its zenith. When we know *ascending life*. Joy, deeper than agony. Love, deeper than hatred. When we know the beauty of the world. When we've said *yes* to everything we want to overcome.

Our music is about the whole, even if there is no whole—that's what we'll come to understand. It's about twisting free, even if we're never free. It's about belief, even if there's nothing to believe in— that's what we'll know. It's about transcendence, even when there's no such thing . . .

★

The band, at the ready. Nietzsche, by his mic-stand.

Marimba tone-clusters. Surging, jagged melody lines over a shifting base . . . The whole band, moving slowly in and out of synch.

Planes of music. Terraced music . . .

A marimba riff . . . Brief solos moving in and out. My guitar . . . Paula's bass . . .

Now I'm playing the riff. Marimba countermelodies. Marimba counter-rhythms, pushing against Bill's beat.

Funky comping. Merv's sound phrases. Swirls, glissanding upward. Semi-pitched electronic sounds from Art. Rising notes, panning across the stereo-field. Tensions, releases, going on at once . . .

A moving tapestry . . . A multilevel web . . . Almost *too* congested. A traffic jam of sound. Make room! Make room!

Simmering down. Marimba and guitar playing cat and mouse . . .

Then quiet. A holy pause . . .

Nietzsche, picking up the mic.

Nietzsche, putting it down: I can't do it. I can't sing.

Stopping playing. Silence.

Looking at one another. Looking at Nietzsche.

I'm sorry, Paula says. About Lou . . . It just happened . . . She's sorry too—Lou, I mean.

We're all sorry, I say. We all wish it never happened.

We're all guilty, Merv says. We should ask each other's forgiveness.

Fuck forgiveness, I say. Fuck apologies. Paula got together with Lou. So what? It's nothing.

Nietzsche, hollow-eyed.

Aren't we supposed to affirm everything that happened—everything in the suburbs? I ask. Isn't *that* the problem? You can't over-come nihilism, can you? You can't leave it all behind . . . Our fucking mediocrity . . . Everyone suffers, right? And suffering is so thick . . . so nauseating. There can never be an Übermensch, whatever happens. There's no way of affirming any of this. Of loving it. We can't believe in anything . . .

We have to believe because we can't believe, Art says. We have to live because it's unbearable to live. Better not to have been born at all—perhaps. But we're alive.

We're not alive, I say.

I'm alive, Paula says.

You're deluded, I say. And don't you start talk about the life of life, or whatever, Merv . . .

You have to sing!, Art says. You have to!

Nietzsche, head in hands, rocking.

Art (to Nietzsche): Don't give in! Don't give up! We have to be severe with ourselves—that's what you taught us, isn't it? We have to secure a mastery—a *strength*: that's what you told us. We have to compose ourselves—that's the real task—that's ethics. Forget compassion, forget compromise, forget feeling sorry for ourselves or anyone else.

The world is nauseating—we know that, Art says. The world is disgusting. We have to let ourselves go under—we have no choice. But then we'll rise again. We'll be reborn. And we'll be creators. We'll create ourselves. *We'll create the suburbs.*

This band—this is the answer: don't you see? Art says. This is the transition. The saving power. Can't you hear it? Every song is a cosmos. We're creating something. Holding it together. Constellations . . . Assemblages of stars and darkness . . .

Every song is a new beginning, Art says. A new chance. A surge. We've shown that fatality isn't fatal. That things don't only fall. There's a rising, too. There's transcendence. There's light along the fucking cracks . . .

TUESDAY

Gig day.

Art's house. Waiting for Nietzsche.

Is he actually going to come? Paula says.

We should be issued with suicide capsules, like in James Bond, I say. *Should your mission fail . . .*

We're not going to fail, Art says.

Waiting.

Art, occupying himself with a medical questionnaire. *Please indicate to what extent these experiences apply to you in the past year.* [Okay.] *I have trouble urinating.* [No.] *I dislike tastes that I usually like. I dislike smells I usually like. I see things around me differently than usual (for example, as if looking through a tunnel, or merely seeing part of an object) . . .* [Oh God, it's not working.]

Art, looking up FailedSuicides.com. This guy shot himself in the face and lived . . . This guy set fire to himself and lived . . . This guy blew out his eyes and lived . . . This guy shot off his nose and lived . . . This guy drank acid and lived . . .

Art, watching videos of animals fucking. Dogs, back to back, panting. Bonobos, slowly, gently (it's how they resolve all communal tensions). A poodle trying to make it with a duck. A giraffe getting fresh with a donkey . . .

Nietzsche, cycling up. Leaning his bike against a tree.

I told you, Art says.

★

Art's pep talk. Remember the cues. Remember the set-list. Wait for the signals. Let the music breathe. Don't screw it down. Be loose-limbed. Find the pulse. Be funky.

And keep still on stage, Art says. Keep it simple. No need for theatrics. We're newcomers. No one knows us. No one expects anything. Be modest. Be unassuming. Dress normal, act normal.

No stage banter (of course!), Art says. Don't say anything (obviously!). No need for introductions. Look to Nietzsche. Keep him in your sights. Be restrained. Give nothing away. Don't smile. Don't look the punters in the eye. We're not *of* them—we have to remember that (except for Reading Youth—who aren't going to come). We're *better* than them (except for Reading Youth—I *hope* they come).

No guitar heroics, Art says. No marimba heroics—whatever the fuck they might be. No drum solos. In fact—no solos. We'll play as one—all as one. We'll have each other's backs. Solidarity . . . We'll maintain the phalanx . . . This is a *war*—remember that.

We'll turn our backs to the audience—figuratively at least, Art says. We've deigned to play, that's all. We happen to be playing, and playing before them, that's all. But we might as well not be.

The van. Bill, driving.

Nash Grove Lane. Barkham Ride.

It's really clean, I say. It doesn't smell of piss, or anything.

Don't throw up, Art says. And don't smoke. We've got to keep it tidy or we'll lose our deposit.

Finch Road, past the garage.

The last day of our old lives. The first day of the rest of our lives.

The touring life, we reflect. We'd better get used to it. The open road. Today, Reading—tomorrow, the world . . .

Drive us past the school, Bill, so we can say a final *fuck you*. Drive us past the arcade. In fact, drive us through Wokingham. Never mind the traffic—we can say the biggest *fuck you* of all . . .

Discussion. Are we going to remember our old friends, when we're famous? *Fuck them!* Are we going to remember our parents when we're famous? *Fuck them!* Are we going to remember Wokingham when we're famous? *Fuck that!*

These nowhere streets. These nothing streets. We're leaving them now. We're striking out . . . We didn't just suck it up. We didn't just *take it*. Maybe we can kick-start some new movement. Rekindle teen rebellion. We'll show them what *death to the world* looks like.

We imagine it: touring relentlessly. Playing in cramped low-rent bars, eyeball to eyeball with our audience. Playing, heads down, as hard as we can. Playing brutally loud—no melody, just rhythm and texture. Counting in each song—one, two, *FUCK YOU!* . . .

★

Wokingham traffic. Perpetual Wokingham traffic.

Wokinghamites, trapped in their cars. Trapped in their *commute*.

Ah, Wokinghamite, how do you hold it together—job, commute, mortgage, kids? How do you keep yourself sane?

Ah, Wokinghamite, are you dreaming of the golf green? Of a walk in the woods? Of a beer on the decking? Of two weeks in Marbella? Do you want to be young again? On your gap year? Back at uni?

Ah, Wokinghamite, do you ever think of leaving it all behind. Of slamming your car door and walking away? Of emigrating to Australia? Of starting all over again? Of the outdoor life? Of big blue skies?

Ah, Wokinghamite, do you know what ails you? Would it help to give it a name? *Nihilism*, Wokinghamite: what does that word mean to you? *Passive nihilism*: is that the name for what you feel?

★

Reading. Parking up.

We're like four hours early. What to do in Reading for four hours?

Nietzsche, walking off. Nietzsche, doing his own thing.

Typical, Paula says.

★

The need to walk. To feel ourselves in motion. We need to go some-where. Just move our legs. Just prove that we're not dead. We're not dead, are we? We haven't died, have we?

Drudge watching in the Oracle Centre.

Look at them—zombies of boredom. The fucking *undead*.

The fucking *unalive*, I say.

They're bored without knowing they're bored, Art says. And they're nihilists without knowing they're nihilists.

Is it weird—the most nihilistic people are the ones who *feel* least nihilistic, I say.

The true nihilists are the ones who oppose nihilism with their more and more faded positivities, Art says. Remember that—from Nietzsche's blog? So we just have to stay with nihilism. Sit with it.

Well, we're good at that, Art says. We've had plenty of practice.

Why so quiet, Paula? I ask.

I just don't hate everyone as much as I used to, Paula says.

Fuck you!, I say. You don't hate Reading?

See—romance makes you lose your edge, Art says.

★

Reading flats, along the river. Reading apartments, on the river. This is where they live, the new internationalists. The fly-in fly-out workforce. This is where they touch down for three months, for six months. This is where they perch for a season.

New Readingites, temporary Readingites, strolling along the river. Flat dwellers, apartment dwellers, just the same as every-where. A stroll along the regenerated riverside here is the same as a stroll along the regenerated riverside there. Public art . . . Apartment blocks . . . Happy déjà-vu. They've seen it all before . . . They know where they are . . . New Readingites, just plugging themselves in and recharging by the river . . .

And not a single Nietzsche and the Burbs poster anywhere. No sense that the world's about to shift on its axis . . . That a new epoch's going to begin . . . That it's the end of the end of history . . . (Laughter.)

★

The *Reading art-trail*, on the river. There really is such a thing as the *Reading art-trail* . . .

Colourful art. Agreeable art. Ready to be enjoyed. Ready to be *liked*.

Tell me you hate this, Paula!, Art says.

Paula, shrugging.

See, romance makes you numb, too, Art says.

Me, reading a plaque. Reading art, providing *a focal point for enter-tainment and shopping*. Generating *creative and memorable experiences*. Stimulating *innovative thinking*. Improving the urban space. Helping *town branding*. Contributing to the *creative economy* . . .

Paula, looking immune.

Art: *JESUS!*

A plaque about the old Kennet, a tributary of the Thames. How they dug out the Kennet. How they made it navigable. How they put locks on the Kennet. Now it's a canal, in all but name. They deepened it so it would run slowly, so it would never flood. And they *straightened* the Kennet, so it wouldn't foam and rage. There was to be no meandering in Reading. Meandering's basically banned in Reading. Just as daydreaming's banned in Reading. Just as *philosophy's* probably banned in Reading. No doubt they spray the city once a year with *anti-philosophy gas*—like that stuff they spray to kill mosquitoes—just to be sure . . .

And they would have banned thinking, if it wasn't for the uni . . . Actually, they probably *did* ban thinking. Reading Uni is probably the first post-thinking uni. The world's first . . .

Look at the river—they're hardly *honouring the topography*, are they Paula? Art asks.

Paula, looking serene.

It's like being with Mother fucking Theresa, Art says.

★

Imagining Rimbaud walking along the old Kennet, writing his last poems about the old Kennet. Imagining Rimbaud, broken by Reading, remade by Reading, throwing his last efforts at poetry into the old Kennet . . .

I am the wound and the knife. I am the blow and the cheek. The limbs and the rack, the victim and the executioner . . .

Imagining Rimbaud studying *advanced mercantilism* at Reading College. Imagining him, studying *joint-stock capitalism*. Studying *double-entry bookkeeping*. Studying *management theory*. Studying *performance logistics*. Studying *quantitative measures and controls . . .*

No wonder Rimbaud never wrote again. No wonder Rimbaud went off gun-running in Abyssinia or wherever . . .

Paula—no response.

I'm actually glad you're leaving the band, Art says. You can fuck off and join Dancin' Star. Disco would suit you better.

Big Hand Moe's Funtime Emporium.

It's *echoey*, Merv says.

Because there's no one actually here, doofus, Art says.

Is that Big Hand Moe, do you think? I ask, nodding at a barman.

He doesn't have particularly big hands, Art says.

It's *metaphorical*—clearly, Paula says. Moe, if that's him, has a *metaphorical* big hand.

What's it a metaphor for? I ask.

Generosity? Paula says. Magnanimity? Go and ask for a free drink.

It clearly refers to his cock, I say. They might as well have called it Big *Cock* Moe's and have done with it.

Is there even a Moe? Merv asks.

Oh, *now* you're interested, Merv, I say.

I just want to know what's so fun about Moe's emporium, Paula says.

We're the fun, I say.

For who? Art asks. There's no one here.

Will we have played a gig if there was no one but us to hear it? Merv asks. Does a band exist if it doesn't have an audience?

Look—there's some *fun memorabilia*, I say.

A girl's school uniform. Supposedly Britney Spears's from that video.

Fuck off—that's a Spinney school uniform, I say.

It's fucking *paedophilia*, Art says.

A jumpsuit, supposedly Agnetha's from Abba. The depressed one.

Obviously fake, too, Art says.

A display case. The *real* stuff. A page of lyrics by Tanita Tikaram, the sound of Basingstoke. A signed photo of Howard Jones, the sound of High Wycombe, with his giant feather-cut . . .

What are we doing here? Who are we fooling? What are we trying to be? Nothing comes from nothing, right?

Just think of all the Thames Valley band legends, Paula says.

What *band legends*? I ask. Name me a band that's come from Reading.

. . . Slowdive, Paula says.

Slowdive—*one* band, I say. From thirty years ago.

Slowdive's reforming, Art says.

Of course Slowdive's reforming, I say. Everyone's reforming.

★

Bill and Merv's equipment. Banks of synths.

Merv, laying out bowls of snacks.

Bill, filling DANCIN' STAR balloons with gas.

★

Enter Tana and Noelle.

Hello, losers, Tana says.

You'd better be good, Noelle says. You'd better not embarrass us.

I can't believe you *play an instrument*, Art, Tana says.

He doesn't *play an instrument*, I say.

Art's our ideas-man, Paula says. Our Brian Eno.

So what's your great idea, Art? Noelle asks.

We've been asking him that, I say.

I only know what it isn't, not what it is, Art says.

So what *isn't* it? Noelle asks.

Reading—in general, Art says.

We've all got *that* idea, Tana says. That's easy.

Being against Reading is part of Reading, right? Noelle says.

That's the problem, Art says. I don't know how to defeat it. I don't know how to crack it open. To get between the fucking molecules.

Between the molecules of Big Hand Moe's Funtime Emporium? Noelle asks.

It's a problem of *perception*, Art says.

It's a problem of *Reading*, Noelle says.

Fuck all this, Art says. Fuck the Reading vintage zone. We're just Reading's pet alternatives—you know that, right? Reading's tame revivalists, serving up the '70s without the vanguard. It's all played out: every rebellion. Every political dream. Every musical dream. There's no new frontier. There's just *Reading* . . .

We can be as negative as we like, Art says. We can hate whatever we like. The system doesn't mind our negativity. It's not bothered by our hatred . . . The system runs on nihilism. It's a nihilism-engine. It converts darkness into light (so-called light). It makes something out of nothing (so-called something). It changes meaninglessness into meaning (so-called meaning).

It's like a *negative miracle*, Art says. There really is such a thing as *nihilist meaning. Nihilist belief* . . .

We'd have Nietzsche, I say.

Yes, of course. We'd have Nietzsche . . .

★

Nietzsche, sitting on his own at the bar, headphones on.

How *contained* he is. Is he composing himself? Gathering his forces? Is he playing *Eye of the Tiger* on his headphones? Is he playing some classical shit? *Ride of the Valkyries*, or something . . .

★

Bombproof, coming through the door.

Art, giving a double thumbs-up to Bombproof.

Was that a sarcastic thumbs-up? I ask.

It was fucking not, Art says. We need the numbers.

Enter Mags. Enter Enid.

Enter Hand Job.

The Valley massive . . . Our audience. The ones we're going to save (laughter). The ones we're going to redeem (laughter).

Enter Lou.

Paula, embracing Lou. Paula, kissing Lou.

Nietzsche, watching Paula and Lou. Nietzsche, sipping on his vodka.

★

Merv and Bill, emerging from the bathroom.

Cycling gear—*very* interesting choice. Quite distinctive. Rod-Stewart-in-the-'80s visors. Matching *Dancin' Star* teeshirts . . . Head-mics, like the boybands. Putting Merv's drug money to good use.

Merv, at the keyboards. The drum machine, starting up. Trills and arpeggios. An early-'80s sound. A disco-via-synth-duos sound, all bleeps and dinky melodies.

Bill, out front. My God, Bill's voice is so high! Bill's falsetto—who knew? It's unearthly. You'd think he was a castrato if it wasn't for that great bulge in his cycling shorts.

Where's the old Bill, the lumpen Bill, out with the beasts at the Phoenix? Where's Trimtones Bill, with his macho guitar?

Bill's dancing. Bill's pogoing. Bill's stagecraft. Bill's stage moves. Bill's *graceful*, that's the thing. The gymnastics has paid off. Bill's got real frontman potential. Bill's really *working the room*.

Angelic disco. Disco songs of innocence. Love-will-save-the-day disco, fresh from the Loft . . .

The last song. The finale. All breakdown. Nothing but breakdown. Nothing but the best bits of the song. Best bits, all the way down.

Merv, coming out from behind his keyboard. Synchronised dance moves, among the balloons.

The desert grows / No one knows / What you're doing to me.
The desert grows / No one knows / Why what is must be—

★

Our set.

What should have happened: Nietzsche, unsmiling at the mic, as a frontman shouldn't smile.

What should have happened: none of us smiling, as band members shouldn't smile.

What should have happened: Nietzsche's song. Nietzsche's singing.

What should have happened: Nietzsche, really singing for the first time. Nietzsche, all melodic, for the first time.

What should have happened: Nietzsche, letting his body resound, the whole animal. Nietzsche's voice, from his deep body. Nietzsche's voice, deeper than thought, deeper than philosophy.

What should have happened: Nietzsche's body singing, not his mind. Nietzsche's body reverberating. Nothing showy, nothing histrionic. Just Nietzsche, using his lungs, his larynx, his vocal cords. Just Nietzsche, letting his voice resound.

What should have happened: Nietzsche's singing, gathering intensity. Becoming richer, darker. Nietzsche's singing, projected on the out-breath, coming from the core.

What should have happened: Nietzsche, singing joy and mourning, both at once. Nietzsche, singing pain and dissolution, both at once. Nietzsche, singing death and rebirth, both at once. Nietzsche, singing fullness and loss, both at once. Nietzsche, singing gathering and dispersal, both at once. Nietzsche, singing tragedy and comedy, both at once.

What should have happened: Nietzsche, singing his cosmic life. Nietzsche, singing his demonic life. Nietzsche, singing of lightning striking above him. Nietzsche, singing of starry fragments, of part-divinities. Nietzsche, singing of sky-roads, of light paths . . .

What should have happened: Nietzsche, singing of blazing shoals, of the cathedral night. Nietzsche, singing of the tears frozen on his cheeks. Nietzsche, singing that his lips were bloody, that his hands were bloody. Nietzsche, singing of the death-day rising. Nietzsche, singing of electric storms inside his head. Of the stars that are falling inside his head.

What should have happened: *kairos*. Transition. The Moment, come. Nothing but Moment.

What should have happened: the world, become threshold. Reading, become all brink. The suburbs, become offering.

What should have happened: losing the world, and regaining it. The world, burning. The world, singing in its flames.

What should have happened: all the gods, singing. All the world, drunk. All of us, living inside the miracle.

What should have happened: the great bells, ringing. The stars, trembling. All of us, knowing what was meant by the music of the spheres.

What should have happened: playing music that said, *I want the world as it is, exactly as it is.* Playing music that changed everything that happened into an *I wanted it thus* . . .

What should have happened: playing music that asked, without answering. Playing music that desired its desiring. Playing music that loved love. Playing music that believed in everything, that wanted to receive everything, that wanted what there is, over and again.

What should have happened: playing music that leaped. Music that *reached*. Playing music of faith, without an object of faith. Playing music that believed, that believed in nothing.

What should have happened: the audience, wowed. Won over. The audience, cheering.

What should have happened: audience applause. Audience shouting.

What should have happened: being bought drinks. Being brought a tray of golden beer.

★

What really happened: never really beginning. Never really getting anywhere.

What really happened: the opposite of creation.

What really happened: Hell came. The end of every world. Madness AKA chaos. AKA truth.

What really happened: noise. Chaos. The unlimited. The unordered. The uncomposed.

What really happened: entropy. Decay of the will. The anti-song. The non-song.

What really happened: music, lost. Infinite cadenza. Free, but too free . . .

What really happened: the mandala, falling inwards. The mandala, collapsing inwards.

What really happened: scattered words, scattered speech-song.

What really happened: Nietzsche, stumbling, staggering.

What really happened: unearthly screaming—from Nietzsche's throat. Quavering, buzzing—from Nietzsche's throat. Nietzsche, fitting. Nietzsche, thrashing.

What really happened: Nietzsche, hitting his head hard. Nietzsche, lips going blue. Nietzsche, eyes completely rolled back in his head.

What really happened: suffering—just that. Pain—just that. Madness—just that.

What really happened: bar-staff, standing around us. Calling an ambulance.

What really happened: paramedics. Nietzsche, bundled up. Carried out on a stretcher.

Noelle and Tana, clambering into the van.

Just so you know—we're not groupies, Noelle says. Don't expect any blow jobs.

Jesus, where's your heart, Noelle? Art says. Even Bill's crying.

Oh, I forgot—you're in *mourning*, Noelle says. I should be more respectful.

It was a fucking freak show, Art says. *See the amazing exploding singer* . . .

Don't cry, Bill, I say. There was nothing you could do.

We would have been good, right? I ask. How did Nirvana do at *their* first gig?

Their first gig wasn't their last gig, Art says.

Nietzsche might get better, I say.

Nietzsche's fucked, Art says. Did you see him?

Maybe his mind only *appears* shot, I say. Maybe it only *appears* to have blown like a fuse. Maybe there's a greater madness. And a greater sanity, that's indistinguishable from it.

Oh, *please*—he just had a panic attack, Tana says.

There's no truth in madness. There's just madness, Noelle says.

We played the wrong music, Art says. Our music should have protected him. It should have been a shield.

Against what? I ask.

Against the truth, Art says. Against chaos.

I thought he wasn't afraid of anything, Merv says. I thought he'd trans . . . trans . . . (*Transfigured*, I say) . . . yeah, transfigured suffering.

It was Lou, Tana says. It was seeing Lou there.

It was seeing Lou *and Paula*, I say.

And now we haven't got a leader, Art says. And we haven't got a band. We're just the Burbs. And the Burbs are just nothing . . .

Now you can be your own men, Noelle says.

We don't want to be our own men, I say.

★

Art's house. Bill, unloading the gear. Roaring off with Merv. Where are they going?

A celebratory fuck, I'll bet, Art says. I can't believe Dancin' Star upstaged us.

Walking through the woods.

Noelle (singing): *Don't be afraid to become what you are. Just remember, baby, you're a dancin' star.* I can't get it out of my head. It was a real earworm.

Tana (singing): *I thought I was a Dionysian dancer / IN TURIN / I knew time was running out for me / IN TURIN* . . . God they were good.

You guys were too heavy, Noelle says. People just want to *dance* at the end of times . . . (singing): *Don't want your apo-cal-ypse / Just want your lips to kiss.*

I was crying, Tana says. Crying and dancing. It was, like, holy fool disco . . . Dancin' Star are going to make it.

People want to dance, Noelle says. They want to dance and cry. They want to dance as they cry. They want to laugh as they cry . . . That's what you guys don't understand . . . Jesus, why does everything have to be so *serious*?

Life is serious, Art says.

Maybe the secret of life is not to take it too seriously, Noelle says. Did you ever think about *that*?

★

The lower woods.

The path, petering out. No more signposts.

Where are we? Noelle asks.

Satan's Crotch—that's what we call it, Art says.

It's the lowest part of the Thames Valley, I say. Everything disgusting funnels down here.

It's so *dark*, Noelle says. I can't see the stars. What's happened to the stars?

This is what Wokingham was like before civilization, Art says. Before the Romans. Basically, a *marsh*.

It still is a marsh, Noelle says. Jesus, it's *heavy*.

What's wrong with this place? Tana asks. I can't breathe. The air's so thick.

It's spores, I say. The air's full of them.

You guys really bring us to the *best* places, Tana says.

The trees look *sticky*, Noelle says. And there's mould everywhere. God—the *damp*, Noelle says.

It's an area of special scientific interest. Art says. There are fungi in the undergrowth that are unique to this place.

We shouldn't have come here, Tana says. No one should be allowed here.

It's the sort of place some new plague might begin, Noelle says. Some new kind of AIDS . . .

It's so fertile—do you see? Noelle says. Look at the way everything's *growing*.

It's because there's so much *death*, Tana says. The soil's black as shit . . . It's basically a giant compost heap . . .

There are weird hybrids here, Art says. Mutations. Strange leaps and throwbacks. Anything goes. Bats fuck birds. Flies fuck slugs. Deer rut with rabbits. It's interspecies. It's interkingdom . . .

It's all so—*indiscriminate*, Noelle says. All these clumps . . .

How was this allowed to happen? Tana asks. What about woodland management?

And what's that *smell*? Noelle says.

That's the fungus, Art says. The famous Satan's Crotch fungus.

It's nature, rotting, Noelle says.

It's like *cancer*, Tana says. This is what cancer looks like.

In the beginning, there was cancer, Art says. In the beginning there were the elements, slipping and sliding. In the beginning, there were *flowers of evil* . . .

Cancer cells are immortal—did you know that? Tana says. They don't know how to die.

Just like nature, I say.

Nature *is* cancer, basically, Tana says. It's death in life and life in death . . .

Low rumbling. Is that thunder? Will there be a storm? Let there be a storm! Let the air be clarified! But the rumbling comes from the woods. From deeper in the woods.

Discussion. Maybe the woods are becoming sentient. Maybe some kind of swamp creature's being born. Some shambling mould. Maybe there's some forgotten branch of the human race living out here. Creatures unknown to science.

It's the land that time forgot, I say.

It's the land that *light* forgot, Tana says.

It's like the woods *know* we're here, Noelle says. Like they're drawing us in. The woods are actually *trying* to gross us out.

I never knew what evil meant until now . . . , Tana says. I never knew evil could *burgeon*.

It's why the Romans built their roads, Art says. It's why the Saxon chiefs cleared the woods. It's what drove the Vikings back. And it's why they built the suburbs in the first place. It's either the suburbs or *this*.

I *much* prefer the suburbs, Noelle says.

Nature basically hates us, right? Tana says.

Nature hates itself, Noelle says.

Nature's blind, Art says. It's chaos, that's all. It's entropy.

I thought entropy meant things coming apart—not, like, *growing*, Tana says.

★

At the bottom of the valley.

You just want to punish us, don't you? Noelle says. For not being miserable enough about Nietzsche. It's part of your depression-cult. Well, fuck you guys. I'm sick of all your gloomier-than-thou *bullshit* . . .

If you gaze long into an abyss, the abyss will gaze into you, I say.

Have you ever let the abyss look into you, Noelle? Art asks. What would it *see*, anyway?

Come off your meds now—*tonight*, I say. Go on, let's see what happens.

And it worked *so* well for Nietzsche, Noelle says.

Just get us away from all this disgusting stuff, Tana says.

Chaos, you mean, Art says. Keep you away from chaos. But chaos is real. Just like despair. Just like madness.

You must have chaos in yourself to give birth to a dancing star, I quote.

Well, Nietzsche gave birth to Dancin' Star, Noelle says. Ironic, eh?

★

Heath Pool.

You guys should swim, Noelle says, stripping down. Why do you never swim?

Because we're not *Mediterranean*, for fuck's sake, I say.

Noelle, wading into the water. Tana, following.

This is where we used to come with Nietzsche, Art says.

Jesus—it's too early to start *reminiscing*, I say.

Swigs of vodka.

All his books—his dad's books . . . , I say. What'll happen to them?

They'll put them in a skip, Art says. For landfill.

Fuck, I say. *FUCK!*

It's not as if we could read them, Art says.

It's not the books. It's . . . it's what Nietzsche was part of. A whole culture . . . He was the *last philosopher in the world*. And the last philosopher in the world's gone mad.

Maybe that's what he wanted, Art says. Maybe that was always where it was going to lead. Maybe madness is what it takes to think—what it takes to affirm everything that is, or whatever. And who knows but that there's joy in madness. Unimaginable joy . . . Like your brain's all light and flame . . .

Then we should go mad like him, I say. We should just blow our minds out. Burn out the filament . . . We don't need our sanity, not anymore. Sanity's just a way of holding back.

Haven't we lived long enough? I ask. Fuck it—haven't we seen more than enough? We should just *EXPLODE* . . . Just offer ourselves up to *NOTHING*. For *NOTHING*. To the fact that God is dead . . .

★

Our campfire.

Noelle, drying her hair.

Tana, smoking.

It's so calm, I say. So still. Have we completed nihilism? I mean—is this it?

It's the hurricane eye of nihilism, Art says. The storm rages all around us.

I don't get it—has the world ended or not? I ask.

The world's ended everywhere but here, Art says. These are the last woods in the world . . ..

★

Dawn. Walking.

The suburbs, again. The suburbs, over again . . .

Something should happen, you know, in honour of Nietzsche, Art says. A miracle. Or the opposite of a miracle. An earthquake. Why can't there be an earthquake?

We should smash a window, I say.

You can't smash these windows, Art says. These double-glazing units are fucking tough. Rocks just bounce off.

We should smash a windscreen, I say.

We'll set off an alarm, Art says. We'll be caught on CCTV.

The suburbs—one, Nietzsche—nil, I say. The suburbs—one, the rest of us—nil . . .

It should all be destroyed in the name of Nietzsche, I say. In the name of fucking madness. When's the terror going to come—the suburban terror? When's it all going to burn?

Discussion. We're already dead—but we want that confirmed. We died some time ago—but we want to re-die, in *fire*. We want to *burn* this time . . .

When will the terrorists strike? When will death come from the skies?

Art and I, imagining it: A great blow. A great hammer-down. A disaster vaster than the suburbs . . .

We imagine it: the absolute event. A terrorist strike by God Himself.

We imagine it: the very sky itself as disaster. The very air itself.

We imagine it: some cosmic fall-out. Some ruination of the cosmos. Some super-death. Some world-annihilation.

We imagine it: something unavoidable. Something cosmic. Something that began several billion years ago.

We imagine it: some abstract war. Between light and dark. Between the world and the void. Some conflict between matter and anti-matter.

We imagine it: some solar flare. Some exploding star. Some demise at the heart of the atom.

We imagine it: the bomb going off. The cosmic bomb. The existence bomb.

They'll scramble the Air Force—too late. They'll fill the roads with troops—too late.

Fighter jets, roaring across the sky. Muffled thuds. Missiles, flying low, hugging the contours . . . But it will be too late—much too late.

The sky, destroyed. The sky, cancelled. No blue of noon. No eye of life . . . Just chaos. Just mumblings in the dark. Just darkness, crawling over itself . . .

★

Outside Paula's house. Tapping on her window.

Tapping again. Stirring inside.

Paula, bleary-eyed: what the *FUCK* do you want?

Save us from this pair of death-boys, Noelle says. They're in full doom-apocalypse mode.

Do you know what *TIME* it is? Paula asks. Why aren't you fuckers in bed?

We're never going to sleep, Art says. Sleeping's for losers.

Yeah, yeah—you've got no one to sleep *with*, Paula says. What about Nietzsche? What's the latest?

No news, I say.

He's probably lying in some hospital bed growing the *moustache of destiny*, or whatever, Noelle says.

He's probably suffering more than anyone us can imagine, Art says. He's been torn to pieces. He's lost in chaos. No—he *is* chaos. He *is* loss.

You've got blood on your hands, Art, Paula says. I'm calling you *murderer* from now on.

But I'm not actually a murderer, Art says. Nietzsche isn't actually dead.

It's a battlefield out there, Paula says. We left a soldier down.

Where's lover-girl, anyway? I ask.

We had a row, Paula says. She went home.

Have you got any weed? I ask. Tana doesn't *exist* without weed.

Who do you think I am—your fucking dealer? Paula asks. FUCK!

Huzzah—we've got the old Paula back!, Art says.

★

The golf course.

Let's just fall asleep here, on the grass, Tana says.

They don't allow it, Art says. They unleash the hounds.

Paula, trying to pull the flag up from the golf hole. I'll spear the hounds with *this*.

Why don't terrorists ever target golf courses? I wonder.

We should drive a bulldozer down here, Art says. Liberate the river. Look at it—all channelled.

I hate all this *fake SHIT!*, Paula says. Fake views. Fake vistas. Fake valleys . . . These bastards. They can't just *destroy* a landscape. They have to *re-create* it, too. They have to remake it in some really stupid way.

I thought we were supposed to hate hate, Paula, I say.

Fuck that!, Paula says. *FUCK IT!* So long as there's hate, there's fucking life.

Art, laughing. We missed you Paula.

★

Merv's.

He's not answering his phone. Throwing stones. Merv! *MERV!*

Merv, opening his window.

We've been up all night!, Art shouts. Come on—make us breakfast.

Bill at the stove in boxer shorts and a Dancin' Star teeshirt.

I'm, like, starstruck, Noelle says. You guys were so good last night. You're going to be famous—seriously.

Bill, plating up.

You do a mean omelette, Bill, Tana says. Jesus—you can cook, too.

Merv, does your dad mind you going out with a giant spermy hulk? I ask.

Merv, shrugging.

Not when *stardom* awaits, Art says. Next stop—Eurovision. You guys could win, you know.

You're so sarcastic, Noelle says.

I'm not—I like Eurovision!, Art says. I like all that Abba stuff!

Yeah, you like it *ironically*, Noelle says. In that bad-taste-is-good-taste kinda way.

But no one could take it *that* seriously, could they? I say. I mean, it's just . . . crowd-pleasing, isn't it?

Sure—crowd-*pleasing*, Noelle says. Everyone *likes* it. Everyone can *dance to it*. Not like *your* stuff. You've got to *entertain* your audience—don't you see that?

We can't all be *X-Factor*, Art says.

Don't listen to Art, Merv—Dancin' Star are genius, Tana says. You've got something they'll never have.

Songs, for one thing, Noelle says. Proper songs.

And moves, Tana says. You've got moves.

Come on, Paula—stick up for us, Art says.

We're just a bunch of murderers—especially you, Paula says. Dancin' Star are *sweet*. There should be room for sweetness . . . Anyway, I don't care anymore. I'm going to get on with my own thing.

Doing *what*? Art asks.

I don't know . . . I might make a film, or something, Paula says. Something set in the suburbs. I'll just shoot stuff. Improvise. Lou can star . . . if she'll talk to me. That's what I'm going to do this summer . . . cycle around, shoot bits and pieces of ordinary life . . .

Why not just *be* a part of life? Art says.

That's what I've been saying all along, Noelle says.

I don't mean swimming or going to France, Art says. I don't mean buying sun-dried tomatoes from some deli. I mean *LIVING*—in capital letters. Setting fire to boredom. *Life, like a pillar of fire. Like a pillar of cloud. Life, that burns with fire and yet is not consumed . . .*

Mysticism!, Paula says. You're no different from Merv.

The band was the obstacle—I see it now, Art says. *Nietzsche* was the obstacle. We should try and go beyond him by just . . . living. That's what he'd have wanted, isn't it?

So Nietzsche was part of a greater plan all along, Paula says. He's just a ladder to be kicked away.

Nietzsche wouldn't want pity, Art says. He wouldn't want compassion—seriously.

That's *his* problem, Paula says. It's the problem with his philosophy.

Me, quoting: *You had not yet sought yourselves; and you found me. Now I bid you to lose me and find yourselves . . .*

So you're just going to let Nietzsche rot? Paula asks. You're just going to step over his body?

NINTH & TENTH WEEK

MONDAY, TUESDAY, WEDNESDAY, ETC.

Exams. Exams. Exams.

(First exams—ease itself, like spiderwebs breaking on our faces. Like dandelion clocks blown into the wind. Like freewheeling down Doles Hill . . .

Later exams. Squalor of the mind. That we should be concerned with this. That we have to feel so trapped. That our concerns should be exam concerns. That our heads should be filled with exam *facts* . . .

And rest days. Cycling to escape. Carving cool tunnels through the air . . . Lying in deckchairs, looking up. The vast sky above us. As though we were underwater. As though the sea-surface rolled above us. As though the breakers broke above us . . .

And more exams. Yet more exams.)

News: Nietzsche's in a mental hospital. In a locked ward.

(Merv and Paula knocked on his door. Merv and Paula dared knock on Nietzsche's door.

Nietzsche's mother, looking worn. Nietzsche's sister, looking gleeful. Nothing like a *mad brother* to manage . . .)

FRIDAY

Before the last exam.

The sports-hall changing rooms.

Merv, sharing out the blotters for our post-exam celebration.

L . . . S . . . D . . . , Art says. Super-fucking-strength.

Fuck that—the Head Boy blew his mind on acid, Noelle says. He's in a fucking *coma*.

He took, like, ten blotters, Art says.

He had a psychotic break, Tana says.

Well, this is going to be a *psychedelic* break, which is different, Art says. We're going to remake our brains—collectively. The brain is plastic, man—it's plastic. Which means it can be remade. We can remake its architecture. Its interconnections . . . And we won't need our old brains after the exams . . .

★

The last exam.

Taking our seats in silence.

The high celling. Light, from the high windows. Climbing frames, folded into the wall.

Desks in rows. Blank answer booklets. Exam questions, placed face-down by teachers.

Hush. Expectation. Solemnity, despite everything. Respect for the occasion.

The exam clock, big, round, old-style, like something from a costume drama. The exam clock, brought out every year to be hung in the sports hall. This is what exam time looks like, all stern and imperious. This is what Greenwich Mean Time looks like, all absolute . . .

But we're dreaming of *our* time, on the other side of the exams. We're dreaming of *summertime*, on the other side of the last exam. Of festive time, with wine on its lips. Of walking beneath time, as under a great sky. Of singing time's songs, with tears on our cheeks.

Soon, our time—real time—will be loosed from its cage. Soon, time will flutter into its sky. Soon, we will become the celebrants of time. Time's drunkards, time's lovers . . .

★

The exam room.

The teachers. Mr Pound, bolt upright, RAF upright, under the exam clock. Mr Saracen, unfamiliar out of sportswear, looking up at the windows. Mr Merriweather, no doubt counting down until his holiday. Until *Bhutan*. Mr Varga, looking amused, full of

Old European irony. Mr Zachary, looking pensive, anxious, fearful of the apocalypse . . . The Old Mole, nearly retired, *craving* the apocalypse . . .

The empty desk where Nietzsche was supposed to sit. *Nietzsche couldn't possibly be here, we'd say if they asked us. Nietzsche's on another path, which he must follow to the uttermost, we'd say. Exams are nothing to him, we'd say. School is of no importance. He's beyond it now, as he is beyond everything, we'd say. Nietzsche's left it all behind. Nothing has any hold on him anymore. Nietzsche is unreachable now, we'd say. Nietzsche is becoming a god, or a beast . . .*

A couple of minutes left. Breathe. At the brink. Just before the plunge . . .

Adrenaline. A sense of unreality. Of distance. Everything around us, shrunk into the distance.

The urge to stand up and bellow, *FUUUUUCK!* The urge to topple your table and chair, and all the tables and chairs . . .

The hour's come. The time's come.

★

Forty-five minutes in. Coming up for air. One question done; one essay written. Refreshing our eyes. Letting them rest on Calypso. Letting them rest on Nicholas Nugent. Another question . . .

Another forty-five minutes. Looking up again. The first pupils raising their hands to be let out. Halfway through, and they've already given up. Dingus, scratching his head. Fatberg, drooling slightly. Sister-Fucker, with the DTs. And has Vince's hair really gone white?

The last half-hour, when no one's allowed to leave. The last half-hour, checking through our answers. Free to look around, to watch the others working. Teachers, pacing the hall. Pupils with hands in the air, waiting for supplementary answer pages.

The sun, aslant through high windows. Shafts of light angled from the windows . . .

The dream of being *out*. Of time that sings. Of drunken time. Of time that smashes. Of time that dances with madness in its eyes. Of sprawling time. Of time-vistas, time-views . . .

After.

Popping the blotters under our tongues . . .

School's finally—*out*, Art says.

I can't believe we survived, I say.

I don't think we *did* survive, Art says.

This is going to be the best day, Merv says. The best day that ever was.

★

The school gates.

No more nihilism lessons for you, Bill, Art says. No more nihilism club . . . We've graduated. Time to fly into the storm. Do you think you're ready, Bill? Do you think you're going to survive?

If we've taught you one thing, Bill, it's that we're not going to survive . . . , I say.

No, people—you can't talk about suicide, Noelle says. Not today.

How about parasuicide? I ask.

I don't even know what that *is*, Noelle says.

Self-inflicted injuries and stuff, I say.

No parasuicide either, Noelle says. I'm tired of death.

This is going to be a good trip, right? Tana says.

It's going to be a good trip, Art says. And it's going to be a good summer. We've been let out to play. This is a *reprieve*. A fucking bonus level . . .

Jesus, I hate it when you get expansive, Paula says.

We're going to see the world as it is, Art says. We're going to see the flame of eternity. *To enter paradise, you first have to be tested by the fire.*

We're just going to fuck ourselves up, Tana says. That's okay. I *like* fucking myself up.

All roads lead to madness, I say. This is the summer when we'll all go mad.

Sure we'll go mad, Art says. We'll *have* to go mad. But it'll be *ecstatic* madness. Death-of-God madness. We're going to redeem the suburbs. We're going to *re-dream* the suburbs.

Oh, here he goes . . . , Paula says. Womb-boy in full flight . . .

It's a holy day, Art says. It's a feast day. It's the world's secret birthday. Today is *our* day. Because we're going to forget how to tell the time. And it's *our* world. Because we're going to reclaim the world as ours. The world as no one's . . .

★

Palmer Gardens, in the middle of town. Flower beds. Flower baskets.

It's definitely hitting, I say. It's fucking whooshing.

I just want to say *wow, wow, wow* . . . , Noelle says. But that's, like, really stupid.

Wow, Tana says. Wow.

Wow, I say. Say, *wow*, Paula.

I'm not saying fucking *wow*, Paula says.

It's beautiful, Art says. Everything's moving. Everything's, like, made of fire. Every blade of grass. Every tree's radiant . . . Blazing.

It's raging, I say. It's a rage of joy. There's power. There's mania . . . It's a carnival of light . . .

God—that's what I see, Merv says. The *fury* of God . . . the *glory* of God . . .

Is this what madness is like? I ask. Nietzsche's madness?

Everything anew, everything eternal, everything interlinked, entwined, in love . . . , Art quotes.

Eternity—*e*-fucking-*ternity*: what does it mean, anyway? Tana asks.

Giving up your life, I say. Sacrificing it. Over and over again . . .

It means life as moving beyond form, all forms, Art says. It means life as all things passing, all things arising. It means life as shattering every limit, every finitude . . .

It means the unfallen world, Merv says. It means innocence, blazing . . . It means the ferocity of love . . .

It means walking on the beach, Noelle says. Swimming in the ocean. It means the light on the waves.

It means waking up from death, Tana says. It means everyone coming alive again . . .

This is life, Art quotes. *This is your eternal life. All joy wants the eternity of all things.*

Fuck this hippie shit, Paula says, rising. Seriously—*FUCK* this. Acid melts your fucking brain . . .

Where are you going? Art asks.

To see Lou, Paula says.

Paula, collapsing. *FUCK!* I can't *WALK*.

Wow, Tana says.

Jesus, even I'm feeling it now . . . , Paula says.

★

What we see: Wokingham, pressing closer to the sky. Wokingham, rising higher from the Valley. Raising itself a little higher above the floodplain.

What we see: Wokingham, squaring its shoulders. Remaking itself. Wokingham, shrugging off the housing estates; shaking off the motorway and distribution centres. Wokingham, letting the corporations slide from its sides.

What we see: Old Woosehill—all wild grass again, all flowering fields . . . Old Earley (without Lower Earley)—all marshland, all water meadows . . . Old Winnersh (without the Triangle)—all woodland, all oak and ash and thorn . . .

What we see: Wokinghamites, knowing that they've been hibernating until now. That they've been drowsing in darkness until now. Wokinghamites, knowing that *this* is happiness—right here, right now.

What we see: Summer vastness. That outstrips our purposes. Laughs at them. Summer generosity. That dissolves all meanness. All economy.

What we see: The summer bonus. The summer boon. It's always the day of rest in the Mediterranean. It's always siesta-time in the Mediterranean.

What we see: The royalty of the sky—*our* royalty. The heavenly cosmos—*our* heaven.

What we see: The *full* day. The *full* sky. Glory for all just as there is light for all.

What we see: Zenith life. Sunburst life. Summer's crown upon all our heads . . .

What we hear: The great organ-chord of summer. On infinite sustain.

★

Lying on the grass.

What's going to happen when we come down? Tana asks. What's going to happen tomorrow?

There is no tomorrow, I say. There's only today, over and over again.

Is . . . that . . . supposed . . . to . . . be . . . a . . . good . . . thing? Tana asks.

Let's actually *do* something, Art says. Let's actually change something in the world.

That's what the band was for, I say.

We've got to carry it through, Art says. Complete what we began. We've got to *live* it . . .

Move into my house—all of you . . ., Art says. We'll start the commune. We've been talking about it—now we can actually *do* it.

Why can't we just live off Dancin' Star? I say. Take us on a world tour, guys. We'll be part of your entourage . . . You could do an end-of-the-world tour . . . Get the whole world dancing with tears in their eyes . . .

We can't just run away, Art says. We've got to confront the beast here, where it's at its strongest. This is where we should dig in. Mirkwood should be our last stand.

What about the bulldozers? Merv asks.

Bill will flatten the bulldozers, Art says.

Will there be, like, running water? Merv asks.

When we dig a well, Art says.

What about electricity? Merv asks.

We won't need electricity, Art says. We'll set up a windmill, or something. Produce biomass energy. Put up some solar panels. We'll live from the land . . . Follow the seasons . . .

The new Bhutanese, Paula says.

The Thames Valley Bhutanese—why not? Art says.

The Bhutanese are *boring* is why not, Paula says. I thought we were agreed on that . . . Fuck all this self-sufficiency shit. Fuck *farming* . . . We should just try to survive off the grid. Live from dealing, grow skunk-weed or 'shrooms or whatever. Scavenge. That's how the real communalists live.

Does that mean you're in? Art says.

Maybe, Paula says. With conditions.

Come on—Nadya Tolokno would approve, Art says. We'll be the children of Dionysus, right? Innocents . . . Speakers of truth . . .

Until I go to uni, anyway, Paula says. And only if Lou can hang out, too.

How about you, Merv?—Bill? Art asks.

Nods. Dancin' Star are in. Dancin' Star can have the outhouse.

Don't . . . even . . . *ask*, Tana says. It's just too disgusting round here . . .

I'm staying at my dads', Noelle says. I value, like, good food. And basic hygiene.

You're going to miss the revolution, Art says.

Noelle, snorting.

We're going to reappropriate the commons, Art says. We're going to take back the means of living. We're going to seize the means of communication. We're going to *not* work together. We're going to be *sovereign* . . .

Yeah, but what are you actually going to *do*? Noelle asks.

We'll be partisans, Art says. We'll lead raids into the suburbs . . . Commit acts of sabotage . . . Plunder . . . That sort of thing. It'll be a war. We'll be at war with *everything* . . .

You'll end up in Guantanamo, Noelle says. They'll jail you for terrorism.

We'll be *spiritual* terrorists, Art says. Joyful terrorists . . . We'll be a shockwave . . . Mirkwood will be the new centre of the world . . .

We could be like Hassan as-Sabbāh, sending out death missions from the mountain, I say.

Count me out, Noelle says. I don't want to be part of your damn suicide squad . . .

Okay, okay, we won't attack anymore, I say.

Yeah, well, civilization will just destroy itself, Art says. We'll be ready, that's all.

Ready for what? Noelle asks. Smoking and talking crap?

Art: We'll be steeling ourselves. Hardening ourselves. (Quoting): *At last the horizon seems open once more. The sea, our sea, again lies open before us; perhaps never before did such an open sea exist . . .*

See—more crap, Tana says.

Macho crap, Noelle says.

There'll be communes like ours everywhere, Art says. In every housing estate, every office block, every distribution centre. It'll be some new kind of aristocracy. An aristocracy of the sun, with light for all. A sovereignty of the sun, where every act is pure and bright . . . Where there's no more death . . . No more cancer . . .

No more cancer . . . , Tana says. I *like* that . . .

A sun cult, Art says. We'll worship the sun. We'll worship *heat*. We'll brew summer vodka. Honey vodka. We'll sip down summer in a glass . . .

I'm in, Tana says. Count me in.

We'll make our own private Mediterranean . . . , Art says. Learn how to take siestas. How to swim. How to live in the nude, without secrets . . .

Then you'll definitely need me, Noelle says. I can be your Mediterranean consultant.

We're going to fail, aren't we? Tana says. We can't just escape from the world that easily.

Sure, we'll fail, Art says. We'll fuck up everything. But we'll do it *gloriously* . . .

No, dillweed—we'll *just fail*, Paula says. But that's okay . . .